RAINBOWS IN THE CLOUDS

First Published in the UK 2013 by Belvedere Publishing

First edition: 2013

A copy of this work is available through the British Library.

ISBN: 978-1-909224-36-0

Belvedere Publishing
Mirador
Wearne Lane
Langport
Somerset
TA10 9HB

RAINBOWS IN THE CLOUDS

BY

ELIZABETH REVILL

Previous titles by Elizabeth Revill include a psychological thriller trilogy:

Killing me Softly,
Prayer for the Dying
God only Knows

And with my current and exceptionally great publisher, Belvedere:

Llewellyn Family Saga:
Whispers on the Wind
Shadows on the Moon

Against the Tide
The Electra Conspiracy

Author's Acknowledgements

This book is dedicated to all those wonderful people who support and encourage me, especially my loving husband, Andrew Spear who persuaded me to write full time.

I must mention my lovely, talented son, Ben Fielder who shares my passion for writing and thanks for all the excellent discussions and ideas we share together. He is a unique and original writer please check him out and his novel, Land of the Awoken. His website is www.benfielder-uk.com

To my dear friend, Hayley Raistrick-Episkopos, who is an amazing lady, a tower of strength and brightens my life. Thank you for the very special friendship we have and all the laughter we share.

My lovely FB friends from around the world, who have bought all my books, read them and wanted more.

And as always very special thanks to my inspirational and multi-talented commissioning editor, Sarah Luddington and her brilliant team at Belvedere who made this possible. Thank you one and all and here's to the next...

Future titles will hopefully include, a Fantasy Adventure 'Sanjukta and the Box of Souls', which is vastly different from anything else I have written and another historical stand alone novel, The Black Rider. Please feel free to contact me on my Facebook Author's page:

If you like my books please click 'Like'. Thank you.

Terms and colloquialisms used in

Rainbows In The Clouds

bach:	male term of endearment - dear.
blas:	flavoursome, tasty.
cariad:	term of endearment – my love, little one.
Duw:	God.
Dadcu:	Grandfather.
esgyrn Dafydd:	bones of David - an exclamation.
fach:	female term of endearment - dear.
fy merch 'i:	term of endearment - little lady.
ie:	yes.
iechy dwriaeth:	an exclamation.
Jawch:	an exclamation like crikey.
Mam-gu:	Grandmother.
nawr yna:	now then.
paid:	don't - stop it.
potch.:	soaking wet.
rhwyn dy garu du:	I love you.
tschwps:	a lot, cried the rain.
Wuss:	friend, mate, pal - local to the region not what it means today.
Yerffyn darn!:	An exclamation like, damn it.

Chapter One

The darkest hour

Footsteps slid and skidded on polished floors as people scurried to safety. The air raid siren wailed its mournful warning and nurses and visitors scattered from the hospital corridors and wards and out into the street dashing for the nearest air raid shelter or tube station.

They didn't scream or yell as they ran, but moved silently and quickly, as they tried to get away from the imminent danger.

Nurses on duty refused to panic as they struggled to move patients that could be transported somewhere where they would be better protected; others that were too ill to move lay and awaited their fate. Word spread quickly that Men's Surgical was in dire need of extra nurses.

Carrie Llewellyn hurried to the under staffed ward. She was determined to help all she could. She rounded a corner and ran straight into Hawtry, who was also on her way to Men's Surgical. She knew that Hawtry had volunteered to remain on duty throughout the bombing. She was unrecognisable as the nurse who had been so unpleasant at Bronglais.

"Lew! What are you doing here? You are not due on the ward yet. Get yourself to safety!" she urged.

"But, I want to see how James Titmus is doing after his surgery."

"They haven't brought him up yet. His operation was delayed because of the bombing last night. I don't know what they'll do now."

"You mean he's still in theatre?"

Hawtry nodded, her face was pinched with worry. A blast went off in the street outside and the building shook. "Quickly you need to hurry and get out."

"No time for that. From what I understand they will need

all the help they can get on Men's Surgical. I'm going to do what I can."

Hawtry smiled, "You never cease to amaze me, Lew. Come on then, I'm right behind you."

Hawtry and Carrie sped against the tide of staff, visitors, and those patients, who were able to walk, who were trying to flee the building. In front of them walking in the same direction was the familiar snowball blonde hair of Pemb.

"Hi, Pemb!" called Carrie. "Wait up!"

Pemb stopped and turned. She waited for the two nurses to catch up to her. She looked at Carrie quizzically, "I didn't think you were on duty now, Lew."

"Not you, too," murmured Carrie. "Men's Surgical is short staffed. We are on our way there, now."

"Better get a sprint on then, as that's where I am headed," grinned Pemb.

"Good job the Morgue's not short staffed," mused Carrie.

"No, if that was hit. There'd be no one to get you out. They wouldn't look there for live ones," puffed Hawtry as they scooted along the gleaming floors.

The crowds of hospital personnel were thinning out now as they turned the corner of the corridor toward the ward. Another blast outside rocked the building and a crack appeared in the ceiling above them. Hawtry slipped and Carrie caught her arm preventing her from falling. They exchanged a look between them. It was enough, and spoke volumes. These were worrying times.

The three nurses hurried toward Men's Surgical, as two orderlies wheeled trolleys complete with drips out from the ward. One of them acknowledged the nurses, "Come to help? That's good. You'll be welcomed in there."

Theatre Sister Kirby was marching from the other direction to the ward with a junior nurse from the theatre, Janet Duggins. James Titmus was on the trolley.

Carrie skidded toward them as they turned through the doors of Men's Surgical, now being propped open by the stern Sister Friend.

Sister Friend looked surprised when she saw the group of nurses approaching, and raised an eyebrow.

"We've come to help," said Carrie brightly. "Thought you'd need it."

"We most certainly do," boomed Sister Friend. "You are more than welcome. Two of our more stable patients have just left. The others are in no fit state to be moved."

Theatre Sister Kirby and Nurse Duggins pushed the trolley to an empty bay and settled James Titmus, who was still unconscious having not yet come round from his anaesthetic.

"How is he?" asked Carrie tentatively. She had a particular interest in this patient after the death of a favourite patient, fireman, Hamish MacDonald. James Titmus was another brave fire fighter. He had been trapped by falling masonry after rescuing a family. His chest and abdomen had been crushed and one lung punctured by a broken rib. Surgeons needed to stop the internal bleeding and assess the damage to other vital organs.

"He's critical," said Kirb. "And he needs careful monitoring. Unfortunately, he has to remain here."

The drone of another German bomber became ear splittingly loud, or so it seemed to Carrie. She looked at the assembled nurses, "Quickly. We need to do something."

Sister Friend nodded in agreement and brusquely instructed, "We'll move the patients' beds as close as we can to the Nurses' Station."

"But, why? We don't know where the bomb could hit," objected Kirb.

"No, but they'll stand more chance of being rescued there with its open access to the stairs and lift."

"Or we'll all be blown to kingdom come," added Kirb.

"Have you any better ideas?" questioned Sister Friend.

"No," Kirb shook her head, "Let's do it."

The nurses scurried around the ward and moved all the patients to the area by the Nurses' Station, close to the stairwell. Once this was done, the nurses huddled together and assessed what to do next. Carrie glanced out of the window and was shocked to see the dust fly up outside and acrid plumes of smoke rising. The smell of burning wood travelled on the breeze and was a warning of the danger they were all in.

At the end of the now empty ward was a huge, high, wooden table, often used by a night nurse at which to sit, work and study, and yet, still be able to watch over the sleeping patients in her charge. Carrie shouted, "Come on, under the table."

There was no mistaking the familiar whistle and whine of a bomb being dropped. They all heard it and they dashed for shelter under the table. Carrie somehow ended up on top of them all, covering the other five nurses with her body. Pemb was directly underneath her and they cuddled together in the small shelter that afforded some protection or so they hoped.

The crash of the explosion as the bomb impacted was deafening and the building rocked. Ward windows shattered and bricks rained down on the end of the ward covering the table under which the nurses were crouched when another bomb blast ripped out part of the hospital wing they were in.

A shocking and immediate silence followed as the bombers having delivered their final deadly load retreated back through the sky. The eerie stillness evaporated with the sound of crackling flames and more dust from the debris clouded up to merge with thicker, more suffocating, billowing smoke. From the nurses there was no sound, no movement, nothing.

Ernie woke from his slumber on his straw bale bed and sat bolt upright. He rubbed his eyes fiercely as if trying to clear some horrific remnant of a dream that still blazed furiously behind his eyes. He muttered one word, "Carrie."

Ernie's expression was serious as he splashed cold water on his face. He knew something had happened to her but he daren't say anything until it was confirmed. It was no good worrying people, he reasoned with himself. But the dream had shocked him and stolen the twinkling mischief from out of his eyes.

Once dressed for work Ernie clambered down from the hayloft into the barn and was greeted by Bonnie, the young black and white Border Collie that had replaced, Carrie's beloved Trixie. She danced excitedly around his feet, "Jawch!" he muttered, "Stop or you'll have me over." But Bonnie wouldn't stop. She jumped up nudging his hand demanding to be petted. Ernie couldn't help but smile and finally gave in, bending down to ruffle and stroke her fur. "So, what's all this about? Eh? Is something wrong?"

Bonnie made some little whimpering noises in her throat and ran out to the yard. The ducks and chickens scattered with a kerfuffle, a clucking and a quacking. As the menagerie of creatures flapped away a rolling duck egg was revealed with part of a beak protruding through the shell.

"Now, what have we here?" Ernie bent down and retrieved the egg. He glanced around him and spotted a magpie eyeing him beadily. "So that's it! Well, hear me, you chatter bird; you won't be stealing this egg away. That's for sure." Ernie waved his arm in an attempt to scare away the scavenger and proceeded to the duck pond where he found a female mallard sitting on a clutch of what he believed were ready to hatch eggs in amongst the rushes.

"Now, how can I get this back under you without scaring you off the whole batch?" Ernie moved toward the reeds but the duck sat tight and still.

Daisy, one of the Land Girls appeared out from Old Tom's cottage. She watched Ernie bending over peering in through the foliage, "Whatever are you doing, Ernie?"

Ernie jumped up, startled, "Iechy dwriaeth! You frightened me half to death, creeping up on me like that. I thought death itself had come to collect me. Duw! Duw."

Daisy laughed and added, "Well, what *are* you doing?"

"Trying to work out how to get this back under its mam," said Ernie indicating the now cheeping egg. "A magpie stole it from the nest. They are not averse to eating eggs or live babies, see."

Daisy's face fell, "Oh, that's horrid."

"If I try to replace it now I may scare the mother off the lot of them but if I don't get it back it will be a little orphan and we'll have another Bandit on our hands."

As if on cue, Bandit came scurrying around the corner of the barn flapping his wings. He stopped at Ernie's feet and quacked. "Now, what do you want?" scolded Ernie. The waddling duck quacked again and toddled to the pond. The mother duck fluffed up her feathers and rose from the nest and she too, glided into the water. "Perfect!" breathed Ernie in relief.

Daisy watched as Ernie deftly placed the emerging duckling still encased in its egg into the clutch on the vacated nest. Ernie turned to Daisy, "See, it's always best to do this at dusk or dawn when the birds are still asleep or settling down. At other times they'll kick the egg out."

"Why?"

"I'm not sure. It may be the smell of us or perhaps when they turn the eggs they feel something is wrong. We'll just watch and see what happens."

The female duck and Bandit both upended on the pond pushing their ducktail bottoms in the air. "I do believe that Bandit may be the father of this brood," observed Ernie.

"Why is he called Bandit?" asked Daisy.

"Because of the little mallard duckling's markings around the eyes when it was a baby. Carrie thought it looked like a little mask. She called him Bandit and Bandit it is."

"Look!" pointed Daisy. "The mother is leaving the water."

The brown mother duck paddled out from the pond and waddled back to her nest. She shook her feathers and settled back down on the hatching eggs.

Ernie and Daisy watched. A smile spread across Ernie's face as he chortled, "Thank goodness for that. She doesn't seem to have noticed. It should be all right now. We won't have another Bandit racing indoors at every opportunity."

Daisy laughed, "That's good. Although, I wouldn't have minded raising an orphan."

"Very time consuming, believe you me! Now, what are you up to?"

"On my way up to Gelli Galed. Laura and I are meeting Sam Jefferies there. Something about pulling the wild oats out from the oat crop."

"Then I don't envy you. Hard work it is. You'll see them easily enough. They stand taller than the crop. The ears of grain are sparser. Better to do it now while it's in its early stage of growing."

Ernie's tummy rumbled and growled, "Duw! Anyone would think I hadn't been fed," he mused.

"And have you?" asked Daisy.

"No," winked Ernie. "I'm on my way to start the fry up, if Jenny hasn't already begun."

"Then, I'll see you later," murmured Daisy. She gave him a mock salute and began to walk to the mountain track. Ernie watched her a moment and then turned to cross the yard and enter Hendre.

The smell of frying bacon assailed his nostrils and Jenny's sweet voice filled his ears as she sang. She turned when she heard the door open, "There you are, Ernie. I wondered where you were."

"I had a hatching duckling to get to safety."

"Pardon?" quizzed Jenny.

"A tale of villainous magpies and innocent little hatchlings."

"What?"

"Never you mind. I'll tell you over breakfast. Where's John?"

"He left really early. Taken Senator into Crynant. Got some errands to run, he said. He also has to arrange with Pritchard the Police to come and witness the slaughter of one of the pigs. He needs to get the licence sorted, too."

"Aye, half the pig for the Government and half for us. People are going hungry; we have to do our bit. Still, I expect the smell of the frying bacon will lure him back. He always seems to turn up when the rashers start sizzling in the pan." And before Ernie could say anymore, the sound of Senator's hooves clopped into the yard. "There you are. What did I tell you?"

Ernie sat at the table to wait for his breakfast and knew he'd have to put on his brightest cheeriest face or John would soon realise that something was wrong. Ernie was aware he had to hide his fears about Carrie and hide them well.

Chapter Two

Aftermath

The German bombers had done their damage; part of the North Wing of the London Chest Hospital was badly hit. Emergency services were out in force trying to extinguish the flames. Patients were being ferried to different wards and space was adapted to accommodate those rescued from Men's Surgical.

Brenda Friend had been right to move them close to the Nurses' Station. They had survived the blast unhurt. The hunt was now on to find the nurses who had been on duty at the time. It was difficult to see how anyone could have survived a direct hit, such as this, and live.

A few hours later, the hall porter, George was standing amidst a mound of bricks and splintered timber. A patient wearing only his pyjamas and a dressing gown, William Taylor, was tearing away at the fallen masonry with his bare hands trying to find survivors.

George had obtained a spade and was digging away at the earth and mess of plaster and loose cement. "According to records, Sister Friend and Staff Nurse Hawtry should have been on duty. There's a possibility that a Theatre Sister and a junior are also underneath that lot. Come on, we have to hurry, but dig carefully we don't want to bring anything else down on top of them."

Underneath the table covered with a mountain of bricks, Carrie groaned. She spluttered and spat out the choking dust from the bomb blast and tried to move. She couldn't. The table was wedged on her head but it had created a tiny air pocket. Underneath her felt soft. She patted her hand around and felt a handful of hair with her fingertips.

"Hey, careful!" coughed a voice.

"Pemb? Is that you?"

"Lew?"

"Yes, it's me. Who else is there?" asked Carrie.

"I don't know, I can't move. I've got someone's foot close to my face and mouth. I hope they don't kick. Is it yours?"

"I don't know, squeeze it, but gently," ordered Carrie.

Pemb gingerly exerted some pressure on the foot minus its shoe, close to her face. "Do you feel that?"

"No," said Carrie feeling concerned.

"Then it's not yours."

"How can you be sure?" asked Carrie.

"It doesn't smell like yours," muttered Pemb.

"Cheeky!" called Carrie. She was about to say something else when she heard a noise from above ground, "Hush, listen!"

The two friends strained their ears for any sound.

"Someone's looking for us," called Pemb a note of hope entering her voice. "We have to let them know we're here. Together now after three. One, two, three."

"HELP!" they chorused together.

George on the surface stopped what he was doing, "Did you hear that?" he asked.

William Taylor stopped and listened, too.

Carrie tried to knock on the underside of the table and both she and Pemb called out once more, "Help!"

"They're alive. Someone's alive down there! Quick! Keep digging. Over here." They moved over the rubble to where the sound was coming from and George shouted down through a small gap. "Hold on. We'll get you out! Keep making a noise, anything. It's George here."

Pemb continued to call out and Carrie kept on knocking on the underside of the table. Another groan joined them. It was Kirb coming to wakefulness,

"Ugh, I can taste blood and I can't feel my feet. They're numb," complained Kirb.

"I know. I've got something sticky pouring down my face. I can't move my hand to feel, but I think it's blood, too," said Carrie in between her knocks and calling out.

"Don't shout too loud. You may bring more down on top of us," chastised Kirb.

"I don't think so," soothed Carrie. "George is trying to dig us out with the help of someone else."

"Who's next to you, Kirb?" asked Pemb.

"I seem to be wedged underneath you and there's two others next to me and one below. God knows… The one under me is really still and feels cold. I hope she's all right."

"Just be careful, we don't want to do anything to make our situation worse," chided Pemb.

"At least, we're alive,' added Kirb.

"Yes, let's hope it's all of us," murmured Carrie. Inexplicably Ernie's words echoed in her mind, 'Just remember that if you go to London, and I suspect you will, be nice to a man called George. He could save your life.'

Carrie shuddered. Suddenly, she began to shake uncontrollably. Her body was in shock and had gone into rigor. "And I thought he had saved me from a rat," she stuttered as she shivered.

"What?" asked Pemb concerned. "Lew, you're not making any sense. What rat?"

But Carrie continued to mumble and then fell quiet. Pemb could feel Carrie's trembling limbs and she called out, "Stay with us, Lew. Stay with us." She felt Carrie's legs fall still. "Over here, hurry, quickly please," she shouted as loudly as she could. And then began coughing violently as yet another brick was dislodged and thudded onto the pile on top of the table.

George and William heard the cry for help and recognised the urgency in Pemb's voice. They stretched down on the pile of rubble and debris and threw aside the broken bricks in a fevered frenzy. Slabs of masonry clattered and smashed to the side of the two rescuers who were now on their hands and knees pawing and scrabbling at the diminishing mound.

"I've found something," shouted George as he pulled off two more pieces of block work. He brushed dirt and cement clumps from the table surface. "What's this?" he cried.

William looked at him and muttered blackly, "Looks like a coffin."

A frantic shout came from Pemb underneath, "We're here under the table. Pull it up and you'll find us."

"How many of you are there?" asked George.

"Six, no, there's seven of us," called Pemb.

"And get a stretcher," called another tremulous voice belonging to Kirb.

The porter and patient struggled together to clear the rest of the masonry and then the table could be seen clearly. They tugged and pulled at the huge, heavyweight, oak table and tried to winkle the legs free without disturbing more of the bombed material. "Got their own little shelter here," observed George.

"Probably saved their lives," agreed William.

They grunted and heaved and finally managed to lift the table clear. Carrie lay unconscious, her body was spread covering a number of other nurses. Blood poured from a gash in her head, and her cheek and neck were badly bruised, her arms and legs had also suffered lacerations.

"Nurse Llewellyn," said George involuntarily and Carrie let out a soft moan. "We need some help here," shouted George above the cacophony of rescue workers and firemen fighting the remains of the flames. "Stretcher here. Now!"

Two male attendants struggled across to Carrie and lifted her onto the stretcher and transported her away to Emergency. George and William helped Pemb up, who was dazed, with cuts and abrasions and a bad graze on her head, but she was able to walk. She stumbled off the bricks and leant against the wall that was still standing. From there they pulled out Kirb. She was shaking but uninjured apart from a cut on her chin. Underneath her was Nurse Janet Duggins. George shook his head sadly. Her neck was twisted and had broken during impact. Pemb bit her lip as she watched them haul out her lifeless body. Lastly, Hawtry and Sister Friend emerged. They were totally unscathed physically, just unnerved and in shock.

"I can't believe it. Lew took the brunt of it, protected us all with her own body," murmured Hawtry.

"What about everyone else, George?" asked Kirb.

"The raid destroyed the North Wing, Chapel and Nurses' Home," said George. "Word has it they are keeping Outpatients open and evacuating the rest until the buildings are repaired. We are all going to be very busy."

William Taylor piped up, "Dr. Bathfield has been helping

the rescue services. He refuses to leave until everyone is out. Dr. Challacombe is at his side."

"Aye and Assistant Matron McGovern is on patrol through the hospital now with a police constable to make sure no one is left inside, even though she's injured herself. Hearts of lions our medics and nurses," added George. "And what about Staff Nurse Marmion? She's been pacifying patients and ferrying them out. She carried one through all the rubble and down the stairs. She's another brave lass, she carried on despite being injured herself."

"I heard they're taking her to Grovelands," finished William.

"What about us?" queried Kirb.

"The hospital is moving to Surrey. That's where you'll be going, I expect, to Camberley," asserted George. "Unless you stay on here to man Outpatients and Emergency."

"Well, if the Nurses' Home has been flattened, there won't be anything to pack," said Kirb wryly.

"No. We'll have just what we stand up in," complained Hawtry. The nurses fell silent as they contemplated their fate.

Chapter Three

Hendre Farm

Ernie managed to keep his misgivings to himself throughout the day and no one noticed the shroud of darkness that surrounded his thoughts and settled like a cloud around his head. John and Ernie sat around the kitchen table as Jenny with the baby, Bethan, tied up in a shawl and held, as if in a sling, close to her mother's body, slept contentedly, as Jenny moved deftly between the range and the kitchen table serving out tea from the big pot. John munched on a culf of bread and butter as he finished wiping it around his plate, to mop up the juices from the hearty casserole Jenny had prepared.

Ernie broke the silence, "Let's have the wireless on, see what's happening in the world."

"Why? It's all doom and gloom and propaganda," protested John.

"I just want to see if there's anything happening. My daughter, Wendy's husband, Oliver has been pulled back from leave and been told to pack for overseas and with a baby on the way… I just want to be sure the Second Battalion of Welsh Guards are not suffering heavy casualties."

"I thought they had it pretty easy," observed John as he rose to switch on the wireless. "Weren't they at the Tower of London and then shifted to Camberley?"

"Er … Yes. That's right," he confirmed.

John twiddled with the knobs as the valves warmed up and he tried to tune into the station. It whistled and wailed until John found the Light Programme.

"We need the BBC Home Service, if you can find it," pressed Ernie. "The news should be on, now."

John twisted the tuning knob again and a voice blared out, "This is the BBC Home Service."

"Turn the volume down. You'll wake Bethan," ordered Jenny.

John grinned and fiddled with the volume. The evening news continued, "The minister of Agriculture has decreed that farmers are obliged by law to grow more wheat. Lack of imports means that we have to work harder to become self-sufficient. To that end a campaign for Digging for Victory has begun and Hyde Park and other green areas in London are to be ploughed up and utilised for the war effort." The wireless began to crackle and John twiddled the knobs once again before the newsreader's voice blared out. "London's East End was badly hit in the night forcing the evacuation of one of its major hospitals, The London Chest Hospital, which lost its north wing during the bombardment. Fortunately, there were few casualties…."

John burst in, "That's where Carrie is!"

"Hush!" cried Ernie and they all fell silent and listened to the report, which minimised the details in case enemy ears were listening. Ernie clenched his fist and his knuckles turned white. Bonnie rose and shook herself before nudging her head toward Ernie's knee.

Jenny looked at John and Ernie's worried faces. "I'm sure she'll be fine," she said softly trying to reassure them. "Carrie's a survivor."

"Yes, but how many times can she survive? She's been through too much already," blazed John.

"Now, now," tempered Ernie. "This won't do any good. We're all concerned for Carrie. She will be all right. I can feel it."

"But how will we know?" asked John rubbing his hands through his unruly hair.

"If it was anything serious the family would be notified wouldn't they, Ernie?"

"Yes, we would," affirmed Ernie. "No news is good news, as they say."

"Don't give me platitudes, Wuss. How can we be sure?" pressed John.

"You could always ring the hospital. You'll have to go down to the village to use the public telephone or go to the Post Office and speak to Gwyneth in the exchange. She might be able to help," remarked Jenny.

John swung her and the baby around and gave her a big kiss on her lips, "Jenny, you're a wonder. Now why didn't I think of that?" John left his tea, grabbed his hat and jacket and hurried out through the scullery and glasshouse and into the yard. Bonnie went chasing after him.

"Do you think she's all right, Ernie," asked Jenny her face puckered with concern.

"Yes, Jenny, I do but it will put John's mind at rest, she might be injured after all, you never know."

"What about your son-in-law? Oliver isn't it?"

"He'll be okay, although I had better drop a line to Wendy just to show I'm thinking of her."

"I'm sure she'll appreciate that."

They both lifted their heads as they heard Senator's hooves clattering out of the yard and across the cobbles. Jenny looked at the remains of John's meal on his plate, "He's not left much. Hardly worth keeping, but too good to give to the pigs."

"That it is, Jenny fach. Why don't you serve him up another portion and pop it in the oven to keep warm. He'll need it after his trek to the village."

"Good idea, I thought I might…." They were interrupted by a fierce hammering on the door and Bethan began to wail. "Oh no, just when she was settled…"

"Never you mind, gal. You sit with Bethan in the rocker and I'll see to this. I think I know who it might be."

Jenny settled into the rocker and began to sing a soothing lullaby in her melodically sweet voice. Bethan's eyes popped open and fixed on her mother's face and gradually lulled by the beauty of her song the infant slowly closed her eyes again and her tiny fist went into her mouth and she sucked it noisily and purposefully.

Ernie returned with a frowning Michael Lawrence, who was leaning heavily on a stick. "I'm sorry to disturb your evening but I just heard on the wireless…"

"Yes, we all did," interrupted Ernie.

"Is Carrie, Miss Llewellyn all right?"

"We'll know soon enough. John has gone to the village to try and ring the hospital. Then we'll be more certain," said Ernie simply.

"I see. Do you mind if I wait?"

"Not at all, Mr. Lawrence, not at all. Do excuse us, we hadn't quite finished our meal."

"Of course, of course," affirmed Michael his face now looking very grave.

"Can we help you to something, Mr. Lawrence?" asked Jenny. "There's plenty left."

"Thank you, but I'm not too hungry at the moment. Maybe later."

"Well, at least have a cup of tea. Ernie, can you deal with that while I get Bethan to bed?"

"Certainly, certainly. Forgetting my manners, I am. Tea, Mr. Lawrence?"

"Thank you, and please call me Michael."

"Very well and maybe you can tell me what's been happening to you. I had heard you were coming back home. Knew it would be soon, of course, from your manager. But not when."

"I'm not surprised, I only arrived this morning. I had to be debriefed first."

"What about your leg?" prompted Ernie.

"Long story, Ernie…"

"I've got time. So, what's with the stick? Can't have been easy walking from Gelli Galed on that."

"I didn't. I had a ride down with Sam Jefferies, coming across the cobbles was none too good but the stick won't be with me forever, just until the leg has fully healed."

"Oh?"

"Bullet wound, behind enemy lines, as I said, it's a long story."

Ernie finished making the tea and poured himself and Michael a cup. Michael began to relate all that had happened in France and how he had ended up in the London Chest Hospital and met up with Carrie, again.

"Meant to be, Michael fach. Meant to be. I don't believe in coincidence."

"No, neither do I now, and what's more," he said shyly, "Carrie has agreed to be my girl."

"Duw, Duw. That is a surprise. A good one mind," grinned

Ernie wondering what John would have to say about this news when he returned.

The two chatted like old friends as they waited for John to come home. They didn't have to wait long. Senator could be heard clip clopping on the cobbles as Jenny entered through the stair door.

"She's asleep, at long last. Hopefully, she'll rest now until later," smiled Jenny. She looked at the two men, "Well, you two look as if you've had a long chinwag," she observed.

The door to the glasshouse opened and John hurried inside. He looked in surprise at Hendre's visitor. "Mr. Lawrence." He greeted Michael with measured tones.

"What of Carrie? Miss Llewellyn? I heard on the wireless…" Michael blustered with a fearful look in his eye.

"As did we all," said John.

"Well?" pressed Michael.

John looked at the expectant faces around him and gushed forth, "She's all right." A collective sigh of relief rippled through them.

"Come on, before we all die of suspense. He's tighter than a tick on Tuesday. Give," prodded Ernie.

John laughed, "What a performance I had. I tried the telephone box first but I couldn't get through. Something about the lines being busy and so, then I decided to rouse the Post Mistress. She was none too pleased at being so rudely pulled from her evening meal but when Gwyneth heard it was about Carrie she couldn't have been more helpful." John then launched into description of how she had patched through to Neath and further afield until she managed to get a line to London.

Ernie, now, was getting impatient, "For goodness sake, Wuss. I'll have a beard like Rip Van Winkle by the time you tell your tale. What about Carrie?"

"I'm coming to that," he licked his lips tantalising them all still further.

"Jawch! This is worse than pulling hen's teeth. If you don't tell us I'll shake it out of you," Ernie muttered about to get to his feet.

"All right, all right!" John laughed, "Yes, she was bombed

with six other nurses, one of them wasn't so lucky but the others are fine. Carrie and Pemb are in hospital."

"Hospital?" shrieked Ernie.

"Yes, they have both suffered a head injury and cuts and abrasions. Nothing life threatening, I'm told. They wouldn't say too much. They have been evacuated to Camberley until repairs can be made to the building."

"Camberley!" repeated Ernie.

"Camberley, it's in Surrey."

"I know where it is," remonstrated Ernie.

"Then stop interrupting me," laughed John. He continued on with his tale finishing with, "Now, I must go and untack Senator and if there's anymore food left, Jenny, I'll have a plate. I'm starving after that ride."

"And I will away," murmured Michael. "I need to pack a few things."

"But you've only just arrived," blustered Ernie.

"I don't care. I need to get to Camberley."

"Why?" questioned John as he turned from the kitchen door.

"To see Carrie, of course," came the terse response.

"And I repeat, why?" asked John, crossing back and bringing his face level with that of Michael Lawrence.

"Because Carrie is my girl," he said boldly.

Silence fell in the room. Ernie studied John's face earnestly. John's expression was hard. Jenny glanced at Ernie and made to speak but John stepped back and extended his hand to Michael, "Why, that's wonderful!" he exclaimed.

Ernie's jaw dropped. He was not expecting that reaction and was flooded with a sense of relief as the two men shook hands, warmly.

"In that case, Jenny? Have we enough to offer Mr. Lawrence something to eat. He has a long journey ahead of him. Please, have some supper."

Lloyd Osmend was in the newly evacuated King Edwards Five Ways School in Monmouth. He had also heard the news of the bombing. He paced outside the headmaster's study nervously and waited for the Head, Mr. Dobinson to dismiss the fifth former who was being carpeted for smoking on the school premises.

A lanky youth emerged and hurried away, rubbing his palms that smarted from receiving the cane. Lloyd cleared his throat and knocked on the door.

"Come," the Head's voice echoed into the corridor.

Lloyd entered. Dobinson looked up from replacing the cane on the shelf above his desk, his spectacles perched on the end of his nose. "Yes?"

"Sir, I want permission to go to London?"

"What? When?"

"Now, this weekend."

"Certainly not. You have duties and classes here. The school cannot spare you."

"I'm sorry, Sir but I am going. I am leaving immediately. My fiancée has been bombed and injured. I must see that she's all right. Hopefully, I will be back on Monday."

The Head's jaw dropped. He was totally lost for words and Lloyd marched out of the study picked up his overnight bag that he had left outside the door and stepped outside to the waiting taxi that would take him to the station and on the train to London. His stomach churned like a maelstrom and he couldn't relax. He just wished he could be there and see Pemb and her friend Carrie. His knowledge was sparse and although he'd telephoned he didn't dare say too much for fear of Pemb getting into trouble. Their engagement was a secret. He did not want to jeopardise her job.

Lloyd was lost in his own thoughts and the streets outside were just a blur as he struggled to blink back tears. He arrived at the station and waited in line at the ticket office. It was a complicated journey starting with the tramway and going across country with a number of changes at Ponytpool, Cardiff and Bristol before he would reach London St. Pancras. Lloyd didn't care. All he was concerned about was seeing his beloved Pemb. He wasn't even worried about his job. Pemb came first and he needed to set his mind at rest.

Chapter Four

Camberley

The nurses evacuated to the hospital in Camberley were more than fortunate to leave the blitz in the heart of London. Some, however, like Kirb and Hawtry, remained, to run the Outpatients department that was still standing and to deal with emergencies. Many of the military were still transported there whilst workmen and women tried to clear the masonry and rubble in order to rebuild and make the rest of the hospital safe.

Many nurses lost everything when their quarters were flattened and there was a free for all of people who looted possessions that were visible and undamaged. Kirb complained bitterly when she saw one of the auxiliary nurses parading up the road to the park in Carrie's best coat. "Why, the little minx. That's Lew's coat, I'm sure of it."

"Are you certain?" questioned Hawtry. "I went to the site to try and recover something, anything, but there were all manner of people swarming over the piles of debris. I've lost everything too, including fourteen pairs of shoes."

Kirb snorted, "I'm positive. I was with her when she bought it. It cost her three month's salary. I bet the little strumpet has snaffled all the silk underwear, too."

"Say something. Get the coat off her back," protested Hawtry.

Kirb sighed, "No, we're all in the same boat. She's not to know. She probably lost all her belongings, too."

"Well, I don't think it's any excuse. It's still theft. She knows it doesn't belong to her."

Kirb raised an eyebrow. It was hard to reconcile Hawtry's changed personality from the one she had known in Bronglais where the staff nurse was not averse to a little light pilfering herself. But with all due credit, Kirb had to agree that Hawtry had undergone one heck of a transformation. She had gone up a hundred fold in Kirb's eyes especially as she was one of the nurses determined to stay on and do her best. It took immense courage to work with nightly bombing raids. It was Hawtry's insistence on staying in London and in the midst of everything that had persuaded Theatre Sister Kirby to stay, too.

"If you won't say something, then I will," announced Hawtry.

"No, don't."

"But, Lew has nothing left according to the others."

"Then if she returns she can do something about it," affirmed Kirb.

"What do you mean, if? She'll be back. She's not one to shirk her duty," confirmed Hawtry.

"No," said Kirb slowly. "No, she isn't. But she needs to get fit first. I have heard rumours that she is still unconscious."

"In a coma?" asked Hawtry with trepidation in her voice.

Kirb nodded, "She'll need all our prayers."

Lloyd was tired and anxious. He'd had an arduous journey with all the changes and when the train finally chuffed into St. Pancras he didn't stop to admire the beautiful architecture of the old station, but like a man on a mission he hurtled to the ticket barrier and searched to find a train to take him to Camberley. His journey of changes was not over yet and he groaned aloud as he was directed to Kings Cross and onto Waterloo where he would catch a train to Ascot and change again for Camberley. He grumbled to the ticket collector, "Would be so much easier coming from Birmingham."

"Certainly would, Pal. You look like you've been run ragged," added the Station Official. "You better put a spurt on, train leaves in three minutes."

Lloyd didn't need to be told. He raced along the station concourse to the platform, his coat tails flying like bat wings behind him. He showed his ticket at the barrier and boarded the train with seconds to spare. He flopped into the first available seat in the carriage and sighed. "That was close," he murmured to no one in particular.

Michael Lawrence looked up from his newspaper and

smiled politely, "You're lucky to have caught it. There isn't another until eight o' clock tonight."

"I didn't know," gasped Lloyd struggling to catch his breath. "Duw, Duw. I just hope the other changes aren't this tight."

"Where are you headed?" inquired Michael, glad of the company. "The train is relatively empty. Most people are getting out of London and as far away as possible." He waited for Lloyd to answer.

"Whew, I haven't run like that since I was at school… me? Oh, I'm off to Camberley."

"What a coincidence, so am I," said Michael in his cultured tones.

"Really?" smiled Lloyd, his voice now more even. "I've had one heck of a journey."

"Where from?"

"Monmouth, I'm teaching at a grammar school there."

"I didn't realise it was school holidays," observed Michael.

"It's not. I just dropped everything and left. In fact, I don't know if I'll have a job to go back to. The head refused permission."

Michael's curiosity was piqued, "If it's not too rude a question, why did you do that?"

"My fiancée has been injured in the bombing. I had to see if she was all right."

Michael raised his eyebrows in surprise, "You're not going to the hospital in Camberley by any chance?"

"I am, indeed," replied Lloyd somewhat amazed.

"Me, too."

They sat quietly for a moment and then both leaned forward to speak at once. "Sorry," apologised Lloyd. "After you."

"Not much to tell really," his voice began to swell with pride, " My girl, was bombed with some other nurses. I just had to see her."

"Mine, too." Lloyd extended his hand, "Lloyd, Lloyd Osmend, and you?"

Michael took the proffered hand, "I've heard of you… I'm Michael, Michael Lawrence."

"Carrie's young man?"

"Yes, and aren't you courting her best friend, Pemb?"

"One and the same. Well, I'm blowed!" Lloyd leaned back and laughed, "What are the chances…?"

"Very useful, we can share a cab," said Michael practically. "Are you staying over?"

"I intend to if I can find anywhere to stay."

"Me, too. Oops! It's our station, all change for Ascot." Michael rose up and retrieved his bag and stick from the overhead net rack.

Lloyd studied the stick, "What happened to you?"

"Long story."

"You can tell me on the way," said Lloyd as he grabbed his bag. "I want to see if I can get any flowers anywhere. More likely to find them here than in Ascot or Camberley."

"Great idea," concurred Michael.

The two young men alighted from the train and hurried through Waterloo for their connection to Ascot. Conversation was short on the ground but they kept an eye out for a flower stall. Michael alerted Lloyd as he spotted one close to the entrance to the underground. They dashed across and each bought a small bouquet of scented blooms before they hurried to their platform.

The train was in and idling at the station, clouds of steam billowed up into the glass roof and the whistle sounded. The glorious smell of the white vapour filled their nostrils. They scrambled aboard and moved along the corridor from First Class to Second Class to find a vacant carriage.

They had no longer sat down than the guard blew his whistle and waved his green flag, and the magnificent iron horse began to chug out of the station. The pistons on the wheels went click and grind, as they began to move, and the rims of metal on the wheels scraping along the tracks began to squeal into the recognised clicketty-clack sound as described in children's story books.

The two young men exchanged pleasantries and Michael revealed to Lloyd his dramatic escape from war-torn France where he had been shot down and ended up behind enemy lines.

"So that's why you have the stick? What an incredible story. That will be something to tell the children."

Michael laughed, "Maybe, if I ever have any."

"Don't you want kids?"

"I haven't really thought about it," replied Michael. And so they continued chatting amiably until they reached Ascot where they had to change again for Camberley.

The journey passed quickly enough and they shared a cab to the hospital. Once inside the main entrance they hastened to the information desk to find out, which wards had admitted Carrie and Pemb.

Pemb was in the Medical Assessment Unit on the first floor but Carrie was in Intensive Care on floor three. The young men went their separate ways eager to see their respective girlfriends.

Lloyd ran up the stairs to the first floor and entered the ward. His eyes searched the line of beds. One of the nurses, a Scot, asked him politely, "Can I be helping you, at all?"

"Please, I'm looking for my f… girlfriend, she's a nurse."

"Och! That could be anyone, don't you have a name?"

"Carol, Carol Pembridge," Lloyd gushed and flushed with embarrassment.

"Aye, the Welsh lassie. She's in a private room along here. Follow me."

Lloyd quickened his pace as he fell into step behind her. She stopped outside room three and knocked on the door. She opened it a fraction and spoke to the patient in the bed, "Visitor for you, Nurse Pembridge." She turned and spoke to Lloyd, "Not too long now, you don't want to tire her," and with that she smartly returned to the main ward.

Lloyd pushed open the door and saw Pemb sitting up in bed against a bank of pillows with a large bandage around her head. She stared in surprise at him, "What are you doing here?"

"That's a great welcome I must say," admonished Lloyd crossing to the bed.

"But, you're supposed to be teaching, aren't you? How on earth did you get time off?"

"I didn't. I told the headmaster you'd been hurt and left. I had to be sure you were okay." He handed her the flowers and bent to kiss her. "So, tell me what happened and what do they say?"

"Oh, I'll be fine. Slight head wound and a bit of concussion that's all. I'll soon be back on my feet, on duty and dancing with the rest of them. This is just a precaution. Thanks for the flowers, they're lovely," she said smelling them.

"Well, it looks serious."

"It's not. Have you heard about Lew? She's the one we're worried about. She's in a coma. It was really weird, she was conscious throughout the rescue and awake when she was pulled out and then she went out like a light, fainted dead away. She hasn't come around yet. As soon as they release me, I'll go and see her. In the meantime, you'll have to find out how she is for me, will you, Lloyd?"

Lloyd studied her pleading eyes, "Yes, certainly. When will you be released?"

"I think they're planning to let me go tomorrow, or the day after, fingers crossed. How long are you here for?"

"I should return on Monday, but as long as you need me I'll stay. Once you're back at work, I'll feel happier to head back. But, I'll come and see you again at the first opportunity. You can tell me when you'll get time off. You know, you quite frightened me."

He leaned over and kissed her, again. Pemb flushed with pleasure, "Now scoot! Come back and see me later. Just remember that I am gorgeous. I don't usually look like this."

Lloyd laughed, "You always look lovely to me." He stood up, "Okay, I'll be back later. Get some rest."

"Huh, that's all I've been doing. I want to get out of here. Now go and see Lew!"

Chapter Five

Repercussions

Michael Lawrence leaned on his stick as he hurried to the Intensive Care Unit. His heart was pounding and his stomach churning with fear. He knew that if Carrie was in ICU then it must be more serious than John had been led to believe.

He pushed through the swing doors to the ward where the patients that needed constant care were under observation. He limped to the desk at the Nurses' Station and coughed. The Sister in charge looked up and over her spectacles, "Yes?"

"I'm here to see Carrie Llewellyn," he offered.

"Yes?" she answered questioningly forcing Michael to stumble on.

"I'm here on behalf of her family and of course, me." Michael didn't know what else to say.

"Are you a relative?"

"No," he answered feeling awkward. "Carrie is my girl… my girlfriend."

"I'm sorry?"

"Her family are in Wales running the farm and unable to travel so I came instead." The woman was infuriating and giving nothing away. "Please, I've come all this way. Can I see her?"

The nurse replaced her pen on the desk and closed the file she was examining, "Miss Llewellyn is in a bad way,"

Michael's heart thumped louder in his chest, "Yes?"

Sister Parsons removed her glasses and looked him squarely in the eye, "After the nurses were dug out, she fell into unconsciousness. She has not awoken since." The anguish in Michael's face was plain to see. His knees began to buckle. "I think you better take a seat, Mister…?"

"Lawrence, Michael Lawrence." He pulled up a chair from the corridor and sat opposite the nurse. "Please, tell me, what has happened, what can be done? Can I do anything to help?"

"It may be fortuitous that you are here. It can sometimes help a patient to hear a familiar, friendly voice or even listen to a favourite song to help rouse them out of their coma." The Sister could see Michael's distress and continued. "Luckily she doesn't have any internal injuries or bleeding; physically she suffered a severe head trauma that needed stitches. There is some swelling on the brain. The coma is nature's way of dealing with the injury."

"How long could she be like this?"

"We have no way of knowing."

"Isn't there anything that can be done?"

"Like I said, we are monitoring her carefully. She is being fed and hydrated through a tube. A physiotherapist comes every day to move her muscles. The fear is the longer she remains unconscious the more muscle damage she will incur. We don't think there are any lasting neurological problems"

"What can I do?"

"Talk to her; a friendly, familiar voice can work wonders. Remind her of happy times past. Even reading a favourite book to her could help."

Michael nodded gravely, he said helplessly, "I bought her these."

"You can tell her yourself. I'll get an auxiliary to put them in water. Chat to her. The more stimulus the better."

"Thank you, Sister."

"Step this way, please."

Michael followed the Sister to a side room where Carrie lay silently in the bed. Her glorious hair showered the pillow, but her complexion was pale. She had a profusion of wires, like small tentacles, and tubes surrounding her. Michael looked anxiously at the Sister who encouraged him with a nod. Michael pulled up a chair and took one of Carrie's hands and began to talk.

The sister nodded in approval and left Michael to it. The pain he was feeling was etched on his face. He gazed at her upturned nose with its sprinkling of freckles and her curling lashes. He touched her spangled curls and sighed, "You have always had such wonderful hair. Do you remember when I confused you with Julie Ann? I never imagined anyone else could have such wild, clouds of untameable tresses. I was so rude to you that day and you had just saved my life." Michael paused, it was difficult to keep talking when all he wanted to do was sweep her up into his arms and hold her.

An auxiliary entered with the flowers in a vase and left discretely. Michael continued, "I've brought you some flowers. Do you know I don't even know what your favourite ones could be? These are scented blooms and very pretty in gold and yellow and pink. It's a poor excuse but it's all I could get with a war on." He stopped again, "I didn't realise how tough it could be just talking, like doing a monologue, but it may give me a chance to say things that I wouldn't ordinarily have the courage to say. Sister told me to keep chatting and fill your head with memories, like the butterfly brooch I gave you for your interview at the Maternity Unit in Aberystwyth, remember? I said it would bring you luck and it did."

Michael continued to chat about Hendre and Gelli Galed, Trixie and Boots, and the new dog at the farm, Bonnie. "Of course, it was quite a surprise when I met your friend, Pemb's fiancé, Lloyd on the train here. Best keep that quiet, she doesn't want to lose her job. He just dropped everything to see if she was okay. You all gave us quite a scare, you know. I know you wanted to volunteer but, in fact, you helped me with my recovery after I came home. I hope I'm making sense to you, it feels like I'm just rambling." Michael sighed. This was more difficult than he had thought.

"I'm still using a stick to walk but once my leg is healed I'll throw the cane away." He laughed, "Remember when you twisted your ankle and I carried you back to Hendre, you were so stubborn. You refused my help, refused to eat and then I caught you sneaking a portion of food. I believe you threw a spoon at me."

Michael chatted on. He had begun to get into his stride but still there was no reaction from Carrie, not even a blink. The physiotherapist arrived and Michael left the room whilst the specialist pulled back the covers on the bed and spoke soothingly to Carrie and began to work her legs by bending and stretching them back and for.

Michael sat outside the room looking forlorn. The Sister approached him and asked, “How’s it going?”

“Tough. I didn’t think it could be so hard to just talk. Do you think she can hear me?”

“Who knows for certain but I am sure that some of what you say must be registering in her subconscious somewhere. You just have to be patient. Why don’t you go and get a cup of tea? You look as if you could do with one,” smiled the Sister. “The physio will be with her for another thirty minutes at least.” Michael nodded gratefully. “Canteen is on the next floor. Go on, if she wakes I’ll send someone to collect you.”

Michael rose from his seat and hobbled out of the unit and made his way to the canteen. He crossed to the counter and ordered a cup of tea. No sooner had he sat down than he saw Lloyd enter. He waved at him cheerily.

“Thought I may find you in here, how’s Carrie?”

Michael shook his head, “Not good. She hasn’t come round yet. I feel an idiot chattering on to her as if everything is all right. But that’s what they advised me to do. What about Pemb?”

“She’s good. Told me off for coming. It looks like she’ll be out in a couple of days and back to work. There’s no stopping her. But, at least there’s no serious damage.”

“Good, good. That will give me something else to tell Carrie. I’m running out of things to say,” he said sheepishly.

“Has she any other injuries?”

“No, physically she seems to be okay.”

“Then it will only be a matter of time. From what I know of Carrie she’ll bounce back better than ever, you’ll see,” said Lloyd trying to be encouraging. “When are you going back?”

“I don’t know. I haven’t thought that far ahead, yet. What about you?”

“I’m going to a guest house close to the hospital, a place called Woodlands near Frimley Park. I’ll book in for two nights and then I have to get back that’s if I’ve still got a job. Unless of course Pemb takes a turn for the worse, but that doesn’t look likely,” said Lloyd wryly.

“I suppose I ought to find somewhere to stay, too.”

"I can try and book you in with me, if you like?"

"Thanks, I'd appreciate that."

"Here." Lloyd scribbled an address on a piece of paper torn from a notebook. "I may see you later, then."

Michael smiled wanly and pocketed the slip of paper. He checked the time. "I'd best get back. Her physical therapy should be completed now. Thanks Lloyd."

"I'm going to find my way to the place but I will pop back at visiting time. I may see you then? I also have to see Carrie. I've had my orders!"

"Yes, I'll look out for you."

"What say, if I don't see you before that we meet here at eight?"

"Fine." Michael nodded, gratefully and finished his tea. "See you later." He started to make his way back to ICU.

Carrie was walking through a field of poppies in dazzling sunshine. Her hair blew behind her in a tangle of fiery curls. She had a half smile on her face as she began to run through the waist high meadow of verdant grass and a multitude of fragrant flowers. She looked down and her beloved Trixie was scampering alongside of her. Every now and then the black and white Border collie would jump up and bat Carrie's hand with her head begging to be petted. Carrie stopped and made a huge fuss of the dog. Eventually, she tumbled down into the sweet lush grass and rolled in loving play with the animal. She scratched Trix behind her ears and pulled out some loose tufts of fur that was waiting to moult and Trixie washed her face with her soft gentle tongue and Carrie giggled. It was then that she heard melodic voices carried on the breeze, calling her name. "CA- RR- IE."

She stood up and looked across the field of wild flowers and saw a path unfolding before her leading to a tunnel that entered the hillside that was filled with a vortex of indescribable white light. Adjacent to the tunnel was a dark copse of trees that looked grim and forbidding and where shadows lurked.

Carrie's movements now became slower but more fluid as she tried to skip forward. She shaded her eyes from the brilliant, whirling, dazzling energy and began to make out smiling figures waving an excited hello to her.

Carrie gasped when she saw her mother, Miri, holding a boy, about eight years of age, by the hand. Her father, Bryn, had his arm around his wife and was laughing delightedly. His face was filled with absolute love and more than that his face was complete, whole and healed. Carrie began to run toward her parents who had opened their arms to her as more people flooded from the tunnel into the meadow. She recognised her grandparents on her mother's side of the family and her father's father, Dadcu who had passed some years before. Gwynfor, too, stepped out from the light and grinned at her. She continued running and the lumbering giant picked her up and swung her around in the meadow until she was dizzy and squealed to be put down.

Gilly stood back from the family watching Carrie whose eyes filled with tears as she saw her friend, "Gilly!"

"I was wondering when you'd be noticing me. I was thinking you'd forgotten me," she admonished.

"Forget you? No, never." Carrie held out her arms and the two friends embraced. The air was charged with emotion and Carrie could feel a lump rise in her throat as she strived to blink back the tears that threatened to spill from her eyes.

"Let me look at you, Carrie Llewellyn. Indeed, to be sure you have a loving future ahead of you." Gilly stepped back and Carrie's family pressed around her more closely.

Carrie could feel them and their enveloping love, which circled around her and, more joyously, she could see them. Her heart swelled with great happiness and as they spoke to her she could hear them clearly inside her head but puzzlingly their lips didn't move. They patted her on the back and congratulated her for visiting when from the shadows in the trees stepped a dark figure wearing a sombre black suit and wide brimmed preacher's hat. He had a lean saturnine face and pearl white teeth with a smile like a film star. He watched Carrie and licked his lips lasciviously. Carrie stopped and stared in horror. She believed her heart would stop such was the terror that filled her. Jacky Ebron touched his forehead in a mock salute and mouthed the word, "Soon."

Carrie shuddered and the malevolent evil figure disintegrated before her eyes. Her father had one finger pointing at where Jacky had stood as if this action had destroyed the presence that had so tormented and hurt her so badly in her young life.

She fell into her father's arms who comforted her and dried her cascading tears. The faces around him began to blur and fade. Gwynfor moved back into the tunnel and blew a kiss. Miri turned with young Gerwyn and was swallowed up by the swirling vortex of bright light.

Bryn took her by the shoulders and held her hard, "It is time for you to go back." But Carrie cried, "No, I want to stay with you, stay with you all. Let me come with you," she implored.

Bryn answered softly, "No, you must not follow, Cariad. It is not your time. Rest assured when it is, we will come for you and cross you over. We will all meet again. I promise."

She watched, unable to move as her father disappeared into the spinning tunnel of light and only Trixie remained, wagging her tail and gazing longingly at her young mistress. A chorus of whispered voices echoed the dog's name and Trixie gave Carrie's hand a final lick and padded into the swirling brightness that closed like a camera shutter and sealed the cliff.

Carrie floated back above the field and back, back through time and space and into the hospital room. She gazed down at her body from above. She studied the wires that monitored her life force and she watched the activity around her as a nurse checked her chart and vital signs and left. She saw a man sitting at her bedside talking soothingly to her. A flicker of recognition stirred in her memory that dissolved and faded.

She felt inexplicably drawn down toward her body as if pulled by a silver cord. She heard a voice echo in her head, a familiar voice that she couldn't place.

"You were less than impressed with me when I brought you back from the doctors, and I lifted you into the cart, telling me to think someplace else, remember?"

Carrie took a huge gulp of air. Her eyes fluttered. Michael called out urgently, "Nurse! Quickly!"

Sister Parsons and a junior nurse ran into the room and Carrie opened her eyes. Michael cried ecstatically, “Carrie.”

Carrie studied the man sitting at her bedside and struggled to recall his name. Her face was filled with confusion. She had returned to her body and still felt the remnants of the incredible unconditional love that had surrounded her moments before and it made her sad.

Her tummy began to feel queasy with fear. She didn’t understand why this man should disturb and unnerve her so much. There was something about him, something that both agitated and excited her and yet the more she tried to remember the more elusive the memories became.

She screwed up her face in concentration and announced, “I am Caroline Llewellyn. Nurse Llewellyn.”

“Yes,” said Michael. “You are, and much, much more.”

Carrie examined the contours of his face and her heart yammered in her chest. She stuttered out, “I live in Wales, at… on…” She stopped and took a deep intake of breath in an effort to steady herself.

“Yes, go on,” said Michael expectantly.

Finally, Carrie turned her face to him and said, “Begging your pardon, but who are you?”

Chapter Six

Getting to know you

To say that Michael was shocked was an understatement. His face dropped miserably and he said, “It’s me, Michael, Michael Lawrence.”

Some of Carrie’s fiery spirit returned and angry with herself for not being able to remember she railed at him, “That tells me nothing.” She bristled further, “Who are you? How do I know you? What are you doing here?”

Sister Parsons watched the interchange and ushered Michael out from the room, “Please don’t worry. This sometimes happens and it is rarely permanent.”

“She doesn’t remember me. How can that be? After everything…”

“She’s suffered severe concussion and has been in a coma. The receptors in her brain are just not connecting properly. The limbic cortex and temporal lobe have swollen slightly due to the injury and in the inner temporal lobe lies the hippocampus, which is responsible for memory, names of people and so on. So, although she doesn’t know you now, it’s more than likely she will remember.”

“Yes, but when?”

“Sometimes it’s a few hours, sometimes a few days. It is very rare for it to continue longer than that.”

“But does amnesia ever become more permanent or have you known it to happen?”

“Not in my experience but I have heard of a few cases that have taken longer.”

“That’s not very comforting.”

“Cheer up! It will be okay. That kind of amnesia only happens in books and films. You’ll see. The important thing for you is not to be put off; keep seeing her and talking to her. Tell her your memories. Now, if you don’t mind waiting we need to get a doctor to check her out.”

Michael reluctantly limped to a day room waiting area and sat. He felt utterly dejected but determined to follow Sister Parson's advice. He was still sitting there when Lloyd found him. He grinned, "Pemb's instructions, before I do anything else I have to see how Carrie is faring?" He studied Michael's face, "What is it?"

"Carrie."

"Is she okay?"

"She's woken up now but she doesn't know me. Some sort of memory loss."

"That's bad. What can you do?"

"Keep talking to her and hope she will remember," muttered Michael philosophically. "Even knowing it's not permanent doesn't help."

"We ought to go and settle in our rooms at Woodlands. I've booked you in. I shall pop back again this evening. What are you going to do?"

"I'll come with you. She's going to be surrounded by doctors, now. Not much point in me hanging around."

"Good. You look as if you could do with something to eat and I'm starved."

Michael rose from his seat and followed Lloyd out to the main corridor and stairwell as Dr. Challacombe came striding past.

He quickened his step and entered ICU and marched to Carrie's room and entered, "Well, well what's been happening to you?"

Carrie responded mechanically, "I think you know better than me," she replied with a half smile.

Andrew Challacombe took out his pencil light and examined Carrie's eyes. He then instructed her to watch his finger as he moved it from side to side. "Follow the movement. Yes, that's it!"

He sat on the end of the bed. "You've given us all quite a fright." Carrie turned her eyes on him curiously. "You have a temporary memory loss, but I bet you remember me, don't you? After all we have a date," he said cheekily and winked at her. Carrie blushed. "Don't you remember?"

Carrie grappled with her confusion but she did seem to

have some fleeting memory of him from somewhere. Or maybe it was because he was her doctor and she had an impression of him that made him seem familiar.

"So what do you recall?"

"I know who I am if that's what you mean," said Carrie.

"Good. That's a start. Do you remember being bombed?"

Carrie shook her head, "No, nothing." She sighed, "How long will I be like this?"

"It's hard to say. Everyone is different but it won't be permanent."

"I hope not. There are some things I remember quite clearly, other memories are fuzzy and I sometimes have fleeting glimpses that I can't quite grasp, yet…. Duw, I sound like an idiot, a goody-oo, as my Aunty Annie would say. How long am I going to be in here for? I feel a bit of a fraud. All I had was a bump on my head."

"It was a bit more than a bump on the head, Nurse Llewellyn."

"You know what I mean. I need to get back to work, to focus on something. I'll go mad in here."

"Patience, just a day or two longer. We need to discover what you do or don't remember."

"It's so annoying, my mind is all of a muddle. I can't seem to think straight. I know I've just upset someone who knows me well but, it's awkward as he is just a stranger to me, now."

"Well, I hope you don't forget me so easily," admonished Dr. Challacombe.

"I'm not sure. I'm getting even more of a headache trying to work it out."

"We will just take things slowly, go through what you can remember and take it from there."

Carrie appeared to accept this and nodded her agreement. She closed her eyes and murmured, "I just want to go to sleep and wake up and everything is all right."

Dr. Challacombe rose and spoke quietly to Sister Parsons, "Let her rest now. I'll be along later. I need to speak to someone in neurology, formulate some sort of strategy to help her regain her missing memories. Meanwhile, don't let her get too stressed."

“What about her young man?”

“Use your discretion. She mustn’t be unduly upset.” Dr. Challacombe turned and left the room and ward.

At the Woodlands guesthouse, Lloyd and Michael were unpacking their bags. They had booked an evening meal with Mrs. Nancarrow who owned the establishment after which they decided they would return to the hospital.

The gong sounded downstairs and Lloyd knocked on Michael’s door. “Dinner’s ready. Are you coming down?”

Michael came out of his room and smiled. “I wonder what’s on offer?”

“We’re lucky to have anything, what with the rationing, but Mrs. Nancarrow grows her own vegetables so that’s a help.”

The two young men walked down the stairs and entered the dining room. Mrs. Nancarrow was waiting. She was tall for a woman, with dark hair and large brown eyes. She had an engaging smile and welcomed them brightly. “Welcome to Woodlands. Dinner won’t be long. Not a sumptuous feast but heart warming, none-the-less. Is there anything you don’t like?” Both men shook their heads. “Good. That makes life a lot simpler. Sit yourselves down and I’ll bring you some soup. Nourishing vegetable soup with the fruits of the garden.”

It seemed that Lloyd and Michael had fallen on their feet. They smiled appreciatively as the landlady returned with two steaming bowls of thick country style vegetable soup. There was no more chat while the men fed their faces. The soup was tasty and they settled back to enjoy corned beef and onions with fried potatoes. It was then they began to talk again.

Michael and Lloyd found they had much in common and a growing respect and genuine liking for each other was soon established. They completed their very satisfying meal, bade good evening to Mrs. Nancarrow, took a key for the front door and made their way back to the hospital.

Megan, Carrie’s childhood friend, was excited, she was on her way to Drury Lane where she was to continue with rehearsals as part of a six strong troupe of three girls and three young men. She had been warned that a doctor would be in attendance through the week to give them the necessary inoculations for visiting both India and Burma, and had suffered three jabs already and was not looking forward to the rest, but she was filled with an almost enjoyable nervous anticipation, too. She never dreamed that when she enlisted in ENSA that she would be visiting such far-flung places.

Megan arrived early at the beautiful old theatre where she had originally done her dance audition and there she met the other members of the troupe as they arrived, who were all keen to begin warming up. They were a lively bunch, Megan thought, and well suited to the revue and cabaret show that had been scripted for them.

They were all as apprehensive as each other but even more so at the prospect of having to undergo nine vaccinations in total. Megan exclaimed, "I'm already like a pin cushion. Just the thought of another needle is enough to make me fall apart. Why do we need all of these?"

The petite blonde dancer and juggler, with a winsome, dimpled smile, called Janet Gregson, explained, "We must be protected. Smallpox is rife in India as well as other horrible diseases like Cholera, Typhoid, and Yellow Fever."

Megan pulled a face, "Sounds dangerous."

"It will be, those are the unseen enemy and then there's the Japanese," added Gary Wilson one half of a brother and sister acrobatic contortionist double act.

"Surely, they won't give us the rest all in one go?" asked Megan.

"No, they'll spread them out," continued James Adams, pianist and singer. "Some of them might make us feel a bit ill or so I've heard. The worst are over, now."

Megan shuddered, "Huh! You wish! Still, we'll have to grin and bear it, I suppose."

"The things we do for our art," complained Bill Bushby the troupe's plump comedian and compere. "Oh well, I'm sure I can use the experience to write some original material. Shall we get a move on? Let's get started. The quack is arriving soon to do the deed."

"And I for one am not looking forward to it," muttered Megan.

"Okay," called Bill, "Starting positions. Please. We open with the chorus song and dance number before moving onto the individual acts. Here's the new running order." He passed everyone a sheet of paper. "Any suggestions before we begin rehearsing the first routine, speak up!"

They gravitated into their opening spots and James ran his fingers across the piano keys and started the introduction. The performers moved on cue into an opening tableau and burst out, coming to life one at a time.

Megan and James began to sing the opening lines of Chatanooga Choo Choo in harmony while Gary and his sister, Lucy rolled in tandem like railway wheels as Janet danced in front of them, juggling. Bill, who played the train guard waved his flag and blew his whistle before stepping out into his warm up comedy routine.

Megan stopped, "There's something missing. It's all a bit flat. I suggest we rethink the opening number. We need to grab the audience from the first moment."

"Actually, I agree with Megan," said Janet, smiling at Megan. "We have our own acts within the show. We're sort of telegraphing what they can expect…"

"What do you suggest?" asked James.

"Let's do a proper choreographed opening number that we can all join in and we need a thread to run through the show so it all makes sense, it's a bit disjointed at the moment," offered Megan.

At that moment the door to the rehearsal room banged open and the troupe gave a collective groan as the company manager who was also their commanding officer entered with the theatre doctor carrying his black bag.

The doctor who wore glasses and had a drooping moustache like Dr. Crippen, and indeed bore a distinct resemblance to the man, who had been hung at Pentonville prison for murdering his wife, stepped to the desk at the front of the room and laid down his bag. He looked at the dismayed faces before him and announced, "Come on, it's not so bad. Last injections today and you'll be fully protected."

"Last ones?" wailed Megan, shaking her shiny conker coloured tresses. "You're not going to give us six needles?"

The doctor laughed, "No! Two combination jabs. But your arm may already be a bit sore so we'll use the other one." The doctor looked at Janet, "No juggling for you today!"

The group fell into complaining chatter and the company manager was forced to call order, "Stop grumbling, it's just a little scratch."

"It's all right for you, you're not on the receiving end," moaned James.

"Yes, well, that's where you're wrong. I shall be coming with you. After rehearsals you all need to convene in the Greenroom where you'll be kitted out with your wardrobe, mosquito nets, malaria tablets, cooking utensils, hurricane lamps and candles, soap, towels and toilet rolls."

"Toilet rolls!" exclaimed Megan.

"Yes, there aren't any in India."

"What?" groaned Bill. "How hygienic! I hope there's enough. What are we limited to? One sheet per sitting?" he joked. The troupe laughed half heartedly as the reality of their situation began to kick in.

The company manager, Major Freddie Sims, called them all to attention, "We set sail on Friday. You are each to look after your own stuff, pack it and get it to the docks on time, where it will be collected."

"Are we really going to India?" questioned Megan.

"We'll be travelling on a troopship, in convoy and should be in Bombay four weeks after we leave. You'll have plenty of time to get the show right, on board. So, make the most of your time left. Now, roll up your sleeves and let's be done with it," ordered Freddie. "Then, take a break and be back at one."

The life seemed to have been suffocated out of the group as they reluctantly shambled forward to face the diminutive doctor whose smile bore a certain amount of enjoyment at their huge discomfort.

Megan dropped to the back of the queue to wait her turn and decided she needed to write to her family and friends at the first opportunity, especially Thomas. Megan didn't know where he was stationed or headed and wondered if she'd be lucky enough to see him at all in the next year.

Thomas had been transferred to HMS Indomitable, an impressive and relatively new aircraft carrier, which was on its maiden voyage to the West Indies. It was rumoured that they were scheduled to ferry the forty-eight Air Force Hawker Hurricanes to engage with and protect HMS The Prince of Wales and HMS Repulse in Singapore in the light of extreme Japanese aggression. None of this had been confirmed but sailors believed they were part of a deterrent force known as Force Orange hoping to quash the advance of the Japanese in the Far East. Further plans had been mooted involving the ship protecting and patrolling the seas around Gibraltar. Sailors waited to hear the truth from their captain, Captain Morse.

Thomas stood on deck taking a much-needed breather. It was hot in the engine room. They all had to take their turn in stoking any of the six boilers below. The navy had discovered practical Thomas' aptitude with motors and he was in training as an engineer working alongside veterans in the field, but his capacity for hard work meant he was often relegated to doing the hard slog. He stared out across the water gaining little respite from the sea air, which blew in his face like a salon's hair dryer. The ship was on course for Jamaica. There he hoped he might be able to get a letter home to Megan and at least let her know that he was all right.

Thomas shaded his eyes in the hot sun and could just make out through the shimmering heat haze the beginnings of a coastline. He heard a cry go up from another sailor who cheered, "Land ahoy!" The illustrious ship turned toward the land and pushed its way through the languid turquoise seas on route for the harbour, a notoriously difficult place to navigate to because of reefs and submerged clumps of rock.

From what Thomas understood the ship would dock in Kingston where some of the crew would be allowed shore leave before they progressed on to help Force Z in Singapore. He took a last gulp of air before returning below deck. The ship roared ahead at thirty knots like a hungry lion, chomping the miles away, carelessly neglecting underwater obstructions.

Once below he was assigned to maintain number five boiler, while the other seaman in charge took a break. Once they were to arrive in dock he was told he would have to grease and overhaul the piston heads before being allowed to step ashore.

Suddenly, there was a huge groan from tortured metal that clunked and grinded against something. The engines struggled to keep going and squealed in complaint as the ship began to list to one side. Chaos appeared to reign where sailors shouted and officers yelled their orders. Men ran back and for, trying to see what they had hit.

"It's got to be rocks!" one able seaman asserted.

"I think it's a reef," assessed another.

"Watch out!" cried another, "We're going over!"

Catastrophically, the ship floundered to a complete halt and the engines whined in protest and juddered to a stop. Water slapped on the sides of the ship as the waves broke against them. The men could taste the salt in the air and the navigation officer could see something pooling in the water below. He hoped it wasn't a ruptured fuel tank.

No one in the engine room knew what was happening. Men had been flung off balance and thrown against scalding hot pipes and machinery. Cries of pain went up from those burned in the accident. They received a call through the communication tube, sometimes called a voice-pipe, from above, telling them that the ship had run aground on a coral reef just off Jamaica. The chief engineer swore softly and cursed the captain and navigation officer claiming that they were culpable and should be relieved of duty.

There would be no shore trips. All qualified men were to report and work together to effect repairs to the stricken ship in the hope of floating it off the reef then docking and finishing mending it in dry dock. Thomas groaned. He knew he would be one of the ones drafted in to do this work. He was feeling lucky that he hadn't been burned or scalded in the incident but now felt his luck had run out. Thomas could see that he and his shipmates would have little or no free time for a while.

Chapter Seven

Hendre and further afield

Ernie was on edge. He yanked off his beret and scratched at the sparse tufts of wiry hair that sprouted from the sides of his head. "Iechy dwriaeth, I need to be busy," he complained as he sat at the table, looking out of the window and watched the unexpected downpour of rain that flooded the yard and ran like a river down the mountain track.

Bonnie watched him lazily as he stood up and peered hard outside and then paced back to the table before sitting again.

"Whatever's the matter Ernie? You're like fiddler's bow, back and fore and up and down," asked Jenny.

"Oh, Jenny fach, I can't settle."

"Why?"

"I'm worried about Carrie."

"But John said that the hospital had said she was all right."

"I don't think they told him the complete truth. I've just had a feeling that's all."

"We all know you and your feelings and we know not to ignore them. What are they? Tell me."

"Oh, I don't feel it's anything life threatening…"

"Then that's all right then," Jenny tried to placate him.

"No, I don't know… I think…"

"What do you think?" asked John as he walked in.

Jenny tried to warn Ernie with her eyes, she knew how upset John could get with anything to do with Carrie. Fortunately, Ernie caught Jenny's look and spluttered an excuse, "It's Wendy's husband, Oliver. I don't know what to do. I've got a feeling he's going to be posted to the Middle East."

"I should keep quiet about it if I were you. Worry about it when it happens and not before. Don't frighten her, Wuss. Aunty Annie is right, what you don't know can't hurt you... Why upset her on a feeling?"

Ernie sighed, "Aye, you're correct. Wise words. I'll keep quiet."

Jenny looked at Ernie and she smiled her thanks saying, "Aye, it's for the best. All of a tremble, he's been John."

"Fleas nesting in his pants," concurred John.

"What?" said Jenny in confusion.

"Another of Aunty Annie's sayings. She was full of them. Now, what's for supper? I'm starved."

Ernie smiled and pulled up his chair to the table. He didn't want to say anymore but something else was worrying him and it was something he couldn't put his finger on but he feared there was trouble brewing.

The four-week voyage to Bombay was turbulent and tough. Megan and the rest of the troupe managed to rehearse and get the revue show slick and professional in spite of the bouts of sickness that attacked and beset each of them at some time during the voyage. The first thing Megan noticed as they approached the Indian continent was the heat that came from the warm winds and the burning sun that sweltered down from the cloudless sky.

The young group of entertainers were filled with delight. They chattered about this wonderful opportunity and looked forward to entering a new land, a new culture, new experiences, and meeting new people. The ship blew its flat single toned honking hooter that blasted in their ears. Troops scurried to erect the gangway leading to the busy dockside, where local men in sarongs, some in white loose tunics over dhotis and others wearing churidars worked at carrying goods from shore to ships.

Megan breathed in the aromas that pervaded the air; spices such as she had never smelled before. Sacks of saffron, cumin, turmeric and garam masala waited with traders eager to sell their wares. Colourful samples sat in baskets on the dockside, which was ablaze with colour. Megan could hardly believe what she was seeing. She followed her company off the ship to the quay and where the baggage would be taken to wait for them to collect.

Megan had never experienced weather like it. The air was

humid and her hair was sticking to her neck and face in sweat laden strands. She wondered how they would perform some of the more energetic acts and dances in this extreme heat. She was sure as she looked at the rest of the company that her face must be flushed with colour. She took out a handkerchief that was tucked in her sleeve and wiped away the droplets of perspiration that beaded on her forehead.

The group waited as their luggage was unloaded and stacked next to them. They each picked up a suitcase but Megan stared in dismay, "Where's my case?"

"It will probably be brought off in a minute, hang on," said Bill philosophically.

The troupe waited until the company manager, Freddie disembarked carrying his own case. "Okay, welcome to Bombay. We must get some transport to HQ. Is everyone ready?"

Megan shook her head, "No! I don't have my case."

"Where is it?"

"I put it outside my cabin door like everyone else but it's not here."

"It will turn up I'm sure. I'll go and check. Wait here."

Megan groaned, "It can't be lost. Everything I need is in there. Some of my costumes, all my clothes, nighties and underwear, even my toothbrush is packed away. Don't say this is all I've got?" She indicated the clothes she stood up in, which were less than suitable in the sweltering heat.

"I may have something you can borrow," offered Janet sympathetically who had become good friends with Megan, "I know it's not the same but better than getting smelly."

Megan pursed her lips and frowned, "This is all I need. Sorry, I don't mean to sound ungrateful, you're very kind." She spotted Freddie striding back across the gangway. "Aw, no! He's empty handed, now what?"

Freddie puffed as he returned to the troupe. "We need to get to HQ. We'll report your loss there. Sorry, Megan."

Megan followed the others miserably off the dockside and they trekked to the dusty road that was awash with peddlers all begging them to look at trinkets for sale and pestering them to buy.

A ramshackle charabanc was parked at the roadside. Windows were missing and coloured rags and material fluttered in the space where glass should be. A lean Indian with a mouthful of extraordinary white teeth hopped off the step and spoke in a singsong tone, "Welcome, Sahib, Memsahib, please to come aboard and I will take you forward to HQ."

The troupe clambered onto the bus, and loaded their bags before finding seats, many of which had the stuffing poking out from worn cushions. Lucy wrinkled her nose in distaste at the state of the inside of the bus, which seemed littered with chicken feathers. The driver called Ravi, started the engine with a clunk and the motor spluttered and coughed before bursting into a throaty rattle. The wheels wobbled dangerously as the bus began its journey and juddered along the rough potholed roads.

The company were mesmerised by the views outside. They passed through the wealthy city with its fine, colourful and exotic buildings and streets that milled with people. Megan thought she had never seen so many people anywhere, not even in London. As the bus clattered on they entered the slums; a large, shanty town of wooden shacks, tin huts and corrugated iron lean-tos where the poorest native families lived in filth and squalor among flies and stench.

Megan ducked her head back inside the window trying to suppress the urge to retch as the searing heat heightened the disgusting odour of human sewage, which freely ran in the gutters and street. They continued on their way past a railway line where a packed train trundled past, overflowing with natives sitting crammed into every available space, on the roof and hanging off the sides of the carriages. They called out for, "Baksheesh, Sahib," as they spotted the Europeans travelling on the coach.

The sun was ferocious as it blistered down coating them all in a slick film of sweat. Their clothes stuck to them and Megan bemoaned the fact that she had nothing else to wear and nothing with which to wash.

A slight breeze blew through the open places where there were once windows; but not a cool refreshing light wind but more like a blast of hot air from a blazing furnace. The excessive heat was debilitating and tiring. The company were exhausted by the time they reached HQ.

Freddie gathered the troupe together and they alighted from the bus. Army trucks lined the yard and they were led away to the barracks, which was to be their home for the next few weeks.

Megan stopped off at the main office and logged a report about her missing case. The officer on duty assured her, "I am positive that it will turn up eventually. It sometimes happens so don't worry."

"But, what am I supposed to do until then?" she questioned.

"We'll kit you out with something."

Megan had to be satisfied with that and she made her way to the women's hut and flopped on a bunk. She made up her mind to write to Thomas as soon as she had rested. She had much to tell him.

She was so relieved to have escaped the obsessive and unwarranted interest of Grainger Mason in her last theatre company. His irrational jealousy was frightening and Megan was only too pleased to have found a place with this new cast. She wondered if the man had been sacked or if he had directed his attention onto some other poor unsuspecting female. In spite of the heat Megan shivered. She didn't like to think what might have happened if Thomas had not arrived, literally, in the nick of time. And thinking loving thoughts about Thomas she fell into a dreamless sleep.

Grainger Mason had settled back into theatre life and was feeling outraged by Megan's rebuff. He thought about the girl with the conker coloured tresses that gleamed and bounced as she walked and it made him angry. The scenes he was currently re-enacting on stage with her replacement, Lucinda, played like a film reel in his head, but in his mind he saw Megan's face, her eyes and lips and he sighed with longing.

Grainger knew it would be risky to chase after Megan and the voices in his head began to argue. He gave himself a stern talking to and came to a flawed conclusion. He convinced himself that it was Megan's loss and he deemed it too dangerous to follow her to another company. Simon Jackson his company manager had already let it slip that she was in a troupe covering the Far East. However, he knew that he couldn't pursue her out of the country. He was aware that he had managed to avoid the routine inoculations and vaccinations demanded by the military for this job with a home troupe but to apply for a different posting would mean that he'd be expected to undergo a whole armful of injections, and needles were the one thing, which made Grainger desperately afraid. He was not going to allow himself to become a living scientific experiment. Certainly, he had never felt better. Immunisation didn't feature in his vocabulary.

Grainger had some leave coming up, which he was required to take, before the rehearsals for the new show would begin. Inexplicably, his thoughts drifted back to Land Girl Laura, his childhood sweetheart. She had been devastatingly upset when she saw him in Wales with Megan, so much so she never wanted to see him again and had transferred to another part of the country. Or had she?

Grainger rubbed his chin, thoughtfully. During his break he decided that he would revisit the Welsh village of Crynant and see what he could learn. Someone may give him a clue as to Laura's whereabouts and he could set things right with her. She used to be his girl. Why couldn't she be his again?

Chapter Eight

Keeping a vigil

Michael Lawrence was feeling utterly deflated, he had sat at Carrie's bedside and chatted to her trying to help her remember. He was putting himself through another hour of torture talking about her beloved Hendre.

"Think Carrie, you loved it more than any place on earth."

"I know, I do. If it hadn't been for that solicitor in cahoots with Jacky we would never have lost the farm."

"The solicitor was acting for me. I bought Hendre in good faith."

Carrie stubbornly shook her head, "No, it was that pompous Mr. Phillips who was the swindler."

Michael sighed and his eyes filled with tears. Carrie was flooded with compassion, "I am sorry, Mr. Lawrence. I can see that this is terrible for you but although you seem familiar I just cannot place you. My mind is totally confused. I'm sure that there must have been something between us or you would not have come all this way. We will just have to wait for nature to take its course for I am assured that my full memory will return. It just may take a while. Until then I suggest you return to Crynant and wait for me to contact you."

Michael took her hand, "It is hard for me to know that you remember so much but yet, you have forgotten me. I can't go back yet. I have to stay."

"But what about the farm? Who will run it?"

"John and Ernie are managing well and Sam Jefferies, my manager is looking after my affairs for the moment."

"I don't remember him, should I?"

"I don't think so. I'm not sure if you met him or not."

The door opened and Andrew Challacombe entered with the physiotherapist and Michael stood up.

"Today's the day," Dr. Challacombe announced. "We are to get you up and onto your feet. We need you back on the wards. Good nurses like you are hard to find," he said cheerily. He nodded dismissively at Michael, "Come back in an hour and young Nurse Llewellyn may be able to have coffee with you in the canteen."

Michael stood up reluctantly and moved to the door, "I'll pop back in an hour."

Carrie smiled in response and Michael stepped into the corridor. He watched through the window. He saw the body language of the doctor, and witnessed him flirting with Carrie. Carrie's smiling response tore at his heart and a wave of jealousy gripped him. He tried to shrug it off knowing that this wasn't the real Carrie.

He observed as the doctor pulled back the covers on the bed and the physio encouraged Carrie to stand. She stepped out of the bed and would have collapsed onto the floor if Dr. Challacombe had not caught her. Michael couldn't help noticing the rapport between Carrie and Dr. Andrew Challacombe and he was envious.

Carrie leaned against the doctor and the physio as they encouraged her to take her first weight bearing steps. Michael had seen enough. He retreated to the canteen for a cup of tea. He felt in deep need of a friend but Lloyd had since returned to Monmouth although he had promised to come back in a few weeks. Pemb was up and about and back at work. Michael was disheartened that Carrie had attributed incidents that he had recounted to her as being done by Gwynfor or someone else. The doctors agreed that this was most unusual and diagnosed a case of Source Amnesia. Since all her learning and nurse training was intact she was able to return to duty, once she was deemed strong enough.

Pemb found Michael in the canteen with his head in his hands, "Michael, please don't worry. It will be all right. It's only a matter of time."

"How often have I heard that?"

"But, it's what you must hang on to. She will remember and then she'll remember everything. I know it. Trust me, the first time we met and talked about our boys at home we wheedled it out of her that there was a gentleman farmer she quite liked but he was somewhat older than her. And Lloyd, don't forget Lloyd, she put us together so she could see you."

Michael gave a half smile, "It can't come quickly enough for me."

Pemb patted his hand and left briskly. She dropped into ICU and was pleased to see Carrie walking; she also noticed a closeness that had developed between her friend and Andrew Challacombe. Pemb waited until the doctor had left to complete his rounds and caught Carrie by the elbow, "Lew, remember what you said about Dr. Challacombe?"

Carrie shrugged.

"He's a womaniser, there were fights between nurses in Birmingham over him. Think back," Pemb prodded.

Carrie turned to her friend, "I'm going back to London."

"What?" exclaimed Pemb in horror.

"Whatever happened to me happened there. It might jog my memory." She studied her friend's face that registered huge concern and added, "I don't want to hurt anyone Pemb. This is something I have to do. I am going to work at Outpatients with Hawtry and Kirb. I'll go for a month and then come back to Camberley. It will be on a rota basis. It may just do the trick. I have spoken to the authorities and they have agreed to this arrangement, even if it is somewhat unusual." She paused as she studied Pemb's shocked face and then continued, "I have to admit that Michael Lawrence disturbs me. He sends shivers down my spine in a good way but I am clearly not ready mentally to recognise him yet. I'm not saying I never will but I have to accept that although he excites me that things have changed and that I may have changed. I may not be the person he remembers and I cannot be something I'm not. I need to return to London to find myself. Please tell me you understand."

Pemb took her friend in her arms and held her in a tight embrace, "You're still the same Lew, you'll see."

Carrie released herself, "I'm leaving later today. Please tell Michael for me. And tell him to go home. I will write, I promise. Here," she passed Pemb her address scrawled on a scrap of paper, which Pemb pockcted.

"I don't think he'll listen to me. Shouldn't you speak to him yourself?"

"I can't. I really can't. Do it for me, as my friend, please."

Pemb nodded and hugged Carrie again, "You'd better go or you'll have me blubbing."

"I'll see you in a month," smiled Carrie and she turned to go.

Pemb stopped her, "Is Dr. Challacombe doing this rota duty, too?" she asked.

"Not as far as I know. I haven't said anything to him. I don't wish to complicate my life further."

"Okay. Good luck. Give my love to Kirb and Hawtry."

Carrie smiled and watched her friend go. She tentatively stepped to the door and ventured out into the polished corridor. She knew there was a train to London later that day as she had already checked with the secretary in the admin office.

Pemb walked through the hospital and back to Men's Surgical. She just caught sight of Dr. Challacombe disappearing around the corner and she ran to catch him up. Of what she was going to say, she was uncertain but she still called out his name, "Dr. Challacombe!"

He stopped when he heard his name called and turned to see Pemb running toward him, Don't run," he reprimanded as she scooted to a stop.

"Sorry," puffed Pemb.

"Well, Nurse Pembridge, what is it?"

"It's Carrie," she blurted out.

"What about her?"

"You must know she's very vulnerable right now. It won't do her any good to confuse her."

"I beg your pardon?" he raised his eyebrows questioningly.

"Carrie, is not quite herself and it isn't advisable to play with her mind or feelings."

Andrew Challacombe pulled himself up to his full height and the ever-present cheeky twinkle in his eyes vanished, "Nurse Pembridge, I don't know what you are suggesting but Nurse Llewellyn has been in my care. I don't know what you think you may or may not have seen but the relationship is purely professional and to think otherwise is to doubt my integrity as a doctor." His tone was sharp and he eyed her as a bird might prey upon a wriggling worm.

Pemb stuttered, “I wasn’t suggesting…”

He cut her off, “Then what were you suggesting?”

“Carrie is my friend. I am just looking out for her, that’s all.”

“And I, too, Nurse. And I, too. I’ll pretend we never had this conversation.” He strode away down the corridor with obvious annoyance and more than a hint of anger in his gait.

Pemb was left floundering and her face was flushed. She spoke crossly to herself, “Well, that went well, Nurse Pembridge. Why won’t I learn to keep my big mouth shut?” She tried to calm her beating heart. Now she needed to find Michael. She supposed he could still be in the canteen and so set off in that direction.

Pemb entered the refectory and scanned the hall. He was sitting where she had left him. She took a deep breath and walked up to the table and sat. Michael took one look at Pemb’s face and he knew. He knew it wasn’t good news.

Her voice echoed in and out of his head as he struggled to take in what she was telling him. “No, she can’t. She’s not safe there. What if something else happens?”

“You know Carrie. She’s twice as stubborn as any mule.”

“Then, I’ll have to go to London, too.”

“No, she asked me to tell you to go home and she promised to write.”

“I can’t risk it. Is… is that doctor going to be there?”

“No. He’s not.”

Michael sighed, “At least that’s something.”

“You do what you feel you have to, Michael. But in my heart of hearts I believe that you and Carrie will be together.”

“Thanks, Pemb, although that’s small comfort now.”

“I know.” Pemb patted his hand and rose. She looked back at him from the door. He was slumped over the table a picture of abject misery. His sorrow brought a very physical lump to her throat. She dabbed at her eyes and hurried away.

Chapter Nine

Outpatients

Carrie had managed to catch the three-thirty train to Ascot where she could change for Waterloo and there she would switch to the buses. It was hard to reconcile her mood with the leafy green countryside flying past her window and the devastation that she knew would greet her back in London.

The journey passed uneventfully and relatively quickly. Which gave Carrie time to ponder on all that had happened to her. She carried a small bag. Her uniforms were provided and the Ward Sister had given her some regulation hospital towels and soap. She also had a couple of hospital gowns and had managed to purchase some underwear with the little money she had been given. Outpatients had been notified and were delighted to be receiving extra help even on a rota basis.

Carrie was looking forward to reuniting with Hawtry and Kirb. It would be like old times and she felt certain that they would help her rediscover her stolen memories. Digs had been organised for her at Bethnal Green, she had a bed sitting room in a house occupied by nurses, she was told, in Robinson Road just a stone throw from the hospital. Until the Nurses' Home could be rebuilt staff were in accommodation that was scattered all over the surrounding area.

Still alone with her thoughts, Carrie took the bus to Bank Station and then changed to another one for Bethnal Green. As she travelled the London roads she couldn't believe the number of bombed buildings and homes that had been reduced to rubble. She alighted at her stop in a little bit of a daze, a myriad of thoughts rambling through her mind. She walked slowly toward the hospital; her legs were still trying to work properly and prone to going into spasms of pins and needles.

She arrived outside The London Chest and saw teams of

women labourers and some older male workers clearing the debris and loading it up into carts to be taken away. She walked to where the chapel once stood and the remains of the Nurses' Home. It looked like a building site. Props had been erected to stabilise the rest of the hospital building that was still left standing after the North Wing had been flattened. A feeling of sadness filled her. She turned back toward the main entrance, trotted up the stone steps and into the functioning part of the building that was running as an Outpatient department. Casualties from the bombings were brought here, as were Service men and women that needed specialist care before being transferred elsewhere.

Carrie walked through a waiting area that was tightly packed with people nursing all kind of wounds from cuts and abrasions to broken limbs. The makeshift admissions desk stood imposingly at the back; it was being manned by a young junior nurse who looked frazzled. She called out names as spaces became available and ushered them through to the two doctors on duty.

Carrie pushed forward through an assortment of people waiting to be seen. Her eyes scanned the area. She caught sight of Kirb and waved, "Kirb! Sister Kirby!"

Kirb turned at the sound of her name and was surprised to see Carrie standing there waving. She hurried across and gave her friend a big hug, "Lew, how wonderful. You're awake. I'm so pleased." She took a step back and scrutinised her friend, "You're intact… no injuries to be seen."

Carrie pushed her wild hair back from her forehead. "Apart from a very small bump and cut that is healing well by the looks of it. I'm doing well. But you're wrong I'm not completely intact…"

"What do you mean?" asked Kirb concerned.

"I've got some temporary memory loss."

"But, you remember me?" stated Kirb.

"I remember most things but not Michael Lawrence… He came to see me."

"But you will, surely? Lew, you were crazy about him."

"So I've heard."

"Are you coming back to work?"

"Yes, I'm on duty tomorrow. Where are you and Hawtry staying?"

"We're in a house in Florida Street. It's only a short walk. What about you?"

"Robinson Road, just around the corner. When do you get off?"

"Eight o'clock. I'd say we could meet up but I know I'll be whacked. We can try and alter our duties to coincide. It would be lovely to catch up. I want to hear all about Camberley."

A woman came rushing in with a small child that was screaming hysterically and whose hand was pouring with blood. His index finger was almost severed. The woman cried, "Please someone, anyone, help. He sliced it on broken glass on a pile of bricks at a bombed building." The child who was now a deathly white went silent. Kirb hurried across and ushered them through to an examination room and Carrie was left standing in the midst of all this urgent activity. She felt strange and as bereft as she had when she had lost her father but she couldn't explain why.

Carrie left the department and made her way back out onto the street. She paused outside and steadied herself against a tree. She felt faint and her head filled with clamouring voices that she couldn't still. People that she loved and had known went in and out of focus in her mind's eye. Their voices distorted and Carrie knew she had to get to her digs and lie down. Perhaps she really had left the hospital too soon? Maybe coming back to London was too much? "No!" Carrie said aloud and remonstrated with herself, "You can do this, Carrie. It's right that you are here," she said defiantly. She stood up straight, and with her head held high, she tilted her chin in her signature style and progressed down the street. She instantly felt better; no bloody German bombing was going to get the better of her.

Michael Lawrence was now making his way to Bethnal Green. He needed to find somewhere to stay. He wasn't going to make his presence obvious but he wasn't ready to return home no matter what Carrie had said. For a start he didn't know what he would tell her brother John. He didn't want to upset her family unnecessarily. He limped off the bus and struggled toward Victoria Park. He stared at the piece of paper in his hand that Pemb had hurriedly scrawled for him with the address of Carrie's digs.

His eyes searched for a Guest House or small hotel. He walked along Victoria Park Road and could see first hand the terrible damage the Germans had done to the East End businesses and properties. On the other side of the road from the park entrance was a parade of small Bed and Breakfast accommodation close to Oxford House. Michael selected one that had a window box of flowers outside. It bore the name Bellevue. He mounted the few steps, rang the bell and entered.

A homely looking woman came down the passage to the hallway, "Yes?" Her voice was of the East End and Michael supposed that she must have been born within the sound of Bow bells.

"I wonder if you have any rooms vacant?" he asked politely.

"Take your pick. Ain't no one looking to holiday 'ere or visit, not with all these bleeding air raids."

"No, I don't expect there is," he smiled.

"Is it just the one night?"

"No, I'm not sure how long I'll be staying maybe a week, maybe a month."

"Right, you are. Breakfast is seven till nine. I'll put you in room four. It's a nice big room overlooking the park. This way."

"Thank you, Mrs…?" Michael questioned as he followed her up the stairs.

"Brennan, Velma Brennan."

"Is there anywhere I can get a decent evening meal around here?"

"Not much doing around here except in the daytime. I'd be happy to do one for you for an extra five bob a night."

Michael smiled, "That would be excellent."

"Right," she opened the door with a key, which she passed to him. "Dinner will be on the table at six-thirty prompt. Is there anything you don't like?"

"No, I pretty much eat anything."

"Good. Dining room is back down the stairs to the hallway and off to the right. I'll leave you to settle in and see you downstairs in..." she checked her watch, "An hour. There's a residents' lounge downstairs and you're welcome to listen to the radio if you want, Mr....?"

"Lawrence, Michael Lawrence."

"Well, Mr. Lawrence you can sign the hotel guest book when you come down and maybe tell me why anyone is mad enough to come here to stay."

Michael nodded and smiled once more. Mrs. Brennan was clearly a good sort. He felt he could have done a lot worse.

Carrie was sitting in her bed-sit. Her head was buzzing. She was tired, and feeling drained. She wanted to take a long hot bath that's if the bathroom was free and the water warm at this time of day. It would help remove the confusion from her head and hopefully she could think more clearly.

Carrie took her towel and soap, stepped out of her room and walked to the shared bathroom one floor down and was pleased to find it empty. She locked the door and began to draw a bath, testing the water as it gushed into the white enamel bath. The room quickly filled with steam and almost as a reflexive action she checked the flame on the boiler. It was bright blue, she sighed relieved, and began to undress.

The water was pleasantly and bearably hot as she stepped into it and sat. Carrie rested her head and closed her eyes. She thought about the time she had nearly drowned in the bath and stiffened. An image of Andrew Challacombe popped into her head and what Pemb had said to her in Camberley and she recalled the incident from outside her room in the Nurses' Home at Birmingham's Dudley Road Hospital. Other occurrences crept into her thoughts. She wasn't sure if they were real memories or imagined ones? Did she really accept a lift to Snow Hill Station with the doctor? Had she accepted his request for a date? She thought not.

The warm water was both soothing and relaxing and Carrie felt it was helping her. She sighed softly and allowed her mind to wander. She wondered about her friend Megan, about Hendre and what was happening at home.

Then, in the distance, the sound of the drone of a German warplane roused her from her half slumber. She was now wide-awake. Carrie pulled the plug out of the bath and stepped out to towel herself dry. The air raid siren joined the hum of the plane's engine. It was a chilling sound. She dressed hurriedly and quickly swilled the bath with the cleaning rag and Vim. There was a knock at the door. One of the nurses called out, "Tube Station now! Gerries are bombing us again."

Carrie hurried out of the bathroom, left her towels and soap and ran down the stairs after the other nurses getting out of the house. People were swarming from their homes and heading for Bethnal Green Tube Station.

Michael, too, was leaving his Guest House. He and Velma Brennan joined the milling throng that rushed to the Tube Station. "At least I've got a good meal inside of me," he said cheerily as he hobbled along, "It could be a long night."

The convoy of people ducked in unison as the pitiful bleat of the air raid siren melded with the throaty rumbling of German warplanes, which droned like alien hornets ready to drop bombs on factories and work places in the East End. A terrific explosion assailed their ears and children began to scream as they ran for the tube station's entrance. Michael stopped to pick up a cuddly rag doll that was getting trampled by the masses of feet running blindly for shelter. A small child was crying hysterically for her dolly as the harassed mother dragged her by the hand to relative safety. Michael half skipped on his stick and caught up with the pair and returned the little girl's doll to the child who stared at him with distracted eyes. The mother shouted her thanks as they swept down the stone steps under cover. Michael was carried along by the sheer surge of bodies all wishing to escape the dangers of the streets.

Snippets of conversations were caught on the breeze, "Can you see Aunty June?"… "I couldn't carry it all"… "You've forgotten your pillow." "It's so hot down here and come midnight it stinks." …

Folks crammed together to find space on the platforms and set up their sleeping bags. The noise from the whistling bombs and explosions were muffled here. Michael and Velma found space on a bench and sat waiting for the all clear. People huddled together and chatted. One elderly gent with white hair and wearing a flat cap started to sing an old song. His voice was strong and surprisingly good and he encouraged everyone to join in, "It's a long way to Tipperary, it's a long way to go…" The volume increased as more voices joined the song. Michael began to sing and children clapped their hands. The strained atmosphere lifted replaced by a bubble of hope and positivity, as more people sang and smiles lit up their faces. The camaraderie was evident as strangers chatted to strangers. They were as one against the doom and gloom pervading the streets outside.

Carrie was virtually carried down the last few steps to the station platform. Her feet didn't touch the floor. She followed the nurses from her house and shook out her wild mane of hair that was barely dry and had sprung into tiny ringlets and curls all over her head.

Carrie looked around at all the people filling the platform and thought that she had never seen so many in one place not even during previous air raids. Yet the mood was stoical and surprisingly light. Men and women were bright and cheerful. They had a warmth of spirit that was difficult to ignore and she found herself forgetting her problems and chatting to strangers as if she had known them forever.

Michael glanced at the influx of new people arriving in the now cramped space and gasped. He felt his heart almost stop as he saw the sweet face of Carrie as she chattered innocently to another nurse, who was in full uniform. He studied her cloud of hair that wilfully behaved like an unruly child and he sighed. He was in something of a dilemma, should he make himself known to her or wait for a more opportune moment to make contact again? He wanted to edge closer but there were too many people in the way so he watched and waited.

Carrie was engaged in conversation with another volunteer nurse who said she came from Newcastle. Carrie was entranced by the woman's Geordie accent. She had heard nothing like it before. Maggie, as she had introduced herself was anxiously seeking her friend whom she had lost in the stampede to the station. "It would be of no matter but the lassie owes me ten bob. I can't afford to lose that and I've a week to go till payday," Maggie grumbled. "She promised to pay me later. If anything happens to her, who's to know? I won't get it back then." Suddenly, Maggie called out and waved, "There she is, Sheila! Sheila, over here."

Carrie studied the woman with short bleached hair worn like the film star Jean Harlow. There was something familiar about the coat she was wearing, a handsome brown and white small dogtooth check with a dark brown velvet collar and epaulettes. Buttons decorated the sleeves up to the elbows and Carrie stared harder, it was *her* coat. She was sure of it. But more importantly on the lapel was a distinctive fine cream delicate lace butterfly brooch. Carrie knew it and knew it to be hers. Almost reflexively she muttered, "That's my coat and my brooch!"

"What?" asked Maggie.

"Your friend, she's wearing my coat and my brooch."

"Are you sure?"

"Positive. It cost me three months' salary. I got it in Bond Street."

"I know she lost everything when the Nurses' Home was flattened. She said she'd managed to scavenge a few things. Your coat must have been one of them. Tell her."

The woman was getting closer and finally squeezed in next to them. Maggie couldn't contain herself, "Wai aye, Sheila. Your coat and brooch belongs to this lassie, here."

Sheila bristled, "What do you mean? I don't believe it. It's a case of finder's keepers. How do I know she's telling the truth?"

"Because the label inside says Fifth Avenue Bond Street," said Carrie.

"Pooh, that means nothing. Lots of clothes come from there. It's just your tough luck."

Carrie was dumbfounded, she caught the nurse by the arm, "Please, listen to me. I understand, I really do. Keep the coat, but the brooch… I must have the brooch back." Suddenly Carrie knew that the brooch was very important to her and yet she didn't know why.

"In your dreams," rasped Sheila angrily and she shoved

Carrie hard who tumbled to the ground amongst all the legs and feet.

"Now, was there any call for you to do that?" remonstrated Maggie.

Sheila merely shrugged, "She's just trying it on."

Michael saw the interchange and when he saw Carrie fall he was on his feet and pushing through the multitude of people blocking his way. He struggled and shoved until he forged a pathway through to Carrie sitting dazed on the floor.

He hurried past the nurses and helped Carrie to her feet, at first she didn't realise who was helping her; she stuttered out, "It's my brooch."

Michael turned to the nurse and recognised his mother's butterfly pin. He said politely, "I believe you have something that belongs to this lady."

"Not you, too," complained Sheila.

"Yes, I know it's hers because I gave it to her. It was my mother's."

Carrie looked at Michael's face and whispered, "Michael…"

"Carrie?" Michael searched her face and saw her fiery spirit ignite in her dazzling green eyes, and more than that there was recognition.

She turned to the nurse again, "I can prove it. If you take the pin off it is engraved on the back, with his mother's name."

Michael and Carrie chorused together, "Isobel."

Sheila removed it and turned it over, Maggie strained to look. It was there clearly for them both to see. "She's telling the truth," asserted Maggie.

Reluctantly Sheila passed the brooch to Carrie. She began to take the coat off but Carrie stopped her, "No, keep it. I can always get another. I'm sure you lost everything, too. But the brooch is special, very special," she added and looked at Michael.

"Carrie? Do you…" he hardly dare say it, "Do you remember?"

Carrie nodded and shook her whirlwind of curls. She threw her arms around his neck and they held onto each other tightly for many minutes. Michael was filled with an intensely impossible joy that defied description. He took Carrie's face in his hands and kissed her tenderly and then more passionately. Tears streamed from his eyes and mingled with hers.

"I'm so sorry," whispered Carrie.

"It's not your fault, you would have remembered at some point."

"But, what I put you through, forgive me."

"Nothing to forgive. But it has told me something. I love you Caroline Llewellyn and I never want to let you go."

They were still holding onto each other when the air raid siren sounded the all clear.

Chapter Ten

Found and Lost

Megan had been at the camp for two weeks and there was still no sign of her case. She was fed up with wearing clothes that didn't fit and trying to manage. She went to the company manager, yet again. "Freddie, you have to do something. I can't keep borrowing clothes from Janet and Lucy. It's not fair on them and the uniforms I've been given are miles too big for me."

"I'm sure the case will turn up, it's probably still in the hold of the ship hidden behind something else."

Megan pursed her lips and frowned, "I can't manage another two weeks like this. Please." She looked imploringly at him.

"No, I don't suppose you can. I've telegraphed home base and they have agreed to let you have some money to buy what you need."

"What? Like an advance from my salary? That hardly seems fair."

"No, not an advance. You will get paid as normal. This is to cover the loss of your basics. You can go shopping."

"Hallelujah! Although, where can I go? I haven't a clue."

"You've been going to the cinema every night, you must have some idea," said Freddie.

"Yes, but that was to keep cool and have an ice cream."

"Every night of the week?" said Freddie incredulously.

"How else do we keep cool?"

"Yes, well you had better think of something and you need to shop soon. We are off to Calcutta at the end of the week. You'll find it much hotter there. We will be doing a week of shows there and then we fly to Burma."

Megan took the proffered money and kissed it. She started to leave and Freddie called out, "Don't be late, you have a show at six."

"I won't. And afterwards, why don't you join us at the cinema at least it's a bearable temperature inside?"

"I might just do that!" smiled Freddie. "I've completed all my paperwork. So, why not?"

Megan shook her burnished hair and left to look for her new friend, Janet to see if she would accompany her on her shopping trip. Bombay had a lot to offer and had shops with Western style clothes as well as those with Indian fashion. They would have fun, Megan decided. Janet had an engaging personality and a giggle to match. Her sense of humour was similar to her own and Megan was delighted to find someone in whom she could confide and share her feelings.

Grainger Mason had six weeks of leave after finishing the evening show this last night in Cardiff. His next round of duty with the current show would be six months long, touring bases all over the UK but rumours were spreading that they may have to travel further afield later in the year. Grainger hoped this wasn't so. He made up his mind to spend this leave in South Wales. He would need to plan his visit carefully.

Grainger sat in the hut used as a dressing room and slapped on some Number Five grease paint. He blended it in over his chin and down to his neck, then took a small brush and rubbed it into a stick of Carmine and placed a red dot under the arch of the eyebrow and blended it slightly. He studied his reflection in the mirror. He wondered how this action opened the eyes up. But it did, the alternative was to put a dot in the corner of each eye near the bridge of the nose, which worked, just as well.

Grainger gazed at his face and his reflection seemed to blur and ripple as if in liquid silver. Lucinda knocked and walked in; she looked at Grainger and asked, "I'd like to just run through our last sketch. I've got an idea and want to see if it works."

"What's that?"

"Let's do it as WC Fields and Mae West, we can use so many of their quotes as one liners, people won't expect that … we can comment on the lines…" said Lucinda.

"I think I get what you're saying."

"Yes, I used to be Snow White and then I began to drift…" Lucinda laughed. "Ta da!" she exclaimed.

"Okay, but it's a bit late for tonight's show. Let's think about it in the break and try it out on the next tour," said Grainger being more conservative.

"Okay, but can't we just slip one line in?"

"Where? What?" Grainger looked perplexed.

"When you tell me I've been a bad girl I can say, when I'm good I'm very good but when I'm bad I'm better. Yes?"

"Okay, let's try it."

They launched into their lines and Grainger watched the performance in the fluid mirror. He wanted to rub his eyes as Lucinda's face changed and blurred into that of Megan's then faded and became Laura. Grainger's eyes flickered and became almost glassy. He caught Lucinda by the shoulders and drew her close. His hand travelled down her neck and shoulders and back to her neck again and he began to squeeze ever so slightly.

Lucinda squealed and pushed him and his hand away, "What do you think you're doing?" she coughed as she struggled to get her breath.

Lucinda's face became her own in the mirror and Grainger looked shocked, "Sorry, I got a bit carried away." He made an excuse, "I was thinking the part through to one of WC Field's lines*, a woman drove me to drink and I haven't had a chance to thank her.*"

Lucinda still rubbed her throat and looked at him warily, "That doesn't fit."

"No, I'd have to change it to *this* woman drove me to drink…"

Lucinda backed out of the door, "Leave it for now. It's something to think about in the break." She left hurriedly.

Grainger stared in the mirror once more. Everything looked normal, but behind him he saw Laura's face and Laura's smile. It was a sign. He needed to find Laura. She missed him.

The all clear had sounded and people drifted out from the underground and back to their homes, some remained, in fear of further raids during the night. The platforms remained awash with people and children but Carrie and Michael began to trek back up the steps to above ground. Michael held tightly to Carrie's hand and she smiled up at him lovingly. "I'd best get back to my digs. I just left everything in the bathroom. I need to pick them up. I'm hard pressed as it is for toiletries."

"I'll walk back with you," said Michael.

"I think it should be me walking back with you," smiled Carrie. "How is your leg?" she asked tenderly.

"Getting better every day. I'll soon be able to lose this," he indicated his cane. The muscle still pulls where the bullet was lodged."

"Well, at least I will know you're safe. When are you travelling home?"

"I think I might stay the week, if you don't mind. Your family will be keen to hear how you are. Ernie is like a broody hen worrying about you."

"Ernie!" she exclaimed. "I miss them all so much. And I can't wait to see how my little niece is faring, she must be growing fast."

"When are you coming home?"

"I'm not sure. There's still work for me to do here."

"We could do with a good nurse at home. Dr. Rees would welcome you on the district, I'm sure."

"I'm sure he would. Maybe, in a few months time; when hopefully this war will be over."

Michael looked up at the now seemingly innocent night sky, "I just have a strange feeling that this war will drag on longer than expected."

"I hope you're wrong."

"Me, too."

They turned the corner of Robinson Road, and strolled to Carrie's digs. They stopped outside where a number of nurses were talking quietly. In the distance the bells of fire engines could be heard hurrying to douse fires in burning buildings that raged like beacons in the dark of night.

Neither Michael, nor Carrie wanted to say goodnight. They lingered on the pavement as the other nurses drifted away; some entered the house where Carrie was living and others moved on down the street.

Michael took Carrie by the shoulders, "Never forget me again, Caroline Llewellyn," he implored.

She whispered up to him, "Never, I promise."

His strong arms crushed her as he kissed her goodnight. She watched him limp off into the dark. He stopped at the corner and turned to wave before finally turning the corner and with lightness in her heart, Carrie ran up the steps into the house. She took a deep breath as she closed the door and leant against it and sighed, "It was meant to be. It was all meant to be," she told herself before retreating to the bathroom to collect her things. Now she knew that Michael Lawrence was indeed the only man for her.

She fingered the butterfly brooch that had been the trigger to all her lost memories and determined that she would never lose it again.

The ENSA troupe took their final curtain call. The show had gone without a hitch and the last sketch was played as rehearsed. Lucinda promised, "Say, Grainger I'll look at a new slant on our final sketch. See what I can come up with."

"I'll do the same and then we can combine our thoughts. It *is* a good idea and should be quite fun," said Grainger. He was pleased that things were more cordial between them.

As they ran off stage, the actors wished each other a good break and hurried to change into mufti to travel home. Grainger dressed smartly, picked up his case and left camp, getting a ride with one of the officers in an Army truck to the station where he was catching the last train from Cardiff to Neath.

He had plenty of time to think on the train and plan his reunion with Laura. He was feeling so much better now, more settled and decided. He should never have been fooled by that strumpet Megan Langtree or Thomas or whoever she was. It was all her fault, dallying with his affections and leading him on as she did and putting between him and Laura. He would get his own back in time. But now, now he had to focus on winning Laura back into his arms. He knew he had upset her, turning up in that Welsh village with Megan. No wonder she was cross with him. Now he needed to find out where she had moved on to from there. That is if she had left at all. But, there he would start his search. Someone would know where she had gone.

Grainger looked out of the window and watched the countryside clicketty-clack by. The light was fading and it would be dark by the time he reached Neath. There he must find somewhere to stay. He wanted to surprise Laura, but when *he* was ready. He would have to ensure that she hadn't turned to anyone else. Grainger knew that would complicate matters, not for him but for her. He was convinced that she would turn to him as soon as he made it clear that he was free to be with her once more.

He was feeling better in himself. He was, he decided, on top of everything, his work, his health, his life and he would soon be in charge of his love life again. He intended to find somewhere comfortable in Neath to stay. Time enough for social calls to Crynant, later on.

Grainger was more than pleased with himself and when a young lady boarded the train at the next station and entered his carriage, he doffed his cap to her and engaged her in pleasantries until the train chuffed into Neath and Grainger stepped out onto the platform while the train idled. He strode confidently to the taxi rank. Luckily there were three in line and nobody in the queue.

"Where is it you'll be going?" asked the cabbie.

"Somewhere in Neath that I can get a room. Do you know of anywhere?" said Grainger.

"Well, well, let's see. Depends what you want. Will it be a hotel or guesthouse? Lots of places are full because of the evacuees until they are placed. They are arriving in their droves."

"I want to be comfortable but nothing too fancy," said Grainger. "And no one too nosey either. I like my privacy."

"That won't be easy. They're all very friendly round here. Let me think. Hop in."

Grainger opened the door, pushed in his case and sat in the back.

"Got it, Betty Jones at The Duke. It's a pub with rooms. They do breakfast. Will that do?"

"Sounds fine. I'll try it."

The driver started the engine and the taxi headed off for Market Street. He dropped Grainger off outside The Duke of Wellington. Grainger paid the man and entered the hostelry, which had its windows blacked out with heavy-duty blinds but the lights were on inside. An elderly man tinkled the piano keys in the corner and played a medley of popular tunes.

Grainger smiled as he approached the bar, "Pint of your best ale, please. And a room if possible?"

"Certainly, Sir. How many nights?" asked the barmaid moulded in the image of Carol Lombard.

"I hope to be here for a few weeks at least. I don't suppose you do meals? I've just left camp. It would be great to have a home cooked meal rather than army rations."

"Oh? You in the army? Where's your uniform?"

"Back at camp. I'm in ENSA. We entertain the troops. Due to be shipped out to the Middle East when I get back," he lied glibly.

"Jawch, there's brave. I'm sure we can rustle something up."

"Thanks, I appreciate that." Grainger looked around the bar. There were a few old codgers, farmer types in there. He would see what he could learn later. But for now, he would enjoy his ale and meal.

John sat with Bethan in the rocker and gently swayed back and fore soothing the infant to sleep. They had spent a tough night, or rather Jenny had. The baby had got her up six times and she was exhausted so John was trying to give her some respite, while he was able.

Ernie walked in yawning; he was surprised to see John in the chair nursing the baby.

"Don't ask," whispered John. "I'm just doing my bit and I don't want any wise cracks from you, all right?"

"I'm saying nothing," grinned Ernie, "Just hope you don't start singing that's all. Bing Crosby, you're not!"

"Cheeky, I think I can turn a tune better than you."

"Yes, but turn it into what?" chortled Ernie.

John laughed and grinned at Ernie, "Can you manage the

breakfast yourself? You're a dab hand with the frying pan."

"That's no hardship. Shall I cook for Jenny, too?"

"No, let her sleep. Just do some for us and then if it's all right with you, can you organise the girls this morning, Daisy and Laura?"

"Duw that's simple enough," said Ernie taking two plates and popping them in the warming oven before putting a knob of lard in the pan on the range. He watched it sizzle and popped in two pieces of bread to fry. "Do you know, I think young Laura is sweet on Sam Jefferies. And he's taken a shine to her."

"Whatever gave you that idea?" said John astonished.

"He took her to the sixpenny hop last week."

"Did he?"

"Aye, and rumour has it they went to the Hall to see Boom Town with Clarke Gable and Spencer Tracey and have to go and see it again because they missed half of it!"

"Never?"

Ernie took out the fried bread and slapped it in the warming oven and then filled the pan with a few slices of home cured bacon. "And he's taking her to Neath on his day off," he said knowingly.

"Ernie you're like the News of the World. How do you know all this?"

"Daisy told me."

"Daisy?"

"Duw, don't start repeating everything like a parrot again. Daisy… Daisy, Land Girl Daisy," said Ernie.

"I know who she is. Thought those two were as close as leaves and twigs."

"They are. Daisy is pleased for her friend after all that upset with that Arthur fellow," affirmed Ernie.

"Aye, bad lot, that chap from what you said," remarked John.

"That he is. Let's hope he stays away."

"Don't you think he will?"

Ernie cracked two eggs in the pan, "I'm not sure. I hope so, for Laura's sake."

Chapter Eleven

Bravery and Repercussions

Carrie was back on duty helping to staff Outpatients alongside Hawtry and Kirb. It was a busy time with all manner of injuries being admitted to be examined from the seemingly mundane to very serious damage that people had incurred from the relentless bombings, and servicemen were still arriving there before being transferred to specialist centres elsewhere. For those with respiratory illnesses, the hospital was still the first port of call.

Carrie worked alongside Dr. Bathfield who was dealing with a small child that was struggling to breathe. The doctor examined the mouth of the infant and saw discolouration and what appeared to be a fold of skin growing down the child's throat. The little one's neck was thick and bullish.

"It's diphtheria. Nurse Llewellyn, quickly prepare a syringe of antibiotics. Sister Kirby, we need anti-toxin now. I am going to have to do an intubation so the little one can breathe."

Carrie raised an eyebrow, as she prepared the correct dose for the child and the doctor caught her questioning gaze. "Is something wrong, Nurse Llewellyn?"

Carrie blushed and stuttered a reply, "No. It's just I don't know what that is. I have never heard of it."

The doctor smiled and explained, "It's safer than a tracheotomy for a child and survival rates are greater with intubation." He continued to explain how it was performed.

Carrie, however had more questions, "Why can't you just remove the fold of tissue growing down the throat?"

"That would be extremely dangerous. The tissue is adherent and bleeds profusely when attempts are made to remove it. The haemorrhage that results can accelerate the trauma and subsequently cause death."

Carrie listened eagerly as the doctor continued to instruct

her on the varied procedures and unsuccessful experiments in removing the membrane that had been attempted.

The intubation was carried out successfully and Carrie was relieved to see that the child could breathe once more. It would last long enough for the drugs and anti-toxin to work and save the life of the child who had to be placed into isolation to prevent the spread of the illness. Patients waiting for attention were given mandatory inoculations as a precaution. People who had been in contact with the child were informed and asked to get booster jabs or vaccinations. No one wanted the disease to spread.

It was a busy shift and Carrie was both tired and relieved when it was over and she could walk back to her digs for a well-earned rest before her next duty.

At night the London skyline was frequently ablaze with fires from blasts; smoke and the odour of burning filled the air. Streets where children once played became rubble, craters appeared in roads making any travel dangerous and the British people carried on in defiance of these brutal acts of war. Women played a major role and could be seen on building sites, maintaining the roads and, some it's said, even went down the mines. Previously male domains were now the responsibility of women; and women embraced the challenge; they were proud to do their bit.

Some young men, randomly picked were forced to work in the collieries, too. Bevin's boys they were called. It was just the luck of the draw. But coal mining was vital to the war effort. In fact some youngsters complained bitterly. They had wanted to serve their country in battle but instead were put to work in the mines.

The next day in the hospital Carrie was tending to a mother and toddler whose house had collapsed and they were suffering with cuts and bruises. The woman's leg was bleeding profusely and needed to be dealt with first. "What I can't understand is why you haven't been evacuated?" said Carrie as she cleansed the particularly nasty gash.

"My other three have gone to Devon," said the mother. "My Jimmy, that's my husband, is across the sea, God knows where… Little April was too small to leave me. I've been struggling to make a living as best I can. But, now my house has been blown apart, I don't know what to do."

Carrie studied the woman's face, weary with pain, and worry etched in every line, and yet she could only have been in her mid to late twenties. Carrie empathised with her and spoke softly, "If your house has gone. I would get out of London. Get you and April evacuated somewhere safe."

"But, what about work? I have to live."

"I have no answers but I am sure that there must be something you could do, if not for the war effort then …" Carrie stopped… "Our hospitals are in great need of workers, why not try somewhere outside London. I can't promise anything, but if you speak to our Almoner she has an office just off the main hallway. She may be able to help you. It's worth a try."

The woman looked at her with gratitude, "Thank you, I will. I don't know what else to do and I would like to do something, anything to help. April won't be any trouble. She should never have seen what she has. Saw the milkman and his horse blown up. It was awful."

Carrie looked at the little girl who had seen so many horrors and tragedy in her short life. It was reflected in her eyes. The child remained silent and stared ahead stonily.

"Hello, April," said Carrie gently but the child remained silent.

"It's no good, she won't talk. She hasn't said a thing since it happened. I'm worried about her," said the woman whose name was Ellen Macloud. "I was thinking of going to my mother's place but she's no better off than me. But at least her house is still standing."

"Then I'm sure she'll want to help you all she can. There!" exclaimed Carrie as she finished dressing Mrs. Macloud's leg. "Now, what about April?

Carrie began to clean up the visible grazes and bruises on the child. She turned her around and noticed blood seeping through the back of the child's dress and cardigan, "What has she done here?"

"I don't know," said Ellen with a note of panic in her voice.

Carrie eased off the child's cardigan and met with no

resistance. She gently undid the buttons on the back of her dress and noticed that the dress had been cut through toward the middle by something and slipped it off her shoulders revealing a deep laceration on her spine.

"How did she do this?"

"I don't know," said Ellen her voice rising tremulously.

"This needs stitches and a doctor to see it. It looks like a piece of metal or shrapnel has lodged close to the spine."

Carrie saw that the mother looked terrified and was going to hug her child. "No don't touch her, it may push whatever it is in deeper." Carrie's voice rang out, "I need a doctor here, now, urgently!"

The curtains around the examination bay were whisked open as Dr. Franks strode in. He studied the child's back and addressed Carrie, "Cleanse the area around the wound. Paint it with iodine and get me a pair of tweezers. We don't know how deep this goes or how big it is. I don't want to damage her spine. What's the child's name?"

"April," said Carrie as she began to follow the doctor's instructions.

Dr. Franks spoke comfortingly to the child who said not a word while Carrie dealt with the injury before leaving to look for the surgical instruments.

She asked Kirb, who was standing at the Information Desk, "Any surgical tweezers?"

"In the sluice. Either being sterilised or they'll need sterilising," said Kirb.

Carrie hurried to the small room and looked about her. She spotted the big stainless steel cabinet filled with surgical instruments and opened it. Steam billowed out. Carrie placed on protective gloves and removed a clean kidney dish, selected a pair of tweezers and covered them over with a cloth. She closed the cabinet and hurried back to the examination bay.

Carrie entered the bay and watched. April was now lying on her front and the doctor was gently palpating the area. "I think I'll numb the area, Nurse!"

Carrie passed him the Ether and he gently daubed the area. He held out his hand and Carrie firmly slapped the surgical tweezers into his hand. "That's a firm placing,

Nurse. I could do with you in Theatre. Better than some limp wristed junior that merely tickles my hand," muttered Dr. Franks. Carrie watched closely and observed, as Dr. Franks manipulated the tweezers and gently grasped the tip of the sliver of metal wedged in April's back and tugged. He finally extracted the offending material. April whimpered and the blood flowed.

"Quickly, cleanse it and I'll staunch it and stitch it."

All the time the doctor worked, he chattered soothingly to the child who never murmured, again. He commented, "She's very quiet."

Carrie explained, "Apparently she hasn't spoken since she witnessed a horrific bombing."

The doctor looked up at the mother, Ellen. "She's not said a word?"

Ellen shook her head, "Not even to me. I thought she'd get over it."

"Hm. Give it time… Do you have a pet?"

Ellen and Carrie were both surprised. Ellen replied, "We did have a cat but she ran away when the street was bombed. Why?"

Dr. Franks finished the final suture and asked Carrie to dress the wound, "I've come across this before. It's very rare but after a severe shock or trauma I have heard of it."

Carrie was more than interested, "What is it?" she asked and listened intently.

"It's like, how do I explain it? The child refuses to speak and acts as if mute. Elected mutism I believe it's called. It often helps if the child has a pet, something to focus their love onto, in order to safely share their hopes, and fears. An animal can work wonders, more than any doctor," said Dr. Franks. "If you can, I would get another cat, something for her to love. Bring her back next week and I'll check if it's healing. Stitches will need to come out in about ten days."

Carrie looked at Ellen's tortured expression, "Dr. Franks, they have lost their home. They may not be able to come back."

"Ah, I see. In that case, take her to another Outpatients or doctor. I'll give you a letter. You can take it with you."

Carrie saw the relief in Ellen's eyes as she spoke to the doctor. "Yes, Doctor. Thank you, Doctor."

"I'll do it now. Follow me. Come on April, hold your mummy's hand."

Ellen buttoned up April's dress and put on the child's cardigan. Carrie watched the little girl clasp her mother's hand and follow the doctor to the Admissions and Information Desk.

Carrie drew back the curtains and called, "Next!"

The next few hours passed quickly. Carrie had never seen so many people with so many varied complaints. She was looking forward to getting off duty and having a good long soak before meeting Michael.

Carrie sighed with relief as another nurse came on duty to take her place. Carrie took off her apron, stuffed it into the washing bin, and signed her name as going off duty in the book.

Carrie grabbed her cape from her locker and left the building. She walked down the road and looked at the devastation around her. Women were knocking off from work after clearing the debris at the side of the building. There was still a mountain of bricks to be removed. Carrie noted that scaffolding had been erected to stabilise the wall.

She walked in the direction of her digs and was startled by Hawtry calling after her. "Lew! Slow down!"

Carrie stopped and turned. "Hawtry!" The two nurses hugged.

"Have you heard?"

"What? No…"

"George and the patient, William Taylor, the ones who dug us out, they are to be awarded with the George Medal."

"Never?"

"For bravery, for rescuing us. Isn't that wonderful?"

"Certainly is, indeed. If it weren't for them, we wouldn't be here. What's happened to them?"

"George is still working here and William has gone to convalesce in Camberley."

"I'll have to look him up next month when I get back."

"Yes, and say thank you for us. What are you doing now?"

"Going back to Robinson Road, take a bath and I'm seeing Michael."

"I thought there was a glow about you," teased Hawtry.

"Give over," laughed Carrie. "What about you? How are the piano lessons going?"

"Fallen off now we're getting bombed to bits. Most of my pupils have been evacuated. I still have two in the area, but for how long I don't know."

"You're not going back to…?" Carrie didn't finish the sentence.

"No, no. No more of that. Never again."

"How is your mam?"

"She's middling. Anything could happen. Her sister has asked her to stay while I am seeing the war out here. She's just lost her husband and wants the company. Saves me worrying about her."

"That's good, isn't it?" said Carrie noticing the expression in Hawtry's eyes.

"Yes, it is. I never thought I'd say this but it's good to be needed, to be wanted. My mother won't be so dependent on me while she's with her sister."

"That's still a good thing, isn't it?"

"Yes. I've just realised why I came into nursing and why I volunteered here. You are a big part of that."

"Me?" said Carrie aghast.

"I don't think you realise, how much you've given me…"

"Oh, tosh! You've just rediscovered your true self that's all."

"No. If it hadn't been for you… You trusted me, taught me to trust again. You gave me back my dignity and helped me to like myself again. That was you."

Carrie blushed, "I think you are over dramatising it. I did no more than anyone else would."

"No. I had no friends; everyone hated me." Carrie went to speak but Hawtry continued, "No, let me finish. Trust takes a lifetime to build, seconds to break and forever to repair. But somehow you managed it. You made time for me, helped me and suddenly, I had a future."

"You've helped me, too," said Carrie. "Getting my

placement at Birmingham, time off. You've been a tower of strength. I've learnt so much from you, not least that I wanted to specialise in Chest."

Hawtry dismissed Carrie's comment with flippant, "Tosh!" She then continued, "To coin a phrase: what goes around, comes around. Trust is a very important facet in an individual's existence, like one's word, if trust and honour are absent then there are only shadows for others to peer into... And shadows are camouflage where people can hide. I hid for a long time." Carrie saw Hawtry's eyes fill with tears, "You really don't know what you have done for me. But, I thank you; from the very bottom of my heart."

Carrie didn't know what to say and hugged the nurse again impulsively. "Duw, Duw! You'll have me in tears if you carry on."

Hawtry laughed and the two began walking toward the park, silently to begin with but without any awkwardness. As they approached the corner, Hawtry spotted one of her piano students a little boy in short grey flannel trousers, skipping in front of his mother.

"Look, there, Carrie!" She pointed at the child, "That's Josh, one of my pupils." Hawtry smiled and waved at the child, "Hello, Josh!" she called out.

The little boy's face lit up with pleasure when he saw his piano teacher and he ran out off the pavement to cross to her. Hawtry and Carrie's faces fell as the child dashed into the road. Coming around the corner at too great a speed was a coal lorry, which was headed straight for the child. The child's mother screamed and Josh stopped in the centre of the road and dithered as if not knowing what to do. Like a flash, Hawtry raced into the road and pushed the little boy hard so that he tumbled out of the way of the thundering wheels of the truck. There was a screech of tyres and a sickening thud as they knocked down, and rolled over the nurse. Carrie's voice resounded in the air, "HAWTRY! NO!"

The lorry driver slammed on his brakes and stopped. He climbed out of his cab, trembling with fear, "She just dashed out. I didn't see…" he mumbled.

Carrie rushed into the road to Hawtry's side and cradled the limp nurse into her arms. She studied the thin-faced nurse's complexion that seemed to shine with more colour than usual and a trickle of blood bled from her nose. "Hawtry!" shrieked Carrie. "Noooo!"

Hawtry's eyes fluttered open. She gazed on Carrie's sweet face and smiled, "I might have known it. With me at the end," she sighed.

"No, no," insisted Carrie. "We'll get help." She shouted out, "Someone call an ambulance, a doctor, anyone."

A crowd had started to gather. The mother hugged her bewildered little boy to her and a man in his fifties wearing a tweed cap ran to get help.

Hawtry coughed and fresh blood frothed from her mouth as she struggled to speak. Carrie tried to quiet her, "Save your energy. Someone's getting help. Stay with me..."

Hawtry managed to splutter, "No, Lew, it's too late for me, now... At least the Gerries didn't get me," she joked.

"No, no, no... Hawtry! Please hang on," cried Carrie in anguish.

"Have a good life... and thank you... for everything... Don't forget me..." Hawtry's breath rattled in her chest and her head lolled to one side. Carrie raised the nurse into her arms and held her tightly, rocking and soothing her as the tears streamed down her face. She remained like that until a doctor arrived at the scene and had to prise her off her friend. Carrie rose slowly; the front of her was smothered in blood. She watched as Hawtry was put onto a stretcher and lifted into an ambulance. She stood there staring vacantly as the crowd dispersed and the ambulance left with its bell clanging.

Carrie looked up at the sky and around her and whispered, "Why, God? Why?"

A policeman approached her and spoke gently, "You'll have to come to the station and make a statement." Carrie nodded dumbly. "You go home, have a cup of tea and change. The statement will wait until then."

Carrie engaged eyes with the copper and acknowledged his request. Then she shuffled onto Robinson Road her proud bearing no longer visible as she was beset by grief. She made her way back to her digs. The joy had left her eyes. When she was in the safety of her room she threw herself onto the bed and sobbed, heart wrenching deep sobs that turned into those hiccupping judders from childhood.

She was still crying when the light faded from the sky.

Chapter Twelve

After the Storm

The funeral was a grey affair. The weather matched the mood as rain drizzled down on St. Matthew's Church, Church Row, Bethnal Green. Nurses in their blue-black capes, in full uniform gathered together. Nurse friends from Camberley added to the congregation, as did doctors, patients and the hall porter, George. Little Joshua and his mother, and another budding pianist with her mother swelled the numbers. Hawtry's mother and Aunt had managed to make the journey, too.

Carrie stood between Michael and Pemb. The strident organ rang out and voices joined together to sing, 'Abide with me'. People settled in the pews to listen to the vicar the Reverend F.W. Ferraro reading a lesson from 1 Corinthians Chapter 13 Verses 4 -7 on love. The assembled people listened attentively as the minister continued with the funeral service. He said a prayer and then invited Nurse Caroline Llewellyn to say a few words.

There was some coughing and shuffling of feet as Carrie left the pews and walked to the front of the church clutching her notes. She addressed the church.

"I first met Ann Hawtry at Bronglais Nurses' Home in Aberystwyth. It's funny but I never knew her name was Ann until this week. No first names for nurses we all used nicknames derived from our surnames. So, she was just Hawtry to us…" Carrie continued to detail things she had learned about Hawtry's life and her accomplishments and how she as one nurse had made a difference. Carrie concluded, "Ann Hawtry was a brave woman and a damned good nurse. She gave her own life to save that of a child; it was the ultimate sacrifice. A light has gone out; without so much as a flicker, and all we have left; is the precious memory of how brightly it burned; and the warmth it gave us. I for one am very proud to have known her. God bless you, Ann Hawtry."

Carrie swallowed hard, blinked back her tears and returned to her seat and saw her friends' and Michael's eyes shining with unshed tears and love. Hawtry may have been a tyrant at Bronglais but she had changed into an exceptional human being and Carrie knew she would keep her unspoken promise and she would never forget her.

The sombre organ struck up with the introduction of another hymn after which the coffin was carried out to be buried in the cemetery adjacent to the church. Everyone trooped out, in a hushed and solemn mood and followed the small procession into the graveyard where the nurse was laid to rest.

People drifted away, some back to work and a few others to reconvene in the Black Bull Tavern to celebrate Hawtry's life. Pemb had to leave to return to duty at Camberley. She wished Carrie goodbye, "See you in a week." The two friends hugged.

Michael took Carrie's hand, "You did well in there. I was very proud of you. What do you want to do?"

"I think I ought to go to the tavern, speak with her mother and aunt but I don't want to stay very long."

Michael looked at his watch, "We've got time. My train leaves at six."

"I know. I wish you weren't going," said Carrie.

"Do you know that's the nicest thing you've ever said to me?"

"Oh Duw! I don't believe that."

"It's true! Come on, give me your hand and we will pay our respects to Hawtry's mother." They hurried on down the road following the rest of the mourners into the tavern.

The pub was dimly lit and tables were laid out with cups and saucers and a large urn of tea took centre stage. Although food rationing had been introduced somehow the pub had managed to put on a few meagre sandwiches and cakes for the mourners. Carrie knew that at home in Crynant people didn't suffer as much hardship with foodstuffs as those did in the towns and cities. Country folk were self-sufficient especially on farms and here everyone was being encouraged to do their bit and 'Dig for Victory'.

Carrie looked around the bar. She soon recognized Hawtry's mother. The resemblance was remarkable. The hair was dark and flecked with grey; she, too, had a thin face with high cheekbones. Carrie approached her.

Mrs. Hawtry recognized Carrie from the church, "Nurse Llewellyn. Thank you so much for all your kind words for Ann." Her voice was soft and mellow. "I have heard so much about you. Ann wrote to tell me she had made a good friend in you. I was so pleased that she had met someone. Ann was always a very solitary child; she never mixed very well. She loved to play the piano." She paused and Carrie could see she was trying to quell her rising emotions.

"She was a very talented pianist," said Carrie. "And nurse."

Mrs. Hawtry sighed and continued in her genteel tones. "She became more outgoing when she went to Grammar School. I was so proud. She won a scholarship and it was there she blossomed. She met Gerard when she was just seventeen. It broke her heart when he died. That's when she changed. She withdrew inside herself until she became friends with you. Thank you for being her friend."

Carrie blushed. For once she didn't know what to say.

"I understand you were with her when… when it happened."

Carrie nodded, "She didn't hesitate. She ran to save Josh. She was a truly remarkable woman."

Mrs. Hawtry patted Carrie's hand, "I'm glad you were with her when she died… that she wasn't alone."

Carrie nodded. A very physical lump had lodged itself in her throat. "I was honoured to know her. I am so sorry for your loss." Carrie smiled and walked away and returned to Michael who had stood back from the exchange.

He studied Carrie's face, "Are you all right?"

Carrie sniffed, as she struggled to keep her voice level, "I will be in a minute. When I've drunk my tea, can we go?"

"Of course. I didn't realize you and Hawtry were such good friends."

"We weren't initially. We became friends, real friends. She was good to me and I learned a lot from her. I shall really miss her." Carrie drained her tea and frowned as she got a mouthful of tealeaves, which she discretely spat back into the cup. "Urgh! Serves me right. Come on, let's go."

Carrie bade farewell to other nurses present and gave Mrs. Hawtry a wave before they stepped out into the street.

"You don't have to come with me all the way to Paddington. I'd rather know you were safe."

Carrie nodded, "I'll walk with you to the tube." She reached into her pocket, "Can you give this to John and Ernie for me," and handed him a letter. "You never know with the post these days. Oh, I know you'll be able to tell him most of the news but he'll still like to hear it from me. I can't believe he was so delighted when he heard about us." She stopped, "I'm babbling aren't I?"

"A bit." Michael smiled, "Why?"

"I do when I'm nervous. Sorry…"

Michael stopped walking, "Babble away, Carrie. I am happy to listen. I thought I'd lost you."

Carrie gazed up at him and he kissed the tip of her nose. "Be safe, my sweet and come home soon," sighed Michael huskily.

"I shall be back before you know it. This war can't last forever," said Carrie.

"Back to your beloved Hendre."

Carrie smiled. "I shall be aunty and nursemaid there, I'm sure."

"Ah, young Bethan… You know, your lips curve softly and beautifully, Caroline Llewellyn." He bent to kiss her and she melted into his arms.

Grainger Mason was learning a lot. He had become a popular figure in The Duke and had engaged many locals in conversation, flirted with the barmaid and he was satisfied that Land Girls were still at work throughout the countryside. What wasn't clear was whether Laura was still at Hendre Farm in Crynant. That was about to change. Grainger made up his mind that he would visit the village and try to be as unobtrusive as possible. He felt invincible and promised himself that he may, at some point, even visit Bronallt and see Megan's mother.

Grainger had eaten a hearty breakfast, washed and had a long chat with the waitress, Bronwyn. She laughed girlishly at his jokes and feeling good in himself he strolled out from the Duke whistling a cheery Glen Miller number and made his way toward the market. He paused and looked in shop windows on the way there and stopped outside a gentlemen's outfitter that boasted bespoke tailoring and he looked at the clothes on display. He was just making up his mind whether or not to venture into the store when he glanced up the street and saw two people arm in arm disappearing into the market. He couldn't be sure but the young woman had a glorious head of burnished chestnut hair. His heart almost stopped and his pulse began to race. He had to see to whom it belonged and the identity of the man who was with her. Window-shopping forgotten, Grainger stepped out and made his way to the market entrance, which in spite of the war was relatively busy. Places here had escaped the bombardment that had affected London, Coventry, Birmingham and other major cities.

Grainger pulled down his hat over his eyes and turned up his coat collar and loitered at the entrance. His eyes scrutinised the people at the stalls. He caught sight of the female with the beautiful deep reddish brown hair. He struggled through a few people and as she turned her head he dropped his and engaged with a young mother with a pram who was passing. The six month old baby was propped up and wide- awake. Grainger leaned over the pram cover and billed and cooed at the youngster, praising the mother for her bonny little girl. He took the baby's tiny hand and kissed it gently, and she gurgled happily, before thrusting her dimpled fist into her mouth and sucking hard.

"She's gorgeous. What's her name?"

"Sian."

"That's a pretty name."

The mother, Janette Roberts, thanked Grainger politely and he tipped his hat to her in a gentlemanly fashion and continued through the market. He bowed down to another small child and chatted amiably with his mother as he fussed the infant learning that the toddler's name was Peter. Grainger moved on and stopped at a home made cake and bread stall and purchased a large custard tart whilst eyeing the couple now standing at the haberdashery stall choosing some ribbon trimmings and other bits and bobs. The girl looked up and laughed at something that the man had said. Grainger gasped involuntarily, it was *Laura*. So, she hadn't moved onto another posting. His eyes narrowed as he studied the man. He had seen him before at Hendre, he thought. He was sure he was a farm worker or manager, but the name escaped him. He was tall and strongly built with a lean face and dark hair. The two seemed to be more than just friends.

Grainger watched jealously as the man slipped his arm around Laura and she smiled up at him. Their lips met and Grainger was filled with an indescribable rage. Suddenly, the man's name came to him. It was Sam. Sam Jefferies the Farm Manager.

Inwardly, Grainger cursed. It was his own fault. He had driven Laura into this man's arms by dallying with Megan Thomas or Langtree or whatever she called herself now. Grainger determined he would change all that. He continued to watch them. They both seemed oblivious to this unwarranted and what would be unwelcome scrutiny.

Laura laughed again and linked her arm into Sam's and they moved across to the stall that did faggots and peas and sat at the wooden tables to eat. Grainger watched. Whether or not Laura was aware of this Grainger was uncertain but at one point she did turn around and scout the area with her eyes. He saw her shiver involuntarily and Sam hugged her to him. Grainger swiftly bent down and chatted to a little boy who was shopping with his mother. He patted the young lad on the head and stood up.

He just caught sight of them leaving the table and disappearing out of the market. Grainger swiftly followed. He didn't want to lose sight of her now. The couple walked hand in hand toward the Neath Empire where Broadway Melody of 1940 was showing with Fred Astaire and Eleanor Powell. It was the last in a series of musicals. Grainger saw them study the poster outside and enter between the white pillars. He hurried after them.

Grainger studied the film times. The show was starting at

two. There was a B movie first, Stranger on the Third Floor starring Peter Lorre, a thriller, and there were bound to be advertisements and trailers. He peered around the pillars and saw them paying for their tickets. They then stepped to the stairs after purchasing some sweets.

Grainger waited until they were out of sight before going inside and buying a ticket. He purchased a seat at the back so he could sit where he liked with impunity. He lingered a while, as other people walked in and he waited until a respectable number had preceded him up the stairs to the cinema auditorium where strains from the organ could be heard playing.

He arrived at the still lit cinema seats and had his ticket torn in half. The usherette put the other half on a spike and pushed it down on a string. He warily looked around the auditorium. He soon spotted the back of Laura's head. She and Sam were mid theatre in the middle of an otherwise empty row. Grainger settled himself in the back row and watched, as he plotted what his next move would be.

The lights dimmed, the organist stopped playing and the instrument sank down into the pit in front of the stage, the curtain rolled back and the screen lit up. The blaring fanfare of voices announced Pearl and Dean's advertisements.

Grainger strained his eyes to see Laura and as his eyes grew accustomed to the darkness he found her and a pulse began to throb in his jaw as he saw Sam place an arm around Laura's shoulders. The adverts passed over his head for Bisto and Ovaltine and other local stores and businesses. Trailers followed and the Pathe News then the certificate for the first film, Stranger on the Third Floor appeared on screen.

The cinema was hushed as they were led into RKO's picture, an urban setting, heavy shadows, voice over narration, diagonal lines, low camera angles shooting up multi-storey staircases and an innocent protagonist falsely accused of a crime and desperate to clear himself. For a B movie it was rather good and Grainger was drawn into the story line and actually quite enjoyed it, although why Peter Lorre had star billing he didn't know when the actor only had a small role.

The lights came up and two smart uniformed girls carrying

trays of ice creams on a ribbon around their necks, paraded to the front of the auditorium as music played. Grainger watched Sam leave his seat and purchase two tubs. Grainger slunk down in his seat and pulled his hat low over his eyes as he saw Sam returning to his row and handing one to Laura.

Grainger watched as they tucked into their ice creams. He seethed when he saw Sam playfully tap her nose with his finger before kissing her. That man had no right to touch his girl. Then Grainger checked himself. No, it wasn't Laura's fault; he had driven her to this and it wasn't Sam's fault either. He'd be bound to step aside once he knew the true sweetheart of her life was back. Then again, he might not and Grainger might have to use other means to get Sam out of Laura's life. The voices raged inside his head, arguing, reasoning, cajoling and fighting. He clenched and unclenched his fists and the lights went down for the main feature.

Grainger was intrigued that the show seemed to parallel his and Laura's relationship in so many ways and as Fred Astaire, playing the role of Johnny Brett, had saved the day numerous times in the film by replacing George Murphy, who was the drunken King Shaw, in order to save the love of his life, so Grainger determined that he would do the same and replace Sam in Laura's affections and thus save Laura. There were parallels, too, between him and Megan, but she was of no consequence now. Laura was his focus and he would win her back, however long it took. After all, he had nearly six weeks to do it and his family weren't expecting him home and he really didn't want to see his mother. He could do this. He was sure that he could.

Grainger could hardly suppress his glee and a whistle almost rose to his lips as he heard Cole Porter's tune, Begin the Beguine. It was very catchy and the tap dancing was superb. He checked his watch He needed to exit the cinema quickly and not linger to watch the credits as he often did. He had to be out before Sam or Laura saw him. As the film drew to a close and the words 'The End' were emblazoned on the screen, Grainger slipped out and left the cinema before the lights came up.

He was soon out on the street and needed a vantage point to

watch the departing filmgoers. He hurriedly crossed the road and stepped into a doorway and waited. People spilled out from the cinema and eventually Sam and Laura emerged and arm in arm they progressed back the way they had come. Grainger followed at a discrete distance. He followed them to the station. They entered the building and stepped onto the platform. Grainger hung back and waited close to the taxi rank, but he couldn't hear the announcements so he ventured closer. He saw them board a train and he waited until it had chuffed out of the station before asking the guard where the train was headed. He was gratified to hear that Crynant was one of the stops. He had been lied to. Laura was still working on the land around Hendre and Gelli Galed. Why did that farm labourer lie to him? Grainger made a decision that the man, Ernie, would pay for that.

Chapter Thirteen

Realisation

Ernie sat upright in the rocker by the range. The hairs stood up on the back of his neck and he shivered. He heard a whistle in his head of a lonely sounding ballad. He shook himself and tried to empty his head of the melody that brought with it an oppressive melancholic feeling. He rose up and ventured into the glasshouse and opened the door to look out. The sun was coming up and there was no one around. Ernie paused a moment and stared out across the yard. An ominous cloud rolled in from the hills and Ernie stood assessing nature's mood. Something was coming.

Jenny breezed into the kitchen singing brightly, with Bethan in the shawl. She hummed a cheery tune as she started to begin breakfast. Ernie stepped back into the glasshouse and into the kitchen. He stood silently in the doorway of the kitchen and admired Jenny's sweet voice. She turned, saw him and jumped, startled, "Duw! You frightened the life out of me stepping in like a wraith. What are you doing creeping about?"

"Sorry, Jenny. I thought I heard something."

"What?"

"I'm not sure. Someone whistling."

"Probably Sam. He's been whistling a lot lately since …" Jenny laughed, "Since…" she left the sentence incomplete.

"Laura," finished Ernie.

"Aye. It's lovely isn't it?"

"That it is," agreed Ernie but he was filled with cold trepidation and he didn't know why. Something brushed past his legs as Bandit came racing in chased by Bonnie and they both settled on the rag mat with a quack and a yelp.

"Iechy dwriaeth! You nearly had me over." He bent over and wagged his finger at Bandit, "Shouldn't you be out looking after your brood? Not in here warming your wings, like you own the place."

The mallard duck eyed him beadily, shook his feathers, quacked and firmly and decisively turned his back and hopped onto Bonnie's back who didn't so much as blink!

"If you think that's going to win you any favours, Bandit. You're mistaken! I'm partial to a bit of roast duck."

Jenny laughed. "Huh! You love that duck like your own. Eat him, indeed. I don't think so."

Bethan began to grizzle and Jenny began singing a little ditty to her daughter as she prepared breakfast. The infant promptly stopped crying and listened, her eyes fixed on her mother.

John opened the door yawning noisily. He stopped and looked at Ernie and Jenny's faces, "What?"

"It's enough to wake the dead," grumbled Ernie. "A caterwauling like a banshee."

"Didn't know you'd ever heard a banshee," said John.

"I haven't but if one was here I'm sure it would sound just like you."

"Give over," laughed John. "And anyway, you can talk."

"What?"

"Woke me up last night with your whistling."

"Not me."

"Yes, you did. I didn't know the song. Some gentle song but a little eerie to hear late at night."

"I don't know what you're talking about," blustered Ernie.

"Selective memory, you've got, Wuss. Who else could it have been?"

"Well, it wasn't me."

"Never mind that old nonsense," admonished Jenny. "Breakfast is nearly ready. Come and sit up."

The conversation was forgotten as they sat at the table and their fry up was dished up. Ernie scratched his head; John had mentioned whistling and Ernie knew he had heard whistling, too, almost as if from another world.

Grainger finished another excellent morning meal. He bade goodbye to the waitress who served him and made his way to the High Street. He spotted what he wanted immediately and entered the store adjacent to the Ironmongers. After some hard bargaining. Grainger emerged wheeling a black bicycle and carrying some rope. He hitched the rope onto a saddlebag, slipped some bicycle clips onto the bottom of his trousers and mounted the machine and began to cycle. He learned from his late night visit that the village was about seven miles away. It would take him less time to cycle there and back. Last night was too much of a trek he thought.

Grainger scooted off and mounted the cycle and headed off for Crynant. He passed the local bus on its way to Neath and one or two other people on bikes and acknowledged them with a friendly wave.

As he reached the outskirts of the village he hopped off the bike and mounted the bank by the railway line. He stashed his bicycle behind the signalman's shed, returned to the main road and progressed to the mountain track.

Grainger weaved in and out of the shrubs and scrub either side of the track so he couldn't be seen. He skirted the fields below Hendre and saw Laura and Daisy loading straw bales onto a wagon. He slipped into a small copse and watched. Laura began raking up the loose straw. And Daisy climbed up into the wagon and shook the reins. Senator began to walk out of the field. Laura was left alone.

Laura continued to gather up the straw and Grainger began a plaintive whistling of Begin the Beguine. He watched Laura continue to work and then she stopped and leaned on her rake and looked around her.

Grainger laughed inside and carried on whistling the same tune. Laura stared about her. She glanced at the trees and shaded her eyes. She called out, "Sam? Sam is that you?"

Grainger stopped whistling. He saw Laura listening and shifting her feet uneasily. He remained still and observed her. A gentle breeze ruffled her hair. Grainger sighed. Laura had such beautiful hair. He waited a moment and saw Laura shrug as if she had imagined everything. Grainger marked time. He observed her continuing to rake up. He admired her figure as she worked, her neat pert bottom, her tiny waist, her gently sloping shoulders and he whistled again, Begin the Beguine.

Laura stopped and frowned. She turned around quickly and called out again. "Who is it? Who's there?"

Grainger didn't respond. He wanted to giggle. He knew they would laugh together about this some day.

"Look, this isn't funny anymore," yelled Laura. She threw down her rake and began to stride toward the gate. Grainger stopped whistling. He peered out through the trees and saw Daisy with the horse and cart plodding back to the field.

Laura ran to the cart and said something to Daisy who stood up on the seat and searched around with her eyes. Laura climbed into the cart and Daisy returned for the rake and threw it into the cart. She clambered back aboard and shook the horse's reins and they moved out of the field. Laura jumped down and closed the gate and stared at the copse. Grainger watched as Laura shivered again and then returned to the wagon. He saw the carriage disappear up the track. Grainger brushed himself down and retraced his steps. He told himself, 'She's there. She's definitely there.' The thought filled him with excitement. He grinned. 'There would be another day and even better, another night.'

"In fact," and Grainger spoke aloud. "Why not tonight?"

Laura sat in the kitchen of Old Tom's cottage as it was still known. She supped a mug of tea and looked at Sam, "It was eerie. Really weird. Daisy had taken the loaded bales to the barn to stack and I was raking up the loose straw when I felt as if I was being watched. That's when the whistling started."

"Whistling?"

Laura studied Sam's face, it wasn't a dashingly handsome face but it was a kind face, a face that could be trusted. "Yes," she said slowly. "It sounded like that song from the picture."

"Which one?"

"Begin the Beguine."

"You weren't singing it and then someone picked it up and began to whistle?" asked Sam reasonably.

"No! It came from nowhere. It sounded like someone was in the copse."

"But, you didn't go and look?"

"No. It gave me the creeps."

"Well, it's gone now." He patted her hand, "If anything like it happens again, come and find me."

"I hope it doesn't."

Sam rose from his seat and pulled her up. "I don't want you ever to be frightened again." He held her close and smoothed her hair. "Now, I must get on I have the milking to do. Will you be all right?"

Laura nodded, "Of course. How could anything happen here?"

Sam kissed her and asked, "When is Daisy back?"

"Not until tonight, later. She's going to the cinema with some of the local girls after she heard how good the picture was from me."

"Okay, then I'll pop by after I've finished. You can make me a cup of tea."

"Fine. I've got to wash my hair and I have letters to write. In fact, I'll make a start on those now. No time like the present. It's a quiet evening in, just me and the wireless."

Laura walked to the door with Sam who retrieved his hat and coat and kissed her gently. Sam stepped out into the cool evening air. He marched off toward the milking parlour. He turned to wave at Laura who smiled and waved back.

Laura closed the door firmly and did something she never usually did. Knowing that she was alone she put the inside bolt on the door and used the big key to double lock it from the inside. Satisfied that it was secure she returned to the kitchen and began to pen a letter home. Laura refilled her fountain pen and paused. She thought she heard the front door rattle. Suddenly alert, she listened. There was nothing. Believing it was just her imagination playing tricks she resumed writing her letter.

Outside Grainger had at first watched events in the glasshouse in Hendre. Not seeing Laura there he stealthily crept to Old Tom's cottage where he saw Sam leave the house.

Colour rushed to his face when he saw Sam embrace Laura on the step. He slipped back into the shadows of the ash trees on the corner of the property. He waited until the farm manager had cleared the area and he moved toward the front door. No one locked doors here. He hoped he might be able to slip inside. He tested the door. It was closed firmly. Grainger rattled the handle to double check. It was definitely locked. Grainger swore under his breath and slunk around the side of the building. He peered into the lit kitchen and watched Laura as she worked. She was beautiful. He sighed and watched as she put pen to paper.

Laura stopped and nibbled the end of her pen. Grainger observed her as she ran her fingers through her hair; her hair that was that glorious, wonderful, burnished coppery chestnut hair just like… he stopped. No, he mustn't think of that or what had happened. Grainger began to whistle mournfully in remembrance of what he had lost. Begin the Beguine shrilled out from his lips.

He saw Laura look up from her writing. He noticed the alarm that had registered on her face. She crossed to the window and swiftly drew the curtains blocking Grainger's view of the young woman.

Grainger stopped the tune and banged on the windowpane, frustrated that he could no longer see her. He decided then to hurry away. It wasn't a problem. He would be back.

Grainger made his way back down, skirting the track and ensuring he was out of the vision of anyone who could be walking up the mountainside. Grainger dropped face forward into the bracken when he heard footsteps on the rough path. He held his breath as the man with the irregular gait walked past.

Grainger peeped up over the docks and ferns and saw the familiar figure of Ernie Trubshawe who had come to a halt on the path. That was the man! He wanted to shout 'Liar'. But, he could wait. His time would come.

"Hello? Is there anybody there?" Grainger watched him. Ernie seemed to be straining his ears to listen. Grainger kept quiet. He waited until Ernie had moved on and let out a slow long breath. He hurried on down the edge of the track stinging himself on the banks of nettles that grew freely in the scrub.

Grainger slid down the last few yards of the slope and rushed to the railway embankment and picked up his bike. He switched on the headlight at the front and cycled back to Neath, whistling as he went. Of course it had to be 'Begin the Beguine.'

Chapter Fourteen

Back on the wards

Carrie was on her way to report for duty in Camberley to Ward Eight - Men's Respiratory Illnesses. But first she went to collect her post, not that she was expecting a letter, but she hoped that there might be something from Michael. She was down at heart after the death of Hawtry and nothing seemed to be able to lift her spirits. A letter from Michael might do that. She didn't want to lose any more friends in this insidious war. It was Hawtry who had encouraged her in her studies to progress. It was Hawtry that had supported her on each move and from whom she had learned so much. The raven-haired nurse's shrewish temperament, for which she was famous at Bronglais, had altered dramatically; she had proven above all that people could change.

Carrie scurried to the pigeonholes in the foyer of the Nurses' Home. She was disappointed to see there were no letters waiting but there was a small packet addressed to her in a hand she did not recognize.

Carrie turned it over in her hand and checked the postmark. It was unclear. The ink had smudged. Carrie opened it and inside was a small box and a letter. Carrie opened it and inside was a neat gold cross on a gold chain. Carrie looked at the crucifix puzzled. She opened the letter. The address meant nothing to her. She read the neat handwriting.

Dear Lew,

I hope you don't mind me calling you that but it is how Ann always referred to you in all her correspondence.

I am sending you Ann's cross that her fiancé, Gerard bought for her before he died. She always wore it and I know she would have wanted you to have it. She believed it was blessed. It is odd that on the day she died she wasn't wearing it because the clasp was faulty and she didn't want to lose it. It was amongst her few meagre possessions that I picked up from her rooms. I have had the clasp repaired and I could think of no one better to pass it on to. She would be very proud for you to have it as would I.

Please wear it in her memory and let us hope it will afford you some protection in these difficult times.

Thank you for being her friend.

With best wishes,

Daphne Hawtry.

Carrie sniffed as her eyes filled up. She undid the catch and with a shaking hand she placed it around her neck and tucked it inside her uniform. Filled with emotion at this touching gift Carrie wiped her eyes and walked briskly to the ward. It seemed as if the cross had filled her with an inner peace and she stepped out more purposefully.

Sister Brenda Friend was on duty. "Ah, Nurse Llewellyn. Mr. Gilmore needs his stitches removed and Mr. Murphy is due to have his dressings changed. Can you see to it before Dr. Challacombe's rounds?"

Carrie groaned inwardly. She did not want to see Dr. Challacombe after he had nearly convinced her that she had agreed to accompany him on an evening out. She was aware of the way he had neatly manipulated her when she had her memory loss and was cross with herself at the fact that she liked the man.

Carrie collected a stainless steel kidney dish, surgical scissors and tweezers, lint, and a cloth and marched toward bed three where Mr. Gilmore waited.

"Ah, Nurse. You're a sight for sore eyes. I can't wait to get out of here. I've got things to do and a life to live."

Carrie pulled back the covers and opened his pyjama jacket, exposing his chest and the neat line of stitches that travelled down it.

"You may feel it pulling a little," said Carrie as she brandished the scissors and cut the first stitch. She snipped carefully along the row and drew out the remaining pieces with the tweezers and deposited them in the kidney dish for disposal. "There's just a little seepage on this last one," said Carrie. "I'll just swab it. Let the air get to it when you can."

"Walk around bare chested, you mean? I don't want to give

folks a fright. Manly chest like mine I'll have nurses fainting at my feet."

"You wish," laughed Carrie as she dabbed at the slightly weeping spot. "Nothing like fresh air for helping wounds to heal. That and salt water."

"Is that an offer?"

"What?"

"To take me to the seaside. I'd go anywhere with you, Nurse Llewellyn," said the patient fluttering his eyes at her.

"Wouldn't we all?" said Dr. Challacombe as he overheard the conversation on his approach.

"Dr. Challacombe," murmured Carrie involuntarily.

"Nurse Llewellyn," he responded and smiled with a twinkle in his eye.

"We weren't expecting you for your rounds until ten."

"Apparently so. Nothing like keeping the nurses on their toes, eh, Sister Friend?" he asked as Sister Friend arrived at the same bedside.

The stern sister frowned in apparent disapproval. Carrie glanced up at them. Their body language was confrontational or so she thought.

"Come, come, Sister. Have you nothing to say? A sister of your calibre and quality must have a view, surely?" he teased.

Carrie kept busy and buttoned up the patient's jacket. She was surprised to see the Doctor melting the heart of the brusque sister and afforded herself a small smile.

"Nurse Llewellyn," said Sister Friend, "I will accompany Dr. Challacombe on his rounds. Please attend to Mr. Murphy and then take your break."

"Yes, Sister."

Also, I understand the new duty rosters are through and you are due some time off. I should imagine you would welcome that. You haven't been home in a while. It will be good for you after all that's happened for you to have a break."

"Yes, Sister. Thank you, Sister."

"Don't thank me. I believe the good doctor here had something to do with that."

"I may have," said Dr. Challacombe giving her a cheeky wink.

Carrie blushed and scurried away to change Mr. Murphy's dressings. 'A break,' she thought. 'That would be wonderful.' She would love a trip home. She could see Michael, her little niece, all the family and of course Ernie. That would definitely be something to look forward to.

Carrie cleaned the operation scar as best as she could in order to redress the wounds in Mr. Murphy's chest but was alarmed to see discolouration at the site of the operation to remove shrapnel from the man's chest and lung. There was also a distinctive odour emanating from one laceration where pus oozed out. "Sister!" Carrie alerted the sister who strode across followed by the doctor and who both saw why Carrie was concerned.

Dr. Challacombe pressed the skin above the lesion and the man jumped in pain biting back his cry. The sound made by the skin around the wound, when it was touched, was distinctive, a definitive crackling signalling gangrene.

Dr. Challacombe ordered, "We must get the man prepped and into surgery. This necrosis must be stripped away before it spreads. Has he eaten today?"

"I can speak for myself, Doc," complained Mr. Murphy.

"Sorry," the doctor apologised. "Have you eaten breakfast?"

"Not this morning. I wasn't very hungry. Just had a cup of tea."

"What time?"

"Seven o' clock on the dot," replied Mr. Brian Murphy. "I'm ready for my elevenses now, feeling mighty peckish, I am."

"Hold that thought," said Dr. Challacombe. "We maybe all right. How do you drink your tea?"

"Black with no sugar, why? Can't always get fresh milk so I sort of cut it out."

"Prep him for surgery. I'll see if I can amend the lists. I'll finish the rounds later." Dr. Challacombe swept away with all the authority others had come to expect of him. Sister Friend addressed Carrie. "I'll have Nurse Harper help me. You go on and take your break. Be back at eleven."

Carrie left the man's bedside. Sister Friend appeared to

know something she didn't. Carrie was puzzled and made a point of going to the main office where the duty rotas were prepared. She waited patiently at the secretary's desk until Mrs. Cummings appeared and grinned toothily at her, "Yes, Nurse?"

"Sister Friend told me to come down and check the duty rosters. I understand I have some leave being given to me."

"And you are?" enquired the secretary pushing her glasses back onto the bridge of her nose.

"Staff Nurse Caroline Llewellyn."

"Ward?"

"Men's Respiratory ..."

"Let me see," She scoured a board at the back. "Ah, here we are... Yes, you have three week's leave."

"Three weeks?" said Carrie amazed, her voice beginning to rise.

"Yes, effective from Saturday," beamed the secretary.

"But that's tomorrow."

"Then you better get your skates on and organise your trains."

"Can you tell me about Nurse Pembridge? Is she off as well?"

"Um, let me see. You want to holiday together, do you? Which ward?"

"Men's Surgical."

"Ah, yes. She has two weeks coming up but not until next month. Sorry."

"That's okay." Carrie turned to leave.

"Oh and Nurse Llewellyn?"

"Yes?"

"You have a letter. It looks important." The secretary retrieved an envelope from her desk and passed it to Carrie.

Carrie thanked Mrs. Cummings and turned the envelope over in her hand. It was an official looking missive bearing the House of Commons Crest and a Home Office stamp.

Carrie was nothing if not curious. She tore open the letter and read its contents avidly. The letter was signed by Winston Churchill himself and invited her to join an organisation and become an SOE Special Operations Executive. She would be contacted again at home during her specially arranged time off. More would be explained to her then.

Carrie felt her mouth go dry with nervous anticipation. She wondered what it could all possibly mean. She glanced at her watch; it was almost eleven. No time for a well deserved cup of tea. That would have to wait. She smiled. She was going home. Home to Hendre and a small sigh escaped her lips. But, now, now she must get back to work.

A song rose to Carrie's lips. She would need to let everyone know. She would slip out later and send two telegrams and pack a bag. Then, she would check the train times. A bubble of excitement was popping in her tummy; she was filled with an intensely nervous delight.

Carrie hurried along the corridor and bumped straight into Pemb.

"Whoa! Where are you rushing off to as if you've got rats nipping your ankles?" asked Pemb laughing. "I thought I'd see you in the canteen."

"Yes, I've missed my cuppa. No time now, as back to work I go."

"I'll see you later, then?"

"Yes, but not for long. I'm going home tomorrow."

"Never?"

"I'll tell all later. Must scoot or Sister Friend will have me doing bed baths and bedpan duty!" Carrie laughed and hurried away leaving Pemb smiling in her wake.

Thomas had been right in his assessment. He was not to get as much shore leave as many of the other sailors had. The seamen had been advised to travel in groups when they visited the town. Most adhered to that rule, those that didn't visited hostelries at their own peril.

Thomas had been assigned to help with the overhaul of the ship's engines. Now it was on dry dock and the breech in the hull was mended; it was due to be floated later that day. The captain was anxious to complete repairs and continue on their mission to Singapore to provide cover for HMS Repulse and HMS Prince of Wales against the onslaught of Japanese aggression.

Thomas had worked in unbelievable heat but his time in Australia had served him well and helped him to become quickly acclimatised. He was pleased to have a couple of free evenings before they were due to set sail.

He and his friend, Able Seaman Jonty Vickers left the ship and entered the port of Kingston and headed for a local bar. Jonty was none too tall, standing around five foot six inches. He had dark short cut crinkly hair, a smiling face, and cheery manner, his name suited him well.

Thomas observed that Kingston had many beautiful colonial buildings and he was told it was further inland that there were slum shantytowns, where poverty was rife and people preyed on others.

Palm trees waved gently in the soft island breeze denying the truth of the sinister side of the island. The sights and smells were tantalising and exciting. The beaches were nothing short of paradise. Sailors enjoyed recreation time on stunning white sand beaches and swimming in tropical turquoise seas.

Jonty and Thomas laughed together in a carefree manner as they explored spice stores, colourful markets with seashells and numerous sponges arrayed for sale.

The sun burnt down and full-breasted dusky maidens touted their wares and flaunted their bodies at the visiting sailors. Some men succumbed to the charms of the ebony women but Thomas managed to remain steadfast in spite of their undoubted allure. But men who had been at sea for so many months couldn't be admonished for giving into temptation. Jonty was one who was unable to resist and he sheepishly left Thomas in the dockside bar while he vanished upstairs with a woman, called Mayleen.

Thomas sat on a stool and drank the local beer where he was approached by peddlers selling trinkets, which he politely brushed away. A strikingly handsome woman with luscious curves and rolling hips, who swayed as she walked, came and stood close to him at the bar. She pressed her more than ample breasts into his arm, tried to engage him in conversation and asked him to buy her a drink.

The bar hostess was of mixed race and as a result was stunningly beautiful, with huge dark eyes and long curling eyelashes. Her long, glossy, wavy, jet coloured hair shone and she asked again, "Handsome sailor buy me drink?"

Thomas studied the woman's face and addressed the bartender, "Get the lady a drink." He slapped down some money and he saw the dark beauty's eyes light up at the sight of the notes in his wallet. A feeling of wariness spread through him. He did not want to be robbed or duped.

The barman poured some sort of fruit cocktail for her and pushed it in front of the woman. He took Thomas' money and handed him some change. Thomas looked at the female, "There's your drink. Take it and look elsewhere for company."

"That's not nice. You being unfriendly to Mimi." Her voice had an interesting tone and the accent was unusual.

Thomas looked her in the eye, "I am spoken for and not a good bet. Try someone else."

Mimi snorted and picked up her drink. She sashayed across the bar and draped herself over another unsuspecting sailor who was half drunk and more than happy to oblige her. He ordered more drinks.

Thomas looked around the bar full of fellow sailors, some involved in card games; others entrenched with dusky women and some rolling drunk. Peddlers still persisted in trying to sell trinkets and handmade beaded jewellery. Other negroes tried to pimp women into sailors' arms while some took charge of gambling games with dice and cards and he made a decision. He drained his glass, tossed down some coins for the barman and left. He felt slightly light headed and needed to get into the fresh air.

Outside the afternoon sun beat down. It was hot and the street leading to the quay was dusty. Strange flowering plants sprouted along the sides of the road emitting a fragrant perfume. Thomas shaded his eyes and moved cautiously down the street. He looked around him and noticed three black men emerge from the bar where he had been drinking. He hurried along the road brushing past begging hands and more women trying to snatch at his hands and body. Thomas turned his head again and the men were closer now and had a determination in their stride. Thomas quickened his step and broke into a run.

A street seller stuck out his foot and sent Thomas sprawling into the dirt. The men were upon him. They dragged him up an alley and knocked him unconscious. Thomas could taste his own blood and then everything went black.

Some time later he came to. The setting sun was low in the sky. He struggled to stand. He was bruised and cut about the face. His uniform was ripped and his ribs ached. He patted himself down. His wallet had gone and there was no one to be seen.

Thomas rolled over and tried to stand. His injuries were not life threatening but hurt like hell. He stumbled to his feet and limped forward to the main street where people ignored his dishevelled state and let him pass. Part of him wanted to return to the bar and search out those who had robbed him, but he thought better of it. He had been warned about frequenting places alone. There was safety in numbers and he worried for the safety of his friend, Jonty. Thomas's left eye was almost closed and his lip split. He winced as he gulped in some air. He wasn't harassed again on his return to the ship. From the look of him other miscreants could see there was nothing left to take.

Thomas sighed in relief at the sight of the ship, he teetered toward the gangway and clambered aboard before collapsing on deck. Men rushed to his aid and he was ushered down to sickbay where a doctor attended to his injuries. The doctor insisted on him staying in the small infirmary.

Two hours later he was joined by his friend, Jonty, who had suffered a similar fate. The two friends commiserated with each other but Thomas brightened up at the rumours that if the repairs were solid then they were to leave port the next day and set sail for Singapore and Burma. Thomas voiced aloud that he wondered if he would be lucky enough to meet up with Megan. He knew she was on her way there to entertain troops but until then, at least he could dream about her.

Chapter Fifteen

Hendre

Dr. Rees scratched his head. He couldn't understand it. There seemed to be an outbreak of a particularly nasty cold or flu virus that was affecting older people and some babies and children. He had another young mother, Janette Roberts, sitting outside in the surgery with her daughter, Sian.

Dr. Rees opened the door and called her in. "What seems to be the matter, Janette?"

"It's Sian. She's been sniffling and bit feverish. Really grizzly. I thought it was just a bad cold but she's having trouble breathing and feeding. She can't seem to swallow. I daren't leave her. I'm holding her all the time so her airways are open. If I lay her down she turns blue. And her neck is swollen. It's like her glands are up."

Dr. Rees looked at the baby in Janette's arms. The skin was turning pale and cold. He took his stethoscope and listened. The baby's heartbeat was rapid. Dr. Rees tried to open the child's mouth. She began to wail. Sian's neck was bullish. He thrust in a spatula to push down the tongue and saw a thick grey membrane covering the back of the throat almost closing over it. He immediately stood up, "The child has got diphtheria. Where, where have you been with her? Whom have you been mixing with?"

Janette's expression changed from motherly concern to one of horror. "What? No. I've only been at home, and around the village. I went to Neath to the market and the shops..." she trailed off.

"We have to get her to hospital. How long has she been like this?"

"Just a couple of days. I thought it was a cold. Oh, Duw." Janette's eyes filled with tears.

"I'll need a list of everyone that you have been in contact with."

Bewildered, Janette stuttered, “I don’t know everyone. I’ll try.”

“I’ll give her a shot of antibiotics and we must get her to hospital.”

Dr. Rees opened his door and looked at the last few patients waiting patiently to be seen. His wife, Millicent, was filing away patients’ notes. He crossed over to her and spoke quietly, “Millicent, contact everyone who has been in the waiting room since Janette Roberts arrived.”

“Why?”

“Just do it, please. Get them back as quickly as possible. I’ll explain later. I don’t want to cause a panic.”

The diminutive Mrs. Rees nodded. She didn’t ask any more questions.

Dr. Rees spoke to the remaining patients. “I have to get this child to hospital as a matter of urgency. I would like everyone to remain here until I get back.”

There were muttered whisperings at this unusual request and Dr. Rees and Janette Roberts left hastily with Sian. One look at Janette’s stricken face and the patients knew there was something seriously wrong.

Carrie had managed to send her two telegraphs home and was now on the last leg of her journey. She was hoping that there was someone to meet her at Crynant. She didn’t fancy a hike home and couldn’t rely on a taxi being there waiting. She needn’t have worried; as the train chugged into Crynant there on the platform stood Ernie with Bonnie at his feet. Carrie pulled down the window and waved madly, her hair blowing in the billowing gusts of steam, “Ernie! Ernie,” she cried out delightedly and willed the train to stop so she could alight and greet him properly.

The screeching pistons finally ground to a halt. Carrie picked up her bag, opened the door and flew out to Ernie and flung her arms around him as Bonnie watched curiously with her tail wagging.

“Oh, how I’ve missed you and your crazy sayings.”

“Esgyrn Dafydd! You’ll strangle the life out of me. Leave some breath in my body, Cariad,” chortled Ernie.

"That's what I mean," said Carrie. She bent down to fuss Bonnie who bore a striking resemblance to Trix, "And you, Miss Bonnie, let me have a cuddle." Carrie leaned over and ruffled the fur on the dog's head that gazed up at her with beseeching eyes. She straightened up. The dog gave a little jump and batted Carrie's hand begging for more. "Just like Trix," sighed Carrie.

Ernie took Carrie's bag and they began to walk off the platform toward the waiting cart. Ernie lifted Bonnie up and deposited her with Carrie's bag in the back and Carrie climbed up to the front.

Ernie flicked the reins and steadfast Senator began to move off along the road toward the mountain track. They hadn't travelled far when they saw someone or something slip off the track and into the undergrowth.

"Did you see that?" asked Ernie shading his eyes.

"I saw something. I'm not sure what," replied Carrie. "Do you think it was a deer or some such?"

"I'm not sure," said Ernie. "But there have been some odd goings on the last few days."

"What?" asked Carrie her curiosity aroused.

"Strange whistling around Hendre, in the fields and around the house. I haven't heard it, dreamt it but not heard it; but Laura has been particularly bothered by it."

"And what have you felt?"

"I have felt a presence." Carrie looked perturbed, "Oh, it's nothing for you to worry about, nothing from another world. Someone is playing tricks and it's a particularly nasty trick to frighten someone like that."

"Who would do that?"

"I don't know, but I am beginning to wonder."

They just began to negotiate a bend in the track when they saw another cart approaching them pulled by a stout ebony mare. The wagon pulled up short. A familiar figure stepped down with a stick that was now more for an emergency rather than a necessity. Carrie whooped in delight, "Michael!"

Michael crossed to them and lifted Carrie down and swung her around in his arms. His overwhelming love for her was apparent to anyone.

Carrie glanced at Ernie whose jaw had dropped open in pleasure. “You’d better close your mouth, Ernie, before you swallow some flying insect,” teased Carrie.

Ernie gulped and swallowed. Carrie could see that he was stuck for words. She laughed, “Ernie Trubshawe, you’re an old softie!”

Ernie blustered and stuttered but couldn’t seem to get any words out. He just sat there holding the reins with an idiotic grin on his face.

Michael let Carrie go and gazed into her eyes, “Is it true? You are here for a whole three weeks?”

Carrie nodded and her hair blazed like fire in the afternoon sun. “Yes, isn’t it wonderful? It’s to give me a bit of respite after the bombing. I have a chance to build myself up again to …” She chose her words carefully, “Prepare before returning to the line of fire, so to speak.” She caught the expression on Ernie’s face and instantly she was aware that he knew there was more to her visit than what she had just said. She also decided she would talk to him before deciding on any course of action regarding the SOE. Her gaze became distracted and she realized that Michael had asked her a question.

“Sorry, I was miles away. What did you say?”

“I asked what your plans were this evening?”

“Oh, tonight I will settle in and catch up with John and Jenny. If you don’t mind?”

“No, no. Of course. They will be as anxious to see you as I have been. What about tomorrow?”

“I thought, I’d pop into the village and see Dr. Rees and then drop by Mam-gu’s and maybe even visit Neath. Although, I may go into town first and then do the other visits in the afternoon.”

“In that case, may I accompany you to Neath? Perhaps we could have lunch?”

Carrie smiled brightly, “That would be perfect. But now, Mr. Lawrence,” she said jokingly, “Now, I must get back to Hendre.”

Michael planted a swift kiss on her cheek, “Naturally. Everyone will want to see you.” He helped Carrie back into the cart and the look that passed between them was plain for anyone to see and interpret, and Ernie grinned.

"Right, then. We'll be on our way." Ernie shook the reins.

Michael called out, "I'll call for you at nine. That's not too early is it?"

"Not for me," said Carrie. "I'll see you then." She waved cheerily at him and watched him as he turned the wagon around and plodded up the track behind them.

"Carrie Llewellyn, you have stars in your eyes," said Ernie with a cheeky twinkle in his look.

"I have not," denied Carrie vehemently.

"No? Then why are you blushing? You've turned redder than a robin redbreast on a holly berry."

Carrie giggled, "And you are cheekier than a squirrel scrumping cob nuts."

"Go on with you," chided Ernie.

Bonnie stood up from sitting and pushed her face over Carrie's shoulder. She gave Carrie a quick slurp and stared ahead. Then as they approached the yard a low growl rumbled in her throat. Her tail stood up challengingly.

Michael continued past the farmyard entrance and called out again, "Until tomorrow!" and he began to sing softly.

Bonnie barked. "Shush Bonnie! His singing is not that bad," whispered Carrie ruffling the dog's fur. Bonnie gave Carrie another lick as Senator clopped into the yard.

Ernie drew the cart to a stop and John emerged from Hendre with Jenny. His face was creased in a huge smile. Carrie jumped down and ran to her brother who picked her up and hugged her tightly while Bonnie danced around their feet, jumping and barking excitedly.

"Duw, you're a sight for sore eyes. Three weeks... How did you manage that, Cariad?" He put her down and she embraced Jenny and kissed her on both cheeks.

"Recuperation. But enough about me, where's my beautiful niece?" asked Carrie.

"Sleeping, thank God," said Jenny. "She's worse than the Princess and the Pea. The least little thing and she's awake. Mam tells me she takes after me and not to expect a full night's sleep until she starts school. It's a horrible thought."

"You won't recognise her, Carrie. She's grown so much. She can pull herself up to stand. It won't be long before she walks, I'm sure. It would be wonderful if you saw her take her first steps," gushed John proudly. "Anyway, come in, come in. Ernie will bring your bag. Jenny's prepared shepherd's pie in your honour with fresh carrots and minted peas, just like mam used to make."

They stepped into the house followed by Ernie carrying Carrie's case and into the glasshouse and kitchen. Carrie gazed around, "You've made some changes," said Carrie admiringly as the enticing aroma of the pie wafted up her nostrils.

The table was laid with Miri's best tablecloth and china in Carrie's honour. Her eyes filled up as she recognised the items treasured by her mother.

"Now, now. No sadness, now," ordered John. "It's a celebration we must be having. You are home! Let's enjoy the time we have. Ernie, leave the bag there and let's sit down. Quickly now, we don't want it to spoil."

Carrie was stunned; her brother was so grown up, so married and so much a father. She began to smile. She was going to love being back. Three weeks. She had three weeks!

Carrie sat at her dressing table in her old room and brushed her wild untameable hair with her mother's silver hairbrush. She mused over her lovely evening with the family. She didn't realise how much she had missed Ernie and John. But Hendre wasn't really hers anymore. She felt like a visitor. It seemed right for John to continue there and raise a new generation of Llewellyns. But, where would she go after she finished her duties in London, when the war ended? She was just pondering this question when a terrific scream ripped through the still of the night.

Carrie tossed down her brush, dashed to the window and opened it. She peered out to the night sky as a wayward moth attracted by the lamplight in her room came fluttering in. Lights went on in Old Tom's Cottage and Ernie emerged from the barn with a torch. John came out of the glasshouse and into the yard with Bonnie at his heels.

Daisy came running out of the cottage followed by Laura.

They sped toward John panting and puffing. Carrie threw on her robe and dashed down the winding staircase through the pine door and out to the yard. She crossed to her brother and the Land Girls. "What is it?" she asked her heart thumping loudly in her chest.

"I'm not sure," said John. "Laura saw something."

"I saw it too," said Daisy.

"What, what did you see?" asked Carrie.

"A face at the window, looking in at us. We were sitting at the kitchen table and that funny whistling was outside. Then it stopped. We looked up and there was this grotesque face squashed against the window."

"Sure it wasn't someone playing a trick?" asked John.

"Who would do something like that?" asked Laura. "It was horrible."

"It's the first time I've heard the whistling. To be truthful, I did wonder if Laura had been imagining it. It always seemed to happen when I wasn't here."

"And you weren't supposed to be here," Laura pointed out. "You were going into Crynant to meet the lad from Bronallt, that's helping out on the farm."

"I know, his little sister is really ill with something horrible and he wasn't feeling a hundred percent, so he left a message for me at Segadellis, and I came home."

"Did you recognise this face?" asked Ernie.

"No, it was all squashed up at the window, like some kind of monster. He slid his face down the window and then disappeared," said Laura. She was shaking. Carrie put her arm around her and the warmth of human contact was too much and Laura burst into tears.

Carrie continued to comfort Laura and heard Daisy address Ernie, "Ernie, what do we do?" Carrie listened to what Ernie had to say.

Ever sensible Ernie cleared his throat and took charge. He began, "Firstly, John and I will check around the cottage, yard and track. Daisy, and Carrie, you check the house. In future, when you come home, when it gets to dusk keep all the curtains shut tight and the windows. You'd best start locking your doors, too. Just until we get to the bottom of this."

Carrie returned to the cottage with Laura and Daisy. Daisy went to check upstairs and Carrie looked through the downstairs' rooms and cupboards while Laura sat silently at the kitchen table. As she checked each room she drew all the curtains. When she returned to the kitchen she crossed to the window and saw a smudge of saliva on the outside of the glass.

Daisy returned to the kitchen, "The bedrooms are clear as are the wardrobes and cupboards. I even checked under the beds. It's safe."

"And here, it's all clear," said Carrie. "You can sleep easy tonight. You're safe. John and Ernie will have checked all around outside. Whoever it was will have gone."

"Probably, someone playing a prank. I doubt it will happen again," added Daisy.

Laura seemed to come to her sensibilities, "But what about the whistling? Someone has been watching me. I have felt it… Why? Who? Who could it be?"

"I don't know, but we'll find out," said Carrie. She turned to Daisy, "Will you be all right now?"

Daisy nodded, "We'll be fine. Laura?"

Laura added, "Yes, I'm feeling a little better now, thank you."

Carrie, walked to the door, "Lock the door after me. Just in case." She left the kitchen and Old Tom's cottage and went back to Hendre. She glanced warily about her as she walked. The whole episode had unnerved her.

Jenny was waiting anxiously in the kitchen and Carrie had to explain the whole thing to her. She set the kettle on the range and set out the cups for tea while they waited for John and Ernie to return. "Duw, there's frightening. I hope Ernie and John are all right out there. We'd better shut our doors tight tonight, too. It's come to a sorry pass that we have to lock and bolt our doors. What's happened to trust and neighbourliness?"

"Aye, but better to be safe. You never know," said Carrie.

"Duw, you sound like Ernie," laughed Jenny.

"Who sounds like Ernie?" asked John as he opened the door, followed by the short portly man.

"Carrie. She's sounding mysterious. Ernie's good at that," said Jenny.

"Jawch, there's an exaggeration. Me mysterious? I'm an open book."

"Aye in a foreign language," continued Jenny. "Come and sit down and tell us what you found while I make the tea."

John and Ernie each pulled up a chair and sat, waiting expectantly for the tea to be poured. John remarked, "I'm surprised Bethan has slept through this. It has to be blessing, though. Would that she would always stay as quiet."

"Don't keep us in suspense. What did you find?" pressed Jenny as she finished pouring everyone a cup.

"Well, I walked down the track, and in the fields. There was nothing, everything was as quiet as the grave," said John. "I was wondering if she imagined it but then Daisy saw it, too."

Ernie looked more solemn. "No one imagined anything. There were footprints outside in the flowerbed outside the kitchen window, and a saliva trail down the kitchen window. No, no. This is no phantom. No prankster but a very real threat. I feel it."

Jenny sat down slowly, as she did so Bethan began to wail upstairs. Jenny rose from the table and hurried to the stair door.

All eyes were on Ernie. He took a mouthful of tea.

"We have to be watchful and careful. There is more than a storm coming." He said no more. John and Carrie stared at him and then at each other and Carrie felt chills run down her spine.

Chapter Sixteen

Neath

Carrie slept the sleep of the innocent despite the traumatic night. She awoke refreshed and remembered her night's vivid dream of her mother and felt somehow that this dream had filled her with tranquillity and peace. She struggled to remember the details but like a slippery eel they wriggled away and escaped but she knew that unlike ordinary dreams these were lucid and made sense. She liked to feel that it was more of a visitation than a dream. She sighed. It felt good to be home with her family and even better to know that she was seeing Michael at nine.

Carrie stepped out from her bed and peered out at the morning sun just beginning to rise. She pulled back the curtains to get a better view and saw Bonnie sniffing around the yard before selecting Trixie's favourite spot by the water butt and settling herself. The day was going to be a good one, no ominous threatening rain or any other kind of storm. But Carrie knew Ernie hadn't been talking about the weather.

Carrie missed the amenities of the Nurses' Home with proper baths and hot water. With her gone John could surely turn her little bedroom into a proper bathroom as they had always envisaged. But enough of her daydreaming, she had to wash and dress for her day out with Michael Lawrence. It was hard to believe that they had been at loggerheads for so long, and now, now she found him the most fascinating man she had ever known. A sigh escaped her lips, "Duw, Carrie girl, this won't knit the baby a bonnet. Shape it or you'll be late," she told herself sternly.

Carrie braved the cold water in the jug and washed thoroughly before choosing something suitable to wear. She sat at her dressing table and brushed her wild tangled locks, before smearing the tiniest amount of Vaseline onto her palms to draw through her hair. Satisfied that she looked half sensible, she pinched her cheeks and took a lipstick from her bag and coloured her lips. The smell of the lipstick made by Yardley reminded her of her mother, not that her mother had worn make-up very often, but when she had Carrie remembered being in awe of her mother's pretty looks. The lipstick had such a distinctive fragrance that Carrie thought it would make a wonderful perfume. It reminded her of times when she had played dressing up games and had sampled the lipstick, smearing it all over her mouth and the laughter she and her mother had shared. Carrie selected a bottle of Rose Water and dabbed some behind her ears and at her wrists. She eyed herself critically in the mirror and thought that she would do. She grabbed her hat and coat and ran down the stairs for breakfast.

Jenny was already at the range; the table was laid, and Bethan was in a stout wooden playpen in the parlour happily playing with a tin lid and a spoon. "Morning Carrie. Did you sleep well after all the shenanigans last night?"

"Better than I expected. I dreamt about my mother. Sort of calmed me."

Jenny turned and saw Carrie all dressed up, "Going somewhere special?"

Carrie blushed, "Mr. Lawrence is calling for me at nine. We are going into Neath. That's all right, isn't it? You don't need me for anything?"

"No, no, not at all. You go and have a good time. Heaven knows you've been through enough. You deserve a little time to yourself. Do you want a full breakfast?"

"No, I'm happy with some toast and some of Mam-gu's marmalade," said Carrie noticing the pot at the table. "But I would love a cup of tea."

"Help yourself, kettle's just boiled. The pot has been warmed. You can make me one, too."

Carrie took the teapot and added the tea before pouring boiling water onto the leaves and letting it steep. Carrie picked up a slice of freshly cut bread and took the toasting fork and held it in front of the hot coals. She'd missed this. Toast somehow tasted better when done in front of the fire.

John and Ernie came in from outside and washed their

hands in the glasshouse sink before sitting at the table. Conversation was limited as Jenny dextrously managed the frying pan, and plates of food.

"Duw, dressed up for this time of the morning, aren't you?" said John.

"I'm going into Neath with Michael and calling to see a few people on the way back." Carrie turned the bread over to the other side and continued toasting.

"That's lovely, you enjoy yourself. But keep your wits about you," advised Ernie.

"What do you mean?"

"I don't know what I mean exactly but I have a feeling you may uncover more than you bargained for," said Ernie.

"You and your feelings," scoffed John.

"I'll pay them attention," said Carrie. "He's never been wrong before." She examined the toasting fork and pushed the toast onto a plate and helped herself to a knob of creamy butter, "You don't know how much I've missed this," said Carrie as she buttered the slices before opening Mam-gu's marmalade and slathering some on. A blob dropped from her knife and just missed Carrie's dress.

"Duw, there's a slop! Need a bib, you do," chortled Ernie. "Better borrow one of Bethan's to take on your lunch date."

Carrie grabbed a tea towel and removed the sticky mess from the oilcloth and grinned, "I know, no finesse, as mam would say." She chomped on her toast and sipped her tea before wiping her mouth. "I haven't seen Bandit, yet. Is he all right?"

"He's a father now, Carrie. Got his own little brood."

"As long as he doesn't bring them all in to warm their wings, as well," said Jenny.

John laughed, "Little did you know the antics of that little chap when you rescued that tiny orphan duckling."

"Aye, but it saved a squabble between you two when you were younger," said Ernie.

John had the good grace to blush but Carrie ploughed on, "Aye, true. You were always a peacemaker, Ernie. I don't know how we would have survived without your steadying influence." Carrie impulsively crossed to Ernie and gave him a big hug, which took him by surprise and he dribbled egg down his front.

"Now who's the messy eater?" laughed Carrie.

"Cwat lawr!" said Ernie, his toothbrush moustache full of crumbs and egg. "Much more of this and I'll need clean clothes, maybe even a new suit…" His eyes twinkled merrily.

"No, you won't," retorted Carrie laughingly as she remembered the Salvation Army incident. "We're not risking you going AWOL again."

"Jawch! Head like an elephant you've got, with a trunk that's twice as nosy."

Everyone laughed together and then John and Ernie settled to discussing their duties for the day and the schedule of work for the Land Girls as they left the house.

Jenny cleared up the debris from their meal and took the plates out into the glasshouse to clean. Carrie looked about her. This was as cosy and as loving a home as she remembered from her childhood and it filled her with conflicting emotions. She determined there and then that she would get legal advice about letting John take over the whole farm and what choices and options were open to her. Carrie just felt that it wasn't *her* home anymore.

Jenny sang out in her sweet dulcet tones and Bethan promptly popped her thumb in her mouth and settled down on the floor of the playpen to sleep. Carrie took a small cot blanket from off the rail and covered the infant over, who sucked her thumb and fist with avengeance. Carrie was flooded with an overwhelming feeling of love for the child and had to take several deep breaths to control a rising tide of tears that threatened to fall from her eyes.

She watched the clock tick around to nine and bade Jenny farewell, "Goodbye. I will be back late afternoon or early evening. And tomorrow I will help you, Jenny, and get to know my little niece."

Jenny smiled accommodatingly, "No need. You work hard enough yourself, putting your life on the line in the capital. Enjoy the time you have off. You'll return more refreshed, then."

Carrie didn't argue but promised herself she would take the

matter up again upon her return. She didn't want to 'ride on anyone's back' as her mother would have put it. Carrie slipped out and walked to the farm entrance and the mountain track as Michael and Sam Jefferies trotted down the trail toward her. Sam pulled the horse up to a halt and Carrie clambered aboard.

"Sam is taking us to the station and he will pick us up later this afternoon."

"That's perfect," smiled Carrie. She felt strangely shy with Michael in the presence of another man and one whom she didn't know too well.

The conversation turned to the events of the previous night. Sam asked her, "I understand you were there, Miss Llewellyn. Laura was really spooked. That's the only way to put it."

"Please, call me Carrie. Yes, it seemed very scary for her. Her fear was real and Daisy saw the face as well. I don't think it was imagined, in fact when I was coming home yesterday, I thought I saw something, no someone, run off the track and hide in the bracken."

"Did you now?" said Sam. "I'm worried. If this is some nutcase on the prowl marauding the hills, something needs to be done."

"I agree," said Michael. "We will all have to keep our wits about us until we can get to the bottom of the mystery."

The cart trundled to the bottom of the track and into the village toward the station. Conversation became more relaxed and Michael made arrangements with Sam to pick them up at the same spot at five o' clock. "That will give you enough time to see your grandmother and Dr. Rees won't it?" asked Michael. "The train from Neath gets in at three."

"Sounds good to me," said Carrie as she clambered down.

The couple watched the cart pull away and Michael went to get the train tickets. Carrie stopped him, "Here, let me pay for mine."

"Not on your life. I asked you. It's my treat."

"But…"

"No buts, I know how independent you are but if you are my girl you have to allow me a little leeway here."

"Carrie turned pink and accepted graciously, "Then, thank you, Michael."

"Good, I'm glad we got that out of the way."

Michael purchased the tickets and offered his arm and Carrie happily linked in. She glanced down at his leg, "Michael you're not limping. You fraud! Is that stick just for show?" she asked giggling.

"I'm nearly there," he replied. "I'm just playing safe as we are going to be out all day. I am hoping to lose it altogether in the next couple of days."

"Why, that's wonderful!" exclaimed Carrie.

"Shush! Don't speak too soon. You don't want to witch it," said Michael.

"What?"

"One of my mother's sayings. She believed words had incredible power and when something is said, it is out there and can manifest."

"Duw, I hope not. Some of the things I have said. Jawch I'm likely to be on bedpan duty for life."

Michael, laughed, "Don't say it!"

"What shall I say?"

"Say… my life will be filled with blessings and love, and Michael."

"That's cheating. You can't tag yourself on the end of a want list."

"Why not?"

"I don't know why not, I just said…"

They were interrupted by the arrival of the train to Neath. They climbed aboard with a bubble of laughter and good feelings surrounding them. They settled down and the steam train pulled out with a hiss and a whistle. They enjoyed watching the countryside clicketty-clack past. Every now and again they would try to speak at the same time whilst at other moments they rejoiced in the silence of words unsaid and drowned in each other's eyes. An elderly lady boarded the train at the next station and watched the couple avidly and unashamedly. Michael and Carrie were so wrapped up in each other they hardly noticed her until the woman spoke.

"Well, well, is it just married, you are?"

Carrie spluttered with laughter, "Jawch, no."

"Then you should be. I can see a rainbow of light encircling you both. It's the sign of true love."

Carrie felt her face flush with colour. For once she was stuck for words. She glanced at Michael who shrugged and listened, too.

The old woman continued, "I see an amazing future for you, with children and animals, and a farm. You will live on a farm."

Carrie stared at the old lady curiously. She was drawn to the woman's mouth and watched the way she formed her words. The woman continued. Her lips were very expressive and Carrie listened fascinated, "You have an offer of a big adventure coming. Think carefully before you accept. If you do, set a time limit. Insist on this."

Carrie stopped her, "What are you? How do you know these things?"

"I know many things. I know your happiness lies in your own back yard."

Carrie stiffened and took a small intake of breath as the woman echoed Ernie's words from so long ago.

"You have a time of hard work, very hard, and some very sad, but you like to be needed. You have skills that will be called for. There is also some danger around you. You will see something or someone that you shouldn't and a secret will be revealed that will solve a problem. Unexpected news, unexpected people…"

The old lady stopped and Michael who had been listening with a mildly amused expression on his face broke in, "And what do you see for me?"

"Ah, you have seen much sadness, and horrors, such turmoil yet so much bravery. You have been brave… Tell me, who is Julie Ann?" Michael's jaw dropped and it was Carrie's turn to look in wonder. "She was your world but she says now is the time for you to start again. She wants you to know she approves of your choice. She wants you to move on. She tells me the new light of your life will dazzle and embrace you. She will lift you to your destiny. But beware of sleepless nights with worry and anxiety. Never fear, all will be well."

Carrie flinched as Michael gripped her hand tightly.

"You are a couple, make it right. Don't leave it too long." With that the old lady stopped and looked out of the window.

Carrie and Michael exchanged glances. Carrie tried to elicit some more conversation with the elderly lady but it was as if someone had waved a wand and the old lady remained silent as if she had never spoken. In fact, she began to hum as she gazed out of the window. It was eerie. She hummed, 'Begin the Beguine', but Carrie and Michael had no idea then what the song was called. They stayed silent, their unspoken thoughts reverberating around their heads. Ordinary conversation was now impossible.

The train soon chugged into Neath station and people stepped out onto the platform. The elderly lady turned to Carrie and Michael, as they waited to exit the carriage, "Make your promises and take your oaths but beware. There is someone out there who would cause harm to you and yours. Beware, beware!"

Carrie shivered and Michael went to speak but Carrie stopped him with her eyes. The door to the carriage opened as the guard turned the handle and helped the woman down onto the platform. She strolled off into the crowds and disappeared through the door.

"How bizarre!" Michael finally exclaimed.

"How did she know your wife's name?" asked Carrie.

"A lucky guess."

"It's not a very obvious name," said Carrie.

"No," said Michael thoughtfully. "Come on, I'm not going to have our day blighted by such gloomy prophecies. Forget it. She probably gets enjoyment out of frightening people. You should have seen your face…"

"Oh, yes? Let me tell you, yours was a picture, too. But, you are right. Come on; let's head for the market. Who knows, we may find a bargain or two."

Michael shrugged, offered her his hand, which Carrie took and she smiled up at him, trying to shake off the remnants of gloom that still remained from the woman's fortune telling.

They strolled to the cattle market and watched the auctioneers at work. Carrie could never understand how they could speak so quickly. They happily spent time looking at the animals for sale and chatting with some of the farmers they knew. Before they realised it, over two hours had elapsed. Carrie nudged Michael and mouthed, 'market'.

They hurried to the pannier market and perused the stalls of bric-a-brac and other items. Many goods and perishables were on sale and Michael surveyed what was on offer before deciding to purchase a bag of apples. Carrie went to the sweet stall and bought some homemade toffee for Ernie and a few other sweetmeats. She was engrossed in examining some old books when Michael touched her arm and asked, "What's it to be? Faggots and peas or lunch at the Castle?"

Carrie laughed, "No contest."

"Right, faggots and peas, it is," Michael began to steer her toward the stall that no visit to Neath was complete without. They settled at the long wooden table and bench seats and Michael purchased two steaming plates covered with gravy. They had just begun their meal when Carrie's attention was caught by someone wheeling a bike through the market. She squinted her eyes; there was something familiar about him. She gasped as the man turned his head and looked around him before disappearing out through the market entrance.

"What is it?" asked Michael, concerned.

"That man, it was Megan's co worker. I'm sure of it. Grainger something or other. Mason, Grainger Mason."

"Who?" quizzed Michael.

"It's a long story."

"I've got time."

"What's he doing here?" Carrie felt unnerved. She started to explain to Michael about the events surrounding the man on her last visit home. "I don't like him. There's something odd about him. Oh no…"

"What?"

"What did that woman say? I would see something or someone I shouldn't… and Ernie said something similar…"

"Are you sure it was him? It may have been someone who looked like him. Don't take everything that old lady told you to heart."

Carrie bristled, "I know what I saw. I am not stupid, Michael."

"No one is suggesting that. Just think, does it make sense for him to be here?"

Carrie hesitated, "No, but…"

"Before we jump to conclusions and ruin our day out. Let's just put those thoughts to one side. Just for today, please?"

Carrie relented and smiled, "You're right. It doesn't make sense for him to be here. But it certainly did look like him and there have been some odd goings on at Hendre and the cottage."

"And we will tell them when we get back. But for now, this is our time. Let's enjoy it while we can," advised Michael.

Carrie nodded uncertainly. She finished her meal but the sighting had somehow taken the edge off the outing.

"I know, let's go to the cinema and see that musical everyone is talking about. Shall we? It means we won't get the three o'clock train back."

"That's all right. Why not? It will certainly cheer me up. I'll still make time to visit Dr. Rees and Mam-gu."

"We will," assured Michael. "I believe the matinee begins at two each day."

"Then we have time for some window shopping in Neath. I want to get a little something for Bethan, but I don't know what. You can help me."

Michael finished his plate of food and the two left the market in a more lively fashion and they made their way to the High Street.

Grainger Mason whistled cheerily as he made his plans. He knew he had frightened Laura but felt certain she would forgive him when she realised that he was only trying to alert her to his presence. In fact, he quite enjoyed her fear. It was a means to an end and he loved the feeling of power it gave him to play with her like that. She would thank him when he removed that farm manager from her life and they would laugh about it together. He was only protecting her. She was his girl. She had always been his girl.

Grainger cycled on toward Crynant. He wondered whether or not to call on Megan's mother but decided against it for the moment. He would call and see her but just not yet. She had made him so welcome before. He was sure she would be pleased to become reacquainted.

Grainger reached the outskirts of the village and made his way up to the signal box on the railway lines and tucked his bike out of view as before. He walked toward the village and the mountain track. He climbed the trail in the direction of Hendre and Old Tom's cottage, ducking out into the bracken and scrub to avoid being seen. It was a long climb but Grainger was becoming more proficient at it and knew where to make his rest stops and where he could watch the girls as they worked in the fields. If only he could get Laura on her own but she always seemed to be in the company of that other girl, Daisy or one of the other workers. He needed to speak to Laura when she was alone and when he knew they would not be interrupted. He would watch and wait. He had time.

Carrie and Michael were enjoying the main feature film and it was when Fred Astaire and Eleanor Powell began their tap dance routine, which Carrie was watching intently when she suddenly recognised the tune that they were dancing to. She nudged Michael, "Listen," she whispered, "That song… it's the one that woman was humming."

"You're right!" exclaimed Michael. "But, what is the significance?"

"I don't know."

Someone sitting in front of them turned and glared at them, putting their fingers to their lips, "Shush! Be quiet."

Carrie whispered an apology, "Sorry," and the woman turned back to resume watching the musical. Carrie pulled a face at Michael and they both struggled to stop themselves from laughing aloud.

They finished watching the film and as the credits rolled they slipped out from the cinema and into the street.

"What now?" asked Michael.

"We ought to be getting back if I'm to see Dr. Rees before his evening surgery. Do you have anything else to do?"

"Nothing that can't be done another time," said Michael. "Right! Let's get to the station. I hope that woman isn't going to be our travelling companion again."

"No. She gave me the shivers. It's one thing dealing with Ernie and his feelings but she was a little alarming, to say the least," said Carrie.

The young couple hurried to catch the next train. There was one waiting on the platform. They clambered aboard and the guard blew the whistle and waved his flag.

"Phew, just made it," announced Carrie as she flopped into her seat. Michael fell into the seat beside her. "You ran those last few yards," said Carrie. "How's the leg holding up?"

"Actually, it's much, much better. I think I can abandon my prop, now."

"Good, I don't want everyone to think I'm walking out with a geriatric," laughed Carrie.

"Cheeky! I don't think a geriatric would do this," and Michael swept her into his arms and kissed her passionately on the lips.

Carrie came up gasping for air. She giggled and was thankful that no one else was in their carriage. Mam-gu would have called her a shameless hussy, she thought. "Pied, nawr, Michael bach. Behave!"

Carrie slipped her head onto Michael's shoulder and he sighed contentedly as he watched the countryside rattle past. There was no need for words. They sat together in their protected bubble of love and lost themselves in their thoughts. Carrie was the first to break the silent harmony. "What do you think that old lady meant? She spouted on like that character in Julius Caesar and the ides of March."

"She did, didn't she?" Michael agreed.

"I wonder who she was."

"It's of no matter now. She's gone."

"You do realise Sam will be waiting for us, when we get back."

"Yes, I thought of that. Maybe I'll send him home in a cab and keep the cart. We can do your visiting and still get home."

"A cab won't get up the track will it?"

"It will as far as Hendre. He'll have to walk the rest."

"You won't be very popular, then. He'll cross you off his present list for Christmas," chirped Carrie.

There was no more time for chatter as the train puffed into

Crynant. Michael rose from his seat and opened the carriage door. He helped Carrie onto the platform. They passed their tickets to the official and left the small station. Sam Jefferies was waiting outside.

Michael strode up to his farm manager and spoke quietly to him. Carrie assumed he was putting his plan into action. Sam jumped down. He touched his cap at Carrie and handed the reins to Michael who dug into his pocket for some money. He handed Sam a ten-shilling note and Sam walked to the sole taxi waiting at the small rank. They watched the cab pull away and Michael lifted Carrie up into the cart.

"Right, first stop, The Crescent and Llwyn -yr-eos," said Carrie.

"What does that mean?" asked Michael.

"Grove of the nightingale, or some would say, the nightingale's bush; my grandmother had a voice to rival that of the upcoming opera star… Kathleen Ferrier. It's still good now. Her mam always compared her to Claudia Muzio."

"Claudia Muzio? She sang like an angel. Her vocal agility had to be heard to be believed. My mother used to trill along to her songs."

"Then we both come from musical families."

"We do. It bodes well for our children."

"Children?"

"Well, that soothsayer did say we'd have children, didn't she?"

Carrie blushed. For once she didn't know what to say. The wagon rolled along the Cadoxton Neath Road and they turned into The Crescent. Michael pulled up outside Carrie's grandmother's house. Carrie jumped down and called out, "I won't be long." Then, she stopped and asked, "Would you like to meet her?"

Michael beamed, "I was hoping you'd say that."

He secured the cart and horse to the lamppost and walked through the gate as Carrie knocked on the door. She could hear her grandmother walking down the passageway muttering, "Who's this coming to the front?"

Carrie knew friends and family went around to the back door but with Michael she wanted to make a good impression.

The door opened and Mam-gu fought with the sun curtain and peered out, "Carrie! Whatever are you doing at the front?" She was about to say something else and then saw Michael Lawrence standing a pace behind her. "And who's this?"

"Mr. Lawrence, Mam-gu. Michael Lawrence."

"Yes?"

"He and I are…" she began to flounder under her grandmother's imperious gaze.

Michael came to her rescue, "I farm at Gelli Galed; we are neighbours and have become friends. Since returning from Service, Miss Llewellyn has agreed to step out with me."

"Well, why didn't you say so," said Mam-gu opening the door wide, "Come in, come in. You'll be having a cup of tea and a Welsh cake now, won't you? Step inside and we'll go into the parlour."

Mam-gu welcomed them into her house and made sure they were settled comfortably in the best room and set about making a pot of tea. She trilled as she busied herself, reaching the high notes with ease.

Michael nodded appreciatively, "I see what you mean. She really can sing. The grove of the nightingale an apt name for the house."

"It was my Dad-cu that named it. In honour of her," whispered Carrie.

Carrie stared around at the parlour. She eyed the large white china Pekinese dogs edged with gold paint that sat on the mantelpiece. By the fire was a young peasant boy holding a bowl of fruit with one hand and in the other he held a bunch of cherries as if he were about to take a bite. But by the hearth were a box of spills for lighting the fire in a round canister that was supported by a black and white dog with its paw in a bandage. Carrie had always loved to play with it when she was small and she smiled at the memory. She revelled in the smell of lavender that filled her grandmother's house and the proudly displayed sepia pictures of the family. The brass that adorned the fireplace gleamed brightly. She knew her grandmother would sit every Friday morning with a tin of Brasso and a polishing rag and clean every single item until it shone.

Mam-gu entered bearing a tray of tea things, cups and saucers, and plates with doilies and laden with Welsh cakes and bread and butter. There was also a platter of bread pudding. She laid it out on the table and went to fetch the teapot, milk and sugar.

She soon returned and began pouring. "Well, well Mr. Lawrence. Tell me a little about yourself. If you are courting my granddaughter it's only right we become acquainted."

The conversation flowed freely between Michael and Mrs. Llewellyn. Carrie was pleased to see her grandmother warm to her young man as he relayed what had happened to him in France and then Carrie filled in the details of her time in London.

Carrie explained that she was gong to call on Dr. Rees and promised that she would visit again before she returned to London. Carrie's next question elicited a huge pause. "How is Aunty Netta? Have you heard from her?"

"Netta!" Mam-gu sighed, when she eventually spoke. "Sadly, Netta is a law unto herself. She fled when she thought the police would come calling. Broke the terms of her probation she did, but yes, every now and then I get a card to say she's all right. So she should be. She swindled me, her own mother, out of my savings. The child Jake is growing, too, she tells me. It's funny, Cariad; I'd welcome her back if she thought to come home. I suppose you think I'm just a soft old woman. But, Netta was grand company and she was good at heart, too. I believe when the war is over she may return but until then I think she's afraid of what may happen. I blame that man Ebron. He was the one who tainted my girl. She would never have done anything like she did. It was his influence."

Both Michael and Carrie nodded. They had all been duped by Jacky Ebron and understood what she was saying.

Michael took a bite of a Welsh cake and exclaimed, "Mrs. Llewellyn this has to be the best Welsh cake I have ever tasted. So light and absolutely delicious."

"Yes," added Carrie. "My Mam-gu makes the very best. There's no one to touch her. Can I take some home with me?"

"Of course you can, Cariad. I'll pack them up for you. John and Jenny will want a taste, I'm sure."

"And Ernie."

"And Ernie," agreed Mam-gu. "Nawr yna. You better get off to see Dr. Rees. Make sure you call again before you go back. You will, won't you?"

"Ie. Yes, of course."

"And you, too, Mr. Lawrence. Don't be afraid to drop in when you're passing."

"Call me, Michael, please."

"Well, Michael please. Just remember what I've said." Carrie stifled a smile as she watched Mam-gu study his face seriously before she cracked into laughter.

They all joined in. Carrie rose and hugged her grandmother. She followed her into the kitchen where Mam-gu took a tin from the shelf and filled it with scrumptious Welsh cakes. "Mind you bring the tin back," she warned.

"I will." She hugged her grandma again and carrying the tin she and Michael filed out of the house to the waiting cart where Mam-gu waved them goodbye.

They boarded the wagon and they trotted off to number ten where Dr. Rees had his surgery. Carrie was surprised to see people queuing up to get in. Carrie looked questioningly at Michael. "What do you think is going on?"

"Only one way to find out," said Michael and he jumped down to secure the horse.

Sam Jefferies had stopped off at Hendre and Jenny had given him a cup of tea. They discussed the latest incident at the cottage and agreed someone was out to unnerve and upset Laura, possibly Daisy, too. Sam played with a loose button on his jacket as he thought. "But why would anyone deliberately target the Land Girls? It doesn't make sense," said Sam.

"Someone who is anti war? A conscientious objector?"

"Not very convincing." Sam paused as he puzzled over the thoughts of an anti-war demonstrator.

"No. But there have been an influx of evacuees to the area. Maybe, it's one of them," suggested Jenny. She pointed at the button. "You'll lose that if you're not careful. Let me get a needle and thread."

"No, it's all right. But, thank you all the same." He

continued pulling her back to the subject in hand, "These evacuees, they are just women and children. The face at the window was a man. They are sure of that," said Sam. "Anyway, I must get on with my work. I've plenty to do. Thanks for the tea, Jenny. I'll say hello to Laura and then get back up to Gelli Galed. See you tomorrow."

Jenny smiled and Bethan began to cry. "Right on cue. Time for her feed."

"I'll see myself out." Sam replaced his cap after deferentially touching the peak to Jenny and left the kitchen. He breathed in the country air around him and walked across the yard toward Old Tom's Cottage. He rounded the water butt sending the chickens flying and passed by the slatted door of the roundhouse where the grain was stored. He twirled his loose button, it snapped off and dropped to the ground. He was about to search for it when he heard a noise and stopped. A feeling of unease rippled through him and he called out, "Hello! Anyone there?"

There was no answer. He pushed the door. It squeaked eerily and swung open but only partially. Dust motes floated in the air where the light filtered through. There was a strange silence that hung in the air, suspended like hanging doom. Sam pushed the door with one finger and it opened further. It creaked complainingly on its old rusty hinges. Sam could feel a presence, as if eyes were watching. He shivered uneasily and moved further into the grain store, "Hello?"

Sam stood in the centre of the store and his eyes searched the shadows. A Hessian sack of grain dropped from the ledge above him and landed at his feet. Sam snapped his head up and saw a cloud of dust billow up in the warm air. He bent to pick up the sack when someone landed on his back and floored him. The air was forced out of him and something hard hit him on the head. Before he drifted into unconsciousness he heard whistling strains of 'Begin the Beguine' and a voice that said, "Laura is MY girl." He heard the roundhouse door bang shut and it being barred.

Everything faded to black.

Dr. Rees was delighted to see Carrie, "My prayers are

answered. I need help here desperately. Can you spare the time?"

"I'll do what I can. What is it?"

"I have set up a make-shift room for suspected cases of diphtheria. I don't know what's happened. We have been clear of the disease here for sometime apart from the case of little Bethan, but she is fine now and safely vaccinated."

"What do you want me to do?"

"The hospital has seen an influx of babies and children, who haven't been immunised, older people, too, with respiratory infections. They are full. I have set up my parlour for the treatment of a few. I need to treat the bacterium with antibiotics in the hope that it will render the disease less transmittable but I have nothing to halt the spread of the toxin already attaching to patients' major organs. I need someone with your skills to monitor those that are here and possibly come with me on home visits when I need help. We have already lost three small infants."

Carrie studied the face of the good doctor who had done so much for her in the past. She wasted no time in making her decision. "I'll stay and help. Michael, can you explain to John for me, please? And can you ask Jenny to fetch my bag with some clothes. She'll know what to put in and bring it to me."

Michael didn't argue. He saw the determination in her sweet face. "Aye, I'll do that for you. Anything else?"

"No, that's all." Michael nodded and took his leave. Carrie continued, "Will it be all right if I stay over, Doctor?"

"Millicent will prepare a room for you." He nodded at his wife, who stood close by. She looked frazzled, Carrie thought, and in need of a rest or some help.

Millicent looked at Carrie gratefully, "Thank you, Cariad. Your help will make such a difference."

"You look exhausted," said Carrie.

"I'll make up the spare room for you."

"And then have a rest," instructed Carrie, before you fall ill yourself."

Dr. Rees agreed, "Yes, Millicent. Do as she says. You have been up all night. We need to take it in shifts."

"You, too, Doctor. You need to take a break."

"But…"

"You won't be any help to anyone if you fall down with fatigue. Go on. I'll be fine. I can give medication where needed and clear your surgery. And I will watch the infants in their temporary accommodation."

"I'll help with the main surgery and then, yes, I will take a break. I promise."

Carrie pursed her lips but she didn't argue. They worked alongside each other and cleared the backlog of patients. Carrie didn't stop but worked unstintingly obeying every one of Dr. Rees' orders.

Most of the adults experienced a milder form of the illness, as their bodies were more able to deal with the bacterium. But the very old and the very young were in the most imminent danger.

"We have to stop the spread," said Dr. Rees.

"Then we will have to set up some sort of quarantine," said Carrie sagely.

"But, how? We simply don't have the room."

"If I were you I would close the village school and set up a unit there. Either that or the police station. Or what about the village hall?"

Dr. Rees rubbed his tired eyes, "That makes sense. But how will we disinfect the place without help?"

"When Michael returns with my things. I'll ask him to set up a task force. There will be plenty of volunteers, I'm sure. This must be contained at all costs."

"I've made everyone make a list of all the places they have visited and people they have seen in the past week."

"And are there any similarities?"

"Some. Neath Market was one, as was the cinema. And a public house in Neath, The Duke."

"Then we need to launch a major disinfection programme at these places. Michael is good at organising. He was a pilot in the Air Force with a whole squadron under his control. He can do this," said Carrie confidently.

There was a shriek from the parlour and a young mother, Bronwen Jones, called out, "Help! Someone, please."

Carrie and Dr. Rees didn't hesitate and both rushed into the make shift ward of baby cots. Bronwen was clutching her young son, William who was blue and appeared not to be breathing.

Dr. Rees grabbed the infant and prised open his mouth. He forced the tongue down with a wooden spatula and tried to clear the baby's airways. A thick grey membrane was partially closing over the child's throat. The doctor forced the wooden implement at the back of the throat causing a gagging action. He wanted to do everything he could to get the little one breathing again.

Other mothers looked on in horror and fascination. The baby took a huge intake of breath and began to cough. Dr. Rees patted the baby on the back to keep the action going and then passed the child to Carrie. "Here. Keep walking him around and patting him on the back. I will prepare another dose of anti-toxin. The poison from the bacteria is releasing through the system and we must try and stop it."

"Antibiotics?" asked Carrie.

"I've been giving him regular shots since he came in to see me. I knew I would need anti-toxin. The hospital has just delivered some to me. I've not used it before. It's very new to me. Just pray we are in time and I administer the correct amount. Damn it! We need to get these children to hospital but there is no room. I fear an epidemic, Carrie fach."

"You need to rest. You can't keep going like this. Take a break."

Dr. Rees sighed and rubbed a weary hand over his brow, "I will, I will. Let's see if we can save this little soul first."

"What do you want me to do?"

"Scrub up and help me."

"Why? What are you going to do?" asked Carrie anxiously.

"This grey black membrane that partially covers the back of the throat is a result of the toxin produced by the bacteria killing the cells. If it continues to grow at the same rate the child will not be able to breathe or feed. He will die."

"What are you telling me?" Carrie pursed her lips in concern, she didn't like where the conversation was leading.

"The membrane is thick like leather. I am going to try and remove it."

"Won't that be dangerous?" pressed Carrie.

"It's made up of dead cells and toxins. They will spread further and could cause heart damage and could spread to other internal organs. If I leave it the child could die." He turned to Bronwen, the child's mother, "It's your decision, Bronwen. What do you want me to do?"

"Please, Dr. Rees. Try and save him."

"You realise that the surgery may not work?"

Bronwen nodded, her eyes filling with tears, "At least he'll have a chance. That's better than nothing at all."

"Then leave us. Go to the waiting room, prepare a notice and pin it on the door advising patients to go elsewhere as we are in isolation. Everyone else present must remain. Perhaps you could make a list of those waiting and take note of those who have been immunised against the illness. They will be free to go, but must wash themselves thoroughly. We can't risk this spreading anymore than it already is."

Bronwen nodded and left the room. Carrie took her opportunity to speak, she said quietly, "I have heard of this being tried before; in London. It will bleed profusely if you try to remove it. It is not recommended, Dr. Rees. How do we get over that?"

"I can't risk the baby swallowing or breathing in his own blood. I shall perform a tonsillectomy and cauterise the site with a Pulvec Medical Induction Coil. That will stop the bleeding."

"Doctor, far be it for me to advise you, but removal of the membrane has always been thought to be highly dangerous."

"Then tell me, Carrie what am I to do? How can I save the little one?"

"The membrane is only partially covering the throat. Use the anti-toxin to stop the further spread of the bacterium and keep on with the antibiotics. We will watch and keep a close eye on further growth. If it continues, perform an intubation or tracheotomy until the medicine has a chance to do its job. A surgeon, I know, told me that cutting the membrane can cause the toxins to spread into the bloodstream and sow the damaging seeds elsewhere."

The good doctor studied Carrie's earnest face and finally

nodded, “As you wish. I have never undertaken anything like this. I admit I am nervous. I’ll go with your experience but, if it’s not arrested then, I will have to try, understood?” Carrie nodded dumbly. “You see, Carrie. Bronwen’s husband has been killed in action. I have to save the child. It’s all she’s got, poor dab.”

“You are sure it’s diphtheria? Not a streptococcus infection?”

“Yes, I took a swab from the membrane. It’s infectious all right and shows the classic signs, variably shaped like rods and arranged irregularly.”

Carrie nodded. She was still holding onto little William, patting his back. “It seems to me that the little one has a raging fever. I will try and get it down.”

“And let’s get as much fluids into him as possible.”

“What about everyone in there?” Carrie gestured to the waiting room.

“I’ll deal with that. You look out for the little ones in here. I’ll also give you a booster vaccine as I will the people waiting.”

Carrie looked at the makeshift isolation room. And laid the baby down. She checked his temperature and prepared some cold compresses and filled a bottle with boiled water. She settled down with the sounds of laboured breathing, the smell of distasteful nasal secretions and ministered to the small children in her care. She kept a close eye on William, bathing his flushed face and propping him up to help him breathe. She struggled to help him take in fluids and regularly checked his temperature. Carrie frowned. She had not seen anything on this scale before and she knew that it would be a long night.

Chapter Seventeen

Drama Continues

Millicent Rees brought Carrie a cup of tea, "Duw. What a night. You look as worn out as a tramp's patch."

"Thank you, Mrs. Rees." Carrie accepted the cup gratefully and took a sip. "How's the doctor?"

"Tired like you. But your young man has rallied the troops. Wonderful he's been. The village hall has been set up for patients. He's called Dr. Allen from Seven Sisters to set up a vaccination programme. They have put up notices all over the village and people are arriving all the time for booster jabs. He's contacted Pritchard the Police who is getting a volunteer task force together to set about the disinfection programme you were talking about." She beamed at Carrie, "He's a bit of a treasure, he is; a tidy young man. You could do worse."

Carrie blushed and took another mouthful of tea. "Ah! You don't know how welcome this is. I am as parched as a rock in the desert."

"I'll get you some breakfast and then you need to rest."

"But…"

"No buts. As I slept yesterday, so you must today. I'm as fresh as a dewdrop so I'll keep watch on your charges. How are they?"

Carrie outlined the condition of the children in the temporary nursery. Most were sleeping fitfully but not getting any worse. Carrie was still concerned about William. I had to get some oxygen to him in the night, as he was turning blue. I nursed him for about two hours. His breathing is still thick and he has a rattling cough." She picked up the infant that was struggling to breathe. "We must get some more fluids into him."

"Mm, his neck is still bullish, too. Leave him with me. The doctor can check his throat when he comes down. He told me to wake him after two hours."

"He can't go on like that, he'll make himself ill."

"Stubborn man, my husband. No one will make him dance if he doesn't like the tune. Now get some rest yourself. It won't do you any good you getting sick as well."

Carrie gratefully relinquished custody of William to Millicent, picked up her tea and stepped into the kitchen where there was a plate of toast sitting on the griddle by the range and a pot of porridge keeping warm. Carrie munched on some toast and helped herself to Millicent's homemade marmalade, before she trundled up to bed and fell into a deep and longed for sleep.

Michael was tucking into his own breakfast and waiting for Sam to arrive to discuss the day's duties. He glanced at his watch. It was ten past nine and highly unusual for Sam to be late for anything. Michael drained his teacup and finished off the last round of toast. He couldn't wait any longer and he put on his overcoat to hurry down the track to Hendre.

He was pleased that he'd managed to organise things so quickly in the village. He was certain that in the village, at least, they wouldn't see any more cases. Prevention was always better than cure. A notice had gone up in the market about the outbreak and the floors had been washed and disinfected and the stallholders' tables scrubbed. It was a start. The cinema promised to spend the morning deep cleaning the upholstery, carpet and rails but wouldn't close their doors. It seemed unlikely that the airborne bacillus would survive this amount of time. There had only been two cases from the cinema and that was from the previous week. Michael hoped it would be enough. He was planning on visiting The Duke of Wellington public house to set something up there, but at the moment he was concerned about Sam.

Michael had left his stick behind and was almost beginning to regret it as he scrambled down the track. He decided to ask Ernie if he could borrow one, he knew there was a canister of canes at Hendre's glasshouse door.

The day was reasonably bright with a few clouds scudding across the sky, but the breeze was fresh. Harvest time would soon be upon them and then everyone would have their work cut out. Michael was lost in his thoughts and plans as he practically stumbled down the last few yards of the track, not least because he was thinking about Carrie. She really was a remarkable young woman. For one so young and so fragile looking with her slim body, pale skin and mane of wild hair she had the ethereal look of a naiad but with the heart and strength of a noble shire horse. Michael determined he would try and persuade Carrie to be more than his girl but he needed the right time to ask her not when she had her hands full looking after the sick.

Michael stumbled around the farm gate and walked toward the house and barns. He met Ernie rolling a milk churn to the collection point.

"Ernie, I was wondering if you had seen Sam today?" said Michael hurrying toward him.

Ernie shook his head, "It's strange you should be asking that. No one has seen him since yesterday afternoon. He had a cup of tea with Jenny and we all thought he'd moved on to Gelli Galed until Laura said he was supposed to come calling last night."

"What?"

"She would have come up to see you if it hadn't been for the strange goings on here with whistling and faces at windows, which has made her afraid to go out after dark unless she's in company."

Michael hit his head with annoyance, "I almost forgot…"

"What?"

"Carrie told me to tell you but with everything that's happened it went clean out of my head. So many things to remember and do."

Ernie pressed again, "What is it? Spit it out, man."

"When we were in Neath, Carrie was sure she recognised someone."

"Who?"

"Some fellow from Megan's ENSA corps, Grainger Mason or Arthur Mason. Does that make sense?"

"Aye, it does. It makes more than sense, it explains an awful lot. I had a feeling… Jawch! Tell me the rest." And Ernie listened as Michael explained what Carrie had told him.

"Carrie thought he was a little crazy. She said he had pestered young Laura before latching onto Megan."

"The man is dangerous and if by some chance he's back then Laura is not safe and nor will Sam Jefferies be."

"What do we do?"

"You carry on with what you have to do with regards to the epidemic and..." Ernie stopped. "Do you know, I think he may be responsible for our outbreak of diphtheria?"

"But how?"

"It was after his visit that little Bethan fell ill."

"But, all military personnel are immunised against everything, diphtheria, polio, tetanus the lot."

"Supposing he somehow escaped all of that? The more I think about it. The more certain I am. I don't suppose you could ask a few questions in Neath? Ask people if they've seen this Grainger fellow?"

"I can do that. But, first, can I borrow a stick? I've left mine at home and I've a feeling I may need it."

"I think we both may need one. If what I am thinking is true. Then this chap has done something to Sam. I can feel it in my water. Now, what could he have done with him? Think, Ernie, think!" Ernie told himself.

"If he was last seen around Hendre..." Michael stopped. "He wasn't at Gelli Galed last night. Jenny was the last to see him."

"Michael, you go on and do what you have to do. I shall get John and we will have a look around the farm and outbuildings. I'll get you a stick first, come with me."

They retreated to Hendre and picked up two stout canes from the umbrella stand by the glasshouse door. He passed a walking stick to Michael who set off for his cart in the yard. Ernie called out to Jenny, who was in the kitchen, "Jenny, where did Sam say he was going yesterday?"

Jenny screwed up her face as she tried to remember. She thought for a moment and then replied, "He said he had a lot of work to do. He was going to check on Laura and then return to Gelli Galed and sew a button on his jacket."

"You didn't say that yesterday," said Ernie.

"No one asked, and anyway, I've only just remembered.

Besides, Bethan was crying, I didn't take a lot of notice. Is everything all right?"

"I hope so, Jenny. I hope so."

Ernie walked back across the yard. He saw Michael heading off down the track and gave him a goodbye wave.

Ernie's eyes hunted the ground as he walked. He turned the corner by the water butt and Bonnie joined him getting up from her slumbers in the yard. Ernie approached the slatted door of the roundhouse and something glinted in the sunlight. He bent down to retrieve it. It was a metal button. He paused thoughtfully and noticed the bar across the door that was usually left off. He looked around and the metal door to the adjacent silo was ajar. This was almost always kept shut.

Ernie started toward the roundhouse door. He lifted up the barrier and pushed it open. It groaned loudly on its weakened hinges and he stepped inside. He waited while his eyes adjusted to the dimmer light and looked about him. There was a low growl as Bonnie followed him. The dog stayed at the door with her hackles raised and watched Ernie as he studied the scene.

Ernie could see footprints and scuffle marks in the dirt floor. A sack of grain lay on the ground that appeared to have fallen from the stacked pile. Ernie followed the trail of what looked like heel marks where something had been dragged in the dirt behind the bank of grain sacks. Bonnie followed and nosed around the back of the bank of sacks. She whimpered and went further into the store.

Ernie walked around the stack and saw Sam Jefferies lying on the ground. He was bound hand and foot and his mouth was gagged but Sam was barely awake. Ernie didn't hear the squeak of the slatted door, so intent was he on helping Sam.

Ernie dashed to him and struggled to remove Sam's bonds. He saw Sam's eyes open wide as if in warning. But too late, something crashed onto his head and he fell onto the dirt floor alongside Sam.

Grainger Mason smiled in satisfaction; he thought he'd killed two birds with one stone, so to speak. Now, he needed to secure the old boy with Sam until he decided what to do with them and then he would visit Laura, but he wanted her to be on her own. He needed that other girl out of the way.

He hastily tied up Ernie's legs and hands, and tugged out Ernie's shirt, tore a strip off the shirttail and used it to stuff into Ernie's mouth. He was just checking the security of his knots when he heard a growl behind him. Grainger turned to face Bonnie, hackles raised, lip curled and teeth bared, snarling threateningly at him. He tried to move past her but the hostile rumbling grew louder. Grainger stopped uncertain as what to do. He snatched up Ernie's dropped cane and brandished it at the dog who stood her ground.

The door to the roundhouse groaned fully open and Michael entered, he called out, "Ernie!"

Bonnie barked and Michael moved around the stacked sacks of grain and saw the two men trussed up on the floor and Bonnie growling angrily. Grainger flew at Michael and the two men tussled with each other rolling around on the dirt floor. Whenever she could Bonnie jumped in and nipped at Grainger's ankles. Grainger's face was a mask of fury and Michael fought hard trying to prevent his adversary from strangling the life out of him. Michael brought up his cane and caught Grainger a hard blow on his head momentarily stopping the onslaught and giving Michael time to catch his breath. Michael felt Grainger's blood drip down on to him. Grainger rolled off Michael and fled out of the slatted door. Bonnie barked after him and then fussed around Michael and Ernie, washing their faces with loving licks.

Michael scrambled up and began to untie Ernie and release him from his constraints before moving onto Sam, who gratefully rubbed his wrists that were clearly without feeling. Ernie was the first to speak, "What I can't understand, Michael, is why you came back?"

Michael's eyes twinkled, "I'd like to say I had a feeling… but the simple fact of it is, I forgot to collect Mrs. Llewellyn's cake tin. I promised Carrie faithfully to return it to her grandmother on my next trip to the village. I saw Grainger sneak out of the silo door and into here."

"Well, thank goodness, you did. I'm not one for combat, unarmed or otherwise. Duw, Duw; I dread to think what would have happened if you hadn't turned up."

"What now? The man must be stopped. Where has he gone?" said Sam who stumbled up rubbing his numb limbs and trying to get the circulation going, "What about, Laura?"

Ernie stood up and brushed himself down, "Aye, the girl could be in danger."

The three men hurried out of the barn, Sam limped as he tried to walk. He stopped and stamped his feet a few times. Ernie looked back at him, "Terrible isn't it? Like sparklers in your leg or as if it's gone fizzy. I know."

The comment, intended to lighten the proceedings, did just that. Michael called back, "Come on, there's three of us and one of him. I'm sure I hurt him with my stick."

"Aye, I'd like to clout him one with this," said Ernie brandishing his own cane.

They hastened down the path toward Old Tom's cottage and heard an ear splitting scream. Bonnie bounded ahead of them, barking angrily.

The men quickened their pace and saw Grainger dragging Laura out of the house. His face was a fiendish mask of blood. His eyes were wild and he looked completely out of control. Grainger pulled Laura down the steep bank. She tumbled and fell as the men gave chase.

Like a wolf salivating for his prey he stretched over her. But Laura was not without fight or courage. She brought her knee up sharply and caught him in the groin. Grainger howled and fell away. He stumbled down the bank and tried to flee.

Sam, his discomfort forgotten, raced to Laura's side and held her close. She wept in his arms. Ernie helped the girl up and together they made their way back to Hendre while Michael gave chase.

Jenny rallied around the unexpected visitors and made a big pot of tea while Ernie looked at Laura's bruises. Fingerprints could clearly be seen on her throat.

"The man's unhinged; that's my opinion," said Ernie.

"But, why, Laura? Why has he come after you?" asked Sam.

"I don't know. I thought he was over his obsession with me now he was chasing after Megan."

"Young Megan didn't welcome his attention either. She's moved onto another unit so I expect the man's thoughts reverted to you," said Ernie. "We must tell the police."

"What can they do?" asked Laura.

"They have your statement from last time. The man was harassing you and now he has assault and kidnap to add to his clutch of misdeeds," said Ernie.

"Kidnap?" said Jenny. "Who was kidnapped?"

Ernie pointed at Sam, "He incapacitated him, tied him up. That sounds like kidnap to me."

"I hope Michael has got him," said Sam. "But the chap was devilishly strong."

"That's because he's not in his right mind," said Ernie. "Something must have made him fixated on women with your colour hair. Do you have any idea, Laura?"

"His mother is the same colouring as me, as was his sister."

Ernie's eyes narrowed, "His sister?"

"Yes."

"You said, 'was'. What happened to her?"

"I don't know, exactly. Everyone thought it was a tragic accident."

"What was her name?"

"Maud. She and Arthur were out playing by the viaduct, close to our village. Maud fell into the water. We'd had a lot of rain and the river was raging. There was some sort of whirlpool in the deeper water; she was swept to it. Arthur tried to rescue her. He caught hold of her foot, her shoe came off and that was all that he had. The water sucked her down and she drowned. He was claimed as quite the hero."

"I bet he was," said Ernie, his eyes gleaming. "How old was he, then?"

"He was about fifteen. Maud was only thirteen. It doesn't make any sense."

"Oh yes, it does. It's beginning to make a lot of sense to me, now," said Ernie.

Someone knocked on the glasshouse door and Michael entered looking frustrated, "I lost him. I caught up with him but he twisted out of my grasp, and shoved me down the slope. It gave him enough time to scramble away. I tried to find him but there are too many places he could hide away. Sorry, Ernie, Sam." He looked at Laura, "Are you all right?"

Laura nodded and the men looked at each other expectantly.

"What now?" said Sam.

"You'd better get on with your original plans, Michael. Get into the village and across to Neath. I think Laura should stay here with Jenny. I'll get down to Pritchard the police. Michael, you can give me a ride down. Sam had better stay and do some work. We can't leave it all to John."

"What can't be left all to John?" said John as he walked into the kitchen.

"You explain," said Ernie to Sam and Laura. "We'll away. Remember to keep your doors locked."

Jenny looked concerned and John put his arm protectively around his wife as Michael and Ernie left.

Chapter Eighteen

Further Machinations

Grainger Mason felt aggrieved and he was in a bad way. His head was thumping, blood was running down his face and the pain in his groin was only just beginning to subside.

He couldn't understand why Laura had reacted like that. He was only trying to help her rid her life of a man she didn't want. She should know he only had her best interests at heart. He convinced himself that this was his punishment for dallying with the harlot, Megan.

He was uncertain what to do. That man had come after him but he'd managed to give him the slip. Grainger was keeping well off the path. He scrambled through the thistles and nettles at the side of the track and flattened himself in the bracken as he heard the approach of a cart.

The iron rimmed wheels rumbled on the stony track and rattled past him. Once the wagon had rolled by, Grainger raised his head from the greenery and saw from the back the familiar head of Ernie in his beret and the man who had tried to apprehend him in the scree.

He lay there quietly until enough time had elapsed to get the men and the wagon clear of the track. He feared they would be lying in wait at the end of the mountain road or somewhere in the village, when he had an idea. He knew what to do. He would make his way to Bronallt and Megan's mother. She would be able to help. He was sure of that. Of course, that was the right thing to do.

Grainger slipped down the last remaining few yards of scrub and ducked behind a stout oak at the edge of the roadside. He peered along the carriageway trying to spot his enemies. He sidled around the tree and sprinted across the road and through St. Margaret's cemetery. Keeping well out of view he dodged along, ducking down between the gravestones whenever he heard voices. He crawled through the fence and skated past the back entrances to a number of houses before coming to the main road.

His breathing was more ragged now and he dived up the embankment and travelled along the railway line and continued up the mountainside until he could see the narrow track that led to Bronallt.

Grainger's head was thumping unbearably. He stopped and wiped his hand across his brow. It was still sticky, although the blood wasn't running freely anymore. He cursed as he caught his coat on brambles with tendrils that climbed through the bracken and bushes and tangled their way through the undergrowth. He tugged hard as the thorns held tight and tore a little piece of his fashionable jacket.

Grainger stumbled on; he passed the outlying fields of the farm empty of workers and he pressed forward purposefully. He clutched at his side; his ribs hurt. He was sure that the man he'd tussled with had cracked one. He took a huge intake of air and winced. Grainger paused in his climb. He could see the stables and paddocks of Nancy Thomas with her preciously bred racehorses and fine breeds.

The big gate that led to the cobbled farmyard came into view. Grainger glanced about him. He couldn't see anyone. He opened the gate and limped toward the front door. He rang the clapper on the outside bell and waited. No one answered. He grimaced and banged on the door. There was no response.

Grainger sidled around the side of the farmhouse and went into the backyard. He saw Nancy Thomas with a basket collecting eggs from the henhouse. For a moment, he stopped and caught his breath from the back she had the same wonderful head of hair that reminded him of… he stopped, no he didn't want to think about it.

He watched her a moment longer and then as if she felt eyes on her she straightened up and stiffened. She turned and saw him leaning against the house and she stifled a scream. Keen to reassure her he spoke, "Sorry, Mrs. Thomas. I didn't mean to startle you. I know I must look grotesque. I've had a bit of an accident."

Nancy Thomas stared at him with a lack of recognition in her eyes.

"It's me, Megan's friend, from ENSA. Grainger, Grainger Mason. Sorry if I frightened you."

Nancy Thomas softened her look and asked, "Whatever happened to you? You need to get that seen to..." She appeared to come to a decision. "Come inside and I'll take a look."

Grainger followed, her inside and Mrs. Thomas unloaded the eggs into a china dish with some straw. "Sit down, Grainger. I'll get the first aid kit."

He pulled out a chair from the kitchen table and sat easily as if he belonged there. Mrs. Thomas didn't appear to be alarmed by him. This was good, very good. He began to play her as a seasoned professional, to manipulate her with his undoubted charm.

"I shouldn't be here really but I was playing in Cardiff with the troupe. We have some leave before the next tour of duty and I thought I'd drop by on my way home."

Nancy filled a small bowl with water and dropped in some disinfectant and dabbed at the gash on his head. "However did you do this?"

Grainger lied, "I bought a bicycle and got knocked over by someone in a delivery van. They didn't stop."

"That's terrible," said Nancy, genuinely sympathetic. "Where's your bike now?"

"I left it at the roadside. The wheel was buckled. I'll have to get a new one."

"Maybe not," said Nancy. "I'm sure Gwynfor's old bike is in the back of one of the sheds. You can have that. He won't be needing it anymore," she said softly.

Grainger winced as she dabbed on some antiseptic cream, "That's very kind of you. Are you sure?"

"Of course, I wouldn't offer, else. It'll need cleaning up, mind." Nancy cut a clean piece of lint and covered the gash and then taped it in place. "There you are, good as new. And now, Grainger, how about a lovely cup of tea and a piece of sponge? You can tell me everything that has been happening to you."

Grainger was feeling quite comfortable and relaxed. He felt pleased that he'd called and felt it was the right thing to do. No one would think of looking for him here. He felt sure that Megan's mother would let him stay.

Michael and Ernie clattered on down the track. They kept their eyes on the side of the road for any sign of Grainger but could not see him anywhere. They concluded that Grainger had managed to hide his tracks in the thick undergrowth, which from their viewpoint showed no trace of broken twigs or flattened grass.

Michael dropped Ernie off at the end of the track. He entered The Crescent and was tempted to call at the doctor's surgery but saw the quarantine notice. He hesitated so pressed on, then to the village hall where all seemed in order. Villagers were going in droves to be vaccinated. Everything seemed on course to ease the developing crisis that was threatening Crynant.

Michael drove the cart along the Neath road. He had time to think on the journey and to organise his thoughts. He would check and see if his posse of workers had disinfected the market hall before he would pop into the cinema and finally, he would visit The Duke of Wellington.

The stalwart shire horse trotted along the street and they soon reached the outskirts of the town. Michael secured his wagon and entered the market, less busy than usual, and he spotted the caretaker manager of the market and called out to him, "Ray!"

The flat-capped man in his late fifties was wearing a brown coat with tweed trousers and he waved cheerily at Michael and strolled across. "Mr. Lawrence, I expect you are coming to check up on me." He grinned and continued, "I've had the whole of the floor awash with disinfectant and each stall holder has scrubbed their display trestle tables and benches. Should be clean as a blade of grass in the dew."

Michael nodded, "That's good."

"Aye. We'll swab the market thoroughly after trading, just to be on the safe side."

"Thanks, Ray."

"That's all right. We don't want any more kids getting sick." Ray smiled and turned away. Michael returned to the cart and proceeded down the street making his way to the cinema. He tied the horse to a post and entered the Empire. He exchanged a few words with the manager and satisfied that precautions had been taken he left and continued toward the oldest public house in Neath, The Duke of Wellington.

Michael settled the horse and wagon before entering the hostelry. He walked up to the bar and spoke to Betty behind the counter. "I am just checking on the clean up regarding the outbreak of diphtheria. It's a long shot, of course, but we are trying to prevent an epidemic."

"Oh, yes. It's Mr. Lawrence, isn't it?" Michael nodded in reply. "Well, we took it very seriously. None of us want the strangles affecting young children, or the old folk for that matter. We did exactly as you said. All surfaces have been washed down and the carpets and upholstery have been cleaned as best we can. We can't understand how some of the cases have related to us."

"The problem is," said Michael. "That if a carrier has been in the pub, then that person wouldn't know they were responsible as many carriers never feel ill or go down with the illness. Of course, some eventually do and that makes it easier. But as this is a sudden outbreak, can you think of anyone who has begun visiting your pub who was not a regular before?"

Betty thought and shook her head, "Sorry. No one springs to mind."

Michael looked defeated, "Well, thank you, anyway. I hope you have advised all your regulars to get themselves vaccinated and those with suspicious symptoms to go to their doctors and get themselves checked out." Michael stopped, "Please think; are you absolutely positive that no strangers have been in here in the last couple of weeks that may have been overlooked?"

Betty shook her head again, "No… Oh, wait a minute… Yes, but that's silly he's in perfect health."

"Tell me, who?"

"We do have someone staying here arrived from Cardiff, on leave from some troop in the army."

"Yes?"

"He's staying here a while having bed and breakfast. Come

to think of it, he didn't come down this morning and I didn't see him last night, you don't think…?"

Betty suddenly looked very alarmed, she took the keys from behind the bar and they went up the stairs to the accommodation area. Betty crossed to Grainger's room and knocked. There was no response. She looked at Michael and he nodded. Betty opened the door.

They could both see that the bed was neatly made and had not been slept in. She opened the wardrobe door. His clothes were all hanging up, tidily and his case was inside. Betty heaved a sigh of relief, "I thought for a minute he may have done a runner without paying his bill. But, it's clear he's coming back."

She closed the wardrobe and they left the room and Betty relocked the door. As they walked down the stairs, Michael began to question her, "Can you tell me the man's name?"

"Yes, very fancy, it is. Grainger, Grainger Mason." Michael stiffened. Betty continued, "He's in the entertainment wing of the army. Very entertaining, himself he is, too. He's had us in fits of laughter with his impressions of WC Fields. And when old Bert has played the piano he's sung some of the popular songs for us. He's a nice chap."

"When did he arrive?"

"Um, just over a week ago."

"Do you know how long he's staying?"

"He wasn't sure. He said he was going to use the time to visit friends in the area. He's spent a bit of time with some of the farmers at market and in here chatting about various things."

"It's too much of a coincidence. The outbreak started just after his arrival."

"What? You don't think he's responsible?"

"It looks like a possibility. But, what I can't understand is that anyone going into the army has to have all vaccinations up to date as a matter of routine." Michael frowned, "He didn't by any chance mention any friends in particular?"

Betty creased her face in concentration, "I seem to remember him being very interested in where the Land Girls were working locally. He also chatted about his friends in

Crynant, other than that I can't think of anymore." Betty smiled at Michael, "Does that help?"

Michael, nodded, "It most certainly does. Thank you, Betty."

Betty beamed with pleasure, "Do you want me to say anything to him when he returns?"

Michael shook his head vehemently, "No. Not a word of what we've discussed must pass your lips. It's extremely important that he mustn't be alarmed or alerted to our interest in him," insisted Michael.

"Very well. But I need you to know, he's very pleasant and utterly charming."

Michael struggled to keep the acid from entering his voice, "I bet he is. Thank you, Betty. You've been more than helpful. You've been immunised haven't you?"

"Yes, and I put a notice up like you asked. But I haven't seen Mrs. Oliver to tell her."

"Mrs. Oliver?"

"She came in the night Grainger was doing a turn with the piano, with her baby daughter. Grainger made a real fuss of the little girl."

"Did he now? Where does the lady live?"

"Out on the Cilfrew Road. Number 18."

"Thanks. I'll pay her a visit." Michael touched his hat and left the premises. He boarded his cart and shook the reins and made for the road to Cilfrew. He hoped he would be in time.

The horse, Buddy, burst into a brisk trot and Michael steered the wagon along the busy road. He noticed that there were a few more motorised vehicles travelling the road than in recent years. He decided that he might even check out a motorcar for his own use. But first things first, he needed to find Mrs. Oliver and her child, and he needed to find them urgently.

Michael drifted off into his own thoughts as the cart and horse continued to plod along the road. He was now convinced that Carrie had indeed seen Grainger Mason and he was more than certain that Grainger was the link and at the root of the outbreak of diphtheria.

Michael looked up at the sky that was clouding over. Black

storm clouds were rolling in. The first few drops of drizzle began to rain down. Michael turned up his coat collar with one hand and spurred the majestic beast onward.

He carefully noted the numbers of the houses and stopped outside number eighteen. Now, the rain was dropping down more heavily. Michael stepped down and tied Buddy up to the gatepost and walked up the drive. He rang the bell and waited.

He waited a few more minutes and rang again. He was just about to rattle the letterbox when he heard someone approaching the front door. The door opened and a young woman looked out suspiciously at Michael, she looked as if she had a touch of flu and her eyes were red from crying.

"Yes?" she sniffed.

"Mrs. Oliver?"

"Yes?"

"There's no easy way to say this. How is your daughter?"

"She's not at all well, how did you know?"

"I have reason to believe that you and your little girl may have been in contact with someone who has diphtheria."

"What?"

"Have you been immunised?"

"I haven't, I don't think."

"Has your daughter?"

"Catherine? Um, no not yet. Oh, Duw. Does that mean she's… ?"

"The only way we'll know is to get you to a doctor. You will both need treatment. Where is she?"

"I've just put her down. She had me awake all night. She's resting now, finally."

"Show me."

Mrs. Oliver opened the door to admit him and Michael followed her up the stairs and into the baby's room. Michael looked into the cot. The infant was struggling to breathe and was turning blue. The mother screamed in despair and Michael picked up the infant and tried to help the little one to breathe. He patted the baby firmly on the back and Catherine took a huge gulp of air, making a strange whooping cry.

"Quickly. We have to get her to the doctor and fast. Come on."

Pamela Oliver grabbed her bag and coat and followed Michael out of the nursery down the stairs and to the waiting wagon. The door swung shut behind her.

Michael handed her the infant and helped her into the seat and then jumped up beside her. He flicked the reins and urged Buddy into his stride and the cart rattled along the stony road. Chips flew up and pelted the undergrowth at the side of the road and birds fluttered from the hedgerows and chirruped in alarm. Michael pressed the steed and wagon on as Mrs. Oliver sobbed and clutched her baby to her.

Hardly a word passed between them. Pam Oliver managed to stutter out, "I lost my first baby. I can't lose another."

Michael pursed his lips, "I'm sure the doctor will do his best."

They soon entered the end of the village and turned left into the Crescent and raced toward the Doctor's surgery. Michael jumped down and helped Mrs. Oliver off the cart.

Michael opened the gate and ran to the front door and hammered on it. Millicent Rees opened the door ajar and peered out. Michael blurted out. "The baby, the baby needs help. Please."

Millicent opened the door wider to admit them. "I shouldn't really be letting you in. We're supposed to be in quarantine."

Michael brushed the protestations aside, "I am protected. But this lady and her daughter aren't and the baby is very ill."

Millicent ushered them into the house and through to the parlour. Carrie was tending to the infants in her care. She looked exhausted and Michael's heart leapt at the sight of her but he was concerned at her appearance and the dark circles under her eyes.

Carrie smiled at Michael and his heart thumped in his chest. "What are you doing here?"

"Another patient for you, possibly two," said Michael.

Pam Oliver stood behind Michael clutching her baby with tears streaming down her face. Carrie held out her arms to take the child but Pam held on tight, fiercely.

Carrie tried to reason with her, "Come on now. We only want to help. Let me see the little one. We have to get antibiotics into her to stop the spread of the infection. And you, you need attention, too."

Pam stubbornly refused to relinquish her bundle. She sobbed out, "We're too late. Catherine is dead," and she burst out into a fresh wave of tears.

"We don't know that," said Carrie. "Let me see."

Michael urged her, "Please, Mrs. Oliver. Let Nurse Llewellyn take a look. You never know."

Pam bit back sarcastically, "Why? Can she raise the dead?"

Michael and Carrie exchanged a look and Carrie held out her arms once more. Slowly, Pam began to offer the baby to Carrie. Michael could see that Carrie was doing her best not to alarm the mother and eventually she was able to gently take the child and Pam crumpled to the floor with heart wracking sobs.

Carrie pushed back the covers from the child's face and they all saw the baby's blue complexion. She unwrapped the child and placed her in an empty cot. Michael touched the child's forehead. The skin was cool and clammy to the touch. Carrie felt for the little one's pulse. "There's something there, faint but it's there. Feel."

Michael touched the pulse point and felt a faint but rapid flutter. He nodded, "There's a chance. Do something, please."

Pam stopped sobbing and looked on in trepidation. Carrie grabbed a small hand mirror and placed it close to the baby's face and there was a very slight misting on the mirror. "Dr. Rees," she cried out. "Quickly, I believe we need to perform an endo tracheal intubation."

Dr. Rees rushed in from the surgery and hastened to Carrie's side. He looked haggard but determined, and he studied the child who wasn't moving and felt the weak pulse. "You're right. We must move fast. But, I will have to take a chance and perform a tracheotomy. I have never done an intubation."

He first checked inside the baby's mouth whose head lolled to one side. The tell tale toxic grey membrane was all too clear for everyone to see. He nodded at Carrie. She hurried to the kitchen where Millicent Rees had concocted some type of sterilisation unit. She took a kidney dish, scalpel, and a small curved glass tube and raced back. Michael was helping Pam Oliver to her feet. He put his arm around her as they watched the proceedings together.

"Please," whispered Pam. "Save her if you can."

Dr. Rees was painting the whole throat area ready for an incision and Carrie passed him the scalpel. The tension in the room was tremblingly tight like the lacing in a corset stretched to breaking point. Michael observed carefully while Pam buried her head in his shoulder unable to watch.

"Carrie keep an eye on the time. Call out the minutes."

Michael shuddered he knew that three minutes without oxygen would mean certain brain death.

Dr. Rees took a deep breath and raised the scalpel to the baby's throat. Michael and Carrie both knew how dangerous this could be, as the anatomy of a baby's throat is very different from that of an adult and the swelling in the neck could give the doctor little room for manoeuvre.

Never the less they all knew this was the baby's last chance. Dr. Rees gently palpated the area, knowing that time was running out. He felt for the soft spot below the bump of the Adams apple and larynx. There was a second smaller bump. He whispered, "I've found it." His fingers pinpointed the valley between the two bumps.

His hand shook and Carrie called out, "One minute." No one dared to breathe as the good doctor made a small incision in an up and down motion and spread the skin tissue apart horizontally. Carrie wiped away the seepage with a clean swab.

Dr. Rees took another gulp of air. He avoided the blood vessels and glandular tissue and Carrie muttered a quick prayer under her breath as the doctor punctured the cricothyroid membrane very carefully and horizontally in the opposite direction of the first incision.

The depth of the puncture was just sufficient to gain access to enter the trachea. "Tube," instructed Dr. Rees. Carrie handed him the small curved tube, which he struggled to insert into place.

"Two minutes!" said Carrie.

Dr. Rees pressed a little more firmly and the tube was in

place. A bead of sweat dropped from the doctor's forehead and splashed onto the infant's chest.

Catherine was able to breathe.

"She's not out of trouble yet," said Dr. Rees, "But at least she's breathing."

Carrie said, "I'll prepare some anti-toxin and antibiotics."

"And something for the mother, too. Don't get the dose confused," warned Dr. Rees.

"That's why I'll do them separately," assured Carrie.

Michael chipped in, "I think I've discovered the source. That is if we can catch him."

Carrie and Dr. Rees looked up, "You were right, Carrie. Grainger Mason *is* here and I am pretty sure from what I have learned that he's our carrier."

Chapter Nineteen

Calcutta, Burma and Beyond

'Calcutta must be the hottest place on earth,' thought Megan. The air was suffocating and clinging like a hot wet blanket. The whole of the troupe were in a constant clammy state of perspiration with beading rivulets of sweat running from head to toe. It seemed to Megan that every day spent there, the temperature and humidity increased without respite. Megan complained to her fellow performer, Janet, "I don't know how much longer I can stick this."

"Stick is right," agreed Janet. "Sticky and stickier with each passing day."

"Even having a shower or bath is no help," grumbled Megan.

"No, I know, the so called cold water is so warm it neither cools nor refreshes."

"Just so. I come out of the shower sweating just as much as before, and need another shower," said Megan.

"Me, too. Thank goodness, we are not here for long. Are you coming on the overnight trip to the mountains, Makaibari Tea Estate, Kurseong and Dilaram?"

"Do you think it will be cooler in the hills?"

"Bound to be."

"Then I will."

"Then we best hurry, the jeeps are leaving shortly," said Janet.

The two young women grabbed their things and hurried through the compound to where the vehicles were waiting. The rest of the group were already on board. Janet and Megan clambered inside. The canvas flaps were tied back to allow the air to travel through the vehicle but it did little to cool them although it did provide some canopy cover for their heads in the scorching heat.

The motors set off in convoy toward the foothills of the

mountains that surrounded Calcutta. They passed through the smart part of the town with their regal stately very English buildings before joining the rough road skirted by peasant shacks that led to the mountain villages. A dense but lush green forest covered one side of the mountain overlooking water and the River Balasun, with tea gardens and plantations spreading over the other slope.

The long drive took them on a tortuous road that snaked its way up through the hills, along high ledges on mountainsides and wound its way up staircases of hair-raising hairpin bends. Megan gulped as she looked down at the drop at the side of the road, which took them higher and higher into the hills.

They passed a hill station of the old British Army that was constructed very obviously in the style of Colonial properties. The European part was built almost like an English country town. Megan sighed with longing as she saw the gabled roofs, bow windows and cross-beamed walls. Cottages stood with roses around the doors and had herbaceous borders skirting the lawn. They passed paddocks and stables with horses and continued winding their way up and up.

The troupe burst into song as they travelled on. There was almost a holiday feel about the trip. They were to travel to the highest point and take in the wondrous view from the peak.

The company manager, Freddie called out, "We will camp at the barracks and spend the night there before returning to Calcutta and our next show. Then, I can tell you we move onto Burma."

Megan clearly wasn't expecting this, nor was Janet. Burma, Burma was imminent. The news was exciting. But on a more mundane level both of them worried that they hadn't brought enough with them for this overnight stay. Still, it was too late to grumble about that now.

They were climbing through the picturesque hills and marvelled at the views and the cascading water that flowed down toward the river. Megan was sure that this water would be cold and longed to get into it, and said as much, "I would love to get out now and fall into that water. It looks deliciously cool, and inviting," and she sighed.

"You're right. It does," acknowledged Freddie. He looked

out, “We’re almost at the camp and I see no reason why we shouldn’t investigate the small cataracts and see if swimming is possible,” he said.

The jeeps pulled off the rough road and into the small barracks, and parked up. The third jeep carried tents and equipment and the group worked together to erect their temporary accommodation. They were allowed to wander off through the small camp and into the dense thickets and rocky outcrops with clear water flowing down looking magical as the spray caught the sun and rainbows projected onto the rocks and in the air. Megan was reminded of home and the hills of Wales with their waterfalls and deep pools. She and Janet stepped out under the gushing water and were relieved to find that the water emerging from the rocks was indeed cool. They allowed themselves to get drenched and enjoyed the feeling it gave them.

Megan lay out on a rock and steam rose up from her wet clothes that dried quickly in the heat. The crystal pool gave them much pleasure and Megan listened to the sound of the rushing water that mingled with the whispering and rustling of the trees. She could hear the cicadas chirruping and calling to each other and bullfrogs honking away further down the water’s tract.

Megan was filled with an unbelievable feeling of peace and contentment. She thought how romantic this place could be if only she could share it with Thomas. Megan reached into her pocket and pulled out her last letter from him. It was creased and tattered from numerous readings. She tried to figure out the blacked out sentences that had been censored but whoever had done it had made too good a job of it. Megan stuffed the missive back in her pocket.

Janet looked at her enviously, “At least your letter is intact.”

“But, I can’t read much of it,” said Megan.

“It’s better than mine,” said Janet. “Look!” She held up a note where the words looked as if they had been removed with a razor blade and it resembled some infantile paper pattern. All that could be read was: ‘My dear Janet, I hope this finds you well…’ There were a few more meaningless odd words and then a signature at the bottom, “With much love, Stephen,” and that was it.

The girls began to make their way back to camp when Megan froze and her mouth dropped open into an oh of horror for the scream that never came as a large snake crossed the path in front of her. It was as thick as a man’s arm and covered the full width of the track. Megan put her arm out to prevent Janet from walking into it. They watched as the reptile slithered into the undergrowth. Only then did they speed up and hurriedly returned to camp to enjoy an alfresco supper of army rations that tasted surprisingly good.

The atmosphere at this camp was carefree. They could forget for a short while that there was a war on. The women retreated into their tents and listened to the sounds around them. Megan sat up, “Do you hear that?”

“What?” asked Janet.

“That thudding noise. It’s going boom, boom, boom.”

“Well, it’s not a bomb, if that’s what you’re thinking.”

“What is it?”

“Coconuts.”

“Coconuts?”

“The local natives are harvesting coconuts.”

“No!” Megan opened the tent flap to listen to the dull sound that reverberated through the camp and she squealed, “Argh!”

“What? What is it?”

Megan pointed to the floor where two scorpions were squaring up to each other. She shuddered and Janet laughed, “Close the flap. They won’t hurt you.”

“What? They’re dangerous, with poisonous stings.”

“We’ll be fine, as long as you close the flap. We don’t want them creeping in when we are asleep. Or you could flick them out of the way.”

Megan picked up a stick and whacked one, sending it into the undergrowth. The second one suffered a similar fate and Megan relaxed.

The dull thudding sound could still be heard as Megan tried to close her eyes. She sat up and asked, “Why does it make such a noise?”

Janet leaned up on one elbow, "Relax, Megan. It's not so bad. It will tune into your thoughts eventually. It can be almost hypnotic and help you to sleep."

"But how do they do it?"

Janet sighed, "They shin barefooted up the tree trunks, cut the nuts loose in their thick husk cases. Then drop them to the ground. It rains nuts! Now go to sleep."

Megan settled down again and tried to slumber. She found it hard. She lay on top of the covers. It was just too hot. The thudding, the heat, the thrum of the insects and whine of mosquitoes all served to pierce her brain and keep her awake. She thought of Thomas, his smile, his kiss, and eventually she slipped away on pillow of dreams.

Megan was the first to wake in the morning, the cries of the birds and sounds from the wildlife in the mountains jarred and served to make her fully alert. She picked up her kitbag, pulled it toward her and stifled a shriek. White ants had eaten through the bottom of the bag and some of the offending insects dropped onto her lap. She shivered in spite of the heat and brushed the ants away. As her hands touched her legs she felt something sticky. She looked down to see blood running from a leech puncture on her stomach. Another bloated leech was still hanging onto her leg. She couldn't quell her squeamishness and a small scream escaped her lips rousing Janet.

"What? What is it?"

Megan gurgled in her throat and pointed at the offending organism. Janet had fared better but had suffered some mosquito bites. Megan went to pull the creature off her leg but Janet hissed, "No! Don't touch it. It could leave the sucker in your leg, which could turn septic. Hold on." Janet reached into her own rucksack and pulled out a pack of cigarettes and lit one. She drew hard on it and inhaled until the lit end was glowing brightly. "Hold still!" Janet placed the burning end on the leech's tail to make it withdraw its sucker and the parasite let go and dropped onto the groundsheet, where Janet squashed it with her boot and the blood spattered the canvas.

Megan felt decidedly sick; she thrust her head outside and

promptly vomited. She pulled her head in, "I hope Burma doesn't have leeches. Horrible things."

Janet started to giggle, "You should see your face. I wish I had a camera!"

Megan looked at Janet and they both burst into laughter. They stopped when they heard a terrific roar coming from the dense forest behind them followed by a rustling.

"What do you think that is?" whispered Megan her face furrowed in concern.

"Some marauding beast. Could be a tiger," said Janet.

"I hope not."

"Well, we are in Bengal."

"I suppose we are. And that rustling…"

"Could be something else, an elephant, the great Indian rhino or even a spitting cobra."

They both looked alarmed. "I think I'll stay put by here, until the others are up," said Megan.

"Me, too," said Janet. "Did you hear Freddie talking with the local guard?"

"No. Why?"

"There was a famous man eating tiger of Calcutta."

"What?" exclaimed Megan her eyes growing wide with alarm.

"Mm, it killed over two hundred people before it was finally captured and put in the zoo."

"They didn't kill it?"

"No. Although that is the usual course of action."

"Then I am definitely not moving until it's time to go."

They didn't have long to wait and Megan was relieved when the troupe was packed up with their belongings and ready to return to Calcutta. From there they were pleased to find that they had one last show before proceeding to Burma.

Thomas was onboard, his cuts and bruises treated, and he was looking at the disappearing coastline of Jamaica. They were, he hoped, on their way to Singapore to maintain a presence in the light of Japanese aggression. The rumour that they would also visit Burma was unconfirmed as was their port of destination. Everything seemed cloaked in so much mystery. Thomas prayed in his heart that they would visit Burma, for he knew that Megan was to be there. He hoped that her tour of duty was still the same and that her troupe's visit would coincide with his ship's company. This knowledge gave him heart and the strength to look forward. Jonty sidled up beside him on deck. He had suffered far worse than Thomas. His arm was in a sling, with a fractured humerus, and he had a broken collarbone.

The two friends acknowledged each other. Jonty asked, "If I am ever tempted to slip away with another woman on shore, remind me of this, please."

Thomas smiled, "Don't worry I will. We must look out for each other and next time…"

"There won't be a next time."

"Never say, never. If we venture to any bars we will make sure we go in a gang. Right?"

"Right!"

Thomas and Jonty stood silently as the ship sailed toward the distant horizon. A few fluffy clouds floated across the azure sky and the coastline of Jamaica became a distant memory.

The two friends retreated below and made their way back to the infirmary. Thomas was due to have the strapping of bandages changed on his ribs and Jonty needed another dose of painkillers. Thomas settled on the side of the bunk and took out Megan's last letter and read it yet again. He sighed, and said a silent prayer that they would be together again, soon.

Jonty looked across and murmured, "Have you heard the latest?"

"No? What's that?"

"I heard from the chief engineer earlier."

"What? Tell me."

"It seems we are on our way to Norfolk to effect more repairs."

"Norfolk, England?"

"No. Virginia."

"In America?"

"The same."

Thomas whistled long and low, as was his way when he

was shocked by something. "So we are going to America."

Jonty nodded, "That'll be something to tell the family."

"Aye," but Thomas' face expressed his dismay. His spirits dropped and he rolled over on his bunk, lost in his thoughts.

Megan and her group had done their last show in Calcutta and returned to camp in the unrelenting heat and she was more than surprised to see a very familiar but battered case waiting for her that had travelled from Bombay. It had journeyed by rail and been returned to HQ in Calcutta. Megan shrieked with glee and ran to the suitcase that was now very much the worse for wear. She picked it up, the lock burst open and her things tumbled out. One glance at the items that littered the floor was enough to tell her that many of her clothes were missing. Her case had been rifled through and garments pilfered. She tried to gather the remaining items up and close the lid but the lock refused to connect.

"Oh no! Now, what do I do?"

"I suggest you go into town and buy another," advised Freddie. "And keep a closer eye on it when we travel. Or maybe, let me look after it. We will be flying out to Burma tomorrow. So make the most of today."

"That doesn't give me long."

"Have a word in the Mess, someone is bound to be going to town later."

Megan nodded and tossed her luxuriant head of hair and walked briskly toward the recreation area and chatted to one of the soldiers.

"Is anyone going into town today?"

"There may be and there again there may not be."

"There's no need to talk in riddles. Is there?"

The young subaltern grinned, "Just joking. Yes, there's a few of us headed in," he checked the time, "In fifteen minutes. "You're welcome to join us. Meet you back here?"

"That would be wonderful. Thank you. I'll just find my friend."

Megan smiled and went to look for Janet. She found her lounging on her bunk. "Come and keep me company, I'm going shopping."

"Now?"

"Now I need another case. Mine is falling apart. And we leave tomorrow. It's now or never."

"All right. How are we getting there?"

"Some of the sappers are heading out in fifteen minutes, "Come on."

Janet rolled off her bunk and the two friends walked out and back through the compound to the jeeps. The young men called them both across and they clambered into the back of the vehicle and in a cloud of dust sped out of camp.

The hustle and bustle of the town and business district of Calcutta were vibrant and alive. They revelled in the native culture, the colour, the sights and sounds and both young women agreed that India was a marvellous place. In spite of the debilitating heat and humidity of the place Megan loved the politeness of the people who treated her with respect and deference. She liked the mild spices that flavoured the food. The very hot ones she couldn't take, as they burnt her mouth, she was also put off these especially when she was told they were used to disguise meat that was on the turn or going off. But, in spite of this she had fallen in love with the beauty of India and vowed that at some time she would return.

Three hours later they were back in camp. Megan had her new case and Janet had purchased some fine embroidered silk. They had feasted on the aromas of street food and dined on vegetable samosas and pakoras and other tasty titbits. They retreated to their quarters and happily fell into their beds and chatted until the wee hours.

The following morning the company boarded the small plane that was to take them to Burma. The journey continued uneventfully as they travelled across the border of India, through Pakistan across the Bay of Bengal. The company were quiet. Gone was the light-hearted banter of the last few days as they realised they were stepping further into the unknown.

As the plane entered the airspace of Chittagong, the light aircraft hit a pocket of turbulence. Megan and Janet both began to feel nauseous, as the plane was buffeted and suddenly and rapidly dropped hundreds of feet before soaring up and falling again. The company watched the pilot with trepidation as he struggled with the controls to manage the flight.

Megan felt as if her stomach had risen up to meet her mouth. She gave an involuntary cry and Janet caught her hand and squeezed it. The pilot groaned as he saw a skein of geese coming into the plane's flight path He held tightly onto the controls holding the plane steady when there was a sudden bang as a bird hit the starboard engine, which stuttered to a stop.

Whoops and cries of alarm were emitted from those on board as the plane continued to shudder and judder through the sky. The engine began to wail in a droning whine as the pilot attempted to guide the plane down to safety. It howled in pain as it spiralled its descent toward the paddy fields that lay beneath them.

The pilot called out shrilly to everyone, "Hold tight and brace yourselves. We're going down." The whistling whine seemed to fill the air and reverberate through Megan's mind. She wasn't a catholic but she crossed herself and said a swift prayer. She didn't want to die. She wanted to live and be with Thomas. The plane dropped faster and Megan screamed.

The pilot fought with the twisting flying machine and struggled to hold it level. It bottomed out and dropped like a stone. The passengers leaned forward and braced themselves against the seats with their heads down. The plane groaned and creaked and fell through the sky as the pilot continued to try and keep the angle of the plane level.

Seconds passed but felt like hours as Megan saw her life flash before her. There was a huge splash as the aircraft met with the water in a paddy field and settled on the mud.

The company waited, hardly daring to breathe. Freddie called out, "Is everyone all right?"

Murmurs of relief went around the troupe as they realised, one by one, that they had hit the ground and had landed in one piece. The pilot was slumped forward on the dash. He sat back and whistled softly between his teeth. "That was close. Hurry, we better get out. The fuel could ignite."

Freddie opened the aircraft's exit door and the group filed out one by one and jumped into the rice field. Freddie grabbed the nearest luggage and tossed it out, which Bill Bushby caught and stacked in the muddy water.

Soon the plane was empty and the troupe stood in the midst of the water logged rice field and took in their bearings. The pilot announced, "We're lucky. By my calculations there's an American camp very close by in Fenni. Come on. Pick up your bags. Let's walk."

"We can't carry everything," said Freddie. "We need to make contact and get a truck back to load the stage and props up."

"Well, I'm not letting go of my case," said Megan stoically and picked it up.

The troupe trudged through the mud and heat. They looked a sorry sight, dirt splattered, and weary. They reached the end of the field and began to travel the earth road, with squelching shoes.

Megan groaned to Janet, "They should make cases with wheels on that you can drag."

"Maybe they will one day," replied Janet. "In fact it could be a great invention."

"Yes, but for now we have to lug them through this miserable sticky heat. First thing I shall buy are a pair of roller skates. I'm going to tie one to the bottom of my case and put a strap or belt around the handle and pull it along."

"That might work. But it might be difficult to control."

"Then I'll experiment and perfect it!" exclaimed Megan.

The troupe kept their spirits up with banter and chitchat under the glare of the sun. Flying insects dive-bombed the group like mini Messerschmitts. They slapped at the blood-sucking tormentors with their free hands and were more than relieved when footsore and in a state of exhaustion they spotted the gate of the American compound.

Soldiers on duty almost fainted at the sight of the women. Their jaws dropped and they gawped at the girls in disbelief. Megan commented tartly, "What's the matter? Have you never seen a woman before?"

"No, Ma'am. Not a white one and not for three years," said a fresh faced soldier who couldn't take his eyes off Janet. "Corporal Bernard D. Sadow at your service. Here, let me help you with that." The young corporal took Janet's case and accompanied her and the rest of the troupe to their headquarters.

Megan mumbled to Janet, "Find out where the lavatory is I am desperate to go."

Janet asked the delicate question and the young soldier answered, "If you're looking for the latrines, there is nothing fancy. Just a hole in the ground, surrounded by canvas to spare your blushes and a couple of posts dug into the ground to hold on to."

Janet blushed and whispered to Megan who responded, "I heard!"

"Be sure to take your Mecoprin malaria tablets, the mosquitoes around here are persistent with a bite to match and they infest the latrines. The patterns they can make on your derriere have to be seen to be believed. Sorry," he added when he saw the distaste register on both Janet and Megan's faces.

Megan sighed and muttered, "Oh boy!" She could see that Burma was going to be full of challenges and trials, and they were there for six weeks.

Chapter Twenty

Crisis Point

Carrie flopped into a chair in the parlour and gratefully sipped the cup of tea given to her by Millicent Rees. She looked extremely tired. Millicent Rees didn't look much better. She appeared emotionally exhausted, and care worn. Finally, Dr. Rees sank into the sofa and sighed.

"At long, long last I think we are over the worst. No fresh cases for twenty-four hours and all our tiny patients are picking up."

"We can't be too complacent, though," warned Millicent.

"No. No one can accuse us of that," agreed Dr. Rees. "But, by all accounts our timely vaccination programme has been solidly accomplished. Your young man has done an excellent job."

Carrie blushed, "He's a good man."

"He is indeed," agreed the doctor. "Talking of Mr. Lawrence, where is he?"

"He went to Hendre to see John and Sam and warn Laura about Grainger. He should be back soon."

As if on cue the doorknocker sounded and Millicent Rees went to admit Michael. He came in and sat on the sofa, "What's happened? How is Catherine Oliver?"

"Stable," answered Dr. Rees but we have still a way to go."

"And Mrs. Oliver?"

"See for your self, she's in the kitchen."

Michael walked into the kitchen and Carrie watched him with pride through the door that was ajar. She felt her heart flutter as he engaged Pam Oliver in conversation. The joy Carrie experienced at the sight of him, his clean-cut lines, chiselled jaw, and rich brown, cropped hair filled her with intense delight.

She searched her heart and mind. Is this what her mother had talked about? Was this strange feeling that excited and unsettled her and filled her stomach with fluttering nerves a sign of true love? She remembered her father's face and voice when he spoke of Miri, his wife and her mother, and the wise words her mother had shared when she was just a little girl. They rang in her head as she continued to watch Michael. "Cariad, you will know when you meet the right one. The confusion of feelings you'll experience will be just the start. You'll know he's the one when you care more about him than you do about yourself. You'll see." At that exact minute Carrie knew. She knew that Ernie was right, her mother was right and the woman on the train was also right. Carrie sat back in her seat with a serene expression on her face lost in her own world.

"Penny for them?" asked Michael as he returned.

"A penny? No. That's too cheap. My thoughts are worth at least ten shillings."

Michael laughed, "You drive a hard bargain, Carrie Llewellyn."

Carrie laughed, "What now? What has been happening?"

Michael gave Carrie a rundown on events at Hendre and Grainger Mason. "The thing is, we don't know where he is. He hasn't returned to the Duke."

"Well, he must be somewhere. I think the police should be informed and a watch kept on the pub where he's staying. He'll have to go back at some point."

"Good idea. I'll call in and see them at the station. Where else could he be?"

"I don't know, there's plenty of places he could hide out; shepherds' huts, old barns, even caves. If he is the carrier he needs to be found and quickly. He could become ill himself."

Michael nodded his agreement, "I'll get on. What about you? How much longer do you need to stay here?"

"I'll remain as long as I am needed," affirmed Carrie.

"I wouldn't expect anything less," said Michael. "But, I hope we will be able to spend some time together."

"I hope so, too," said Carrie.

Michael took Carrie's hand and embraced her, "Don't wear yourself out. You came home for a rest, remember?" He enfolded her in his arms before moving toward the surgery door. "But, I have to say that things seem better here, now."

"Yes, I feel we are over the worst, don't you doctor?" said Carrie. "We don't want any more deaths."

"I hope that this crisis is almost over," said Dr. Rees. "But we mustn't be complacent."

Michael nodded in agreement and left blowing a kiss to Carrie who blushed as Millicent Rees smiled at her knowingly.

Grainger Mason was in his element. He was being fussed over by Mrs. Thomas who had tended to his cuts and abrasions and she was in the process of making him a meal. He sat at the kitchen table and watched her while she worked. From the back, Nancy Thomas looked young. She was slim-waisted with smooth lines and her hands were fine and tapering. Grainger studied her movements, which were graceful and elegant.

Nancy shook her head and her burnished copper hair shone in the afternoon sunlight and he sighed.

Mrs. Thomas placed a steaming and hearty plate of food in front of Grainger. He looked up at her cheekily and winked. Nancy Thomas took this in good part and smiled back, when there was a knock at the door.

"Excuse me, Grainger. There is someone at the door. I can't think who it can be."

Grainger stiffened. He was about to stop her from leaving but was not quite quick enough. He frowned as he heard Mrs. Thomas welcome someone inside. He sat back in his chair as Mrs. Thomas returned with a young woman and small child.

"Ellen, this is a friend of Megan's, Grainger Mason, he's just passing through and stopped by to say hello. Grainger this is Ellen and William. William is just three years old." Grainger smiled in acknowledgement and William hid behind his mother's skirts.

"Hello, Grainger. William is not usually as shy as this. He's normally bouncing around. He'll come out of his shell in a little while."

Grainger turned on his smile and his charm, "I'm sure he will. He is a handsome little chap."

"Ellen lives at the next farm along the track. We try and

have a cup of tea together one morning a week. Today's the day," said Nancy Thomas.

William peeped out from behind his mother and Grainger proceeded to play a game of peek-a-boo before emitting a huge sneeze. "I do apologise. I don't know where that came from," said Grainger wiping his mouth with the back of his hand before fishing for his handkerchief. "I think I must be coming down with something."

"That's why I called," said Ellen. "There have been three deaths in the village. All babies. Rumours are flying about that there's an epidemic of diphtheria. People have been queuing up to get immunised and get booster jabs. I should imagine we're pretty safe where we are but I thought I'd tell you."

Grainger was sympathetic, "That's terrible. I understand it's a horrible disease."

"Yes, people in Neath, Crynant and Cilfrew have been affected. It seems little ones and the old folk are most at risk," said Ellen. "I heard on the wireless that Wales is planning a mass vaccination programme. It can't come quickly enough really."

"Well, we don't get the odd caller out here so we should be fine. Still it's better to be safe than sorry. I shall go down to the doctor's and get my booster," said Nancy.

"I believe they are doing that at the Village Hall. I shall stay home until it's deemed safe and then go and get us immunised. You never know."

"I think that's wise. Come and sit down have a cup of tea. I've made some bread pudding. It was Gwynfor's favourite," she sighed. "I can't seem to get out of the habit of making it for him. You'll have some, won't you, Grainger?"

"I won't say, no. I'm partial to a bit of bread pudding myself," replied Grainger whose mind was working overtime. He needed Nancy Thomas to remain at the house. He couldn't risk her saying anything to anyone about his visit or indeed anyone mentioning him to her. Ellen sat at the far end of the table and little William began to play with a Dinky toy car he had brought with him. He pushed it along with his little chubby dimpled hands and made a sound like a motorcar revving its engine.

Nancy poured Ellen a cup of tea and placed the bread pudding on a plate in the centre of the table. Both Grainger and Ellen reached out for a piece at the same time. Their fingertips nearly met. Grainger withdrew his hand, "After you."

Ellen smiled and took a piece and then Grainger helped himself. The little lad propelled his car along the floor, which hit the table leg and spun around close to Grainger's feet. Grainger half rose from the table to bend and retrieve the little car for William who was still a little shy of approaching the stranger but Nancy picked up the vehicle and handed it back. Grainger relaxed in his seat.

"That's a very handsome car," said Grainger to William. "Can I see?" The little boy shook his head and darted behind his mother's chair.

"His prized possession that is. His father bought him a set of six, but this one is his favourite. He prefers playing with this over his farm animals. We may have a future mechanic in the making," smiled Ellen. "Will you let the gentleman see, William?"

William stopped and looked from one to the other uncertainly.

"I won't hurt it I promise," said Grainger.

William still shook his head fiercely. Grainger smiled, "Not to worry, maybe when he gets to know me a bit better."

"How long are you staying, Mr. Mason?"

"That will depend on Mrs. Thomas," smiled Grainger.

Nancy looked surprised, "I thought you were just passing through before returning home?"

"I am. But if there's some sort of epidemic, maybe I had better sit a few days out here. Just until it's safe to travel."

Nancy spoke slowly, "I don't suppose that would do any harm. You can come with me for a booster when I travel to Crynant."

Grainger just nodded affably. He took a bite of the bread pudding and exclaimed, "This is absolutely delicious. Best I have ever tasted."

Nancy flushed with pleasure at the praise and offered him another piece.

"I won't say, no." he took another slice before sneezing again. "Dear, dear. I think I am getting a cold."

"It will be the shock of your accident, it will make you more vulnerable to things like that," said Nancy.

"Accident?" queried Ellen.

"Ah, yes," said Grainger and reiterated the lies he had told Nancy.

"You poor thing, how awful. What a thing to happen," murmured Ellen.

Grainger could feel another sneeze coming on. He reached in his pocket and fumbled for his handkerchief but dropped it on the floor. Little William came running to pick it up but Grainger retrieved it and grinned at William who had stopped in his tracks and darted back behind his mother.

Ellen stood up, "Well, Nancy we'll be off. No disrespect, Mr. Mason but the last thing I need is to catch your cold. No offence."

"None taken," assured Grainger pleased that they were leaving.

Ellen smiled, "I'll see you again soon, Nancy. Goodbye, Mr. Grainger. We may see you again. If not, have a safe trip home."

Grainger nodded his thanks and Nancy went with Ellen to the door to see them out. She soon returned. Grainger was standing by the kitchen window gazing out at the fields and yard. "It's a beautiful spot," said Grainger mechanically. He turned toward Nancy, "You have the same colour hair as Megan."

"Yes, I know. Like mother like daughter or whatever the saying is," said Mrs. Thomas with a smile. Grainger didn't answer but just stared at her with an odd look on his face

There was an awkward silence between them, which Nancy Thomas eventually broke. "Well, Grainger, if you are to be here for the night. You had better use Gwynfor's room. I think I can find you some spare clothes."

"Where is Mr. Thomas?" quizzed Grainger his eyes like steel flint.

Nancy Thomas was at first reluctant to answer, or so Grainger thought, but she managed to stutter a reply, "He was called to his mother's. She's not been very well."

"So, you are alone here?" His eyes had begun to gleam with a baleful light. He studied Nancy Thomas carefully. She appeared uncomfortable under his scrutiny and Grainger didn't trust her rushed answer.

"Not completely alone. I expect Huw back any day now and I have a farm worker who is labouring and helping us out. He comes every day and so, too, do a couple of Land Girls..."

"Land Girls," sighed Grainger. "What are their names?" he asked almost dreamily. "Is Laura one?"

Nancy was flummoxed, "Laura? No. No one of that name; Barbara and Nora, I believe."

"Do any of them have hair like you?"

Mrs. Thomas blinked in surprise, "Why, no."

"Good. It is good." Grainger suddenly turned on his dazzling smile, "Gwynfor's room, you say? That will be grand."

Nancy Thomas hesitated before replying, "Yes, yes. Gwynfor's room."

"Thank you, Mrs. Thomas. I think I'll just settle down for a short nap if you don't mind. I may feel better then in an hour or so."

"Yes, yes of course."

Grainger Mason beamed beatifically at her again as Nancy Thomas watched him curiously. He turned away and strode to the stairs whistling Begin the Beguine.

Chapter Twenty-One

Under Siege

Nancy Thomas was on edge. She didn't understand why, but she was finding that Grainger Mason disturbed her. She was beginning to realise why her daughter, Megan was not particularly pleased to see him when he dropped by when she was on leave from ENSA the previous year. Nancy had dismissed some of Megan's claims as fanciful dramatics knowing her daughter as she did but now she felt that maybe she had misjudged Megan's claims and she was beginning to regret inviting him in, especially now that he was staying the night.

Nancy felt an urgent need to do something. She didn't feel comfortable in her own home and was just pondering that thought as she stared out at the yard absorbed in stilling the cries of alarm surfacing and screaming in her mind. Nancy went to the hall closet and took out her riding coat and boats before returning to the kitchen where she puzzled and argued with herself some more. She placed her coat over a chair and lined the boots up alongside.

She was trying to convince herself that she was being irrational that there was nothing to be feared of and to that end she delayed leaving the house. Instead, she pulled out her Singer treadle sewing machine from the kitchen alcove and began to hem a new thick sun curtain for the back door to seal out drafts.

The material was cumbersome and difficult to deal with and Nancy soon forgot her worries and became involved in trying to tame the awkward swatches of cloth and she chased her misgivings about Grainger Mason from her mind. Time ticked on and the old portrait photographs of people long past that hung on the kitchen wall watched impassively as Nancy struggled on in the now fading light.

Nancy was so concentrating on the task in hand she didn't

hear Grainger step into the kitchen behind her. He laid a hand on her shoulder and she jumped startled by his sudden presence. She attempted to laugh it off, “Duw, Grainger. There’s a fright I had; you stepping in like that. It was enough to put me in the grave.” She almost regretted her choice of words as she turned to look at him. He looked clammy and was sweating. His face was flushed and his eyes looked malevolent and staring. “Are you all right?” she asked concerned at his appearance.

“I only meant to sleep an hour. You let me sleep on,” he said almost accusingly.

“You must have needed it. I didn’t want to disturb you,” Nancy said feebly.

Grainger looked at the coat and boots, “Been out have you?” and the way he said it sent a shiver down her spine.

“No, no,” she flustered. “I need to exercise Cobalt. I was going to do it after I finished with more chores,” she indicated the curtain she was struggling to sew.

“That wouldn’t be a good idea,” said Grainger. “Besides it’s getting dark. It could be dangerous to ride in the fading light. You never know what might happen.” He spoke slowly and deliberately. His cultured tones held the suggestion of a threat and Nancy tried to brush off his comment.

“No. That’s true.” She hoped her voice sounded normal. “I’ll leave it till the morning. I didn’t realise it was so late. Serves me right for getting involved with this,” she pointed at the sewing. She knew she might start babbling at any minute and bit her lip to stop herself chattering inanely. “Gosh! Is that the time? I must get supper for us and shut the hens up. I don’t want Mr. Fox having a tasty meal of my chickens. The problem is that the fox doesn’t take one chicken. It wouldn’t be so bad if he did. But if he gets in he would kill the lot.” She was rambling and she knew it. Grainger swayed slightly and Nancy rose from her seat, “Why don’t you sit down and I’ll get you a drink? You look as if you could do with one.”

“No, thanks.” His voice cut through the air like ice. Nancy flinched.

Nancy sat still a moment, uncertain as what to do. She

stood up and began to pack away her sewing. She needed something to do to allow her to think.

"Here, let me help you with that," said Grainger pointing at the machine as Nancy attempted to manoeuvre it back into the alcove. He smiled at her. His forehead was now beading with droplets of sweat.

"Grainger, you don't look well. Let me get something for you or at least get a doctor."

"I'll be fine. Just a bit of a fever from a cold. That's all." He looked out of the window and Nancy watched him staring at the yard and fields beyond. The trees were bowing and bending in the rising wind.

"Much better we sit and enjoy each other's company, don't you think? You don't want to be out on a night like this. The wind is getting up."

Nancy walked to the window. Her legs felt weak and wobbly like liquorice sticks. She leaned against the sink for support and her hands were trembling. Grainger crossed to her and placed an arm around her shoulder.

"Why, you're shaking. It has turned chilly hasn't it? The range needs stoking up with some more coal."

Nancy watched as he tipped the slag ends of coal from the scuttle into the fire, which greedily danced up to devour the fuel. He sat in the wooden carver chair by the range and rubbed his hands. "If I remember correctly, you are an excellent cook. I am sure one of your tasty homemade meals will do the trick and I'll be feeling better in an instant.

"We need to get more coal," observed Nancy.

"Yes, more coal, I believe there is another scuttle full in the parlour. And of course you want to close up the henhouse. But first we must eat. I shall watch and learn." He smiled at Nancy who felt that his smile was somewhat predatory like the yawning gape of a crocodile.

Nancy crossed to the larder and took out some potatoes, onions and corned beef. She placed two plates in the warming oven before she settled herself at the sink and began to peel the spuds.

Nancy smiled brightly attempting to be cheerful in her conversation. Grainger had begun to cough and she chattered on banally as if it was of no consequence. "You're developing a bit of a cough. I should check the medicine cabinet in the bathroom. There should be some cough mixture in there. That will soothe it." Grainger didn't respond. Nancy didn't know where to look. She could feel his presence behind her as he stepped closer and touched her hair. A feeling of revulsion rippled through her, which was mistaken for shivering.

"You're still cold. I shall have to bring the coal in after all. Can't have you going down with a chill, can we?" Grainger moved away and left the kitchen for the parlour. Nancy looked about her. She grabbed a sharp knife from the block and stuffed it in her apron pocket then hurried to the back door. The bolt securing it ground squeakily against its casing as she tried to open it.

Grainger returned carrying the coal bucket. He dropped it by the range and proceeded to the back door where Nancy was fumbling with the lock. He placed his hand on hers to stop her opening it.

"Dear, dear," he tutted. "You really are worried about those chickens, aren't you? Very well, we'll go together and gather them in."

Nancy's heart was racing as Grainger opened the door and ushered her outside. She collected a pan of grain from the sack at the back porch. They walked to the far end of the yard and Nancy called to the chickens and filled the trough in the run with corn. The hens came running and began to nibble at the corn, before walking up the wooden slope inside the henhouse. When the last one went inside she closed the sliding flap that would keep them safe until morning.

"There. I am sure you feel happier now," said Grainger and Nancy nodded dumbly. He put his arm back around her and ushered her back inside the house. Nancy crossed to the sink in the kitchen and continued to prepare the vegetables. The light was fading outside and getting dimmer inside. Nancy tried to speak, her mouth was dry and no sound would come out except for a small squeak.

Grainger smiled again at her as she turned to face him, "What? What is it? Is there something else?

Nancy blurted out, "The mantles. We need to light the gas."

"Don't you like the dark?"

Nancy shook her head.

"I find the all embracing cloak of night a comfort, protecting and watching over me. But if you want light I suppose it's not unreasonable to ask." Grainger went to the wall lights in the kitchen and turned on the gas, he used a spill from the fire to light the lamps and the gloom that was settling like a shroud was lifted.

The normality of the sound of frying onions and mashed corned beef did little to lift Nancy's spirits but she carried on stoically trying her best to keep calm.

Ellen had changed her mind and she and William had made it down to Crynant in their wagon to queue at the village hall for her to get her booster jab and for William to be inoculated. The doctor from Seven Sisters, Roderie Hughes, smiled at her. "Thank goodness you've come. I believe we have seen everyone now from the outlying houses. One more day here should do it and then I believe we can all have a rest. And not a day too soon."

"I nearly didn't come. Thought I'd wait it out at home but I needed provisions from the village so decided to come along after all."

"I'm glad you did. We were only talking last night about setting up some home visits to those who haven't been seen for the booster programme."

"Thank you doctor. We'll be on our way."

As Ellen was leaving Michael Lawrence entered with Ernie and spoke to the doctor. "We've done as much as we can now, Doctor. There shouldn't be any more cases. At least we hope not. The main problem is that Grainger Mason can't be found. He has not returned to the Duke. Either something has happened to him and he has succumbed to the illness himself or he's left the area."

Ellen stopped, "Grainger Mason, you say?"

Michael and Ernie exchanged a glance, "Yes? What do you know of the man?" asked Ernie.

"Why, I met him this morning."

"This morning? Where?"

"He's staying at Bronallt with Nancy Thomas. Called to see her on his way home after a nasty accident. I think he's staying the night." She studied the expression on Michael and Ernie's faces, "Is everything all right?"

Michael nodded, "Thank you. I hope so. Quick, Ernie, we must get to Pritchard the Police."

The two men hurried out of the door and left Ellen and the doctor looking flummoxed.

Storm clouds were gathering ominously and rolling in across the mountains. A dense bank of dark clouds obliterated the stars in the night sky, and a wind was blowing up and whirling the fallen leaves from the trees into a frenzy. A crack of thunder rumbled in the distance following a jagged fork of lightning that hit the ground and momentarily flash lit the sky.

Grainger and Nancy sat with the remains of a meal in front of them. Nancy had not touched much of hers but Grainger had managed to eat everything on his plate in spite of his frequent bouts of coughing. There was an awkward silence between them.

"Why don't we adjourn to the parlour. It's more comfortable in there. I'll leave the dishes until later," said Nancy stuck for something to say. "We'll have a drink together. What do you say?" Grainger looked up from his plate and nodded his agreement. "Of course, we may have to fetch more coal," advised Nancy.

It was as if Grainger hadn't heard and like an automaton he followed Nancy into the parlour and sank into a chair opposite her by the fire. Nancy went to the cabinet and poured them each a large whisky. She placed it on a small table next to his chair and left the bottle there, too.

There was another closer growl of thunder as the storm drew nearer. Nancy shivered. She felt that if she could keep him talking she would be safe. She knew the night would be long and prayed that he might fall asleep, especially if she could feed him some more to drink, and she could then make her escape. "So tell me, Grainger. Tell me about you and your family," she enquired with a forced smile.

"Not much to tell really, " he wheezed. "Grainger isn't my real name, you know."

"Isn't it? I did wonder," said Nancy willing him to keep talking.

"It's Arthur. But whoever heard of an actor called Arthur? Art wouldn't be bad, but no one would call me that. I needed to get away from home and that name and start again."

"I see."

"The name Grainger came from my mother. It was her maiden name. It sounded much more theatrical."

"It does. Megan did the same."

Grainger bristled, his voice rose up a notch from the quiet placating tones he had so far employed. "I don't want to talk about Megan. It's all her fault."

Nancy fell quiet. She wanted to ask questions but felt that now was perhaps not the right time.

Lightning flashes lit the sky outside and once more the thudding boom of thunder was heard and Nancy stiffened and shifted in her seat.

Grainger continued, "My mother has hair like you," he coughed and took a sip of whisky, "So did my sister. She was younger than me."

"Was?" questioned Nancy unable to help herself.

"She's dead," he said matter of factly. "Died when she was thirteen. I was just fifteen."

"I'm sorry."

Grainger's eyes ignited with abnormal fire as he bit back. "Sorry? Why should you be sorry? You don't know what happened." Grainger scowled with anger and took another swallow of his drink.

Nancy remained silent and waited for Grainger to continue. She listened to his words as they tumbled out. It was as if Grainger was cleansing his soul by letting everything fall away from him, his façade had dropped, his one sided conversation filled the difficult space between them.

"My mother wasn't normal," he broke into a severe coughing fit and spluttered loudly before picking up his glass and draining it of drink. He poured himself another and Nancy remained quiet and watchful. When Grainger caught her eye she smiled at him as if unconcerned, keeping her expression friendly and bright and Grainger proceeded to explain. "I never had a normal upbringing. My relationship with my mother wasn't like that of any of my friends. My mother treated me as an equal, a grown up. She taught me to do manly things."

He paused, and picked up his crystal glass tumbler and swirled the amber liquor around in the glass before smelling it and coughing once more. His voice became bitter, "She did things to me that no mother should do to a son. She told me she was preparing me for manhood and that when my father died I should be head of the household in every way."

Nancy swallowed. She didn't like the confessional tone that Grainger employed and with each admission he made she felt less safe. She experienced an alien tremulous churning that twisted and writhed in her stomach like an injured snake that threatened to rise and crawl out of her mouth.

"My mother taught me how to please a woman… Are you shocked? I would have been, had I known. I thought it was all perfectly normal. I thought these activities took place in every household, in every home, when it was just the machinations of my mother's twisted mind. The death of my father had made her that way. But that's no excuse. I wasn't to know. It started when I was just ten. Ten years old. Most boys played in the street, climbed trees, or went collecting frogs and lizards at the local reservoir. I learned how to serve; to cook, to clean, to please…" A small sob escaped Grainger's lips and he was suddenly wracked with coughing.

Nancy moved forward, touched at Grainger's tale, and wanting to help him but he snarled, "No! Stay." Nancy eased back in her seat and Grainger dabbed at his nose that was bleeding and dripping mucus.

There was another thunderclap. Nancy flinched.

"She wasn't completely evil and I loved her, in an odd way she loved me, too. I know she did."

Nancy remained silent.

"Did you know I had a sister? Of course you do, I told you. She had hair like my mother; the same colour, the same thickness, the same style…"

Nancy ventured to speak her voice little more than a whisper, "What happened?"

"We were out by the viaduct, skimming stones across the river. It was deep and running quickly that day. We'd had a lot of rain that week and the sky was threatening another downpour. In the bank by the bridge was a small cave and when the first drops began to fall I persuaded her to come into the cave for shelter. When we were in there…"

"Yes?"

Grainger looked up and across at Nancy, "What do you think? What do you think happened?"

Nancy spoke slowly trying to keep her voice level and without conveying any emotion, "I don't know."

Grainger screwed up his face like a spoiled child and his tone altered, "She didn't want to play. She didn't want to be pleased like my mother had taught me. She shouted at me and said she was going to tell, tell our friends and tell our teachers. But when I told her it was what our mother had taught me she screamed that I was a liar. She slapped my face. I caught her hands and twisted them until she dropped to her knees. I pushed her onto her back and then I fell upon her. Her hair shone like my mother's and it covered her face. It was then she threw back her head and spat in my face, which filled me with rage and I hit her. She stopped fighting me then and I could show her what I meant but she just lay there."

Grainger sobbed again and spittle dripped from his mouth. Nancy remained still and quiet, her eyes wide with fright. He began to cough and struggled to breathe. Nancy still didn't move.

The storm was coming closer. This time the crash of thunder outside was ear splittingly loud. Grainger stopped his hacking cough and took a huge intake of breath. He recovered and took another swig of his drink and wiped his mouth and resumed as Nancy shifted uneasily in her seat.

"She pushed herself up and head butted me hard in my middle. I rolled off her winded and she scrambled up and ran out of the cave. I chased after her. She slipped and fell into the water. I waded into the water, too. I knew she couldn't swim. Her hair covered the water and her face. I caught her by the throat and forced her under the water and I squeezed until she stopped moving. When I let go, she sank beneath the surface. I realised then what I had done and tried to pull her back but all I could grab was her shoe…"

Outside there was a sudden hammering on the door, Nancy jumped in fright and Grainger looked wildly about him. "Who is that? Who is coming calling now?"

"I don't know."

The door rattled again, "Mrs. Thomas? Mrs. Thomas, it's the police. We're looking for Grainger Mason… Mrs. Thomas?"

"Don't answer," hissed Grainger as he rose from his seat and pulled Nancy to her feet.

"Mrs. Thomas, we have reason to believe that Grainger Mason is ill. He's carrying a disease and may even have fallen ill himself. Please open the door."

Grainger put his hand over Nancy's mouth as he backed toward the back door, dragging her with him.

"Mrs. Thomas?"

Grainger fumbled with the bolt at the back with his free hand and it complained with a grinding screech as he slid it back. Nancy was fighting for breath, Grainger's hand covered her nose and mouth and she knew she would black out if she didn't do something and do it quickly. She slipped her hand into her apron pocket and her hand found the handle of the knife. Grainger opened the door, as there was a flash of jagged lightning followed by a crashing bolt of thunder. The storm was now overhead. Large raindrops powered down from the sky.

It was clear to Nancy that Grainger intended to drag her with him. She pulled out the knife and slashed it across his hand. He let go of her and shrieked, "Bitch!"

She gulped a mouthful of air and ran. Grainger was seized with another coughing fit and it gave her time to dash back indoors and lock the door. She was now sobbing in fright. She dropped the knife and ran to the front to admit Constable Pritchard, Michael and Ernie. She fell into Ernie's arms, who pacified her and led her back inside.

Michael asked, "Grainger Mason, where is he?"

"He's gone out the back. God forbid, I slashed him with a knife. The man's deranged."

Michael and Trevor Pritchard ran to the back door as Ernie settled Nancy in a chair and tried to comfort her.

Moments later Michael returned, "It's no good. He's gone. There's no sign of him anywhere."

Chapter Twenty-Two

On the Run

Grainger cursed as he slipped on the wet grass underneath the bank by the hedgerow to the field at Bronallt and waited. His hand was badly gashed, 'Bitch!' He should have silenced her while he could. He lay flat on his stomach as he heard feet clatter through the cobbled yard and the back door banging in the buffeting wind. The rain was falling more heavily now. Thunder rain the size of ball bearings was coming down steadily that soaked him through. He hadn't had time to collect his coat, which was left in Gwynfor's room. A severe pain was gripping his chest like the bony fingers of a devil skeleton squeezing at his heart.

He could hear and see someone looking for him. A flashlight played over the yard and beyond to the field. Grainger tucked himself in closer to the hedge and held his breath and prayed that he wouldn't be attacked by another fit of wracking coughs. He wondered what the policeman had meant. A disease, what disease? Yes, he had a bad cold with a fever but nothing that most folks didn't get at this time of year leading into the winter. Grainger took a gulp of air, his throat was irritated and he struggled not to cough. Fortunately the cracking thunder and lashing rain served to mask his presence and whoever it was who had come after him had retreated back to the house. The pain in his chest was coming in waves and once it eased, he decided to move on.

Grainger slid out from his hiding place now running with water. He was covered in mud more so than a player in a rugby scrum when sliding on the field in a torrential downpour. Grainger headed for a barn to wait out the storm but then worried that it would be the first place they would look. No, he had a better idea. If officials were searching for him here, then Hendre would be less guarded. He would be able to reach Laura. He was sure she would be horrified when she saw what they had done to him. She would protect him. After all she was his girl.

Grainger felt he needed a little respite from the weather, he would wait just a few minutes in the shelter of the barn and see what he could find there to help him on his way. He stumbled through the field to a stone barn close to the mountain track and dived in through the door and was besieged by a bout of hacking coughs.

They eventually subsided and Grainger wiped a bloody hand across his face making him appear more like a butchering psychopath than any stage or film set actor made up by a talented makeup artist. His throat was raw and he was uncomfortable and wet. He searched around him for anything that might help.

Although Grainger's eyes had adjusted to the dark he still couldn't see clearly in the prickling black of night in a dark barn banked up with straw and hay. Another lightning flash tore across the sky with jagged spikes shooting to the ground. Grainger used the sudden light to help him look for something, anything that could help.

Leaning against a bank of straw bales were some farm implements, a fork, rake, spike and yard broom. Grainger crossed to them and removed the broom handle from the head. He now had a stout stick to help him move through the slippery and muddy terrain and it would double as a weapon. The next burst of bright light made Grainger halt in his tracks as he saw a figure hunched in the corner. He stopped in alarm. But when the figure didn't move, Grainger ventured closer, a discarded scarecrow lay in the hay. 'Oh joy of joys, dry clothes,' he thought.

Grainger stripped the straw man. He snatched the hat and placed it on his head, ripped off his jacket and shirt, and donned the striped collarless cotton ticking shirt, waistcoat and long dress coat. It was a little tight but it was dry. He grabbed the ragged trousers but dismissed the idea of wearing them. He didn't want to look like a tramp and frighten Laura. Grainger watched through the open stone window of the barn. He could see Bronallt was well lit and moving lights were sweeping the ground outside. No doubt they were searching for him. He needed to move and quickly. He gasped sharply as another stabbing pain ran through his heart. He forced himself to recover and looked out across the land.

The deluge that had nearly drowned him was easing now and the moon that had been previously hidden by thick clouds began to shine its ghostly silver light across the land.

Cattle stood like sentinels in the fields. Horses in the stables could be heard whinnying their complaint at the ravages of the storm. Grainger grabbed his stout staff and left the relative comfort of the dry barn and continued through the fields keeping close to the hedgerows that skirted the track and mountain road. Water streamed down the road like a river. It was awash with sticks, stones, mud and other debris. That gave Grainger some comfort that anyone in pursuit would not find the way easy. He trekked on driven by an insane resolve. His eyes were now wildly manic and he looked barely human, but more like a character from Bram Stoker's Dracula. His blood streaked muddy face, the coat tails that flapped like an avenging crow foretelling the approach of death, and his laboured gait all served to make him look even more demented. Ignoring the agony that seemed to be hitting his vital organs, he pressed on.

In spite of everything Grainger made good time. He had to pause frequently to recover from bouts of severe coughing and griping pains first in his chest and then his kidneys. His throat felt as if it was gummed up with something. He suspected his glands were up.

Grainger tumbled down the last few yards of the track and darted across the deserted road. He hurried toward the Crescent where gas lamps shone their muddy hue pooling their dim light on the rain-stained road. He dodged through the cemetery, past the village hall until he found the back road leading to the farm, Hendre. Grainger began to climb through the undergrowth as if the Angel of Death was chasing him down.

He stopped on the slippery scree and stared at the boiling, swollen black river that rushed through the valley. He would have to take care; one false step could send him tumbling down into its murky depths. His pace was slower now and more considered but his breathing was becoming more difficult. He climbed with his mouth open, gasping for air. His chest hurt and his hand was now stinging like hell. Grainger swung up onto the overhang of a rock and paused to try and catch his breath when another fit of coughing assailed him. He spluttered so much he began to retch and spat up an inordinate amount of phlegm. During the process he lost his stout staff, which fell from his hands and out of sight.

The noise of his coughing was carried on the wind and Bonnie stood up from her slumber where she had sheltered in the overhang by the water butt and growled. She bared her teeth and her hackles rose and she began to bark. The coughing stopped and Bonnie ceased barking but was still alert, she settled down her eyes watchful and her ears pricked.

Grainger wiped the bloody mucus from his nose that dripped. He moved on and arrived at the gate at the end of the yard. There he stopped and narrowed his eyes searching the night for any movement or activity on this evening where Mother Nature had wreaked havoc on the land.

Grainger sneaked silently into the cobbled yard.

Bonnie stood up again.

Grainger looking like a harbinger of death crept along the path to Old Tom's cottage.

Bonnie raised her tail challengingly; her limbs were quivering with excitement.

Grainger skulked around the cottage searching for a way in.

Bonnie raised her hackles and stood rigidly still.

Grainger tried the back door.

Bonnie began to growl a low throaty rumble that developed into a full-blooded snarl.

Grainger stealthily moved toward the front door and rattled the doorknob.

Bonnie's keen ears picked up the sound and she began to bark.

Inside Old Tom's cottage, Laura was alone and mending a tear in her shirt. She could hear Bonnie barking. She stopped, lay down her sewing and stood up. She carefully moved toward the curtained window, turned off the gas at the wall lights and peeped through a chink in the curtains into the darkness outside. She couldn't see anything.

Laura walked down the passage to the back door and listened. There was nothing. She could still hear Bonnie barking in an agitated fashion. Laura shifted position and tiptoed toward the front door, wishing that someone else were at home with her.

She was undecided as what to do. Should she flee the cottage and run to Hendre? Or stay put?

She moved closer to the front door and waited. There was nothing, no sound except for Bonnie who was still barking. Laura tried to reason with herself, "Come on, Laura; stop dithering. You can't go through life jumping at your own shadow." She picked up an umbrella by the front door and unlocked the door. Gingerly she opened the door a tiny fraction to peep out. She was just about to call out when the door was wrenched out of her hand. She dropped the umbrella and screamed as hands grabbed her and dragged her outside, her legs scraped along the stone path and she kicked and struggled but his grip was too strong. Grainger pressed his hand over her mouth to stifle another scream and he hissed at her, "Laura, stop. Stop, it's me Arthur. I won't hurt you. I love you and I have so much to make up to you. Nod if you understand me."

Laura's eyes were wide with fright and she slowly nodded.

"Good, because we need to talk. You're my girl. You've always been my girl. I know I hurt you before when you saw me with that Welsh harlot, Megan. Believe me, I'm sorry. We are meant to be together. Don't you know that?"

He paused and Laura thought it best to try and humour him and she nodded again.

"I knew you'd understand. I knew you'd care. We can be together, forever. You and me, just like I've always planned."

Grainger was slowly propelling her away from the house. Laura was in a state of panic. Grainger spoke softly again, he was finding it difficult to speak, "I'm not feeling too good. I have a lump in my throat the size of a golf ball. Pains are spreading through me. But you'll take care of me, won't you?

If I let you go, promise me you won't be frightened. You won't scream."

Laura nodded again, she could detect the weakness in Grainger's voice he was struggling to breathe and speak. He was suddenly beset with another bout of coughing. He couldn't stop and he wheezed as he tried to gulp in some air. This time, Laura could see he was choking; mucus ran from his nose and phlegm flecked with blood sprayed from his mouth. Grainger fell to his knees, trying to catch his breath. His face was a horrific bloody mask. He gestured to his throat, swollen and bullish. Laura froze and at that moment Bonnie came hurtling down the cobbles and launched herself at Grainger, full force, knocking him forward onto the stones. She snarled and bared her teeth keeping him pinned on the ground. Grainger struggled for air; his face, underneath the mud and blood spatters, was turning blue. He emitted a strange squeaking cry and lay still.

Bonnie remained on his back still growling. Laura found her feet and she ran up the path and along the yard toward Hendre and hammered on the door.

John came to answer it and alarmed by Laura's dishevelled appearance, he rushed out to help her inside. Relieved at seeing John, Laura burst into hysterical sobs and fell into a chair in the kitchen crying "He's dead, I think he's dead."

John ran out toward the path to the cottage. Laura followed him at a discrete distance. She watched as he called Bonnie off who came to Laura's side and licked her hand affectionately. John rolled Grainger over and felt his pulse. There was a faint flicker of life. He shouted to Laura, "There's a faint spark. Fetch Senator and the cart."

Laura ran to the barn and brought out Senator, who whinnied in surprise at being disturbed this night. She hastily tacked him up to the wagon. John hauled Grainger's dead weight up into his arms and with Herculean strength that he found from somewhere; he loaded him into the cart. Laura dashed back to Hendre to fetch a coat for John while John lit the lamps on the side of the cart and he set off for the village.

Laura ventured back to Hendre where Jenny was now up

and they sat together in the warm kitchen waiting for John's return.

"I didn't want to stay alone," apologised Laura.

"Nor should you. It's an ordeal you've been through. I'll make us both a lovely cup of cocoa." Jenny put a pan of milk on to boil and stoked up the fire on the range.

"Do you know? I hope he dies. Isn't that awful of me? I just have a feeling that if he lives he'll come looking for me where ever I go. Is that wrong of me?"

"I'm sure, Laura that I would feel the same. The man is obsessive and it seems he is also off his head."

"I don't want to spend the rest of my life looking over my shoulder and being forced to move on from place to place in fear of him finding me." Laura's eyes filled with tears and it looked as if she might cry. "Just when I've met Sam. He's a good man, Jenny. He's kind and understanding. He's funny and makes me laugh. I've been so happy these last few months. I thought I was safe."

Jenny made them both a soothing drink and passed a cup to Laura, "There, there. You are safe now. The man is ill and it's uncertain what will happen to him now the police are involved."

Laura nodded and sipped her cocoa. "Perhaps you're right. What is it John always says? Worry about it when it happens. I think it's good advice."

The two young women with thoughtful, solemn faces settled down to wait for news.

Chapter Twenty-Three

Resolutions

John drove the cart as fast as he dared down the track to the mountain road. He pulled up Senator sharply as another wagon's lights came into view. It was Michael and Ernie returning to Hendre and Gelli Galed. They exchanged words and information and John went on his way. John was stunned to learn that Grainger Mason was possibly a murderer.

He soon arrived outside Dr. Rees' surgery and he pounded on the knocker. Millicent Rees, opened the door and John indicated the man in the cart. Millicent called for her husband and Dr. Rees came out to help John unload Grainger onto a gurney and wheel him in to the doctor's waiting room.

Carrie looked up in surprise, "John, whatever are you doing here?" At first she looked distastefully at Grainger Mason lying so still on the portable bed but then her nursing training took over and she looked more compassionately at the man who was still and barely breathing.

Dr. Rees opened the man's mouth the acute discolouration at the back on a fold of skin that stretched down his throat had done its worst. The airway was completely closed. Dr. Rees felt for a pulse and shook his head. There was nothing he could do. Grainger Mason was dead.

"You say, this man was the carrier?" asked Dr. Rees.

"Aye, or so we thought, said Carrie. "What now?"

"I'll ask Evans the death to come and collect him. I will write out the death certificate. His family must be informed and his regiment. Do we have any of that information?"

"Laura will be able to give you his family's address and we must have a record somewhere of the ENSA troupe that Megan was in," said John. He looked at Carrie, "What about you, Cariad? How much longer do you need her, Doctor?"

Dr. Rees shook his head, "We are over the worst of it. Carrie can return with you if she wants."

Carrie shook her cloud of hair stubbornly, "I'll stay as long as you need me, Dr. Rees," she assured.

"Then, I think it's time you went home. We will be all right now. You need to rest. You can't go back on duty in the capital the way you are now. Go back with John, and rest. And that's an order."

"But…"

"If I need you I promise I will send for you. But I am sure we can manage now. I'll tell you one thing though…"

"What's that?"

"When you finish your time in London and when the war is over, whichever happens first, you will be more than welcome to join us on the district. We need good nurses like you."

Dr. Rees took Carrie by the shoulders and looked deeply into Carrie's startling green eyes, "Thank you, Carrie fach. I don't know what we would have done without you. We wouldn't have been able to cope."

John looked proudly at his younger sister, "Well, then, there's an accolade. Get your things and I'll be outside with Senator."

"If you're sure?" Carrie's steady gaze held that of the doctor.

"I'm sure. Now be on your way and at least have some of the holiday that's owing to you."

Carrie smiled and left the room to retrieve her bag and the few belongings that she had upstairs. She soon returned and bade farewell to the good doctor and his wife and climbed into the cart alongside John.

"I could sleep for a week," she said as they clip-clopped out of the village. "How is Laura?"

"Rattled."

"Well, she'll be better now she knows he won't be coming back. Horrible man. And to think all this could have happened to our Megan. Even so, it's a hideous way to die."

"Aye, but the man was demented. You should have heard what he confessed to Megan's mother."

"Tell me," pleaded Carrie, suddenly wide-awake.

So John began to recount what he had learnt from Michael Lawrence and Ernie when the wagons met on the road. "That's just the potted version. I couldn't loiter to hear it all. I had to get the man to the doctors. I dare say Ernie will tell us all later."

By the time they reached Hendre, Jenny had a houseful. Laura was there and Sam Jefferies, Daisy, Ernie and Michael Lawrence. They were huddled in the kitchen and Ernie was recounting the events that had occurred at Bronallt.

"Well I, for one, am glad he's dead. Dead and gone. Good riddance! To think all those years we thought his sister's death had been a tragic accident and it was him all along. Not only that, his mother has a lot to answer for, too."

Well, he'll not come calling again. You are safe now," said Sam putting a comforting arm around Laura who smiled up at him, "Which reminds me," said Sam. "Two men came calling for you, Miss Llewellyn."

"Me?" said Carrie in surprise.

"Yes, they looked official, from the government and wanted to speak to you. I told them you were busy helping the doctor. I believe they are staying at the Star and Garter. They said they would call again as soon as it was convenient."

"What's all that about, then, Cariad?" asked John curiously.

All eyes turned on Carrie who fidgeted nervously underneath everyone's gaze. "Before I left London I had a letter, from Winston Churchill himself. It said someone would be contacting me during my three weeks leave."

It was Michael's turn to look concerned, now. "What's this, what do they want?"

Carrie blushed, "I'm not supposed to talk about it. It's something to do to with wanting to draft me into the SOE."

"SOE?" queried Jenny.

"I believe it stands for Special Operations' Executive," said Carrie quietly.

There was a short silence while people weighed up Carrie's words. "Well, I for one don't like the sound of this," said Ernie with a worried frown on his face.

"Me neither," added Michael.

Carrie studied the expressions of those around her, who were all staring hard at her. Daisy was the next to speak, "I've had a letter, too."

It was time then for all eyes to switch to her.

Daisy shrugged, "I don't know what to say, but I believe they will want to talk to me as well."

John piped up, "But Daisy, we need you here. Can you refuse?"

"I think so. It has to be my choice. Yours, too, Carrie."

"Well, we will have to wait and see what they've got to say."

"You have a big adventure coming. Think carefully before you accept and if you do, put a time limit on it. Insist on this," said Ernie.

Carrie shivered and caught Michael's eye. Ernie had used the almost exact same words as the woman on the train. Carrie felt a nervous flutter awaken in her stomach, but she said no more.

Thomas looked out from the deck of the ship. Land was in sight. So, this was Virginia, America. There they were to dock and finalise repairs at Norfolk. There was no visible sign, now, of the beating he'd received. He and Jonty discussed the changes in their mission. "To say that I'm disappointed is an understatement. I was hoping to visit Singapore and maybe Burma," said Thomas wistfully.

"Yes, in the hope of seeing your girl," said Jonty. "But if we had been deployed to Singapore as intended we'd probably be dead. And I know, I'd rather live."

"Aye, bad luck that was. We should have been there covering their backs with good air cover. How many poor young men like us died?"

"And those that survived the sinking were captured by the Japanese. I have heard they are tyrants to their prisoners."

"I can hardly believe that both ships were sunk. Did you know anyone on HMS Repulse?"

"No. Did you?" asked Jonty.

"No, but I knew someone on the Prince of Wales. I met him on the dock at Cardiff when I enlisted. I just pray he was transferred or …"

"Pray his end came quickly. I have heard tales of the terrible cruelty enforced by the Japanese."

Thomas sighed and became more reflective, his hope that the war would soon be over looked unlikely. His eyes misted over and he sighed. "Maybe, I was wrong to sign up. Maybe, I should have stayed on the farm with John and Ernie. Who knows? Megan wouldn't have joined ENSA and we would have been together."

"Come on, Tom. Don't think like that. You should be proud to serve your country. Don't look back. If you question your actions with 'What if' or 'if only' then that way, madness lies," said Jonty trying to reassure Thomas.

Thomas said nothing but stared ahead stonily until the ship's hooter blasted out calling all hands to their posts. Thomas and Jonty beat a hasty retreat below deck. They would finish this discussion another time.

Carrie knelt on an old wicker chair and looked out at the early morning sunrise. The sky was awash with colour of the dawning. The vicious storm that had rampaged through the valley had moved on leaving the land looking innocently lush and sparkling clean. Raindrops glistened with the dew and the field looked bedecked in jewels. Carrie opened her window and breathed in the early morning air. Her eyes closed in delight. There was nothing quite like the fresh smell of country air after the rain. Her senses were sharpened and all remnants of her previous fatigue were chased away.

A handsome red-feathered cockerel crowed and strutted proudly across the slowly awakening yard. He called to the female chickens as he scratched and uncovered a wriggling worm allowing his harem to cluck in argument as they tussled for the prize.

Carrie threw on her clothes and jumped on the cold oilcloth anxious to be out and reliving her childhood memories of the joy of being at Hendre. She somehow felt that this would be a last joining with the land. Something inside her told her she wouldn't be calling Hendre home for much longer. She tried to chase the thought away but her feelings of just being an occasional visitor persisted.

Carrie slipped on her shoes, and grabbed her coat. She tiptoed quietly down the stairs not wishing to disturb her brother and Jenny. She knew they would soon be up and then the kitchen would be bustling with life, as would the farm.

Carrie crept through the kitchen and her mind flooded with memories that echoed in and out of her head playing like a film reel. She stepped into the scullery, out through the glasshouse and out into the yard.

Carrie blew into the air watching her breath steam like smoke into the crisp morning and she giggled. She felt again as if she was ten years old and laughed at the thought. Carrie hurried to the five bar gate that led to Maes-yr-onnen, the meadow of the ash tree, and clambered over. For a moment she just stood, taking in the magnificent views, the fields, the woodland and beyond.

To her surprise something touched her hand. She looked down and Bonnie looked up at her and gave a small bark. It was like stepping back in time and Carrie felt tears prick at the back of her eyes as she looked at Trixie's offspring who was so startlingly similar to her beloved Trix. She bent down to the dog and fussed and hugged her. At that moment a bond was made between Carrie and the Border collie dog.

Carrie kicked off her shoes, "What the heck! Come on Bonnie, let's run." Carrie and Bonnie raced through the grass and darted around the ash tree. Carrie squealed as she tumbled and rolled down the slope as if she was a carefree child once more.

She eventually stopped roly-polying and Bonnie jumped all over her trying to wash her face. Trying to dodge her warm moist tongue proved fruitless and so Carrie succumbed and ruffled the dog's fur that was now ecstatic at this early morning romp. Carrie laughed as she stood up, "Jawch! I'm potch! Soaked to the skin. That'll teach me. Come on Bonnie, we best head back. How am I going to explain this? You are drenched, too."

Carrie and Bonnie made their way back to the yard. Carrie put on her shoes and met Ernie emerging from the barn.

"Well, well, I see you two have finally hit it off. Like a fob watch and chain, meant to be together. It's good to see. But look at the state of you and Bonnie."

At that moment Bonnie decided to shake herself and

showered both Ernie and Carrie with the droplets of water that had settled on her coat.

"Duw, Duw. I've had my wash, Bonnie. Pied!"

Carrie giggled, "Oh Ernie, I've missed this."

"What me getting sopping wet?"

"No, silly. This," she gestured to the farm and surrounding land, "You, Bonnie and just being here. Although, it fills me with sadness, too."

"And why's that, Cariad?"

"I don't know. Maybe, because things will never be the same again. Hendre doesn't feel like my home anymore. I'm just someone who visits now and again. Somehow, I feel that my life here has come to an end."

"Oh, Carrie. Your heart is here as are the bones of your ancestors. You will return, maybe not to Hendre but you will return."

"So speaks the oracle," teased Carrie.

"Jest all you may but your roots are here and you will grow new shoots and spread your knowledge and learning. You have education. Educate a mother and you educate a family and the next generation."

"Now, you are getting ahead of yourself, Ernie Trubshawe," scolded Carrie and she blushed.

Bonnie sat at Carrie's feet and listened to the exchange tilting her head on one side, and then the other, with one ear up and the other down, in that engaging way, all collies have. Ernie took a moment before he spoke and he bent down and patted the dog.

"Cariad, I think you know your future as well as me, as long as you don't change paths."

"What do you mean?"

Ernie fell silent for a moment and stood. He then became more serious, "I'm not the one to influence your decision but I will tell you to think carefully, Cariad."

Carrie stopped, "You're being cryptic again, Ernie. What do you mean?"

Ernie sighed heavily, "Carrie, I don't know, exactly. I just feel that something is about to happen. Something big and it could be life changing. That's all I can say."

"Sometimes, Ernie Trubshawe, you can be so annoying but Duw, I've missed that too. Come on, let's get some breakfast."

They proceeded to the farmhouse with Bonnie in tow. Carrie left Bonnie drying on the rag mat in front of the fire while Ernie stoked up the dying embers and placed more fuel on the range while Carrie went upstairs to change into something dry and not grass stained.

She met John on the stairs. He looked at her in surprise, "You are up early."

"You know me. It was one of those mornings and I just had to be a part of its new dawning."

"I can see," he said smiling and indicating the green streaks on her skirt.

Carrie laughed and retreated to her room. She flopped down her bed, contented and feeling at peace with herself for the first time in many years. She puzzled over Ernie's words and sat up. Retrieving the official letter she read it again. She supposed the signature was real and that it wasn't a hoax. It was interesting that Daisy had also received such a letter. Carrie made up her mind to discuss it with her at the first opportunity. With that in mind, she undressed and washed, flinching at the cold water in the ewer as she poured it into her bowl. The one thing she could say was that cold water certainly brought her fully alert.

Carrie hummed as she changed and she trotted down the stairs to breakfast. Ernie had begun the fry up and was singing, less than tunefully, some song that was rendered totally unrecognisable. More to shut him up than anything else, Carrie asked, "No Jenny this morning?"

"Not yet," answered John. "The little one is teething and Jenny has had a few problems feeding her."

"Then I may be able to help," said Carrie recalling all her training at Bronglais and the Maternity Home. "Save me some breakfast. I won't be long."

Carrie retreated back upstairs and politely knocked on Jenny and John's door, "It's me, Carrie. Can I come in?"

"Yes, do," called Jenny and Carrie curiously entered what had been her mother and father's room for so many years. She hadn't set foot in there since the time she had nursed

Michael Lawrence through his bout of malaria.

Carrie crossed to the bed where Jenny was nursing Bethan, and sat on the edge of the bed. Jenny looked flushed and upset, "Don't mind me," said Carrie. "John said you were having problems and I thought I could help."

"I don't know how anyone can," said Jenny wearily.

"Let me try," pleaded Carrie, "I want to help if I can. I can guess what ails you, is it that Bethan has teeth and is she biting you?"

"Yes," said Jenny surprised. "How did you know?"

"Oh, I helped a young mother in Bronglais. Her baby was born with a mouthful of teeth ready to come down. Far too early. It was most unusual. I was taught when helping mothers to get their babies to attach that if they bit the nipple you had to remove them from the breast instantly, hold their face in your hands look directly into their eyes and say, 'NO!' very firmly. It nearly always worked."

"And for those that it didn't work for?"

"Try again, it usually worked the very first time. Plus the fact that if the baby is older like Bethan, start introducing them to solid food."

"I tried that. She just spits it out. All she wants is me to feed her."

"Then in that case she'll learn. I remember mam saying she fed John until he was three and a half. She thought he was never going to be weaned. It would have looked well him still wanting a feed when he was all grown up."

Jenny laughed, "My mam told me I was five. I didn't stop until I started school."

"Well, you're not alone. Many mothers feed for as long as they can especially in these difficult times. But some mothers aren't as lucky as you and find it very difficult."

"I love it but not at the moment. It's making me very sore, because of Bethan's biting. But I'll do what you say. Thanks, Carrie."

Carrie beamed and left Jenny with Bethan, who was still half asleep, and went downstairs.

She arrived in the kitchen just as Ernie was dishing up breakfast. Carrie took in the aroma of frying bacon and sighed,

"Mm. That smells really good."

They settled down to breakfast and the conversation turned to the recent diphtheria epidemic and the demise of Grainger Mason. "I'll write to Megan and let her know. She can always return to duties in this country then, where she will be safer, not in some far flung place," said Carrie.

"Good idea," said John. "Laura can relax now. She's been through a lot. It's a wonder it hasn't put her off men for good."

"No, she's got Sam. He'll look after her," said Ernie confidently.

"What are you going to do today, Cariad?" asked John.

"Make the most of the time I have left; that's for sure." Bonnie came and placed her head on Carrie's knee and gazed at her.

"Made a friend, you have," said Ernie indicating the dog. "She gets more like Trixie every day."

"She does," agreed Carrie. "Every time I look at her I think it is Trix." She sat back in her chair and ruffled the fur on the dog's head. "So, what's it to be, Bonnie? Do you fancy coming back with me to London?"

Bonnie put her head on one side and listened to Carrie and she gave a little yelp as if to say, yes. Everyone laughed.

There was a knock at the door. They all looked at each other. Carrie glanced at the clock. It was only seven thirty.

John stood up, "Someone's either very early or very keen." He made his way to the door. Ernie gestured to Carrie, "Someone here for you I think," he said.

Carrie raised an eyebrow in surprise, as John entered with a man in a trench coat and trilby hat. "Someone for you, Cariad," said John.

"Miss Llewellyn?" He had a rich dark brown voice.

Carrie nodded, "That's me."

"Could I have a word? In private."

"Certainly." Carrie stepped up from the table and grabbed her coat from the coat stand in the hall. She followed the man outside leaving John and Ernie looking questioningly at each other.

Carrie and the man walked through the scullery and glasshouse in silence and walked across the yard. The man stopped, “Matthew Reynolds, Miss Llewellyn.” He extended his hand, which Carrie took. He had a warm firm grasp. His eyes were warm nut brown with a very obvious twinkle. He indicated a smart chocolate and tan Daimler Straight Eight parked by the farm gate. Carrie noted the number FYP 555.

From the direction of Old Tom’s Cottage came Daisy in the company of another man, also in a trench coat and a trilby hat. They stepped out together along the path, into the yard and followed Carrie and Matthew Reynolds to the car.

The man with Daisy opened the front passenger door for Daisy while Mr. Reynolds opened the rear passenger door for Carrie and she noticed the pillarless body of the vehicle. She hadn’t seen a car like this before and thought it very elegant and grand.

The two young women sat in the car. Matthew Reynolds was the first to speak. “You both received letters from the Baker Street Irregulars?”

Carrie shook her head, “What’s that?”

Matthew Reynolds laughed, he had an infectious smile and engaging laugh, “Sorry, it’s the nickname given to our organisation because that’s where we have our headquarters in London,” he explained.

“It was just fortunate that Daisy here was working on the land and you had leave scheduled,” said the other man who introduced himself as Simon Lever. He had a sallow complexion, very dark hair and an impressive Roman nose that gave him an air of authority.

Daisy sat quietly for the moment without a word. Carrie was not so backward in coming forward as her mother or Aunty Annie would have said. “I don’t understand, what is this organisation and why us?” The questions were bald and demanded answers.

Matthew Reynolds cleared his throat, “We in the United Kingdom are allied to other countries in a Western Alliance against the onslaught of the Germans who, in our belief, are set to conquer Europe.”

“Yes,” continued Simon Lever. “We are part of an elite group whose role is to wreak havoc with the Germans in occupied territory, in espionage, and what can be described as irregular warfare, especially sabotage, raiding parties and in some instances special reconnaissance."

They were like a double act with carefully rehearsed speeches intended to enflame patriotism and excite the young women's sense of adventure.

"Why us?" asked Carrie.

Simon turned to Daisy, "Daisy here is fluent in both French and German. She is an accomplished linguist and represented her school in French speaking competitions and won at university level. She lived in France for a while. That makes her an ideal candidate to drop behind enemy lines or into occupied France. She could pass as one of the locals and work with the Resistance. We can do more damage to the Germans with operations against them on their own turf. so to speak."

"Yes, this is specifically a British World War Two organisation; the brainchild of the Minister for Economic Warfare, Hugh Dalton. Following Cabinet approval in July this somewhat secret group, one could say, is Churchill's secret army, we aim to recruit at least thirteen thousand to this cause and an important part of that are women. Women are less suspicious and able to move more freely than men. And we want you," finished Matthew.

"Then why me?" asked Carrie.

"You have come highly recommended. You volunteered yourself to nurse in the capital throughout the Blitz doing your part for your country. You are a brave woman. You protected six other nurses with your own body during a vicious air raid. We have seen you put your life on the line. You are just the sort of person we need. Someone who is proud to do her duty and help her country," answered Matthew.

Carrie paused reflectively while the two men studied her face. She attempted to keep her face impassive. "But I speak only average French, and no German. How could I function in either country?"

"We will train you. You will do an accelerated refresher course of language development. Records show that you have the intelligence and already know enough of the French language and you are quick to learn. You speak both Welsh and English don't you?" asked Matthew.

"Yes, but I grew up with both languages. It's somewhat different having to return to the classroom and revise a language I haven't studied for years," argued Carrie.

"Let us worry about that," said Simon.

"And what if I don't make the grade?"

"We could still use your services, you could be deployed to the Balkans where a clandestine existence is not so important as the rebellions in those countries are strong and visible. Your nursing skills would be invaluable," replied Simon.

Daisy eventually spoke up, "What about my job here?"

"We would deploy someone else in your place, to pick up where you leave off," said Simon.

"To all intents and purposes for information divulged to friends and family you would be working for your country in a new capacity for The Joint Technical Board or Inter-Service Research Bureau; names that are a cover for the real business of espionage. I needn't tell you that this is secret organisation," added Matthew.

"I don't know," said Carrie thoughtfully, "I like my job, and what I do. I don't know if I would be any good at this."

"You keep your head in a crisis, you show initiative and have leadership qualities. You would be ideal," Matthew tried to persuade her and Carrie fell quiet.

Daisy, however had more questions, "And in the event of capture, how would I be protected? Would I have the same rights as prisoners of war?"

Simon remained quiet and Matthew said slowly, "We hope that wouldn't happen. But I must admit you would be operating outside the scheme of accepted warfare."

"Therefore, I could be shot or executed with impunity..." Daisy studied the faces of the two men. "If I said, 'yes', and I am not saying that, yet, mind. Tell me truthfully what I can expect."

Simon engaged Daisy with his eyes and detailed what would be expected of her, "We would let you work out your week here to give you time to teach your replacement her expected duties. Then into London for registration and paperwork before moving onto Station Fifteen, the Thatched Barn at Borehamwood. This camp is devoted to camouflage, equipping agents with authentic local clothing, and personal effects. You will learn methods of hiding weapons, explosives, radios and other devices in seemingly innocuous items. From there you will move onto Station Fourteen near Roydon in Essex. Here specialist teams will assist in the forgery of identity papers, ration books and so on."

"What about combat?"

"I'm coming to that. Once you have successfully passed all the tests you will be assigned to Arisaig in Scotland to be taught armed and unarmed combat. Finally, you will attend courses in security, demolition or maybe morse code telegraphy before completing your training with learning how to parachute at the RAF school at Ringway. Then we wait for a slot and over you go." Simon Lever waited for Daisy's response.

Daisy pulled off her beret and shook her blonde hair. " That's a heck of a lot to take in. I don't know if I can remember all that. You've obviously checked my home circumstances. You know both my mother and father are dead and that I live with my mother's sister. I have no one to speak of, no siblings. This Welsh community has become my family, my home..." she stopped and Carrie stared at her guessing at what she would say next. "I'll do it. Where do I sign?" She smiled brightly at those around them.

Carrie burst out, "But you may not come back. Are you sure?"

"Carrie, unlike you, I have nothing to lose. It would be an honour to serve my country and utilise my skills; that is if I make the grade." She turned to Simon, "How long is the term of duty?"

Simon replied cryptically, "That depends on you."

"You mean, how long I live?"

Neither man said anything. Daisy volunteered, "I am happy to serve my king and country and use any skills I possess for the good of the war effort."

Both men, smiled agreeably. Matthew turned to Carrie, "Miss Llewellyn?"

"I don't know. I need time to think about it. Can I give you my answer tomorrow?"

Matthew doffed his hat, "But of course. We will stop by the farm tomorrow morning and let you think on what we've said." He got out of the car and opened the front passenger door for Daisy to alight and then did the same for Carrie. He touched his trilby again and sat in the front passenger seat as Simon started the car and it travelled away down the track as Carrie and Daisy watched.

"Well, what are you going to do?" asked Daisy.

"I don't know yet," admitted Carrie. "I really do need time to think."

"Whatever you decide will be right for you. It has to be," said Daisy stoically. "And now I must get on, I wonder when my replacement will arrive?" she mused and then burst into a cheerful bout of whistling and made her way back to Old Tom's Cottage.

Carrie stood in the yard and watched her. There was a sharpness in Daisy's stride, an energy that appeared all consuming, which gave her an air of authority. She felt that Daisy had made the right choice for her. Now she had to make up her own mind and she could think of only one thing, Michael.

Chapter Twenty-Four

Decisions

Carrie looked back at Hendre she knew that John and Ernie would be anxiously awaiting the outcome of her meeting, but she was not ready to face them yet. She wanted to see Michael and so she began the difficult climb to Gelli Galed.

Carrie hadn't totally forgotten how steep the climb was but she was delighted to see that she had a companion on her trek as Bonnie must have been let out of the farmhouse and had chased after her up the hill.

Carrie stooped down and spoke to the dog, "So, what do you think I should do, Bonnie? Go back to London? Or do I quit and train for the SOE?"

Bonnie cocked her head on one side and gave a small yelp of excitement.

"Hm; that's no answer. I think you'd like me to stay in Wales, help Dr. Rees or sign up at the local hospital wouldn't you?"

Bonnie barked again.

"Well, I will but just not yet." Carrie stood up and continued the hike to Gelli Galed, followed by Bonnie who periodically bounded forward her nose exploring all the new scents the walk had to offer. Carrie's mind bubbled with memories of her father when they trekked for the first time to the house known as Hard Living and she remembered with affection the time she spent there with her brother and Ernie. She had to admit that she was a little apprehensive, as she hadn't set foot in the house since Michael had moved in.

Carrie stopped to catch her breath, it was quite a climb but the fresh crisp morning air was helping her to focus and channel her thoughts and desires. What she had been told and was asked to do was becoming much clearer in her mind.

Filled with a new energy she quickened her pace and stepped out more eagerly. She soon reached the path that led to the once rickety gate that John had fixed and painted. Bonnie stopped and growled as she saw the tiny figure of Boots scampering toward the gate.

"It's all right, Bonnie," soothed Carrie, "This is Boots. You'll have to make friends with him. He's Michael's dog."

Boots stopped when he saw the Border collie. He snuffed the air tentatively but his urge to welcome Carrie who had saved his life was too much and he padded toward her making soft noises in his throat. Carrie bent down and called to the little terrier cross and Boots eagerly danced to her side making little jumps around her and licking her hand. He was so excited to see her.

Bonnie watched warily before sniffing the ground but seeing Carrie's easy manner with the little canine she wagged her tail and attempted to get to know the small dog. Within minutes the two were playing a game of chase and gambolling across the meadow. Carrie laughed in delight as she watched them tearing around in a mad half hour as she had always called Trixie's manic circular dashes.

Boots yapped in pleasure and Bonnie joined him in a frenzy of excited barking. It was to this cacophony that Michael emerged from the farmhouse with Sam Jefferies. He stopped when he saw Carrie at the gate and caught his breath. He strode toward her, "Carrie?"

Sam touched his hat and moved off, "I'll be getting on then." He smiled at Carrie and proceeded to the outlying barns.

Michael took Carrie by the shoulders and gazed into her jewel green eyes and asked, "To what do I owe this pleasure?"

"We have to talk. I'm not sure what to do."

Carrie saw Michael's expression change as he recognised the seriousness of her tone. "Come on in. I'll make a cup of tea. Bring Bonnie, too. She can have a nice drink of water."

Carrie walked with Michael up the path to Gelli Galed. Her emotions were bitter sweet. She felt a strange gnawing trepidation that nibbled at her insides and took a deep breath to calm and still the bubbling nerves. He ushered her inside and she couldn't help herself she had to look around.

Michael tried to suppress a smile, which didn't escape

Carrie. She wagged her finger at him. "Now, Boyo, don't go making fun of me for looking around. What else would you expect? I'm bound to be curious. Remember, I used to live here."

Michael laughed, "I'll take you on a guided tour, I promise. But, first tea! Sit yourself down. Boots! Bonnie!"

Bonnie obediently padded to Carrie's side and lay down. Boots fussed around his master and then sat up and begged as Michael fetched his dog bowls. He filled one with water and placed some dog biscuits in the other. Boots helped himself to one and crunched it up on the floor.

"I don't know why he does that. Why can't he eat it over the bowl and save dropping crumbs everywhere?"

Michael took a biscuit from the bowl and offered it to Bonnie who looked for permission from Carrie.

"Go on, you can have it," urged Carrie and the collie immediately snacked the biscuit.

Michael poured them both a cup of tea and sat next to Carrie. "Now then, you look very serious. What is all this about?"

Carrie began to explain about her and Daisy's visit from agents wanting them to enlist in the SOE, "Daisy will be useful as she speaks both French and German; she's a true linguist. She's also going to go."

"Does she realise that if she's captured she won't be in uniform and therefore the Germans won't be bound by the rules set up by the Geneva Convention. They could just execute her as a spy. It's very dangerous game."

"I believe something like that was said," said Carrie. "You know, this is exactly what the woman on the train was talking about."

"Yes, and she told you to think carefully. She also said that if you agreed that you should put a time limit on it. Not have to serve out the whole war. Do you speak French?"

"Only averagely, I wasn't bad at school and got my matriculation. I can read it better than speak it. Welsh and English are my languages. No German or anything else. They thought I could do an accelerated course to refresh and learn. But, I have my doubts. If I can't manage they said they could send me somewhere in the Balkans to be as disruptive as possible. In fact, anything to stop the advance of the Germans were some of the things said. What shall I do?"

Michael paused and Carrie could see he was choosing his words carefully, "It's not for me to say. I believe you are in enough danger nursing in London. Look what happened to you there and you know there will be no let up in the bombing."

"You want me to go?"

"No, I didn't say that. I'd far rather you were here in the Dulais Valley helping the local hospital or working the district and that we could be together. But, I know you well enough. You are strong willed and stubborn and will always do what you think is right."

Carrie pursed her lips and frowned, "Michael Lawrence, you are no help whatsoever."

"And if I told you not to go would you take any notice?"

"I might."

"Then, don't go."

"But, I want to do my best for my country…"

"See what I mean," laughed Michael. "You can be infuriating, Caroline Llewellyn."

Carrie had the good grace to blush, "I know. But, I really don't know what to do…"

"Only you can make the decision. I suggest you talk it over with your family and sleep on it. When do you have to make up your mind?"

"I promised I'd let them know tomorrow."

"Then in the meantime how do you want to spend today? Michael leaned across and tilted her chin, "With me, I hope. I have had your company just once since you've been back."

"That's not true," murmured Carrie.

"Once exclusively," reiterated Michael.

Carrie was forced to agree, "Exclusively… yes. And on that note, I must go." She stood up and finished her tea.

Michael stood and crushed her to him enveloping her in his arms. He kissed her tenderly, before nuzzling her neck and whispering, "When will I see you?

"Call for me tomorrow afternoon."

"Not today?"

"No, much as I would love to see you, tomorrow will be better."

Michael sighed he knew there was no point in arguing, "Time?"

"Let's say two o'clock. I want to spend some time with Jenny and Bethan. Also, I need to go to the village and see Dr. Rees."

"I'll take you down there. Two o'clock it is." He reluctantly let her go and laughed as he saw Bonnie watching them both curiously. "Look at her face. She really is a replica of your Trix."

Carrie started for the door.

"Wait! Don't you want to see the house?"

Carrie nodded, "I almost forgot. Yes, please." Michael took her hand and they left the kitchen and entered the passageway that led to the downstairs reception rooms. Carrie was surprised that so much of the house was as she'd remembered.

"I've repainted but in the same colours. The soft shades mean I can splash colour with the furnishing, curtains and cushions."

Carrie nodded appreciatively. The rooms were welcoming and she felt at ease here. She mounted the stairs tentatively and was pleased to see that he had continued with the colours that she and John had chosen so carefully. She smiled up at him, "It's like I've never been away."

"I wanted to keep it as I knew you would like it…" he stopped momentarily and turned her to face him. "Carrie…?" he stopped.

"What?"

"I've done it all for a reason…" he paused again. Carrie could hear that his tone was serious and his eyes searched hers. She gazed back at him questioningly. "Don't look at me like that you make me forget what I was going to say," said Michael with a smile. "Come and see the bedrooms."

"Why, Michael this is so sudden," she teased.

Michael flushed with colour and Carrie laughed, "Sorry. Yes, please, show me the rest of the house."

Michael took her into the spare double bedroom. Carrie nodded approvingly. He then showed her Sam's room that was masculine in its appearance and in its furniture and was the one room that had changed from when she and John had resided there. Next, was the master bedroom. This was a mixture of styles but nevertheless elegant. Michael spoke, "This is my room and hopefully will be to your liking." Carrie didn't answer. He continued, "And now I have a surprise. Wait." He put his hands over her eyes. "Come with me, I've something else to show you. Let me guide you."

Michael walked her out of the room and across the landing and opened another door to a room that had been used by John and Carrie for storage. "Keep your eyes closed until I say." He removed his hands from her eyes and said, "Now, you can open them."

Carrie did as she was asked and gasped in delight, "I don't believe it. How wonderful. You never said."

"You never asked."

Carrie beamed in pleasure, "A bathroom and with fancy taps. It's just beautiful. When did you do it?"

"I had Sam organise the work when I was flying. He did a good job. So, Miss Llewellyn, does it meet with your approval?"

"It most certainly does. It's everything and more than anyone could wish."

"So, is this house somewhere you could live, Caroline Llewellyn?"

If Carrie had understood what Michael intended to say, she ignored it. "I could. It has happy memories for me. A bathroom! I am stunned. You are a lucky man, Michael Lawrence. That's the one thing that's missing at Hendre. And now, I really must be off."

Michael bit back his next question and pulled himself upright, "Of course. I'll see you out."

They retreated back down the stairs where the dogs were waiting. Carrie stepped up on tiptoe and brushed her lips across Michael's cheek. "I'll see you tomorrow at two. Come on, Bonnie."

And before Michael could say anymore Carrie had left the kitchen and stepped out onto the veranda. Carrie walked out into the cobbled yard followed by Bonnie. She turned back at the gate and saw Michael watching her, an inscrutable expression on his face. She smiled brightly and waved. Michael raised his hand. Carrie slipped through the gate and made her way back down the track to Hendre with Bonnie following close on her heels. Her heart was filled with love for the Englishman. Something she would have deemed impossible when they had first met.

She spoke sternly to herself as she trundled onward, “Now, my girl, you must make up your mind. What are you going to do?”

By the time she reached Hendre. Carrie had made up her mind.

Chapter Twenty-Six

Bitter Sweet

The family sat around the table at Hendre over their evening meal. Ernie kept glancing at Carrie eventually he could bear it no longer and just had to speak. He removed his beret that almost always remained glued to his head and scratched his head where a wiry tuft of hair sprouted. "You have something to tell us, Cariad?"

"Do I?" Carrie raised an eyebrow and looked cryptically at her family.

"Yerffyn darn!" Ernie exclaimed, "You are as inscrutable as a Chinese puzzle or indeed the sphinx itself. You know you have something to say, Caroline Llewellyn."

Carrie laughed and looked at the expectant faces around her, "I'm thinking I shall be doing more for the war effort."

John looked alarmed, "What do you mean?"

Carrie laid down her knife and fork, "Very well. I can see I'll have no peace, else." She took a deep breath, "As you know, Daisy is leaving the farm to go to the Home Counties and train at a special centre to take part in missions in France. The aim is to cause as many problems for the occupying Germans as possible." She stopped and took a mouthful of cordial. "But this is all supposed to be top secret. You are not to be going into the village and discussing this with anyone." Carrie took another sip of her drink.

"Yes?" prompted an anxious Ernie leaning forward and willing her to speak.

Carrie cleared her throat, "Well, there's no other way to say this… I am going with her."

"What?" said John, horrified. "You can't do that!"

"Why not?"

"Because… because… you are a woman."

"Eighteen months ago you would have said women wouldn't work in factories, go down the mines or be in ship building, John. Times have changed," said Carrie and picked up her knife and fork again in order to close the conversation.

"But, Cariad. This will be dangerous," John's tone was concerned and serious.

"And being in London with all the bombs isn't?" said Carrie wryly.

"That's not what I meant," said John looking to Ernie and Jenny for support.

"Don't look at me. Carrie makes her own decisions and I respect her wishes," said Jenny.

"Ernie?" said John helplessly.

"You'll have about as much luck changing Carrie's mind as persuading a bull that red is a calming influence," said Ernie.

"Haven't you anything to say?" queried John in an irritated tone glaring at Ernie.

Ernie was intransigent, "You know Carrie. Nothing we do or say will make a jot of difference. We can only hope that she uses her common sense and asks the right questions. We cannot ask for more."

Carrie looked bemused at the interchange, "When you have all finished, thank you." She studied their faces, "What Ernie says is right and unless I have the common sense of a sprout you can be sure I will ask all the right questions. Now, can we drop it and enjoy the rest of my time here?"

John scowled and went to say something more but thought better of it when he felt Ernie and Jenny's eyes on him. He finally relented, "As you wish, Cariad. But don't expect me to like it."

The meal continued in a subdued fashion, somehow the joy had gone out of the family gathering. Carrie put down her knife and fork and rose, "Excuse me for now. I think I will take a walk with Bonnie."

The others watched as she left the table and collected her coat and called to the dog slumbering by the fire and they disappeared into the cool evening air.

They heard the click of the glasshouse door and fell into a fevered discussion about Carrie's proposed plans.

Carrie wrapped her coat tightly around her and walked to

the mountain track. She stepped out with the dog toward Bull Rock. She hadn't been there in a long time but felt a need for solitude. Bonnie followed faithfully in her steps.

The moon shone brightly that night. There were few clouds and stars littered the sky like a thousand brightly lit punctures in the velvet ceiling. She slid on the slippery slope but managed to hold her balance and sat down on the mossy stone. Bonnie snuggled up to her and Carrie hugged the collie tightly. She talked to the dog as she had to Trixie when she was a child. "Oh, Bonnie. Am I doing the right thing?"

The dog looked up at her with her soft brown eyes and put her head on one side. Before lovingly licking Carrie's face as a stray tear rolled down her cheeks, "I don't know why I am crying or why I am feeling like this. I just have an urge to be out there doing what I can. The sad thing is that it alienates me from my home, family and friends." She smoothed the dog's fur and the white ruff at Bonnie's neck and nuzzled her face into the animal's coat. "I wish you could talk. I bet you would have something to say about it all."

Bonnie's tail began to thump against the rock and Carrie scratched her behind her ear, which set the dog's back leg off in a motion of scratching and Carrie laughed in spite of her mood.

She gazed down at the rushing water of the Black River and what began as a trickle of memories turned into a raging torrent and Carrie wept. She cried for her mother and father, her lost friends Gilly and Hawtry, and those who had their lives taken in hospital in Birmingham and London. Bonnie made a soft whimpering sound in her throat and tried in her own way to ease Carrie's distress.

"Duw, Duw, Bonnie. I am all cried out. Now where did that come from?" Carrie carefully rose from her precarious perch and started back up the slope. She struggled up the last few feet and stared into the enveloping night as she made her way back to the farm gate. There she stopped as she saw someone entering Hendre. The figure looked familiar but Carrie was in no mood for uninvited guests so instead she walked down the path to Old Tom's Cottage and knocked at the door.

Laura opened the door to admit her and Carrie asked, "Is Daisy here? I have a need to speak with her."

"She's in the kitchen, come on through."

Carrie followed Laura into the kitchen where Daisy was sitting in discussion with both Simon Lever and Matthew Reynolds. They each had a cup of tea in front of them. The two men stood up as Carrie entered, "Please don't stand up," said Carrie embarrassed.

"I'll leave you to it," said Laura and went through to the sitting room.

The men retook their seats and Daisy poured another cup from the big brown pottery teapot. She pushed it toward Carrie and indicated that she join them at the table. Matthew raised his eyebrows questioningly, "Am I to assume that you have made up your mind, Miss Llewellyn?" he said with half a smile. His eyes had an irrepressible twinkle and Carrie found herself smiling back.

"I wasn't expecting to see you today. I told you that you would have your answer in the morning," she replied with pursed lips. "I came to see Daisy but seeing you here has confirmed my thoughts."

"Well?" asked Matthew.

"I have thought over what you have said."

"And?"

"And I think I would like to be a part of your operations."

"Excellent. In that case you may as well join the discussion." Matthew looked back at Simon who had obviously been in the middle of some sort of briefing. He nodded his agreement and Carrie sat at the table and Bonnie lay at her feet.

"To recap, a new girl should be arriving at some point tomorrow to replace Daisy. Daisy will have a few days to wind up her affairs and show the new girl the ropes and then she must travel to London. Tickets will be provided and she will be met at the other end and taken to headquarters and then onto Station Fifteen at Boreham Wood and trained for three weeks in the art of camouflage, explosives and weaponry, before getting her identity papers and parachute training. Once we are satisfied she will be flown to France and dropped into occupied territory, where she will be met by members of the Resistance. They will receive their orders by wireless transmission. Her job will be to cause maximum disruption to the Germans."

Carrie looked from one to the other, "Are you sure about this, Daisy?"

"As sure as anyone can be, Carrie. I know what I am getting into if that's what you mean."

"Then that's all right. As long as you are sure," affirmed Carrie.

"So, Miss Llewellyn. You have decided to accept our offer," said Matthew.

"Yes, but I have questions."

"Fire away," smiled Matthew.

"Why me?"

"Pardon?"

"Why did you approach me?"

"You came highly recommended."

"You have already told me that. I want to know who put my name forward?"

"That I can't disclose," said Matthew cagily. "But, I can tell you that there was quite a paper trail leading to you."

Carrie frowned, "What would be my programme of training?"

"Our boffins have devised an accelerated refresher language course. So, in effect you would go back to school to revise your knowledge of French and see if you really do have an aptitude for speaking the language, which is what we have been led to believe. If you have, then you will receive the same training as outlined to Daisy."

"And if not?"

"You will still receive the same training but the placement may be different or we may take a chance and drop you in France, anyway."

"Won't that be risky for me?"

"We hope you won't get caught. And anyway, I will be there," said Matthew.

"Oh?"

"Why? Is that a problem?"

“No, no of course not,” said Carrie hastily as she was somewhat flustered by the agent’s disturbing gaze.

“Your talents as a nurse will also be very useful to us in the field.”

“That’s as maybe, but how long will I have to serve as an SOE?” asked Carrie raising her chin and head defiantly. She didn’t know why she did it but felt that she needed to assert some of her own authority on the proceedings.

“Missions are variable. I can’t answer that. But, we have had operatives engage in a mission, return home and be called up again. Some never see action again. You can appreciate we do not wish the training to be wasted.”

“So, once I agree I will be forever at your beck and call?”

“I wouldn’t put it quite like that.”

“Then how would you put it?”

“You will be enrolled and given officer status and commissioned into the First Aid Nursing Yeomanry. That will afford you some protection.”

“But not full protection?”

“You won’t be in uniform, so no, I cannot promise that. Whether we reuse you after a mission will depend on your success and reliability in the field. You could say that you will be striking a blow for equality. It is decidedly true that women can move about more easily in occupied territory than men.” Matthew paused, “Do you still want to enlist?”

Carrie looked at Daisy whose eyes glowed bright with ambition and anticipation or so Carrie thought. She was measured in her response and spoke slowly, “Yes. I think I do.”

“Think?”

“I am a woman of my word, I will do it.”

Both Matthew and Simon beamed. Matthew really was quite attractive and Carrie wished that he wasn’t.

Carrie rose from the table, “If you will excuse me, gentlemen, Daisy.”

“Your orders will arrive in the next few days and the formalities will be dealt with in London,” said Matthew. He stood up, as did Simon when Carrie left the room.

“I’ll see myself out. Come on, Bonnie.”

Bonnie followed Carrie out into the all-embracing darkness

of the night. As she emerged and began to walk up the path back to the farmyard, spots of rain began to fall.

Carrie began to run with Bonnie following closely at her heels. The rain was light and nothing like that of the storm from before. In fact, Carrie felt it was a soft refreshing rain.

She crossed the yard and noticed a bicycle propped up against the yard wall. By the time she reached the house the short-lived shower was over. Carrie ran up the steps to Hendre and inside.

She entered the kitchen where Trevor Pritchard, the local constable from Crynant, enjoyed a cup of tea. He looked up as Carrie entered, "Ah, Miss Llewellyn. I would be obliged if you could come to the station before you return to London to complete a statement regarding the activities and death of Mr. Grainger Mason. It is just a formality. The rest of the family will also give one, as will Mr. Lawrence, if that's all right?"

"Certainly. In fact, Mr. Lawrence is calling for me tomorrow to come into the village. We will stop by."

Pritchard beamed, "Then that will make my life easier. I didn't relish the climb to Gelli Galed and it's too steep for me on the bike."

"It's about time they gave you a motor car isn't it?" said John, "Or at least a motorbike."

"Funds won't stretch to that, yet," said Trevor, "But, I live in hope." He grinned, revealing a mouthful of crooked teeth and took another swig of his tea. Jenny offered him a Welsh cake. "I was wondering when they would be coming out. You have the touch, if I remember," said Trevor biting into one. "Mmm," he muttered appreciatively, "You do!"

John laughed, "I'm a lucky man. I have a wife who can cook, sing, housekeep and is a wonderful mother."

Jenny blushed. "That's an exaggeration. I manage," she said modestly.

"Well enough for me," said John with pride.

Trevor finished his tea and cake and took his bicycle clips from his pocket and clipped them on his trousers. "Thank you, Jenny, John." He stood up and Ernie rose, too.

"I'll see you out, Constable and bid the rest of you good

night," said Ernie. He walked to the kitchen door and turned back, "And, Carrie. We'll talk again."

Carrie nodded without saying a word as Ernie and Pritchard the Police left the house. John started to clear the tea things from the table as Bethan began to cry upstairs.

"You go and see to her, Jenny. I'll see to these. Carrie will help me."

Jenny smiled, "If you are sure?"

Carrie replied, "Go on. We can manage." She turned to John, "I'll wash and you can wipe. I don't know where to put the things away." Carrie took the kettle from the range where it was bubbling and took it to the glasshouse and poured it into the sink before filling the kettle and replacing it back on the range. She added cold water and frothed up the detergent in the water and began to wash the dishes.

John extended his hand for the first cup as she rinsed it out. "Cariad, when do you think this war will be over?"

"Your guess is as good as mine. The papers said last year that it would be over by Christmas. It didn't happen then and somehow I don't think it's going to happen soon."

"Me neither."

"John?"

"Yes?"

"You do understand, don't you? I had to follow my heart, find my place..."

"Aye, it was best for both of us. I know that now."

"But you don't think I'm doing right by joining the SOE?"

"No. I worry for you, Cariad. What does Michael say?"

"He's not happy. But, he knows I will make up my own mind. He's calling tomorrow afternoon to take me into Crynant. I expect we will talk more then."

She finished washing the last of the plates and stacked them on the draining board. While John completed the drying up Carrie wiped down the table and tucked in the chairs.

"No, you're right, Michael won't be happy. I'm sure of that. He's looking to whisk you away to Gelli Galed at the first opportunity."

"I wouldn't say that," said Carrie coyly.

"Well I would. If you don't see it, Cariad you are blind."

Chapter Twenty-Seven

Loose Ends

The next morning was as bright and crisp as any Carrie had seen. She felt stronger in herself and in her decision. She looked out across the yard and decided that before she spent time with her little niece that she would venture outside first. As she passed her dressing table she spotted the little wooden toy that John had made for her all those years ago sitting forlorn and forgotten. She picked it up and pulled the string that set the gaily-coloured acrobat spinning on his trapeze and smiled. She popped it in her pocket and ran down the stairs.

Ernie had avoided her that morning or so she had thought and in that she was not happy. She determined to seek him out when he returned from milking and ask him some searching questions. But for now she was content to run out in the yard and across the meadow with Bonnie at her heels.

Carrie felt liberated and free. She instinctively knew that her life would change and she was determined to embrace it all. Carrie sped through the grass crunchy with a light frost and played with the collie dog. It was as if Trixie had been reborn and Carrie relished the trust that was growing up between them.

In wild abandonment she laughed delightedly and ran with the dog forgetting that she would soon have to turn around and clamber back up the slope. The climb home was steep but Bonnie raced ahead as if on the flat. Carrie was puffing as she reached the farm gate. "Duw, I am not as fit as I was. I know what Ernie meant when he said his knees were out of breath, mine are now, too."

Bonnie barked happily and Carrie opened and swung on the gate as if she were a child again. She crossed the yard to the house and stepped lightly inside where Jenny was cleaning the inside of the windows. Bethan was in her playpen and had pulled herself up and was toddling around the wooden frame like a miniature prisoner. Carrie smiled and lifted her out. She held onto Bethan's tiny hands, which allowed her to walk a little way before she sat down with a bump onto the parlour carpet. Carrie sat down with the child and began to play. Carrie grabbed the colourful spinning top lying on its side and pumped the handle until it whirred and spun and little Bethan clapped her hands and gurgled with laughter. Carrie chattered to her niece constantly telling the little girl everything that she was doing, like a running commentary.

It was then she remembered the little toy in her pocket and pulled it out to show Bethan whose face lit up in wonder at the tiny acrobat. Carrie offered the child the toy. Bethan's plump dimpled hands clasped it and she tried to copy the action to make the trapeze artist spin. Her little mouth quivered in dismay when she was not successful so Carrie paced her hands over Bethan's and helped her to pull the string and showed her where to hold the toy so that it would work and Bethan's face immediately creased into smiles of glee.

They sat together for sometime playing with Bethan's few toys, her rag doll and wooden bricks. Carrie made up her mind that when she could afford it she would buy her niece the dolls' house she had never had. She remembered being envious of Megan's little wooden house and the games they had played together with setting out the mini furniture items in the rooms and resolved to ask her friend if she could perhaps purchase it from her if she still possessed it.

The minutes clicked by happily for aunt and niece until Bethan became sleepy. Jenny whisked her away to her cot and Carrie began to prepare lunch for everyone. She was anxious to see Ernie and she didn't have long to wait, as he was the first in from his work followed hotly on his heels by Bandit.

"Jawch, Bandit! Anymore fluttering around my feet and I'll make a headdress of your feathers and a tasty pie from the rest of you."

"Go on with you," admonished Carrie. "You're as likely to do that as I am to mint my own money."

"Maybe, or maybe not. If I could get oranges I fancy he'd go well roasted with a drop of sauce," said Ernie with a twinkle in his eye.

"You don't mean that," laughed Carrie. "But talking of sauce, we need to have a bit of a chat."

"Aw, what now, Cariad?"

"You've said nothing to me about my plans. In fact you've been avoiding me and the whole topic."

"Have I now?"

"Yes. Come on, tell me what you think, please."

"And would it make any difference if I did?"

"Probably not."

"Then there's no point."

"Surely you must have some words of wisdom for me?"

"I'll say this and no more. What adventure you are embarking on will be exciting and dangerous. Don't do more than you should and come home safe."

"Ernie! That tells me nothing," exclaimed Carrie.

"Carrie, trust your heart. But don't forget us at home or those who love you, for there are many. I for one couldn't bear it."

Carrie crossed to the little portly man and gave him a hug. "Ernie, I will never forget you, or any of you at Hendre and I fully intend on coming back. You will see."

"Iechy dwriaeth!" he blustered, and blushed. "Cariad, I am just worried that something may happen and you won't want to come back to us."

"That's not going to happen. As you so rightly said, my happiness lies in my own back yard."

The conversation was halted by the arrival of John, who went to the sink to scrub his hands clean in readiness for lunch and Jenny came down stairs."

"She's asleep. Thanks for playing with her, Carrie. You have tired her out that's for certain."

Carrie smiled, "It was a pleasure. I thoroughly enjoyed myself. And now, come and sit up. I have prepared a feast for the workers in your honour."

The kitchen in Hendre was filled with lively chatter as they sat together and shared the meal Carrie had prepared. Carrie studied the faces of those around her talking animatedly and she was filled with an indescribable longing and tender affection for them all. Her heart was full and it was clear to her that in no other place would she find such peace and love.

John was fired up and began telling a series of jokes that Carrie had never heard before. She really felt that she had never seen everyone so happy and joyous since the time her Aunty Annie had come to stay and her father was alive, and a virtual lump rose in her throat and she struggled to blink back the wave of emotion that flooded through her.

It was to this scene of frivolity that Michael arrived. He gazed bemused at the assembled company just in time to hear the last of John's jokes.

"Now think, what do you call a cow with no legs?"

Jenny offered, "Sad."

"No, Ernie?"

Ernie took a guess, "Dead?"

"Come on, John tell us," pleaded Carrie.

"Ground beef!" and he roared with laughter and everyone groaned and then joined in.

Carrie rose from the table and bade them goodbye, "I am not trying to get out of the washing up."

"Go on with you, it was all arranged and what you were thinking all the time," laughed John teasing her.

Carrie went to say something but thought better of it and giggled. "Think what you like. I am away. Come on, Michael." She grabbed his hand, snatched her coat from the stand and skipped outside with him and they made their way to the waiting wagon.

"Crynant next stop," she called as Michael helped her up and off they went. "You have to make a stop at Pritchard the Police. He wants statements from all of us over that Grainger Mason business."

Carrie and Michael chattered and laughed all the way down the mountain track and road. It was as if they were both avoiding the subject of Carrie and the SOE. They arrived in the Crescent and made their way to Dr. Rees' surgery. Michael jumped down, "I'll wait here. You're not going to be long, are you?"

Carrie hopped down and shook her head, "Just a few

minutes, that's all, I promise." She hurried to the door and was admitted by Mrs. Rees.

"Carrie, there's lovely. Is everything all right?" she asked.

"I just wanted to check that the worst is over. I shall be returning to London soon."

Dr. Rees came out from his consulting room and his face broke into a smile when he saw Carrie, "You're a welcome sight."

"Why? We're not in trouble again, are we?"

"No, fy merch 'i. We are over the worst now, thanks to your help. But, I would welcome you back at any time. If you change your mind about staying in the capital I'm sure we could find you a position here."

"Thank you, Dr. Rees. When I come back I shall need your help, as return I will. Of that you can be sure. I just came to say goodbye."

Dr. Rees crossed to her, extended his hand and then forgetting his usual reserve he embraced her and gave her a peck on the cheek. "Good luck, Carrie and come back safely."

She stood back, "I will. I'll certainly do my best." Carrie smiled at Millicent Rees who also hugged Carrie.

"When are you off?" she asked.

"I'm not sure, but it won't be long. I didn't want to miss seeing you."

Dr. Rees placed his arm around his wife's shoulder and nodded, "Be well."

"Aye, safe journey," added Mrs. Rees.

Carrie was quite touched and didn't trust herself to say anymore. She smiled and left quickly rejoining Michael outside.

Michael looked at her, "Where next?"

Carrie shrugged, "I haven't thought."

"Then in that case, may I suggest something?"

Carrie looked at him expectantly. He took her hands, "I know you promised to be my girl but with you venturing into the unknown I would like to put things on a more official footing." Carrie frowned and went to speak. But Michael stilled her unspoken protests by raising his hand. "No, let me finish, please." Carrie remained silent.

"Caroline Llewellyn. I know this is sudden but I know what I want. I want to spend the rest of my life with you. Will you marry me? Please say, yes."

Carrie was stuck for words. She looked helplessly around her.

"Please, say something."

"Oh, Michael. You are so special to me and I feel for you as I have felt for no other but is it fair on you that I am going away and we do not even know if I will come back?"

"Don't say that!" exclaimed Michael, horrified.

"I hope it won't happen but we can never be certain. I have loved you for so long."

"Then, marry me. Wear my ring."

Carrie looked deeply into his eyes, those eyes in which she felt she could drown and she caught her breath. Her heart beat rapidly and as he bent to kiss her she dissolved into his arms and softly breathed his name, "Oh, Michael, yes."

Michael stopped, "Did you say yes?"

Carrie nodded and he picked her up and swung her around. She giggled, "Yes, yes, yes!"

Michael shouted aloud and punched the air in victory, "She said, yes! She said, yes!" He caught her hand and propelled her to the cart and lifted her up, "We are going to Neath."

"Now?"

"Now! We have a ring to buy!"

"What about the police station?"

"Ring first, police station afterwards."

Chapter Twenty-Eight

Pastures New

Carrie studied the sparkling solitaire diamond on her finger and smiled to herself as she paused in her letter writing. She sighed as she remembered her excitement in buying the ring. Her heart began to beat more rapidly just with the memory. She was carefully penning a letter to Megan relating all of the events that had happened in Crynant. There was much to tell.

Carrie announced that she couldn't believe she had agreed to become Mrs. Michael Lawrence; or that the reaction of her family would be so positive. John, Jenny and Ernie had all been delighted at the news. Carrie was ecstatic. But now, the further she travelled the more anxious she became. For now, she was venturing into the unknown.

She thought back to her departure from Crynant. It had been hard to say goodbye, not least to Bonnie with whom she had developed an unbreakable bond, and of course Michael whom she had clung to in a final embrace and promised to return to as soon and whenever she could.

The last few days at home had flown by. A new Land Girl, Mavis, with a freckled face and bright red hair, had arrived to learn Daisy's duties and the workings of the farm. She seemed to fit into life at Hendre easily. Mavis had a girlish charm and impish sense of humour that would fit in well with everyone else.

Carrie and Daisy were now on their way to London as part of Churchill's irregular army. Daisy was absorbed in her journey and Carrie involved in her thoughts.

Carrie read through what she had written so far. She didn't want her letter blacked out and censored so it became unintelligible nonsense when it reached the other end. She was careful in what she said about her proposed training merely hinting at the change of direction she was taking in life. It seemed the safest thing to write.

She glanced at Daisy who was gazing out of the window at the countryside flying past. Daisy's face was positively glowing with anticipation. She turned from the window and exclaimed, "Not long now, Carrie. We'll soon be in London."

Carrie hurriedly finished her letter and popped it into the addressed envelope ready to post when they reached the station. She sat back in her seat and waited for the train to complete its journey. The smell of steam filtered back through the partially open window. Carrie drank it in. She loved the smell.

Daisy grabbed her bag from the rack. "I've never been to London, before. I'm so excited." She pulled down the window over the door and secured it with the leather strap and stuck her head out, just as the train gave a shrill whistle. She pulled her head back inside the carriage and Carrie tried to suppress a giggle.

"What? What is it?"

"You've got smuts on your face," laughed Carrie. "Look in the mirror."

Daisy peered in the compartment mirror just above Carrie's head underneath the mesh rack and saw the sooty marks on her nose and cheeks. She took out her handkerchief and spat on it to rub away the dirty marks. "Nothing a bit of spittle and a hankie won't cure. My mother swore by it," chuckled Daisy practically.

Carrie laughed in agreement and added, "I don't expect you will get to see much of London with all the training we have to do."

"No? But, surely, we're bound to have some time off, aren't we?" Carrie shrugged in a non-committal fashion. "What are you doing about your job?" asked Daisy. "Aren't they expecting you back in Camberley?"

"According to the agent they will keep my position open for me. It's me letting my friends know that could be difficult."

"Yes, I'm sure that could be tricky," agreed Daisy. She peeped out of the window again, "We're coming into the station, now." She peered in the mirror again to check there were no more grimy stains on her face.

They waited for the train to stop and unloaded their bags to the platform. There to meet them were Matthew and Simon who soon spotted them. Carrie's hair even though it was squashed under a hat was a complete give away.

Matthew picked up Carrie's battered case that had seen far better days as Simon helped Daisy with her bags. They walked to the end of the platform and outside to where their official car was waiting.

"Amazing the train was on time. That's no mean feat in today's circumstances," said Matthew.

The luggage was loaded into the back of the Daimler and Simon took the wheel and started the vehicle, which purred into life. Again Carrie noticed the elegant design of the car with its Vanden Plas pillarless body. She sat back in her seat a feeling of nervous trepidation running through her. She could feel Matthew's eyes on her and became disturbed by his scrutiny. Sounding braver than she felt she addressed his gaze coolly, "Yes? Can I help you?"

"Sorry. Was I staring?"

"Somewhat," replied Carrie.

"It's just you look different. There seems to be a glow about you…"

Carrie blushed and felt a need to set things straight with him. She held out her hand displaying her engagement ring purchased so lovingly in the jewellers in Neath. "Perhaps it's because I have become engaged."

"Really?" Matthew raised his eyebrows, "Was that wise? After all you never know what might happen."

Although Carrie was flustered she tried not to show it, "No, maybe not, but I think you will agree that it is no one's business but my own."

"Of course," Matthew replied perfunctorily and turned his eyes to the window.

Carrie didn't know why but she felt uncomfortable about her admission and her brusque comment to the man. She was cross with herself in being drawn to him and couldn't understand why she felt like this when she knew how much she loved Michael.

Carrie couldn't help the involuntary sigh that escaped her

lips and instead of further conversation she focused on the route outside that they were taking. They soon arrived at the main offices in Baker Street. Simon parked outside and Matthew indicated that Daisy and Carrie follow him inside.

The agent showed his ID at reception and the two young women followed Matthew up the stairs to the first floor. They entered a corridor with numerous office doors leading off and Matthew headed for one situated at the far end. It was a large office with a massive, ornate oak desk. Behind it sat a man, the nameplate read, 'Gladwyn Jebb Assistant Under Secretary Ministry Economic Warfare.'

He was an imposing man with an impeccable upper crust accent. Carrie was impressed with his powerful charisma and stood by listening shyly. Matthew introduced the two young recruits and an attractively fashionable secretary prepared the necessary paperwork for the young women to sign.

They were interrupted by the arrival of Major General Colin McVean Gubbins. Carrie watched this man with proud military bearing, sporting a neat moustache and wearing an army uniform decorated with medals and ribbons. He acknowledged the new recruits and Carrie noted his formidable presence, his manly stance and the glint of steely determination in his eyes and set of his jaw.

He, too, spoke English like the aristocracy and had an engaging manner as he explained what would be expected of them in war. The knowledge imparted was disturbing. All too soon their official welcome was over and the paperwork completed. Carrie ensured she signed up for one named mission with an option for more.

They soon completed all the formalities and were on their way to Station Fifteen.

Carrie studied the route they took out of Central London and became absorbed in the green scenery flying past. Carrie had a lot on her young mind, not least what she was allowing herself to do, but thoughts of home and Michael dominated.

In the background she could hear Daisy's excited chatter and Simon Lever's enthusiasm for the training on which she was about to embark but the words drifted in and out of her consciousness and Carrie made little sense of it.

She was lost in her own thoughts.

The car quickly ate up the miles and before long they passed the sign that read Boreham Wood. Simon clearly knew where he was going and they soon entered a compound that the women were informed was Station Fifteen. This is where they would report each day.

Accommodation was at a requisitioned Stately Home that housed a number of recruits. The facilities were far better than Carrie expected as she had imagined dormitory styled barracks with sparse furnishings. This was more than a step up. The magnificently grand dwelling was luxurious in both space and style. Carrie took her time in looking around the entrance hall and the admissions office. She searched for the outgoing post tray and laid her letter to Megan amongst the rest of the waiting mail, before climbing the grand staircase and entering her room, which was elegant and opulent in furnishings and design.

Carrie moved to the window and stared outside. A cloud hid the brightly shining sun and a shadow crossed her face as she wondered for the umpteenth time if she had done the right thing. She spoke sternly to herself, "You have made your decision. No going back now. So live with it."

The weeks in training galloped by. Her French improved to a more than acceptable standard. And in order to help her, Daisy agreed to speak to her during most of their recreation time together in French. Orally, Carrie was becoming very proficient in the language, her accent was good and her schoolgirl foundations had boded well for reading the language, too.

Carrie had succeeded in writing to her closest friends, Kirb and Pemb, without giving too much away, to explain that her work had taken yet another turn on life's path. Daisy was three weeks into her camouflage and explosives training. Carrie was the same time into her language course.

Daisy moved onto Station Fourteen to be equipped with her documents, fake ID and ration book before travelling to Scotland for her paramilitary training. Carrie spent two more weeks perfecting her French until her superiors were happy.

She underwent an oral test and was deemed fit to complete the rest of her rigorous training.

Carrie was selected to be a wireless operator and spent days in the classroom learning ciphers and how to operate the equipment. She learned the rudiments of weapon training, the manufacture of explosives and bombs and the art of camouflage. There was much to learn but Carrie was an able and willing student. She was tested in the field and approved as a telegraphic engineer.

She was soon ready for her fake documentation and ID at Station Fourteen. It was then onto Arisaig, Scotland for the final part of her training. Now, she had to learn how to jump from a plane and parachute down to earth safely.

Carrie's new identity was Madame Yvette Dupont her background was to be a married nurse on the district services in and around Le Havre. She had to be solid in her cover story and endured strict and exacting questioning. Carrie began to understand how an actress felt learning lines and in playing a part and her thoughts turned to her friend Megan.

Megan was suffering in the extreme heat of Burma but coping… just. Several of the song and dance numbers had been changed to suit the climate and the show had undergone a complete overhaul. The concert had become more of a cabaret and revue with an active sing-a-long of well-known songs from films and shows that had proved to be popular amongst the servicemen. They had been ordered to have their stay extended beyond the initial six weeks. Problems in transportation meant that they had been stranded in Burma for nearly ten weeks and had two more weeks left to run before a plane could be landed to fly them out.

Megan sighed. She hadn't received a letter from Thomas in a month and wondered how he was faring. Her friend Janet had become involved with the young soldier, Corporal Bernard Sadow they had met on arrival. In fact, he had taken Megan's idea of a suitcase on wheels and designed a prototype, which the young women thought was excellent.

"Now, Bernard you can fit my case with wheels and then I won't question the patent when you register it," laughed

Megan. "And if you make a fortune don't forget me!"

Bernard drawled, "Rest assured, Megan I won't forget where the idea came from. You never know…"

Janet laughed, "You'll be millionaires. I'll bet."

Megan smiled, "I live in hope! And now I must leave you, I am so hot I think I am about to melt. I need to get cleaned up before tonight's show. I had heard that we have a lot of sailors being transported from the docks, this afternoon. Do we know what ship they're from?"

"I'm not sure," said Bernard. "Two ships are supposed to have docked on their way to Singapore."

"Do you know which ones?" questioned Megan.

Bernard shook his head, "Why? Is it important?" Janet piped up, "Megan's beau is in the navy. She hasn't seen him in almost a year."

"Ah!" nodded Bernard sagely. "Then we will have to wait and see." He grabbed Janet's hand and they ran off together to the edge of the camp.

Janet looked back and called, "See you at the half."

Megan waved and nodded and made her way back to their hut slapping at the dive bombing insects that proliferated in the heat and that pestered and annoyed.

Megan flung herself on her bunk and pulled the mosquito and fly net around her affording her some protection against the bloodsucking insects. She glanced at her watch. She had a couple of hours before she had to get into costume and her half hour call. She closed her eyes for a moment and relaxed.

It was too hot to sleep. The heat was debilitating and Megan truly believed that she would never become acclimatised to the severe temperature. How she longed for the soft refreshing rain of home.

There was a barrage of knocks on the door. Megan opened her eyes and called for whomever it was to enter. Freddie poked his head around the door. "Letters for you, Megan."

Megan sat up, pulled back her net and received three letters. She turned them over in her hand and pulled the net back to cover her. One was in her mother's hand, one in Carrie's and one from Thomas. She decided to save Thomas's letter to last and opened Carrie's first. She was aghast at the account of events in Crynant and amazed at her friend's actions in London although Carrie had been more than modest in her description of her activities. Some words had been blacked out like the name of the hospital, which had been bombed. Megan was somewhat unsure of all the changes that were happening in Carrie's life. It sounded as if Carrie was embarking in a totally different direction, which Megan found hard to believe.

Megan oohed and aahed aloud at each new revelation but had to confess that she was somewhat relieved by the knowledge that Grainger Mason would no longer torment any other woman.

Her anger rose when she read her mother's missive, which described all that Grainger Mason had put her through. She now wished she had reported the man sooner and stopped him before he had wreaked such havoc.

Lastly, with a trembling hand she opened the final letter and sighed with longing at the opening endearment. "My dearest, darling." Megan read on trying to piece together the censored information. She understood his ship had been repaired and wondered what had happened so it needed repairs. That knowledge was denied her. She also worked out he was somewhere hot and travelled extensively seeing much of the world. She looked up and said a swift prayer, "Oh Lord, I pray that I may see my Thomas again before the end of this war. Please put an end to this strife and warfare so we may all live in peace. Even more importantly protect and keep him and all my family and friends alive, oh and me, too. Amen."

Megan flopped back holding her letters to her heart and closed her eyes drifting into that netherworld bordering between consciousness and dozing sleep. She felt she had only lain there for ten minutes but she came to when the hut door opened and Janet breezed in.

"We better get a move on, don't you know the time?"

Megan looked at her watch and squealed, "Goodness gracious! I must have dropped off." She fought with the netting as she scrambled out and hastily tucked her letters into her locker. "Come on! I want to warm up before the men take their seats."

"You'll be lucky!" chortled Janet. "They are already arriving in their droves. It's a big audience tonight. They are being bussed into camp."

Megan fled the hut amid Janet's laughter and hurried to the stage area. Janet had been right and sailors were already occupying some of the seats. She flew around the back of the stage to accompanying wolf whistles and cheers and changed into her first costume. She tried to apply some makeup in the sticky heat and she brushed her hair that was already slightly damp with sweat.

The cicadas chirruped and the whine of insects could be heard harmonising with the hum of mosquitoes as the females hunted for their favourite brand of blood to give them strength to lay yet another batch of eggs.

Janet hurried to her place in the makeshift dressing room next to Megan and began to change.

"What kept you?" asked Megan.

"I know, I know. I got waylaid. Can you do me up at the back?"

Megan dutifully, hooked up the back of Janet's spangled costume, as she twirled her hair into a topknot and decorated it with a freshly cut Myanmar flower and a sprig of Jasmine blossom.

"Gosh that Jasmine is just divine!" exclaimed Megan. "What a beautiful perfume."

"Here," said Janet, "I cut a piece for you, too."

Megan slipped the proffered bloom into her hair and clipped it in place.

Freddie popped his head around the curtain, "Act One beginners. This is your five minute call."

"What happened to the rest?" asked Janet.

"Been and gone," said Freddie. "You were both late," he said accusingly.

"I was here for the quarter," said Megan. "Sorry, Freddie. I fell asleep."

"As long as you're ready now?"

"Raring to go," said Megan sounding more confident than she felt.

Megan and the rest of the troupe waited in the wings for the official opening announcement from Bill, then James Adams, the pianist, struck up the introduction to the opening number.

Megan stepped out and stopped Bill with his whistle and flag, and she sang, "Pardon me, boy – Is that the Chatanooga choo choo?"

Janet tap danced across from the other side and joined in, "Track twenty-nine – Boy, you can give me a shine."

Gary Wilson somersaulted on waving his polish and duster. The whole troupe filled the stage with activity and the number flowed on finishing with rapturous applause from the servicemen in the audience who went wild at the sight of the attractive women on stage.

The show progressed without a hitch and in spite of the sticky heat they all managed the energetic show with panache. They took their curtain call and ran off stage. Megan shoved her head and hair into a bucket of supposedly cold water that was in fact air temperature and therefore warm. Megan shook her locks like a dog shedding water after a swim as Freddie called out, "Megan someone to see you."

Megan looked up surprised, her bedraggled locks sticking to her head. She popped her head around the curtain and gasped in delighted surprise as she saw Thomas standing before her. She promptly whooped and then burst into tears as Thomas caught hold of her and lifted her up in the air. He nuzzled her neck in spite of her wet hair and kissed it passionately. "So sweet the flesh of the neck…" Megan threw herself into his embrace and wrapped her legs around his waist. He lifted her up and deposited her on the trestle table top housing her makeup and hair adornments used in the show.

Megan whispered, "My prayer has been answered. Thomas, I love you so much."

They held onto each other as if their very lives depended on it. Megan slipped down his body and felt Thomas's pressing desire. She was filled with sharp needles that set her belly on fire. Megan had never felt such a desperate yearning. The pupils in her eyes dilated and she swooned into his arms and they clung together as if they would never part.

"I know we were going to wait," whispered Thomas his

voice throaty with emotion. "But, we don't know what is going to happen. Why don't we get married now?

"What, here?"

"Why not? There's a chaplain in the camp. What do you say?"

Megan was stuck for words. She looked around her wildly and exclaimed, "All right. Let's do it."

Hand in hand they ran from the back stage area and into the milling throng of servicemen. Megan could see that Thomas was searching about him crazily looking for the ship's chaplain. It was clear from his expression that he was filled with euphoria. Megan couldn't help herself and she giggled mischievously. She spotted Janet hand in hand with her corporal and called out, "Janet! Over here, quickly."

The young couple pushed through the crowd toward them. "What's the rush?" asked Janet. "Oh… Is this…?"

"Yes. Have you seen a chaplain anywhere?"

"A chaplain, why? Oh… you're not…?"

"Yes," Megan suddenly spotted a man with a dog collar in uniform. "There. Over there! Is that him?"

"Yes, come on!" called Thomas. They dashed hand in hand to the minister, who stopped short when Thomas assailed him, "Sir!"

The Navy chaplain turned around to see the two couples and responded, "Yes? Is there a problem?"

"Sir, can you marry us? Please?"

Megan could see the chaplain studying their earnest expressions and she hoped his answer would be favourable.

"Are you sure?"

"More sure than of anything else in my life. This here is my girl, my sweetheart from home. We want to be married, please." Thomas pulled Megan in close to him.

"You will need the permission of your commanding officers, both of you."

Janet burst out, "Megan, Freddie…Major Sims has gone to his office."

"I'll go and see him there," cried Megan. "What about yours, Thomas?"

Thomas scanned the retreating crowds. "I can't see him."

"How long have you got?" asked Megan.

"We leave tomorrow." Suddenly, Thomas caught sight of his friend Jonty. He called out, "Jonty! Have you seen the Commodore?"

Jonty turned at his name and waved brightly at his friend and pushed through the throng of sailors to his friend. "I did earlier. But, I believe he's already left for the ship."

The chaplain looked at the young lovers, "Then I am sorry. It can't be done." He turned and walked away.

Megan's eyes registered her disappointment. She turned her face up to Thomas and whispered, "It can't be helped. I can and will wait for you."

"And I you," murmured Thomas. "Let's spend what time we can together, now." He took her hand and they walked toward the edge of the camp; to the groves of spreading plants and banana palms. Megan determined she would make the most of these few precious moments. She didn't know when they would see each other again. She nestled into his arms as they stood under a fragrant Jasmine bush when she was interrupted by the urgent shouts of her friend Janet.

"Megan, Thomas, come back. Hurry, quickly. Report to the stage area now." The message was relayed on an internal tannoy, which boomed about the camp. Thomas and Megan looked at each other puzzled as Janet called out. "This is an emergency. Please return now."

No one had to call them twice; they hurried back to the camp and stage area where to their surprise the chaplain stood smiling. Freddie, and Thomas' commanding officer stood side by side with Jonty, who it seemed had chased after both the chaplain and the commodore and explained the situation. He had an idiotic grin on his face, as did Janet and Bernard.

Freddie asked, "I take it you still want to get married?" Megan and Thomas nodded eagerly. "Permission has been granted. Do you have a ring?"

Megan rushed back stage and rummaged through her prop jewellery box and removed a brass band she used during the show in a sketch when she was supposed to be married. She thrust it at Thomas, who handed it to Jonty to give him at the right time.

The service was quick and simple. The music came from the sounds of the insects thrumming in the jungle and the beating of their hearts. They signed the paperwork and were decreed husband and wife. Thomas swung Megan around in his arms and everyone applauded.

Thomas's commander had one instruction, "Be back on board ship at nine o' clock sharp, tomorrow morning. Congratulations both of you."

Thomas was ecstatic, "Thank you, Sir. Thank you Jonty, all of you. I don't know what to say."

"I think you had better find somewhere to lie up for the night, don't you?" grinned Jonty.

"That's easy," said Freddie. "There aren't any empty huts but we do have some tents. I'm sure something can be arranged."

Janet smiled, "Lucy and I will take the tent and you can have our hut. Go on now before I change my mind."

Megan grabbed Thomas' hand and headed for her hut. They barricaded the door and fell into the tiny, but neatly made single bed. Megan's bravado and confidence eluded her and she became modestly shy as Thomas kissed her tenderly whilst gently removing her clothing. He gasped at her beauty and the softness of her skin, allowing his lips to brush over her naked body. Megan burned with fire. She helped Thomas out of his uniform exploring his chest with her tongue. The young lovers entwined and in the all-consuming passion of their embrace Thomas thrust against her and entered her.

Megan made small sounds, which were soft and yielding, and filled with love. They moved together rhythmically until Megan cried out and her body strained and shuddered against his. They fell back together their union consummated and the seed planted. Through the ensuing night they made love again and again, with increased trembling excitement as if for the first time. They didn't want the night to end and finally fell asleep as the first light of dawn crept through the dusty windowpanes of the hut.

With the morning would come their parting, but it would be filled with a joy that would carry them through until they could see each other again.

Chapter Twenty-Nine

The Jump

Carrie was standing at the open door of a plane contemplating her first jump from an aircraft. She had already done one practice jump from a static balloon using a secure line, which had gone well. But this one was different and from a moving plane. There was no line. The noise from the wind was overwhelming. Her clothes fluttered as the aggressive air currents tried to rip them from her. Her camouflage trousers rippled manically around her limbs. A small spade was strapped to her leg in order for her to bury her parachute when she landed. She could feel it biting into her skin. There were five other recruits waiting their turn behind her. She was filled with adrenalin and nervous trepidation with the knowledge that she had to jump, now.

Carrie's hair tangled in the buffeting wind and she glanced down at the West Highland landscape below her of heaths, mountains and moors. She caught her breath and for an instant questioned her own sanity in being there and of what she was about to do. Her heart was pounding rapidly. She took a deep breath and on being given the signal prepared to leap.

The countdown began. There was no more delay, no more prevarication and no more hesitation. The call came and Carrie jumped. She plummeted out of the plane, falling dramatically like a rock. She counted as she'd been taught and felt for the cord to release her parachute and tugged. The chute flew up halting and slowing her descent. She floated down, stilling her initial alarm and she endeavoured to land on the marker laid out in the land below. The experience was exhilarating and one could say excitingly enjoyable. Now she had to focus on coming down without injury.

However, Carrie knew her next jump would be at a much lower altitude. She had to learn to land safely from three or four hundred feet. These thoughts and many more tumbled through her mind as she tried to guide herself towards the marker.

Carrie hit the ground feet first and knees bent and had full control. She gathered in the billowing silk and glanced about her. She took her spade and dug at a patch of peat as if to bury her chute, but of course she didn't. She had to practice the action and so she dug a suitable sized pit that would have secreted the evidence from her jump.

She was soon joined by the other trainees who also worked at finding a hiding place for their parachutes before they filled in the holes and gathered together to await their pick up and return to camp.

Carrie and Daisy had overlapped in their training at Arisaig and Carrie had been more than delighted to see a friendly face in the Scottish camp, where different nationalities were segregated from each other, but Daisy had since moved onto her placement in occupied France. Carrie wondered how the former Land Girl was faring in the field, but she didn't have too much time to think as her days were filled with numerous assorted activities.

Weeks passed. She endured gruelling training in the highlands, crawling like a snake on her belly, overcoming the difficulties of the terrain, trekking up mountains and learning how to kill silently, which Carrie hoped she would never have to do. It was against all her principles. She had a duty to care for people and she said so. Carrie reluctantly accepted that she could be put into a life and death scenario, which may necessitate using one of these methods to save the lives of many.

Carrie completed her physical training satisfactorily. She became proficient in weapons handling, unarmed combat, elementary demolitions, map reading, field craft and basic signalling. Two other student agents fell at this hurdle and were sent to the 'cooler' at Inverlair in Invernessshire. That left three in her group.

One other young woman was finding the working of telegraphy and Morse Code too complicated and she was to be sent to Inverlair to be debriefed. Carrie, however, had proved to be an apt pupil in this technology and she was to complete her last jump in this final week. She was nervous about that. Her previous jumps had been in daylight; this one was to be at night and at a much lower altitude.

A new influx of recruits had arrived at their training centre. There were just two left in the original group of six with whom she had begun the course. She was glad that she had not formed any attachments with her fellow trainees. In some ways, Carrie almost wished she had failed and could return to her job in London but it was not to be.

As Carrie lay in her bed that night nursing her cuts and bruises from her last bout on the assault course in the pouring rain; she thought back to how she had gone on to lay dummy explosives and fog signals on a West Highland rail track, all done with the Railway's cooperation, and then she walked away and hid. The West Highland line had even supplied a train to the school for these exercises.

Carrie thought of home, of her family and of course, Michael and she sighed. She had begun to question her decision to enlist into the SOE, but she had made her up her mind. She would have to live with that and all it entailed. Carrie turned over and struggled to sleep. She tossed and turned and even punched her pillow trying to settle. She just couldn't seem to get comfortable. It was no good. There were too many questions swirling around her mind. She sat up and rubbed her eyes before getting up and crossing to the window and looking out at the dark night.

Carrie decided to write two last letters home. She knew she might not have that privilege once she was in the field. She watched as an army lorry turned into the driveway with the latest batch of arrivals returning from their first night excursion all looking footsore and weary.

Carrie crossed to her desk and lit the lamp and began to pen a letter to John and the family. She poured out her heart with things she had never said and knew she should in case she shouldn't return. She told them how she felt and in her postscript she added that if she returned from her mission, which she hoped she would, that she would relinquish her share of the family farm to John, as it was now expected that she would indeed marry Michael and live at Gelli Galed. Her love for them all shone boldly through every word and she was pleased with the result.

Writing a letter to Michael was not so easy. She felt constrained by her position in the SOE and the unknown path lying ahead of her. Quite simply, she was absolutely terrified of the thought that she may never see him again. On that last day together they had made many plans and now she didn't know whether or not they would be fulfilled. That thought alone troubled her but she strived to put away any encroaching pessimism and wrote in an upbeat fashion finally concluding that should the worst come to the worst then he was to move on with his life and find someone else to love and marry. Carrie so desperately wanted Michael to be happy, as she loved him with every fibre of her being.

Satisfied that she had done the right thing she sealed up both letters and addressed them ready to put into the post tray the next day. Now, now she could sleep and she returned to her bed and settled down more peacefully. Tomorrow would be a tough day.

Dawn broke and Carrie's alarm shrilled out dragging her to wakefulness. The day was blessed with sunshine although bitterly cold. The skies were clear and a fine icy sheen of frost covered everything. The pink hues in the distance suggested snow was on its way, which would further complicate her night jump. But first breakfast, before she was to report for more tests and training.

She had two hours that morning on the range increasing her familiarity with the Colt .45 and .38 and the Sten gun, which Carrie felt strongly, was not the most reliable of weapons. She had been taught to fire by 'pointing' the gun, tucking her firing arm into her hip, rather than the more orthodox method of taking aim. She had been told to always fire two shots to be certain of her target. This was referred to as the double tap system, which was specific to SOE agents. Carrie mused in her head the old adage, 'better safe than sorry'.

Carrie did well. She was a sound and accurate shot in spite of her misgivings about the Sten gun. The smell of lead shots and gunpowder filled the air and the noise was deafening as students rattled off shots at a life size figure on a winch that came at the agents at speed. Carrie believed that this was good training as the enemy was hardly likely to stand still and pose waiting to be shot!

Carrie had been dreading her next appointment. It was most unwelcome as she was to have her hair ruthlessly cropped short. She watched as the floor around her was littered with her clouds of curls and she bit her lip nervously. Her hair said something about her and made a statement of who she was but it was also very recognisable and likely to attract undue attention and so it was cut, layered and razored thin. When Carrie saw her reflection for the first time she hardly recognised herself but the master barber assured her that it would, indeed, all grow back again but for this mission she needed to look as inconspicuous as possible.

The afternoon was spent in more one to one close combat training. Oh, how Carrie wished that she had learned this when she was a child. She would have had no need then to fear Jackie Ebron.

Jackie Ebron! The memory of that man would suddenly slip into her thoughts when she least expected but Carrie felt it could be a useful tool for her. If she were attacked by an enemy soldier she would simply imagine it *was* Jackie Ebron and then she would have no hesitation in defending herself. She determined that if ever she was lucky enough to have a daughter that she would encourage her to learn self-defence. The confidence it would give would mean no child of hers would ever be mistaken for a victim.

Carrie could handle the small FS fighting knife that was used mainly by Commandos. She learned the Fairbairn Fighting System that two ex Shanghai municipal police officers had given their name to and Carrie surprised herself in her natural ability, dexterity and agility in this test. Her superior officers were pleased with her. She avoided attacks using her opponent's own strength against him. Her skill with the knife was ably demonstrated and Carrie knew she had performed well passing the test with ease.

One of Carrie's specialist subjects was burglary and the picking of locks. Her instructor, 'Killer' Green had learned his skills from master figures of the underworld. He was an entertaining companion regaling his students with tales from inner city gangland and stories of master criminals. One of the first things she learned was that you didn't pick a lock, instead you manipulated or pushed it back using a protractor and the door popped open. Carrie often wondered if her geometry teacher at school knew of the instrument's other use.

Taking moulds of keys was also a simple matter. Agents would carry a matchbox full of plasticine, which could take an impression of a key. It was easy then to make a copy. No one knew which skills would be needed and an all round knowledge was deemed necessary.

Carrie's day had been full and there was more to come. Darkness had long fallen. The skies were again clear and snow threatened but Carrie and the remaining student from her group were to go out to complete their final jump before last minute revision in 'finishing school' techniques that dealt with the use of quick disguises, and then the briefing of their mission. This leap was to be the most difficult of their jumps and without the use of a static line, which they hoped they would have when they jumped into occupied territory.

The time had come. The plane flew low as if to evade the radar of the Germans. It was flying at only four hundred feet and they had to jump, get their chutes up and land safely all within ten to fifteen seconds. Carrie went first. She cleared the plane and pulled her cord, the parachute only marginally slowed her descent so she hit the ground running. She pulled in her chute as she had been taught and found a place to hide the silk. Her companion was not so lucky.

The other student agent, whom Carrie only knew as Morag had a problem releasing her parachute. Just a few seconds lost made the world of difference and although Morag operated her chute she hurtled to the ground and smashed her ankle and broke her leg in two places. There would be no mission for her if at all. So Carrie was the last woman standing.

Morag was transported to the medical facility and Carrie didn't see her again. She had a final class in the use of quick disguises joining another group of British recruits. The instructor was an actor, Peter Folis who impressed on them, "When thinking disguises men, don't think false beards instead make small changes to your appearance; wear glasses, part your hair differently, change the way you walk and stand, alter your voice."

He demonstrated how to use scars as a disguise, using Culloden a wax-like substance that dried quickly. Women could wear wigs and do much with the use of makeup. He told them, "We even have a list of plastic surgeons who can alter the features of agents if you get your cover blown." He pulled photographs from a file to show before and after pictures of such agents and went on, "We have one dedicated Jewish man who has had radical facial surgery to make him look more German. He has since been parachuted back into the Reich to wreak more havoc there than he did before." The instructor paused while he removed another sheaf of photographs and laid them out on the desk. "Here are ten photographs of just four agents. See if you can put them together and identify which ones are the same people."

The class did as instructed finding the task difficult. They all agreed that they looked like ten separate people. Peter Folis exclaimed, "My point is made. That's all for now. Good luck."

Carrie's time at Arisaig had at last come to an end and she was to move on for the last, but not least, important part of her training. Her progress would be tested at Beaulieu where she would take part in what they called 'schemes' lasting forty-eight or seventy-two hours. These tested the agents' ability in making contact with a 'cut out' or intermediate; tailing someone in a city, and learning how to lose someone who was following. Longer schemes involved making contact with a supposed resistance member. The student was given a secret number to call in case the task ran up against the local police force who would then receive an explanation from SOE about the agent's true identity. Instructors thought more of the students who brazened out their cover at the police station than those who quickly resorted to the emergency number.

Carrie bade goodbye to those who had trained her in Scotland. She felt no attachment to anyone.

She gathered her things together and boarded the train that would take her to Southampton; from there she would be driven to Beaulieu in the New Forest to undergo the last test.

She passed well.

The day dawned. Carrie was to be collected from her holding flat and accompanied to the airfield by Ernst Van Maurik who was assigned to the Air Liaison section. Carrie was ready and waiting.

There was a polite knock at her door and she admitted a smart man with a military moustache, a full head of dark wavy hair. He introduced himself and added, "People call me Van."

"Yes, Sir. Van," Carrie hastily added. It was at this final briefing that the severity of what she was about to do really hit home. He checked the equipment she would be taking with her and unfolded her map explaining her drop off point just outside Le Havre. He then studied Carrie's sweet young face and his tone became more serious.

"Here are two sets of pills. *Don't* confuse them." He placed them on the table in front of her and opened one bottle. He shook a tablet into his hand. "These are Benzadrine. They keep you awake. You need to be alert at all times but if at any point you are tired these will pick you up. Understood?"

Carrie nodded, and indicated the other bottle, "And those I presume allow you to sleep?"

Van's expression became grim, "If you take it to sleep you will sleep for a very long time." Carrie looked concerned as he continued. "There is only one pill in that bottle." Van removed it and handed the 'L' tablet to her. It was encased in a little rubber cover. "That is a suicide pill. If in the event of capture and possible torture and only if you feel there is no way out for you bite down on it and you will be dead in fifteen seconds."

Carrie visibly trembled and bile rose into her throat.

"It is of course only to be used in an extreme emergency." Carrie remained silent. Any questions she may have had stuck in her throat.

"You will be fully briefed at the other end where you will be met by members of the French Resistance and two of our other agents. Are you ready?"

Carrie nodded. She took a deep breath and lifted her head proudly.

"From now on, you are Yvette Dupont, a married district nurse. You have your papers?"

Carrie still didn't trust herself to speak. She nodded again.

"Good. Then we must go. Don't do anything foolish like asking for a café noir. One agent has already blown his cover by doing just that. Milk is rationed. The only coffee you can buy will be black. Understood?"

Carrie nodded again. She had heard the story that had circulated about the agent who had been captured over a very simple mistake.

"My advice is always to say as little as possible. Think first and speak only when you have to. That way you should remain safe."

Van looked Carrie up and down. She was dressed in typical French attire for the time, "Well, Madame Dupont. It is time to leave. Upon your return I will meet you at the airfield and escort you back. Understood."

Carrie finally found her voice, "And how long will that be?"

Van said cryptically, "As long as it takes."

Carrie sat in the plane silently contemplating her fate. She knew now there was no going back. She gazed in puzzlement at the crate with two pigeons sitting cooing in it. "Why do we have pigeons?"

The dispatcher a fresh-faced freckled soldier passed Carrie a hot drink, as he replied, "Reliable messengers. If anything goes wrong with the flight we will release them. They are ringed with a number and there is a history of their missions. HQ will know something has gone wrong with our flight. SOE's also use them to get messages back in emergencies. I expect there will be a couple waiting where you are headed."

"What's this?" she asked indicating the drink.

"Standard procedure; a hot toddy with a liberal amount of rum in it. It's a cold night."

"I don't know if I can stomach it," protested Carrie.

"I should drink it down. It will help," said the dispatcher. "We are nearing the target area for the drop. We should hear from the pilot soon."

Carrie winced as she swallowed the warming liquid. She was not used to alcohol and hoped it wouldn't make her feel sick. But she drank it down and passed the mug back. It did indeed seem to steady her nerves.

Almost immediately the intercom buzzed and the dispatcher took the expected call from the pilot. The young man opened a hole in the fuselage and hitched the static line of Carrie's parachute onto a hook in the plane. "As you can see, you're well attached. You are perfectly safe and secure. The red light has come on. Now sit here, please."

Carrie thought he went to an extraordinary amount of trouble to show her she was well attached. She did as she was asked and sat with her legs dangling over the edge of the hole and the wind rippled around her legs. She watched the red light, staring at it steadfastly, as if mesmerised, waiting for it to turn green.

Carrie struggled to remember all she had been taught. She thought it was quite eerie sitting there, looking down and waiting for the plane to cut its engines. She knew this would slow the plane down so she could jump out straight and avoid the slipstream. She would freefall until the static line opened her chute for her. She had done two such jumps out of the five like this and prayed that this one would go well for her.

Suddenly there was no more time for thought. The light turned green and Carrie dropped off the edge of the hole and fell into the dark. When the parachute opened she had a feeling of euphoria and felt as if she was floating for quite a time. There was an impression of not falling very fast when all too soon the ground seemed to be rushing up to meet her and she thought, 'God, I'm going too fast.'

Carrie kept her body straight and upright; she bent her knees and hit the ground safely as she had been taught. But this was no exercise. She quickly pulled in the billowing silk of her parachute and attempted to bundle it up before looking around her for somewhere to hide the chute and a place to bury it. She had landed in a clearing surrounded by trees and quickly ran for cover. Her breathing was fast and she was almost wheezing with nerves.

Her eyes were now accustomed to the dark. She froze as

she saw figures on the other side of the clearing creeping toward her. She slipped behind a tree, wondering where she could lose the parachute now cumbersome in her grasp.

Carrie remonstrated with herself to stay calm. She reasoned that they couldn't be soldiers as they would be marching and obvious, not covert and stealthy. She believed that this was the team that had come to meet her and taking a deep breath she came out from behind the tree and face to face with Matthew Reynolds. Behind him stood Daisy and three members of the French Resistance, who she would learn was Andre Leroux, Annie Davide and Honore Bertrand.

Annie stepped forward and retrieved the parachute expertly rolling it up and stuffing it in her rucksack. "Too good to bury. We have a use for these." She smiled and extended her hand, "Annie Davide."

Carrie almost introduced herself by her own name but she whispered, "Yvette Dupont."

"Ah, Matthieu's wife."

Carrie's eyes widened as Matthew smiled and winked at her as if this was so. She was too stunned to respond.

"Further introductions will have to wait. We need to get out of here," he whispered in her ear.

Annie beckoned to them, "Quickly. This way. We have a jeep the other side of the woods and a safe house where you will be briefed. The Germans will soon be upon us, if they saw the plane or the drop."

The small band skirted around trees, covering their tracks as they made their way through the wood to a stone strewn path littered with small twigs and leaf detritus. They hurried toward the jeep and Annie jumped in the driver's seat with Honore alongside. The rest of them bundled into the back under the canvas. Daisy winked, "Good to see you," she hesitated, "Yvette. I am Therese Blanc."

Annie drove like a mad woman. The jeep careered along the track and swung out onto the road. They hurtled along, bumping over the potholes on the uneven rustic road. They passed derelict buildings, barns and motored through a small village. No one was about or visible. It was after curfew.

They travelled on for another two miles and turned up a

long track leading to a secluded farmhouse with numerous outbuildings and Annie drove inside a stone building where her passengers alighted.

Carrie followed the others into the house. Annie gestured to a room down two steps, "That's the kitchen. I've got some game stew cooking slowly. We'll get to know you over supper. Follow me and I'll take you to your room."

For a moment Carrie was uncertain. She wondered if she would be required to share a room with her 'husband' but was relieved to discover that Daisy was to be her roommate.

Annie explained, "Keep your cover. Don't use your real name, ever. You never know who might be listening. If we are ever inspected you will have to stay in Matthieu's room. There are some clothes hanging in the closet in there, and other items, which make it seem that you are sharing. There is also a selection of items in your own room and a district nurse uniform. They should fit. If not, I understand Therese is good with a needle."

Daisy was right behind Carrie and added, "They should be fine. You are a similar build to me." She studied Carrie more closely, "Hm, maybe you have a smaller waist. I almost didn't recognise you without your hair. Get changed and come down into the kitchen. That's where Annie will brief you. At the back of the closet is a panel. You can hide your camouflage clothes and equipment there safely until needed."

Carrie nodded. She hastily changed into working gabardine and brogues that were a trifle loose. She elected to stuff some paper into the toes to stop them slopping off at the heel and hoped she would be able to obtain some decent fitting shoes at some point. She didn't want to live in the boots in which she had landed."

Carrie made her way to the kitchen where a delicious aroma awaited her. The group were all sitting around the table tucking into a steaming bowl of the tasty fare. Fresh crusty bread lay in a basket in the centre of the table to which people helped themselves. Carrie noted there was no butter. That was a French thing. She would have to get used to it.

She struggled to follow the rapid fire of the conversation in French. They all spoke so quickly but she knew that was something else she had to get used to. She would need to practice all she could in case she was caught. Although she did have an idea that she could perhaps claim hearing loss if she found herself in any trouble in order to give herself time to think and assimilate what was being said.

The motley group filled their bellies and pushed away their plates. Honore rose and grabbed a mug. He filled it from a cask on the counter. Matthew followed suit. They sat back down and Annie leaned forward confidentially. She spoke slower for Carrie's benefit having been made aware that she was not as fluent as Daisy or Matthew.

Annie had the voice and air of authority about her. She rose from her seat and all faces looked at her expectantly. "Intelligence tells us that an isolated house on the edge of the cliffs at Bruneval has a built in radio-location receiver there. British RAF reconnaissance flights have photographed it. We believe that this receiver is responsible for the loss of many British bombers. It also gives the Germans early warning of any Allied ships and aircraft approaching the coast of Western Europe. It is vital that this receiver is destroyed as soon as possible."

Honore took a swig of his ale, "Why can't they send in the Commandos to raid the place?"

"Too risky. The priority of any raid is to get back to Britain as much of the receiver as possible for analysis and if possible any technicians that operated it. Any commando raid would give the Germans too much of a warning and it is very probable that the receiver would be destroyed. The building is very heavily defended from the sea so it is just too dangerous."

Therese asked, "So what's the plan?"

"We are to survey the area and observe." She indicated Carrie, "Yvette here will operate the telegraph messages to C Company of the Second Battalion. It's believed that 51 Squadron will be delivering the men to Bruneval. They are planning a combined attack with the Royal Navy. I have contact codes for the Chief of Combined Operations and Major John Frost."

"What about the Paratroopers of First Airborne Division?" asked Andre. "I thought they were involved in the operation?"

"Not enough man power. The players in this game have changed a number of times as you well know and now you know as much as me."

"So what now?"

"Matthieu here and his wife here," she nodded at Carrie, "Yvette, will get as near as possible to the house on the pretence of a cliff top picnic."

"What if the weather is bad?"

"Then you are out together to meet up with your cousin and her fiancé." She nodded at Daisy and Andre. "We work in pairs. We need to take pictures and get as close to the property as possible without suspicion. Our last recce showed increased activity around the house and delivery of building materials. We need to see what they are up to."

"When do we go?" asked Carrie.

"Tomorrow afternoon. We need to get you out and about, beforehand. Maybe, some shopping in the morning. Get you seen and noticed as Matthieu's wife. People need to see you not to notice you, if you understand what I mean."

"Do not worry," said Matthew. "The seeds have been sewn. You have been away on a midwifery course. It's time you were back," and he winked at her.

Carrie had rumbling feelings of discomfort at the implications of her cover relationship but as always, she would make the best of it or so she hoped.

Chapter Thirty

In the field

They set off early, complete with wicker hamper and goodies and of course, well hidden essential equipment, binoculars, camera and a radio transmitter. Matthew also popped in a sketchpad, watercolours and a pencil with completed drawings of landscapes and birds. He drove Carrie in the jeep into Le Havre. He parked in the main square and jumped out. Carrie climbed out and Matthew took her hand. Carrie knew she had to play along and so smiled up at him but the smile didn't quite reach her eyes.

He took her to a café close to the theatre and ordered two coffees. He sat opposite her and gazed in her eyes as if she was everything to him, which Carrie found more than disturbing. She avoided his gaze as she sipped her coffee, which was bitter in the extreme and there wasn't a sugar bowl in sight. Somehow or another she managed to force it down realising she would have to get used to strong French coffee. She would have preferred a cup of tea at any time.

Matthew studied a shopping list and pretended to consult with Carrie over its contents. They prepared then to shop for the items listed and Carrie went on a small tour of shops where it seemed some shopkeepers knew Matthew. He introduced her as his wife and she smiled obediently. People were friendly and Carrie began to feel less on edge. Her first big test came in a shoe shop. Uncomfortable with the shoes provided by the Resistance, which were the wrong size, Carrie went shopping for something practical but smart and essentially comfortable.

The shop assistant was a big burly man with a twirling black moustache who had an unfortunate habit of winking one eye when he spoke. Carrie felt drawn to the eye with the tic, as people are drawn to stare at horrific accidents or anything out of the ordinary. She tried hard to stop herself from doing it and forced her eyes down. She finally found something to her taste and realised that she didn't know the shoe sizing in France. Could she ask for a size four? Or would this be a blunder?

Carrie tiptoed up to Matthew and brushed his cheek with her lips and whispered, "What's a size four?"

Matthew immediately caught on and advised Carrie, "My darling, you really ought to have your feet measured, as the last pair you purchased chafed and blistered your feet. All the walking you do…"

Carrie nodded in agreement and the shopkeeper duly invited Carrie to sit down, "Asseyez vous, Madame." He placed Carrie's foot on a rubber topped wooden tile and measured the length and width of her foot. All the while he chattered on and Matthew engaged with him and the man's winking eye worked overtime. He selected her choice of shoe in her correct size and they fitted perfectly. Carrie sighed in relief and exclaimed, "Oui! Très jolies chaussures."

Matthew agreed that they were indeed, pretty. The shoes were purchased and Carrie elected to wear them. Her others were placed in a bag and they left the shop. Matthew took Carrie's hand and squeezed it tightly as he espied two German soldiers strolling through the square to the café. Carrie felt a tingle of fear ripple through her.

They hurried back to their jeep, packed the shopping in the back and left the square on route for Arque-la-Bataille. This was a village with a history of resistance and rebellion intended as the first line of defence against the invasion of Le Havre and where men were brought in to cover an evacuation of four thousand men to Cherbourg. Matthew knew that if they needed 'friends' it was there they would find them.

Matthew drove out of the square and Carrie noted the firm set of his jaw and steely determination. She glanced away and out of the window. Her face changed as she saw the arrival of German military vehicles into the square and German soldiers alighting from the vehicles fully armed and lining up in rows preparing to march through the town. Her stomach churned at what she was embroiled in and she was relieved that they were driving out of Le Havre. Regret was a word that sprang to mind. Carrie knew her stubbornness and sense of justice had brought her here but she didn't feel competent with the cloak and dagger work in the field and she smiled ruefully to herself. Michael was right, she thought, she would have been better off working on the district in Wales or returning to nurse in the Blitz. But, it was too late now and Carrie knew she had to accomplish her best as many lives depended on it. It was a responsibility she was prepared to face but didn't like and said as much to Matthew.

"You underestimate yourself. You have a strong will and sense of right, which sets you apart from many. Believe. I do," and he smiled at her endearingly. This, too, perturbed Carrie. Was it an act or something more? She wasn't certain and, of course, she couldn't say anything.

They travelled along leafy lanes and passed the odd solitary farmhouse before they came to a small hamlet consisting of a tiny church, some twenty or so houses, a little shop and a bar café. Carrie was engrossed in her thoughts and the fleeting countryside. She was hardly aware of Matthew scrutinising the landscape around him and was surprised when he pulled up in the small village square and parked. "We'll get some lunch here and see how easy it is to walk to the cliffs and reconnoitre this building with the radio receiver."

"But, I thought we were headed for Arque-la-Bataille."

"We may still move on there. I didn't realise that this place had cliff access but I noticed a path traversing the churchyard and leading up to the cliffs. Seems sensible to check it out. Is that okay with you?"

Carrie nodded, "Anywhere there are less likely to be Germans on patrol. They scare the hell out of me," she admitted.

Matthew peered in his rear view mirror, "Unlikely we'll see them here, but you never know. Come on, we'll grab a coffee and some refreshment. See what we can learn."

Matthew jumped out of the jeep and Carrie did likewise. They proceeded to the small café and bar where an old wizened Frenchman sat smoking a clay pipe drinking strong roasted coffee. Carrie could smell the aroma.

She thought he eyed them suspiciously and gave him a nervous smile.

He touched his hat with a perfunctory greeting, "Madame."

"Bonjour, monsieur," she responded, and cast her eyes down to prevent further interaction.

Matthew, however, took full advantage of the half-hearted introduction and after ordering them each a coffee he engaged the old man in conversation. Carrie listened politely speaking only when spoken to directly. She tried hard to follow what was being said without making it too apparent that she needed to concentrate. Listening to Matthew she had to agree that he was good. He fairly gushed with the news that he had his wife back home at long last and painted a rosy picture of Carrie's exploits on the district explaining that she had returned from Paris after completing a midwifery course and had been caught up in the invasion of Paris.

Carrie and Matthew soon ascertained that the old man hated the Germans. He grumbled, "Bastard Gerries. Did for my Madeleine. Heart attack she had with the fright of the bombs and the ransacking of the house. Pity you weren't around then, Madame," he spoke to Carrie. "You may have been able to help her. No doctor here, more's the pity. My daughter, too, is pregnant with my first grandchild; her husband Philippe taken away by the Gestapo. There is no one to help." He shook his head in a mixture of sorrow and anger.

"Then perhaps my Yvette may call and see her sometime to check on her? What is her name?"

"She is Adele. Adele Bellard. I am Josef Dupre."

Carrie warmed to the old man and smiled sympathetically. She allowed Matthew to answer for her. He patted her hand affectionately and explained, "Yvette nearly lost her life. It has made her very nervous of the Germans."

The old man looked aghast and Carrie stared curiously. What *was* Matthew going to say? Matthew took the opportunity to place his arm around Carrie and launched into a tale of heroism that Carrie didn't recognise. He squeezed her shoulder affectionately as he invented a story of Carrie delivering a baby for a woman married to a member of the French Resistance, while the Germans were searching the house. Carrie had to suppress a smile such were Matthew's dramatics and histrionics.

The old man nodded empathetically. He leaned forward conspiratorially, "The Gerries are doing something up yonder." He indicated the cliffs beyond the churchyard path. "Comings and goings at all hours of the day and night. Been unusually quiet today so far. Won't be for long. They're building something and whatever they're building you can guarantee it means trouble. Trouble for us and the allies."

Carrie and Matthew looked at each other. Their fears had been confirmed. Now they must try and get the evidence to find out exactly what was happening there.

Matthew finished his coffee and urged Carrie, "Come on, drink up."

Carrie drained her coffee and attempted to hide her distaste at its bitterness.

"Thank you Monsieur Dupre. We will call to see your daughter on the way back."

"Merci beaucoup."

They bade goodbye to the old man and Matthew threw down some money on the table. They walked back to the jeep.

"Are we doing this task alone?" asked Carrie.

"Yes. Let's get the picnic basket, blanket and your rucksack and get onto the cliffs."

"What about Daisy and Andre?"

"We don't want to attract undue attention. Let's see how successful we are. If we fail then we move onto plan B and we will meet our *cousins*," he winked at her. Matthew grabbed the basket and gave Carrie her rucksack. They left the jeep and walked down the street toward the church. Matthew opened the gate for her. They were startled to see two German soldiers exiting the side entrance of the church pushing out a French priest before them. They were forcing the priest behind the church and out of sight. One of the soldiers was shouting angrily at the priest. Carrie's heart fluttered nervously. She didn't understand the German or what was being said. Matthew caught her by the hand and pulled her into him swiftly. He crushed her in an embrace and his lips burned down on hers while he manoeuvred her into a position where he could watch the path and listen.

Carrie was taken by surprise and wooden in her response as

the kiss continued. He broke off and nuzzled her neck whispering, “Play along. You’re my wife remember.”

Carrie softened in his grip and allowed the embrace to become tender. To outside eyes they appeared as a loving young couple. Carrie, however, had a rush of feelings, which confused her. She knew she loved Michael but she felt the danger of the situation and her admitted attraction to Matthew was leading her in a direction that she did not wish to go.

A shout went up and a gun shot reverberated around the stone tombstones that stood like petrified sentinels on watch in the afternoon light. Carrie flinched at the shocking sound and it seemed as if the warmth was stolen from the sun and she choked back a sob.

“Not now, Carrie. Not now. Hold it together. Just pretend I’m the love of your life. We must be so absorbed in each other that we will be ignored. Quickly now.” Matthew spread out the blanket on the grass behind a leaning gravestone. He set down the basket and her pack and pulled her down. They settled on the rug and Matthew gazed into Carrie’s face. “Just focus on me. Shut out everything else.”

Carrie forced herself to bury her misgivings and did as she was asked when the sound of German jackboots invaded her ears as they marched down the path. Matthew smothered her face in kisses and ignored the world until he felt a prod in his back. He broke off and faced the two soldiers. One was leering down at them and Carrie shivered.

“What have we here?” asked the German with a long scar down his cheek in his guttural accent.

Carrie was becoming more alarmed as she didn’t understand a word that was being said. She fought to keep her face impassive and smile. She was determined not to show any weakness in their presence.

Matthew stood up and chatted affably to the men in their own language. He explained that they were going off on a picnic and hadn’t got very far. He joked with the scarred man and told them that she was his wife and they had been apart for a while. Matthew translated in French to Carrie and she nodded and smiled in acceptance. The two soldiers laughed at Matthew’s banter and strutted out of the church gate.

Carrie heaved a sigh of relief. Matthew hissed at her, "Stay put. Keep pretending."

"Why?"

"Just do it. You'll see." He kissed her again and enfolded her in his arms and Carrie reluctantly succumbed. The embrace continued. Matthew rolled her over on top of him and her eyes fluttered open as she drew away for a gasp of air and was shocked to see the two Germans watching them over the gate. She rolled off and sat up. The soldiers laughed and walked away.

Matthew put his fingers to his lips and paused. He nodded at Carrie and stood up pulling Carrie to her feet. She brushed herself down and picked up the blanket and folded it. They gathered their things together and strolled hand in hand down the church path.

"I've seen it before. We lost two agents in similar circumstances, pretending to be a couple and they got caught out. They were transported away to God knows where. It's not worth the risk. Like it or not we are supposed to be married, we have to be convincing."

Carrie said nothing. They rounded the corner of the church where they had seen the minister propelled outside. They walked around the back and found the priest slumped against the church wall. Carrie ran to the man's side and tested his pulse. He was alive but in shock.

Matthew helped the man up. He bore the marks of a blow to the head and stood there dazed. Carrie saw that the front of the man's trousers were wet and her heart went out to him.

"I thought they were going to kill me," croaked the priest.

"We heard gunshots," said Matthew.

"They blindfolded me. One pressed a pistol to my head. They told me I was going to die. He took off the lock and then the other one fired into the air before hitting me with the butt of the gun. I collapsed with fright. They just laughed."

"You poor man. Let me see." Carrie examined his wound and snapped her fingers for the small first aid kit in the rucksack.

"My wife is a nurse," said Matthew. "Let her see to your head."

Carrie could smell the coppery odour from the seeping blood and swallowed hard. Wanton violence such as this sickened her and she said as much. "Damn Germans!"

"Ah, Madame. Where will this war end? I know not. I just fear that many more will die and divisions between countries will spread like a canker. I fear the whole world will become embroiled in this. We must pray to God for deliverance."

Carrie didn't quite follow all that the priest said but realised her agreement was needed and she nodded her head making positive sounds and allowed Matthew to speak for them.

Carrie swiftly and competently cleaned the man's wound although inside she trembled. The old minister took her hands and kissed them, his rheumy eyes filled with tears and he added, "I weep for the children of war, our soldiers and the land. My soul cries, too for the invading forces, who blindly follow orders with no conscience of their own. Go in peace, Madame and thank you."

"Will you be all right?" asked Matthew.

The priest assented, "I will now. Your names? May I know your names?"

"I am Yvette Dupont and this is my husband Matthieu," replied Carrie.

"God bless you both." The old man entered the back door into the vestry and vanished from view.

Matthew and Carrie packed up their things and proceeded to the path that led up the hillside to the cliff top. The path was steep and the blades of grass rippled like water on a lake in the breeze.

Matthew left the path and spread the blanket out on the fragrant carpet of green and there they sat, taking in the extensive view of the sea and waves driving into shore to smash against the cliff. He opened the picnic basket and removed the artist pad, pencil and paints placing them to the side.

"There's a road on the other side of that isolated house," observed Carrie.

"That's the one we have to watch. I'll take out the picnic things, you keep an eye on the property."

Carrie removed the binoculars from her rucksack and swept

them across the cliff and studied the house. "Lorries are unloading what looks like building materials. Whoa! There are a whole squad of German soldiers."

"What are they doing?"

"I can't tell. Too many of them moving around."

"Keep looking."

"Oh, Duw!"

"What?"

"There's a …"

"What?"

"It looks like they *have* built a radio receiver there."

"Then it's confirmed. No wonder we are losing so many bombers. They have advance notice of any Allied aircraft or ships approaching these waters. It must be destroyed."

"I said it looks like it. I can't be certain. Too many bodies keep getting in the way."

"You will have to radio base and inform them. We need RAF reconnaissance planes to photograph the thing to be absolutely sure."

"I thought they had already done that?"

"It won't hurt to be absolutely certain."

"If it is they could be blown out of the sky. I've just caught sight of some type of machine gun. It's huge." Carrie hurriedly put down the binoculars. "I think I've been spotted. One of them has just pointed our way."

"Give me the glasses," ordered Matthew.

Carrie passed them to him and he secreted them in the false bottom of the picnic basket. "Come here." Matthew swept her into his arms again. "This will just confuse them. They may not have seen the binoculars."

A shout went up from the Germans on guard that echoed across the cliffs to them. It seemed they had spotted something, whether it was the glint of glass in the afternoon sun or not they didn't know. Four soldiers jumped aboard an army vehicle and started out of the grounds. One kept a close watch on the couple, Carrie and Matthew, who remained on the cliffs and were acting with innocence as if oblivious to the stir they had caused.

Matthew picked up his pad and pencil and began to sketch the cliff top and the church building below them at the bottom of the path. Carrie poured out a drink from the Thermos flask and set out some bread and cheese, reinforcing the idea they were a picnicking couple interested in the beauty of the countryside.

Carrie tore off a hunk of bread and piece of cheese. She nibbled at it as she watched Matthew draw. He was good, she thought. He had real talent. She was finding it difficult to still the churning in her stomach. She didn't feel like food but knew the picture they made had to be convincing so she took another bite with more enthusiasm fully aware that their every move was being watched.

Matthew placed down his sketchpad and helped himself to some bread and cheese. He sipped from the proffered drink before throwing the rest away and taking Carrie in his arms once more. He whispered, "Be brave and still. I can hear the engines approach."

Carrie felt that her heart would leap out of her chest it was pounding so hard but she submitted to Matthew's embrace and allowed herself to be enfolded in his grasp. He kissed her again. The turbulence and confusion of her feelings was exacerbating her inner turmoil and nerves. She knew she had to trust and in her head she prayed to her mother to calm her fears and still her beating heart.

The roar of a jeep churning up the grass and earth beside them filled her with horror. Only Matthew remained calm. Four German soldiers alighted and shouted angrily at them and Matthew broke away from Carrie and put his arm around her protectively as the soldiers surrounded them and drew their pistols.

One soldier with a lean saturnine face yelled gruffly at Matthew and hauled him to his feet while Carrie shivered miserably and silent. He bellowed in Matthew's face and a torrent of questions and abuse hurtled from his lips. Matthew was apologetic to the men and Carrie watched fearfully and listened not understanding what was being said.

Another soldier picked up the sketchpad and rifled through it. He alerted the officer in charge who snatched the book away and examined its contents as Matthew tried to explain. He was rewarded with a savage blow to his cheek, which sent him reeling and instinctively Carrie rushed to his side. The German ripped out the pictures and tore them to shreds. He kicked over their Thermos and grabbed up the bread and cheese passing it to another who chomped on it, his grin like the maw of a shark. The officer littered the cliff top with the torn sketches. Some pieces fluttered down sadly toward the sea like lost confetti. Carrie did not know what to do.

The one chewing the bread and cheese tossed it down and roughly yanked her up he pulled her close to him and held her face between his bony fingers and blew out the food from his mouth into her face. Matthew made a move to help Carrie and was bludgeoned again.

Matthew rose up defiantly initially but then his tone became one of concern, questioning and apologising. A tirade of expletives spat out from the officer's mouth and Matthew delicately attempted to placate the man. Carrie caught one or two words and recognised the name Adele Dupre, as Matthew indicated her. Carrie's eyes widened in shock; she had never felt so terrified in all her life.

Matthew continued to soothe the German's anger as he reiterated apologies and explanations. Finally, they were ordered to pack up their things and move, gesturing them away and back to the small hamlet.

Matthew hurriedly gathered their things together. His face was swelling from the blows and his right eye was half closed and turning blue with bruising. He picked up Carrie's rucksack and handed it to her while he gathered the blanket and few items that remained intact. Matthew took her hand and they began to return to the cliff path.

Carrie froze as the officer shouted after them, "ALT!"

They stopped and turned to see the man making an obscene gesture to which all the Germans laughed before ordering them away again.

Carrie and Matthew half ran and half stumbled down the cliff path toward the church and were infinitely relieved when they were not followed or stopped again.

Chapter Thirty-One

Keeping up the pretence

Carrie and Matthew hurried past the church and back into the small village. Matthew ran to the jeep and stowed away the picnic basket. He took Carrie's hand, "Come on."

"Why? Where are we going?"

"Back to the café. You are going to check out Adele's health…"

"But…"

"No buts. We said we'd drop by and you need to maintain your cover, if they decide to check."

"I heard you mention Adele's name."

"Then you know we must follow through."

Matthew entered the café as Josef emerged from out the back. He took one look at Matthew's face, "Germans?" Matthew nodded. "Come in. Entrez."

Josef ushered Carrie and Matthew through to the back of the café and sat Matthew down.

"Non, no. Yvette will see to your daughter first. I can wait."

Josef pursed his lips and acknowledged Carrie urging her to follow him. Carrie progressed out through the kitchen into a back scullery where a heavily pregnant young woman was scrubbing some clothes. Josef explained, "This is Yvette. She is a nurse. She will check you over."

Adele wiped her hands. Her face was flushed and she looked exhausted and worried. Carrie noticed that Adele's feet were puffy, her legs swollen. She spoke to her slowly and gently, "We need to get you on a bed with your feet elevated. Leave what you are doing. Where is your bedroom?"

Adele pointed at the crooked staircase hidden behind a pine door reminiscent of the one at home at Hendre. Carrie followed Adele up the stairs and into a prettily decorated bedroom. Carrie waited until Adele was on the bed and removed two cushions from the bedside chair and placed them under Adele's feet. She checked her pulse, which was rapid and placed a hand on her brow.

Carrie frowned, she opened her rucksack and removed a thermometer from its steel case and shook it hard. "Open up and pop this under your tongue. Try not to bite it."

Adele did as she was asked and tried to speak. Her tone was garbled and Carrie had a hard job understanding her. "You have an interesting accent, Madame. Are you from Alsace?"

Carrie shook her head, and followed through on her cover story, "I was born in Belgium and grew up there before moving to Luxembourg and further schooling and then onto Geneva before studying in Paris." Carrie placed her finger on her lips to stop the conversation while Adele's temperature was taken.

Adele seemed satisfied, "That explains it. You have a certain something impinging on your accent. I thought for a moment you were working for the Resistance and had come from abroad."

Carrie stiffened as she removed the thermometer and read it. She tried to appear impassive as if nothing was wrong but inside she began to churn again with the coiling snake of twisted fear.

She laughed and then her tone became serious. "You must rest. You have a slight temperature and oedema." Carrie pressed Adele's foot and the imprint of Carrie's fingers remained as if she was kneading dough. "I suspect your blood pressure is up although I have no way of knowing, without my..." Carrie paused. She couldn't think of the word for monitor or machine and frowned.

Adele supplied the missing word, "Appareil."

Carrie brushed over it as if she had been concentrating on Adele's condition, "Mais, oui, bien sur. Appareil, machine," and she smiled. Inside, her heart thudded. She knew she had come close to giving herself away. She took a deep breath and continued. "Adele, I am very concerned. I believe you have a condition called Pre- eclampsia. If left untreated it could result in you losing your baby."

Adele looked stunned, "What do I need to do?"

"You must rest, completely. Stay in bed with your feet elevated and pray that the swelling goes down. You should really go to hospital or have a doctor to see you."

"But, Papa… how will he manage?"

"He will have to. It could be dangerous for you."

"But, I feel fine. A little tired perhaps. I feel a fraud."

"Trust me on this and do as I say. Please. I will explain to your father." Carrie, filled with compassion tenderly stroked the young woman's forehead and brushed away her hair. "We must get you help."

Adele turned her face away and bit her lip. Carrie could see the pain etched in the young woman's face. "À bientôt, Adele."

Carrie retreated back down the narrow staircase and into the café. She spoke briefly and quietly to Matthew who understood what had transpired. He spoke to the old man and crossed to him, and Carrie listened, "Josef?"

Josef was cleaning his coffee maker. He looked up, immediately understanding the concerned tone, "What is it? Is it Adele?"

"I am afraid so." Matthew steered the old man away from his chore and explained the situation. "It's not just the baby, Adele could lose her life, too."

Carrie nodded in agreement and support.

Josef's expression turned grave as he listened to Matthew's account of Adele's condition. "What can I do?" Josef's voice was low and filled with pain.

"She really needs to be in hospital. She must be seen by a doctor. Yvette does not have the necessary equipment to do a full examination or the means required to treat her."

"But, there is no doctor here."

"Then, we must do what we can to help. What is best?" Matthew looked at Carrie.

She was just about to answer when a German military vehicle drew up outside the café and two soldiers came marching in. One had a swagger in the way he moved and wore a monocle. The other was the officer from the hillside who had destroyed Matthew's sketches. Carrie froze.

The officer began questioning Josef and Carrie recognised Adele's name being mentioned. The old man confirmed everything that Matthew had told them but the German wanted to see Adele for himself. Matthew translated this to Josef and Carrie whose face filled with alarm.

"No! It could be dangerous for her. She must not be put under undue stress. If she becomes upset she could fit and lose the baby."

The soldier with the swagger removed his baton from under his arm and circled the group menacingly before poking the stick underneath Carrie's chin, forcing her head up and shouting her down. Carrie looked bewildered and her eyes filled with terror as the officer continued with his tirade in German. Matthew stepped forward protectively trying to explain, "Please, my wife does not speak German, she doesn't understand. You should speak through me."

For that he received a sharp blow on the side of his head that brought him to his knees and it was Carrie's turn to be defensive. She dashed to Matthew's side and allowed a few French expletives of her own to explode from her lips. Matthew tried to stop her but Carrie being Carrie felt her temper flare and she called the man a German swine, "Porcine allemands!"

The man understood and laughed mockingly and to her shock he spoke in English. "So, Frau Dupont; you do not understand German. Maybe you know a little English, n'est pas?"

Carrie's green eyes flashed with anger as she feigned incredulity, "What idiot language is this? Quelle langue est-ce imbécile?" She continued to heap French insults upon the man's head who watched and listened with amusement as Matthew attempted to placate her.

"Yvette, Yvette, calm down. Please."

But Carrie was infuriated and all the French slang and swear words she had learned in her French class came hurtling out. She hoped it was one way to silence the man for her fear of being discovered was bubbling underneath her show of bravado. She waved her arms agitatedly as she thundered her abuse.

The officer listened and clapped his hands scornfully with a smirk on his face, "So, we have a spirited filly here," he remarked to Matthew. "I hope you have better control over your wife than this."

Matthew grasped Carrie's hands and shouted, "Assez! Enough!"

Carrie fell silent and the German continued contemptuously, "A remarkable performance, Madame. I will believe you for now. But…" The man stopped and ordered a soldier to go into the house and up the stairs to corroborate the story of a pregnant woman being treated by Carrie. The soldier clicked his heels and obeyed. "We will wait and see what is to be reported."

The motley group remained silent and in waiting until the young soldier returned to confirm that there was indeed a heavily pregnant woman who had been attended to by District Nurse, Yvette Dupont. The Commandant nodded and ordered his men to leave. He marched swiftly to the door, turned and spoke again in perfect English, "For now, Madame, you are safe. But I will be watching you, Yvette Dupont. And you, Sir, if all is as you say then you have no need to worry. If not…" He left the sentence unfinished and studied their faces. Carrie held tightly to Matthew's hand and followed Matthew's lead who shrugged and shook his head as if confused. Carrie pretended to look completely bewildered and glanced at Matthew questioningly.

They watched as the officer returned to the jeep that already had its motor running. He patted the side with his baton and the vehicle sped off back to the cliff road. Carrie and Matthew heaved a sigh of relief. Josef stared stonily ahead.

"And now I must attend to you," said Carrie indicating Matthew's injuries.

"Not now. We have to go," said Matthew.

"But what of Adele?" asked Josef despairingly.

Carrie pleaded, "We have to get her to hospital, now. Please, Matthew."

The old man added his entreaty and Matthew hesitated, "We really should get going." He looked again at Carrie's sweet face and buckled. "This is against my better judgement."

"You will have to carry her downstairs I will fetch a blanket and pillow. Where is the nearest hospital?" asked Carrie.

Josef looked surprised, "You do not know, Madame?"

Carrie flustered, "Yes, yes, of course. I just wondered which was nearer. My geography is not brilliant."

Matthew came to her rescue again, " Definitely Le Havre and we have a choice of two. I will get Adele."

Carrie stood uncomfortably before following Matthew up the stairs. She could feel the old man's eyes on her watching her curiously. Carrie disappeared through the door and went to the bedroom where Matthew was attempting to lift Adele. She grabbed a pillow and warm blanket. They exchanged a look between them and they both knew things were going to become more difficult.

Matthew struggled down the twisting stairs with Carrie close on his heels. As soon as they reached the café she dashed past him and ran to their vehicle and wrenched open the back door. She placed the pillow down and waited while Matthew settled Adele and Carrie covered her with the blanket. Josef had followed them out as Carrie stepped into the passenger seat he touched her arm, "Thank you; merci beaucoup, Madame." Carrie nodded and gave a half smile as Matthew started the motor. She was convinced that Josef suspected that she wasn't French.

The drive to the hospital was fraught with tension and anxiety. She tried to attend to his wounds as best she could while they travelled and succeeded in patching him up somewhat.

Each time they passed a German soldier Carrie stiffened. She understood now more than ever that she was not secure in her characterisation of Yvette Dupont but with Adele in the back of the vehicle she was unable to talk to Matthew freely. Conversation was stilted. However, she managed to convey her need for him to be present whenever she was questioned, "Matthieu, my ears are getting worse. I simply cannot hear what is being said to me a lot of the time. I need you to be with me until I get some sort of hearing aid. I have this awful problem of noises in my ears. Tinnitus and it is getting worse."

"Ah, your tintement, my poor sweet. Of course."

Carrie relaxed back in her seat, momentarily, believing that for now she would be reasonably secure, but at the back of her mind she had an inkling that she would be tested to her limits.

Matthew motored into the town of Le Havre and made his way to the hospital. They drove to the accident and emergency entrance and Matthew dived out demanding help and a trolley. Carrie spoke soothingly to Adele trying to keep her calm. Matthew explained as best he could.

"Hurry, vite! I have a woman here pregnant and with eclampsia. She needs a doctor now."

Adele was whisked away and Carrie prayed that they were in time and that she wouldn't have a fit and lose the baby. A nurse on reception ushered Carrie and Matthew to the desk and asked a succession of questions, which Matthew answered promptly saving Carrie any embarrassment. He covered his tracks with the explanation they had rehearsed that Carrie's hearing was none too good. The nurse appeared to accept this as she completed the admission form.

Carrie and Matthew stepped away from the hospital knowing now that Adele was in good hands and began to walk back to the jeep. Carrie kept her eyes lowered. She did not want to engage with anyone else at the hospital for fear of being questioned. Two German soldiers outside the hospital watched them with interest as they left and Matthew alerted Carrie to this. It was with great relief that they arrived at the vehicle without being stopped or challenged.

Carrie heaved a huge sigh of relief as she sat back in the jeep.

"We're not out of the woods yet," warned Matthew. Carrie's heart began to flutter. "It's clear that you can't stay on here. It's too risky. We must try and make arrangements to get you out of here and back home. If you are caught it could put us all in jeopardy Even though I don't want you to go."

Carrie remained silent. She knew there was nothing to say and in her heart she wanted to return home to what she knew best, nursing. She was also disturbed by Matthew's comment and did not want to respond or press him on it. She could feel an undercurrent of attraction between them, which confused her because she totally believed her heart lay with Michael. She had never kissed a man other than Michael. She also began to understand how someone could be drawn to another in difficult times especially when they shared danger. Quietly contemplative she was lost in her own thoughts and jumped nervously when Matthew spoke again.

"We need to find somewhere where you can use the radio. The sooner the information is transmitted the happier I will be."

Carrie nodded and Matthew started up the engine and pulled away from the hospital forecourt. They drove as fast as they dared out of Le Havre and were relieved not to be stopped. Matthew relaxed as they reached the country road.

"Where are we going?"

"Back the way we came."

"Then where?"

"We will stop off at the village and tell Adele's father where she is and put his mind at rest."

The jeep travelled down the country lanes on the approach to the small village. Ahead was a German vehicle part way across the road. Matthew was shocked when two Germans stepped out from behind it and waved them down ordering them to stop. Matthew skidded to a halt and hissed, "Let me deal with this."

The soldiers walked toward the vehicle. One opened the back and began poking around inside. The other tapped on the driver's window, "Papers." His tone was brusque and officious.

Matthew tried to appear at ease and as he reached in his coat for his documents he asked casually, "Is there a problem, officer?"

The German ignored him and held out his hand for Carrie's papers, too. He snapped his fingers at her. Carrie fumbled in her bag and removed them. Her heart was thumping wildly and she was certain everyone could hear it so loud was the pumping in her head.

The officer inspected Matthew's identification and

scrutinised the photo, looking backward and forward between the picture and Matthew's face. Seemingly satisfied he placed Matthew's papers underneath Carrie's and began the same close examination. This time he walked around to Carrie's window and rapped on it for her to open it. Carrie's mouth went dry. She tried to smile but her lips stuck to her teeth. The soldier muttered something in German and finally folded the papers up and slapped them in her hand when a shout went up from behind.

Carrie froze. The soldier ordered them to wait as he moved toward the back of the jeep. Matthew whispered to Carrie to remain calm. The officer returned with Carrie's rucksack and Carrie tried to appear unemotional. He drew out the radio transmitter and asked in officious guttral tones, "What is this?"

Matthew was flummoxed and struggled to think of something to say.

Carrie spoke, "That is my X-Ray machine."

Matthew shot a look at Carrie and translated into German. She continued, "I am a nurse on the district and I have been attending to a pregnant woman who has eclampsia. I needed to X-ray her to see that the baby was alive and not in distress."

Matthew translated but the soldier looked unconvinced.

"We are on our way now to report to her father, she has been taken to the hospital in Le Havre. Please, it is an essential part of my equipment. I cannot do my job without it." Carrie looked pained and concerned. "See, I attach these wires to the mother's stomach. It sends a read out to the machine, which then helps me diagnostically." Matthew duly translated.

The German considered what he was being told and spat on the ground. He muttered something to his companion and thrust the equipment back in the rucksack and passed it back to Carrie with the papers and waved them on. Carrie mumbled her thanks and Matthew slowly manoeuvred the jeep around the military vehicle and into the village.

Carrie was shaking. Matthew eyed her in admiration, "My God, how did you think of all that?"

Carrie shrugged. Her palms were sweating and her stomach felt as if it was doing somersaults. "Let's get this over with. Please."

Matthew pulled up outside the café and leaving the engine running he went and spoke quickly to Josef, who looked across gratefully at Carrie and mouthed his thanks. He clasped Matthew by the hand and Carrie could sense the old man's relief but all she wanted was to get as far away from the place as possible.

Matthew clambered back inside and the jeep moved off through the village and past the church.

"What now?"

"We don't have much time. Remember, we passed a deserted building on the way here?" Carrie nodded. "I'll drive in around the back and you can send a message to HQ. We need to get you out of here as soon as possible. Especially after today, you are attracting too much attention. And your hair…"

"What about it?"

"It is beginning to grow back. It is just too distinctive and too noticeable."

"I can have it cut again."

"I can't take the risk."

They travelled in silence until they reached the building in question. Matthew left the road and drove around the back of the old house and into a derelict barn and stopped the engine. He turned to Carrie, "Before you radio HQ there is something I must say."

Carrie saw his eyes searching her face, "No Matthew, don't say it."

"I have to. I don't know what is going to happen. I only know that from the first time I laid eyes on you I knew you were someone special." Carrie went to speak but Matthew stopped her, "No, let me finish. I have never met anyone like you. You are amazing and it has been a privilege to have you work so closely with me. To be your husband in these identities has been more than wonderful. I only wish..." He stopped and took her hands and gazed deep into her eyes. "If anything changes between you and your Michael. Think of me, please."

Carrie tried to speak again but he placed his fingers on her lips to stop her. "Caroline Llewellyn, let me kiss you one last time, without fear without subterfuge but as our real selves."

Carrie bit her lip. Her confusion was apparent. Matthew clasped her in his arms in a crushing embrace. He kissed her shamelessly and with passion. Carrie fought against responding but eventually relinquished herself into his yearning hold.

She pulled away, "We have to get down to business." She tried to sound professional and not in the turmoil she was experiencing.

"Yes," agreed Matthew. "After the war, when it is over. I will come and find you."

Carrie shook her head vehemently, "Matthew, the situation and the danger we have shared has brought us closer together and yes, I admit I am attracted to you but I truly love my Michael. My happiness lies with him and in the words of another, in my own backyard."

Matthew dropped his gaze and her hands; "All I ask is a little hope to see me through this war."

Carrie was stuck for words. Memories of Gwynfor rushed to the surface and with it a flush of regret. Matthew's words were like Gwynfor's plea all over again. And as she remembered her last meeting with the gentle, lumbering giant and what happened to him she relented, "As you wish."

Matthew beamed, "That's all I ask. Thank you. And now, to work." He instantly became professional again. "You get the equipment up and running. I will keep watch."

Carrie delved into the rucksack to remove the transmitter; "I'll hook it up to the jeep's battery. From my understanding it's safer and harder to track by the German high frequency direction detector vans than by using an electric supply or generator."

"Good idea. German D/F vans are bound to be on patrol in these lanes."

"What should I say?"

"Tell them about the radio receiver and the building work, warn them of the radar. They will have to set up an operation to destroy them. The building is heavily defended from the sea. A commando raid would be too risky. It appears there are three blockhouses being built only two hundred metres from the radio receiver. Other defences are six feet thick barbed wire to stop any entrance or exit to the beach, machine gun posts and a garrison of what we assume to be thirty men. The Resistance have also reported that the Germans keep troops at a nearby farmhouse in Bruneval."

"Anything else?"

"Yes, tell them your position is compromised and ask for arrangements to be made to get you out."

"Are you sure about that?"

Matthew's eyes locked onto hers, "Yes. We need to get you out."

"How do you explain my absence?"

"If it comes up, which I doubt. You have gone off on another training course." He shrugged, "I'll worry about that when it happens."

Carrie nodded. "Open the bonnet."

Matthew lifted the engine hood and she quickly attached the transmitter to the vehicle battery. "I still can't believe they bought your story of an X-ray machine. Wonderful stuff." He laughed and winked at Carrie as she began to relay the information to HQ.

The reply came back; her message had been received and understood. They would be contacted again regarding the operation to destroy the radio receiver and plans would be made to get Carrie out. She would need to report in again at the same time in two days. Carrie quickly signed off and dismantled the equipment and packed it away. They waited until dusk had fallen when Matthew deemed it safer to move.

"What now?"

"Back to base camp and reconvene with the others."

Chapter Thirty-two

Escape

The group sat pensively around the scrubbed kitchen table. The fervid discussion had lapsed into silence. Their mood matched the drizzling rain that spattered the window on this murky day.

Carrie had been busy on the radio receiver and still chose to operate using a car battery, which was proving very effective against German detection. Matthew now knew more about the proposed raid at Bruneval and how Carrie was to be got out of the country.

"So," said Matthew, "We must pray for decent weather. If not, it could scupper the plans. It was thought that Para-troopers from the First Airborne Division supported by the Royal Navy would carry out the attack. That's now changed."

"Yes, C Company of the Second Division led by Major John Frost," added Daisy knowingly.

"No, he can't," continued Andre Leroux, "Major Frost has not had time to complete his parachute training, yet."

"So?" asked Honore Bertrand, "What *is* the plan? I must admit, I don't like all the chopping and changing. It doesn't bode well."

"And yet," said Carrie, "If we have to be kept on full alert, then that could make us more careful and ensure the safety of the mission."

"I am always careful," added Matthew especially when it comes to our lives. And you're wrong, I believe that Frost will lead the raid."

"This is all very confusing. Just what is happening?" asked Andre. "And who will replace Yvette?" asked Andre nodding his head at Carrie, "How is she to get out?"

"First things first," remonstrated Matthew. "It's true many of the men have not yet completed training and the means of delivering them to Bruneval, using the Thirty-Eight Wing of the RAF, is not yet operational. Therefore, Fifty-one Squadron, under the command of Wing Commander Pickard, has been given the task. Frost will also be involved."

The group remained silent while they digested this new information. Honore shook his head, "I don't like it. Too many changes, too many times."

Matthew slapped his hand on the table, "The details are unimportant. All we need to know is that the raid will go ahead and will act as a suitable diversion to the landing of a small craft that will take our friend back to England."

Carrie smiled gratefully at him, "It will also bring my replacement, won't it?"

"Yes, of course. For who will operate the radio when Yvette is gone?" asked Honore who began to tap his fingers in irritation at the uncertainty of the facts being relayed.

Matthew sighed, "I feel it is better not to overload you with all the details. Then, in the case of an emergency; you will not know anything."

"You mean, if any of us get caught," Honore pointed out.

The group fell into silence once more as they contemplated the validity and seriousness of the statement.

Finally, Andre spoke, "Yes, I agree. The less detail we know, the better. We just need the time and place where we get our friend to safety," and he smiled reassuringly at Carrie. He looked around at everyone, "Then, it's agreed. I will just say that on paper, the paratroopers have all the advantages – surprise, skill and the knowledge that failure would either end in either death or years as a prisoner-of-war. That should be incentive enough for success."

Matthew nodded, "At the designated time, we will gather in the clearing. There should be enough going on at Bruneval to mask the arrival of the plane and the drop of the new operative. We will have a window of only a few minutes to get you aboard," he indicated Carrie, "Get our new SOE to safety and to wait for news of the success or failure of the raid."

No one spoke.

Matthew studied the faces in the group. There was no dissension. "Right. Better get prepared. You will need to lie low for a few days and only take what you need."

"What about my papers?" asked Carrie.

"Keep them with you, you never know," advised Matthew.

Carrie nodded silently.

Annie added, "It may be useful to keep them with us. We can change the photo."

"As long as Yvette, here, doesn't make herself wanted by the enemy," laughed Andre.

"Is that it?" asked Daisy.

"That's it," affirmed Matthew.

The group moved away from the table chattering amongst themselves. Carrie rose thoughtfully before Matthew stopped her. "Yvette, may I have a quick word?"

Carrie looked surprised as Matthew steered her out from the kitchen and into the scullery. "I know we have already spoken briefly, and I had been meaning to say something for a long time but now … well, now I must speak out again. The thought I may never see you again is too much to bear."

Carrie looked at him seriously, "We have had this discussion, Matthew. There is no more to say."

"No, please. Tell me, you must have felt it, too? It wasn't all play acting, was it?"

Carrie didn't like where the conversation was heading and didn't know what to say. Matthew ploughed on, "You know I have feelings for you. I felt it as soon as I met you and since we have been here and what we have been through together you must know that I care."

Carrie put her hand up to stop him, "I know. I don't deny it, but I don't really know you and you don't know me. As I said, we are in an artificial situation and we both know my heart is at home with Michael."

Matthew lowered his eyes crestfallen, "I know. I just didn't want you to go without me saying anymore. I would have regretted it forever. I had to speak again, forgive me."

"Another time, another place it may have been different…"

Matthew sighed, "I understand. But, I said it before, and I will say it again; don't be surprised if I come looking for you after the war is over and if I am still alive."

The night of February 27th leading into the 28th was good with regards to the weather. The group had received confirmation that the naval force had sailed. The Whitley bombers of Fifty-one Squadron had taken off from Thruxton for the two-hour journey to Bruneval. Whatever would happen next was in God's hands.

The chosen Resistance members, Annie, Andre, Matthew and Carrie travelled watchfully in the jeep toward the designated drop and woodland clearing, keeping a wary eye out for German soldiers. They had to pass through heavily occupied German territory. As the jeep drove through a small hamlet Matthew was aware that the daylight was fading and they would soon be in breach of the curfew.

The monocled German Officer that Carrie and Matthew had encountered at Josef and Adele's café was exiting a terraced house with two of his guards. On the steps sat a French woman sobbing and crying with blood streaming from her head.

The Commandant turned his head as the jeep drove past and stared into the window and recognized Carrie. He looked thoughtful and began a slow tattoo into his hand with his baton. Carrie lowered her eyes averting his gaze, her heart beginning to pound in her chest as they continued out of the conurbation. She remembered the German's threat and she began to worry. In her anxiety she hugged her small, strapped purse containing the few items she was taking home including her papers.

The monocled German slapped his baton decisively into his hand once more and swaggered to his vehicle before shouting to his guards, "Schnell! Folgen Sie dem jeep. Quickly, follow that jeep."

The men scrambled to their vehicle and jumped in. They started it up and hurriedly turned around in the road before speeding off in pursuit. But the jeep, with the Resistance, now had a good lead.

"He's seen us," warned Carrie.

"Who?" asked Annie, so Carrie explained their previous encounter with the brutish officer. Annie listened in horror and expostulated in anger, “Diable, bâtard!” She shuddered in disbelief at the account.

“Oh, he was a devil and a bastard all right,” affirmed Matthew as he turned off the road, extinguishing his lights and onto a track into the woods. Matthew watched in the rear view mirror. He could just see the lights of the pursuing vehicle diminishing to black as he drove deeper into the wood. “Let’s hope we’ve lost him.”

Matthew drove cautiously to the designated spot and parked the jeep amongst the trees and out of sight to wait. The central clearing was large enough to land a plane and trees had been cleared to make a temporary runway from the spot. So far, this had escaped detection but Matthew felt it would not be long before it was discovered and alternate arrangements would need to be made. He said as much to Carrie, “Let’s pray our devil friend doesn’t find us. It will complicate everything.”

Carrie didn’t speak, her eyes revealed the fear she was feeling.

Over at Bruneval the planes had succeeded in flying under the German radar. The actual jump from the air was surprisingly uneventful and the men from C Company hurriedly gathered at the designated rendezvous point and prepared for the assault. The attack on their target was swift and clinical. The occupants of the house and the radio pit with the receiver were dealt with and killed. Then an attack came from Germans staying at a nearby farmhouse who had witnessed the action. Whilst a specialist worked to dismantle the receiver, Major Frost took twelve of his men to attack the Germans at the farmhouse.

This action served two purposes, which was to capture the receiver and hopefully help thwart the German attempts at maintaining an early warning system when the Allies came across on any bombing missions and to allow another plane through to drop a new radio operative and to airlift Carrie to safety.

The Resistance waited quietly, tense and nervous but ever watchful for the enemy. The sounds of bomb blasts ripped through the night air, shaking the trees and ground around them. The hill at Bruneval lit up in a blaze of fire that bled rapidly through the night sky. The Resistance remained hushed knowing this raid could be a major turning point in the war, which seemed to be dragging on longer than any had expected.

The monocled German Commandant and his pursuing contingent had continued down the road at speed toward the next village. Suddenly he rapped his baton on the dash and ordered the armoured car to stop, which halted leaving its wheels spinning.

"Turn around. Drehen Sie sich um wir sie muss verpasst haben. We must have missed them," he roared.

The young soldier, spun the wheel and repositioned the vehicle and they proceeded more slowly back the way they had come searching for a sign, anything to show where the jeep had gone.

Another blast rocked the ground and the Commandant's eyes took on a steely glint as he twisted his mouth into a cruel snarl. He stood up in his seat and scrutinised the night sky alerting his men to a low flying plane that seemed to be skirting the tops of the trees. The Germans moved off looking for signs of disturbance among the leaf detritus and for wheel tracks.

Matthew signalled to his people as a thudding droning hum was heard and a low flying craft swooped down into the clearing. Keeping its engines running, the pilot held the craft fast until a young man emerged from the plane carrying a small bag. He jumped down and looked around before running for the trees and where Annie was standing. Carrie made to break out into the space but Matthew caught her by the arm, he whispered, "One last time," and pulled her into him kissing her full on the mouth. She didn't resist.

Carrie touched her burning lips and gently touched Matthew's face, shaking her head sadly, "I'm sorry," she mouthed and started for the plane.

As she broke cover the German military vehicle came blazing from out of the trees and the monocled Commandant took aim.

Carrie ran in fear and haste, dropping her purse, which snagged on a branch, as she sprinted to escape. Annie ran out behind her and raised her pistol at the German.

A shot rang out followed quickly by another.

Chapter Thirty-Three

Notification

John was trekking back to Hendre clutching a tiny orphan lamb in his arms. Ernie was at his side. "Jawch! This reminds me. Duw, Duw!"

"Ernie, stop being so cryptic. What are you talking about?"

"It takes me back, it does. Remember? My first winter here. You and the sheep in the snow. It was a little lamb that saved your life."

"Yes, Lucky."

"Aye, Lucky. Lucky for you and lucky for the little scrap of a thing."

"Not so little now," chortled John. "Lucky grew up into a big fat ewe."

"A big fat ewe that is still going strong, and will mother many more. Like a dog she is, only bigger," said Ernie.

"Talking of dogs, where's Bonnie?"

"She skulked into the house with Jenny and Bethan. Sitting in front of the fire I expect with Bandit," Ernie said.

They crossed the yard, their breath clouding the frosty air in front of them. John stepped lightly up to the glasshouse door and tried to kick off his Wellingtons. He managed to manoeuvre one off but the other stubbornly refused to budge. He hopped on the steps and Ernie suppressed a grin.

"Duw, and I thought I had two left feet. Give me that little scrap and you can get the other boot off," he laughed.

John passed the little bundle to Ernie who scratched his head in amusement at John's antics removing his boot. He laughed even more when he saw the large hole in John's sock with his big toe poking through. "Jawch! All he needs is a face painted on it and he'd be saying hello. I should tell Jenny to get the darning needle out."

They trooped into the house and kitchen and little Bethan toddled toward John, "Dada!" her little face crumpled into a delighted smile and she put her arms up to her father. He scooped her up and swung her around until she laughed in glee.

Jenny scolded him lightly, "Give over, John. You'll excite her before bed and she'll never get to sleep," but she smiled broadly and with adoration as she watched her husband play with his little girl.

There was even more excitement when Bethan saw the tiny lamb. A bed was made up by the range and the baby animal was loved and fussed over while Jenny prepared a bottle for the orphaned creature. She joked, "Doesn't look like I'll get much sleep anyway, if this one has to be fed!" She ushered Ernie to the table, "Come on sit up. Tea's ready and I have made some hearty rabbit stew. Sam dropped a couple into us. If you close your eyes you'll think it's chicken."

"Smells wonderful, Jenny bach," said Ernie appreciatively. "Makes me want to lick my chops, the aroma has me salivating like a dog tempted with a meaty bone."

"Talking of dogs, where's Bonnie?" asked Jenny. "I have some tasty morsels for her."

"Nosing round the yard, she was, when we came in," said John.

"After the bacon rind I threw out for the birds, I expect," laughed Jenny.

Suddenly there was a terrific barking and squawking, "If she's chasing the chickens, she'll have real scolding," grumbled John.

"Aye, your bark is enough to blow a parrot off its perch," Ernie teased.

Bonnie's agitated yaps continued and John placed Bethan in her playpen. Her little face crumpled and she snivelled a little. John soothed her, "I'll not be long, Bethan bach. Daddy will be back and it's a lovely game of rough and tumble we'll be having."

Ernie frowned, as there was a stout knock on the door. John walked slowly and curiously toward it and opened it. Outside were two members of the military in full uniform bearing a letter. Ernie strained his ears to listen but could not hear what was being said.

John took the envelope and turned it over in his hands. The soldiers saluted him, turned on their heels and left smartly, returning to their military car. John's knees buckled and he dropped to the floor. Ernie rushed to help him to his feet whilst Jenny watched anxiously biting her lip.

A deep-rooted sob escaped from John's lips and he looked at Ernie in utter despair.

"What is it? What is hurting you so badly?" questioned Ernie and he struggled to support John to a chair. John was silent and just passed the envelope to Ernie indicating he should open it.

Ernie glared at the official brown envelope with the Ministry of Defence insignia and with a trembling hand opened the missive. He stared at the stark writing on the page before dropping it and letting it flutter to the ground. Jenny scrambled to pick it up. She read the words and looked up in horror, "What? Carrie's dead?" She shook her head in utter disbelief.

"No. I'll not accept it. There's been some mistake. I would know. Jawch! I would *know*!" insisted Ernie.

John ran his fingers through his unruly hair. He appeared to have aged in a twinkling. His pallor was grey, his shoulders hunched and he began to weep silently. Jenny was instantly at his side, comforting him and showering him with kisses. John rose roughly pushing his wife aside and disappeared through the pine stair door and up the stairs.

Jenny's face was white and she looked after her husband her emotions in turmoil. Ernie took Jenny in his arms, "He doesn't mean it, Jenny bach. It's the shock. Leave him be. He needs to be alone with his demons. Just remember, this is wrong. It's all wrong. Carrie is alive. I feel it. I know it."

Jenny looked up at Ernie sorrowfully, "But the letter…"

"Letter's can be wrong. Mistakes have been made before." Ernie's expression remained grim.

"Someone needs to tell Mr. Lawrence," murmured Jenny.

In the small cemetery next to the church a small band of people surrounded a graveside. A temporary cross had been erected until the ground had settled and a stone could be made.

It simply said, "Yvette Dupont beloved wife of Matthieu."

Adele stood with her father Josef and her newly born baby, "Such bravery. She had the heart of a lion."

Daisy stood with tears streaming down her face, "It should have been me. I have no one. She had a wonderful family who loved her."

Andre put his arm around her, "No, we need you more than ever now. We are your family."

Matthew stood silently his arm in a sling. His face was flushed unhealthily and he sighed before replacing his hat and moving away from the site. Honore solemnly patted him on the shoulder.

Andre pressed Daisy to follow, "Come, we have much to do. And we need to find a new radio operator."

Daisy nodded dumbly, "I know. It was all going so well, but to lose the new SOE so abruptly."

Later that day at the house, the mood was subdued. Andre, Daisy and Matthew sat with a pot of coffee. Rucksacks and a few small cases stood by the door.

"What's next?" asked Daisy.

"We will wait for the others to get back, and leave together," said Matthew. "But we can congratulate ourselves. The mission was a resounding success." Matthew wiped away the beading droplets of sweat forming on his brow.

"Yes, but at what cost?" interjected Daisy looking at him in concern. "Are we sure the plane didn't reach safety?"

"I have it on good authority that after dealing with the attack, Frost led his men down to the beach. I'm told that at two-fifteen a.m. the paratroopers assembled on the beach but no contact could be made with the naval force, which had its own problems."

"That was the time the plane was landing to deliver the new operative and take Carr… Yvette to safety," added Daisy.

"Everything happened so fast. Two German destroyers and two E-boats had passed less than a mile from British boats. As our plane was taking off Naval motor gunboats were brought in under extraordinarily heavy German machine gun fire from the cliffs. This fire hit our plane, which went down in the water. I know that Frost, his men, and their valuable cargo, which included German prisoners, were hauled aboard from their landing craft. The pilot never got out. I'm told there were no survivors. The motor gunboats then powered their way back to Portsmouth. As daylight broke, fighter planes from the RAF gave cover in case of a possible attack by the Luftwaffe. The rest you know," finished Matthew drawing a clammy hand across his brow once more.

"So, how do we work the radio now?" asked Andre.

"We will have to try and muddle through until they can send someone new."

"We can't use the usual clearing," said Daisy.

"No. We need to find another safer place."

"What about the Germans?" asked Andre.

"They were all dispatched. It's only a matter of time before someone comes looking for us. That's why we have to move out. If the others are not back by dark we will move on alone." Matthew's hand had begun to tremble and he started to shiver.

"You need to get that bullet removed. You don't look well. If it festers you could lose more than your arm..." Daisy left the rest of the sentence unfinished and stared at the table.

Andre continued, "I will drive. I know the way to Dieppe and our next stop. Help will be waiting there." Andre glanced at his watch, "The others are cutting it fine. I say we get ready to go, now."

Matthew nodded. He rose from the table and swayed. Daisy steadied him and helped him to the door. She accompanied him outside and settled him in the back of the jeep. "I'll get the rest of the bags," she nodded at Andre.

Andre sat in the driver's seat and started the engine while Daisy retrieved the final two cases and clambered aboard. "Right. Let's go."

Sam Jefferies walked into the kitchen at Gelli Galed where Michael was preparing a meal, whistling happily. Boots was at his feet and raised his head at Sam's entrance. Michael glanced back, "Just in time. You can lay the table and butter the bread while I..." he stopped and turned taking in Sam's grave expression. "What? What is it?"

Sam pulled off his hat and remained standing, "You need to get down to Hendre."

"What? Why?"

"Just do it… I'm sorry, Michael."

Michael's face froze and the colour drained from his cheeks, "Tell me, please," he paused, "Is it Carrie?"

Sam shook his head, "You need to see the Llewellyns." Sam refused to say anymore.

Michael left the kitchen, grabbed his coat, hurried out of the house, and down the mountain track. His feet could hardly keep up. His knees were wobbly and he was feeling sick to his stomach. He lurched forward almost tumbling over.

Boots yelped and yapped as he followed him. Detecting the urgency in Michael's demeanour the little dog determined to keep pace with his master and tried to offer his loyal support as he ran alongside. Every now and then he would jump up and try to lick Michael's hand.

Michael scrambled down the last few yards of the mountain track to the gate that led to Hendre's yard. He stared at the house. The sun that shone down that crisp fresh day on the farmhouse and the Dulais valley belied the tension Michael felt and his mood.

He paused at the gate and Boots slipped through, dancing and barking dementedly around Bonnie. The two dogs began a playful game of chase, tearing around the yard in sheer joy.

Michael took a deep breath, steadied himself and walked toward the path that led to the glasshouse door. He had barely taken two steps when the door opened and he saw Jenny's concerned face looking out at him. Michael quickened his step and entered the house. The door banged shut behind him with a finality that reminded him of a tolling funeral bell. Michael was swallowed up inside.

Ernie was sitting on a kitchen chair minus his beret scratching at the wiry tufts that sprouted from the side of his head. Michael thought he had never seen him look so miserable. Jenny was nursing Bethan in the rocker. The little girl was struggling to get down but somehow Jenny's mood transmitted itself to little Bethan and the child became perfectly still and stared curiously at Michael Lawrence.

Jenny's eyes were puffed and red from crying. She began to rock in the chair, a metronome click and grind that accentuated the melancholic feeling in the air.

John was standing in his shirtsleeves leaning against the mantelpiece over the range with his back to Michael. Strong, capable John appeared cowed and broken. He turned to face Michael and held out his hand containing the fateful letter. Not a word was said.

Michael took the envelope with fear raging in his heart and tremblingly opened it up and read the contents. He gulped back a sob and his eyes filled with tears. A gamut of emotions ran through him culminating in a painful cry that was echoed by John. The two men fell into each other's arms as they shared the misery of those who had lost the love of their lives. The men clasped each other united in a brotherhood that had never existed before and would never leave them.

Jenny watched dully and Ernie said nothing. He just shook his head in abject sorrow and disbelief. Jenny opened her mouth and began to sing, slowly and hesitantly at first and then with more confidence. Her sweet clear tones appeared to soothe the two inconsolable young men who still held tight to each other.

Bonnie barked outside. The two dogs set up a fierce barking that filtered through into the kitchen with the sound of a motor running and a door slamming. Ernie raised his head and listened, "Isht! Listen!"

Jenny stopped rocking and singing and Ernie rose from the table replacing his beret. John and Michael broke free from each other stifling their heartfelt sobs. The dogs continued to bark and the agitated yaps turned into a frenzy of welcoming whimpering cries.

Ernie strode briskly to the door and opened it wide closely followed by John, Michael and Jenny, still carrying Bethan. It was then that Ernie let out a howl and a shout, "Esgyrn Davidd!"

Michael pushed past Ernie and his eyes filled with tears anew as his gaze settled on Carrie standing by a military vehicle that turned and drove out of the yard scattering the ducks and chickens in a feathered fluster. Carrie looked on the faces of those she loved, who stayed still in awe and silence until Michael scrambled toward her. He sprinted to her side and gathered her up in his arms showering her face and neck with kisses whilst the others slowly came to their senses hardly daring to believe what they were seeing and ran to them both surrounding them with cheers of joy.

Michael finally set her down as the others crowded around. He whispered, "We thought you were dead."

Carrie laughed at their solemn expressions, "Well, I'm not. Do I look dead? Do I sound dead?"

"But how…?" asked John in amazement as he sniffed back a tear.

"I told you," pronounced Ernie. "I knew she wasn't dead. I *knew*."

"Is the kettle on? I'm bursting for a cup of tea."

Carrie stepped out toward the house trying to answer the dozens of questions being hurled at her. "One at a time, one at a time," she laughed amiably as they entered the house.

The letter stained with tears sat on the pine kitchen table and Carrie picked it up. She read it quickly, "Well, the best place for that is on the fire," and she tossed it into flames on the range, which eagerly devoured the forbidding message of gloom and death, along with the envelope, which she scrunched up and threw into the fevered flames.

"But, I don't understand," said John. "How could they say you were dead?"

"I can understand that." Carrie launched into an explanation of the events that had happened on that fateful night. "When I managed to dive into the plane I lost my bag with my forged papers as Yvette Dupont. Annie stepped out to save me from German fire from the swine with the monocle giving me time to scramble aboard and my replacement to tumble out. Sadly, she was shot in the chest as was my replacement. And my… our…" she chose her words carefully, "leader, Matthew, took a bullet. I still don't know if they are alive or dead." Carrie stopped. A catch of emotion had entered her voice. "As we flew off I remember being filled with both dread and excitement. I watched in anguish as those who had… become close to me… fell. I remember the euphoria of getting out being marred by the fact that some of those I … had meant so much to me… could be dead." Carrie stopped and Michael put a protective arm around her. She continued, "The pilot started out across the channel heading for Portsmouth when we were hit by German gunfire from the cliffs. I remember screaming as we took a direct hit and with an engine on fire we started droning down and hit the water."

"How terrible," murmured Jenny fascinated by the drama of the story.

"I was pulled out unconscious and remember very little. Apparently, I spent my time in sickbay on board the boat and made no sense. Apparently, I was rambling in a strange mixture of French and something else. They thought I was part of the German contingent from the Bruneval farmhouse. It was only when I fully came to my senses in a hospital in Porstmouth that I was able to make them understand who I was. By that time, the notification of my death had already gone out."

There was a pause while they all digested the details of Carrie's escape. Michael finally spoke, "What now? I suppose you'll be back to London to continue nursing?"

"…No."

"No?" everyone chorused.

"I thought… I thought …" she eyed Ernie locking with his gaze, who blushed furiously under his toothbrush moustache and beret, which he had now replaced.

"I thought I'd settle for happiness in my own back yard and see if I could work out the rest of the war on the district and help Dr. Rees, if he will let me."

John stood up and whooped, dragging Jenny to her feet and they danced around the kitchen table. Ernie for once was stumped for words and just kept spluttering, "Duw, Duw! Jawch!"

Michael's face filled with indescribable joy and he pulled Carrie in close to him and kissed her. She melted into his arms. "There's only one thing I want now all my other prayers have been answered," whispered Michael.

Carrie gazed up at him, "And what would that be, Mr. Lawrence?"

"To make you Mrs. Lawrence as soon as I possibly can. We've wasted too much time already."

Carrie stood up, "Let's walk, Michael. We need to talk."

John and Jenny looked at her in surprise and Ernie shook his head, apparently knowingly. Michael seemed worried.

Carrie took Michael's hand and they stepped outside to be joined by Bonnie and Boots. A gust of wind blew and Carrie removed her hat, allowing the wind to blow through her growing locks.

"What happened to your hair?"

"I was shorn. It was too distinctive. A dangerous thing in the game I was in. It's growing back now. It won't be long before it's in its usual wild state. You should have seen me when it was first done. You wouldn't have recognised me."

"Oh, I would. I would know you anywhere."

"Maybe."

They walked on toward the mountain track with the dogs at their heels.

"Where are we going?"

"I have so missed this place. And everyone in it. I want to drink in the views of the valley and the river. Best place for that is Bull Rock."

They continued in silence until they reached the spot. Carrie gingerly made her way down to the mossy boulder and perched on it. She looked out across the valley's sweeping view, while Boots and Bonnie went off exploring with their noses and chasing each other in a game of doggie tag.

Michael studied her impassive expression. Carrie's eyes now seemed much wiser. It appeared her wartime experiences had etched themselves into her manner and on her face. He noticed faint little frown lines that had not been present before. She sighed and Michael began to look concerned, "Carrie?" She faced him and turned her startlingly green eyes on him and searched his, revealing her own untold bottomless depths of pain. "Carrie, what is it?"

Carrie took his hands, "Michael you have to know that I love you. I love you like I have never loved anyone."

"Carrie, you're frightening me."

"There's something I have to tell you. I don't want you to

hate me and I need you to understand…" Carrie stretched out her hand and stroked the contours of Michael's face. "In France I was given the identity of Yvette Dupont, *Madame* Yvette Dupont…."

"So?"

"My cover was that I was a married district nurse."

"Yes?"

"I had to pretend to be the wife of another operative."

Michael studied Carrie's face. "What are you saying?"

"We didn't share a room or anything like that but we had to look like a couple when we were out. We had to appear married." Carrie struggled to speak, "Matthew, he… he fell in love with me."

Michael became silent and a pulse began to throb in his temple. "Did you? Do you…? Did you fall for him?"

"No."

"That's all right, then. You didn't do anything wrong. It was something you had to do."

Carrie shook her head slowly; "I couldn't come home to you and marry you, without telling you. Our love is built on honesty and trust. I never want to damage that. I had to set things right. The truth is… If I am truthful, I was also attracted to him. But, I never stopped loving you…. You were always on my mind." She stopped again and swallowed hard, "We did no more than kiss and that was for the purpose of fooling the Germans." Carrie now had tears streaming down her face, "I don't want to hurt you, but I can't lie to you either. I will understand if you no longer want to marry me."

Michael sat back and perused her face. He took a handkerchief and wiped away her tears, "Oh, Carrie. If you hadn't have told me. I would never have known. My darling, things happen in wartime that we can't avoid. I had to kiss a member of the Resistance when I was trapped in France to avoid the scrutiny of the SS. I didn't mention it because it wasn't important. It was a necessity to evade questioning and capture."

Carrie looked at him curiously her tears had now stopped, "You never said…"

"No, and you didn't have to tell me, but you did. It really

doesn't matter as long as you still love me and want to marry me. But, did you tell me because a part of you has doubts? Or maybe Matthew came to mean more to you than you thought?"

"No," Carrie protested. "I have no doubts. I just wanted no secrets between us. I felt… I thought it was the right thing to do."

"There's something to be said for the old saying that what you don't know can't hurt you. The thought of anyone else holding you makes me as jealous as hell but I know you, Carrie and I trust you. If you say nothing happened I believe you. What you had to do to save your lives… you had to do. Now, stop alarming me and come here."

Michael enfolded her into a tender embrace and she nestled into his shoulder as the dogs came hurrying back and danced around them. Bonnie deposited a piece of wood at Carrie's feet, her eyes beseeching her to throw it.

"If you think I'm chucking a stick down here for you to chase it into the water, you're mistaken. Wait till we're back on the path."

Michael picked up the wood and hurled it to the top onto the mountain path and the two dogs scampered after it. He stood up and gently coaxed Carrie to her feet, "Come on. Everyone will wonder what's happened to us. I am sure they all will want to hear of your adventures."

"I don't think I'm ready to talk about that, yet. In time maybe… I saw some awful things…"

"So you won't be enticed back to another mission?"

"No," Carrie said firmly. She passed a hand out sweeping across the vista before them. "This is where I belong and where my heart is… where you are…" Michael smiled down at her and she felt drawn into him. "This is right."

Michael helped her up the remaining few feet of the bank and they walked back to Hendre in that silence that only true lovers enjoy. Bonnie and Boots ran ahead; the stick was momentarily forgotten as swirling leaves whirled up before them and the dogs barked joyfully as they jumped and dived at the leaf debris. Carrie looked up at Michael and all that defined him. She gazed at the budding new growth on the trees and the lush green valley that was her home and at last she was content. She turned to Michael, "I have one last thing left to do…"

Dr. Rees peered up questioningly over his half spectacles perched on the end of his nose as there was a knock at the door.

"Enter," came his crisp tones.

He looked in wonder as he was faced with the vision of his new district nurse.

"District Nurse, Carrie Llewellyn reporting for duty," and she smiled that inscrutable smile of a young woman who had at last found her place in society and where she rightly belonged.

Lightning Source UK Ltd.
Milton Keynes UK
UKHW04f0013130918
328781UK00001B/12/P